"NOBODY DOES IT BETTER THAN CLIVE CUSSLER. *NOBODY.*"
—Stephen Coonts

"JUST ABOUT THE BEST STORYTELLER IN THE BUSINESS."
— *New York Post*

"CLIVE CUSSLER HAS NO EQUAL."
—*Publishers Weekly*

#1 *NEW YORK TIMES* BESTSELLING AUTHOR
CLIVE CUSSLER DELIVERS...

"ACTION, INTRIGUE, AND BEAUTIFUL WOMEN."
—*San Antonio Express-News*

"PURE ENTERTAINMENT."
—*People*

"A NEW CLIVE CUSSLER NOVEL IS LIKE A VISIT FROM YOUR BEST FRIEND."
—Tom Clancy

Clive Cussler's explosive *Oregon* Files novels have been hailed as "honestly fabulous" (*Kirkus Reviews*) and "action-packed" (*Publishers Weekly*). Now, the author of the bestselling NUMA® and Dirk Pitt® series delivers an explosive *Oregon* Files novel featuring his unbeatable hero of the high seas—Juan Cabrillo . . .

1896: Four Englishmen flee for their lives across the merciless Kalahari Desert carrying a stolen fortune in raw diamonds, and hunted by a fierce African tribe. The thieves manage to reach the waiting HMS *Rove*—only to die with their pursuers in a storm that buries them all under tons of sand . . .

Today: Juan Cabrillo and the crew of the covert combat ship *Oregon* have barely escaped a mission on the Congo River when they intercept a mayday from a defenseless boat under fire off the African coast. Cabrillo takes action, saving the craft . . . along with beautiful Sloane Macintyre. Sloane is looking for the now-submerged *Rove*, and her search has attracted unwanted—and lethal—attention from unknown forces. But what surprises Cabrillo is her story about a crazy fisherman who claims to have been attacked on the open sea—by giant metal snakes—in the same area.

What begins as a snake hunt leads Cabrillo to the trial of a far more lethal quarry—a deranged enemy whose cadre of followers plans to unleash the devastating power of nature itself against all who oppose them . . .

PRAISE FOR CLIVE CUSSLER'S *NEW YORK TIMES* BESTSELLING NOVELS OF THE *OREGON* FILES

DARK WATCH
SACRED STONE
GOLDEN BUDDHA

"Ablaze with action." —*Kirkus Reviews*

"Readers will burn up the pages following the blazing action and daring exploits of these men and women and their amazing machines." —*Publishers Weekly*

"Fans of Cussler will not be disappointed." —*Library Journal*

continued . . .

SKELETON COAST

CLIVE CUSSLER

WITH JACK DU BRUL

BERKLEY BOOKS, NEW YORK

THE BERKLEY PUBLISHING GROUP
Published by the Penguin Group
Penguin Group (USA) Inc.
375 Hudson Street, New York, New York 10014, USA
Penguin Group (Canada), 90 Eglinton Avenue East, Suite 700, Toronto, Ontario M4P 2Y3, Canada
(a division of Pearson Penguin Canada Inc.)
Penguin Books Ltd., 80 Strand, London WC2R 0RL, England
Penguin Group Ireland, 25 St. Stephen's Green, Dublin 2, Ireland (a division of Penguin Books Ltd.)
Penguin Group (Australia), 250 Camberwell Road, Camberwell, Victoria 3124, Australia
(a division of Pearson Australia Group Pty. Ltd.)
Penguin Books India Pvt. Ltd., 11 Community Centre, Panchsheel Park, New Delhi—110 017, India
Penguin Group (NZ), Cnr. Airborne and Rosedale Roads, Albany, Auckland 1310, New Zealand
(a division of Pearson New Zealand Ltd.)
Penguin Books (South Africa) (Pty.) Ltd., 24 Sturdee Avenue, Rosebank, Johannesburg 2196,
South Africa

Penguin Books Ltd., Registered Offices: 80 Strand, London WC2R 0RL, England

This book is an original publication of The Berkley Publishing Group.

This is a work of fiction. Names, characters, places, and incidents either are the product of the author's imagination or are used fictitiously, and any resemblance to actual persons, living or dead, business establishments, events, or locales is entirely coincidental. The publisher does not have any control over and does not assume any responsibility for author or third-party websites or their content.

Copyright © 2006 by Sandecker, RLLP.
Cover photography—Desert: Ron and Patty Thomas/Getty Images. Ship: Hulton Archive/Getty Images.
Cover design by Richard Hasselberger.

PRINTING HISTORY
Berkley trade paperback edition / October 2006

Library of Congress Cataloging-in-Publication Data

Cussler, Clive.
    Skeleton Coast / Clive Cussler, with Jack Du Brul. — Berkley trade pbk. ed.
       p.   cm.
    ISBN 0-425-21189-4 (trade pbk.)
    1. Cabrillo, Juan (Fictitious character)—Fiction.   2. Mercenary troops—Fiction.
3. Treasure troves—Fiction.   4. Skeleton Coast (Namibia)—Fiction.   I. Du Brul, Jack B.
II. Title.

PS3553.U75S54   2006
813'.54—dc22   2006020588

PRINTED IN THE UNITED STATES OF AMERICA

10 9 8 7 6 5 4 3 2 1

KALAHARI DESERT
1896

H E never should have ordered them to leave the guns behind. The decision would cost them all their lives. But had there really been a choice? When the last remaining packhorse went lame they'd had to redistribute its load, and that meant leaving equipment behind. There was no debating the necessity of bringing the water flasks the animal had carried, or the satchels bursting with uncut stones. They'd had to abandon the tents, bedrolls, thirty pounds of food, and the Martini-Henry rifles each of the five men had carried, as well as all the ammunition. But even with these weight savings the surviving horses were severely overburdened, and with the sun beginning to rise once more to pound the desert no one expected their mounts would last the day.

H. A. Ryder knew better than to agree to lead the others across the Kalahari. He was an old Africa hand, having abandoned a failing farm in Sussex in the heady days of the Kimberley rush hoping to make himself a millionaire in the diamond fields. By the time he'd arrived in 1868 the whole of Colesberg Kopje, the hillock where the first diamonds had been discovered, was staked and the fields around it, too, for several miles. So Ryder turned to providing meat for the army of workers.

With a pair of wagons and hundreds of sacks of salt to cure the game, he and a couple of native guides ranged over thousands of square miles. It had been a solitary existence but one that Ryder grew to love, just as he came to love the land, with its haunting sunsets and dense forests, streams so clear the water looked like glass, and horizons so distant they seemed impossible to reach. He learned to speak the languages of various tribes, the Matabele, the Mashona, and the fierce, warlike Herero. He even understood some of the strange clicks and whistles that the Bushmen of the desert used to communicate.

He'd taken work as a safari guide so that rich Englishmen and Americans could adorn their mansion walls with trophies and he had spent time finding suitable routes for a telegraph company stringing lines across the southern third of the continent. He'd fought in a dozen skirmishes and killed ten times that many men. He knew and understood the African people and knew better still the savagery of the land itself. He knew he should have never accepted the job of guiding the others from Bechuanaland across the vast Kalahari wasteland in a mad dash to the sea. But there was always the lure of the big payoff, the siren song of instant wealth that had drawn him to Africa in the first place.

If they somehow made it, if the uncaring desert didn't claim them, then H. A. Ryder was going to have that fortune of which he'd always dreamed.

"Think they're still back there, H. A.?"

Ryder squinted into the rising sun so that his eyes nearly vanished into his weathered skin. He could see nothing on the distant horizon but curtains of shimmering heat that formed and dissolved like smoke. Between them and the fiery sun marched dunes of pure white sand—shifting waves that rivaled towering hurricane swells. With the sun came the wind, which lashed at the tops of the dunes so that sand blew off their crests in stinging clouds.

"Aye, laddie," he said without looking at the man standing next to him.

"How can you be sure?"

H. A. turned to his companion, Jon Varley. "They'll follow us to the gates of hell for what we did to them."

The certainty in H. A.'s raspy voice made Varley blanch under his tan. Like Ryder, the four other men in their party were all English-born and had come to Africa to seek their fortunes, though none was as seasoned as their guide.

"We'd best get going," Ryder said. They'd been traveling under the relatively cool cover of darkness. "We can cover a few miles before the sun climbs too high."

"I think we should make camp here," said Peter Smythe, the greenest member of the group, and by far the worst off. He'd lost his swaggering attitude shortly after entering the sand sea and now moved with the shuffling gait of an old man. White crusts had formed at the corners of his eyes and mouth, while his once bright blue eyes had grown dim.

Ryder glanced at Peter and saw the signs immediately. They'd all shared the same water ration since filling their canteens and jerry cans ten days earlier at a brackish well, but Smythe's body seemed to need more than the others. It wasn't a question of strength or will, it was simply the lad needed to drink more to stay alive. H. A. knew to the drop how much water remained, and unless he could find another desert well, Smythe would be the first to die.

The thought of giving him an extra ration never entered Ryder's mind. "We go on."

He looked westward and saw the mirror image of the terrain they'd already covered. Sand dune piled upon sand dune in endless ranks that stretched seemingly forever. The sky was turning brassy as light reflected off the infinite desert. Ryder checked his mount. The animal was suffering, and for that he felt guilty—worse than his feelings for young Smythe in fact, for the poor animal had no choice but to carry them across this cruel environment. He used a clasp knife to remove a stone from the horse's hoof and adjusted the saddle blanket where the pannier straps were beginning to chafe. The animal's once glossy coat was dull and hung in flaps where its flesh had begun to waste away.

He stroked the horse's cheek and muttered a few soothing words into its ear. There was no way any of them could ride their mounts. The animals were already struggling under their lightened loads. He took up the reins and started off. Ryder's boots sank to the uppers as he led the horse down the face of a dune. Sand shifted under them, hissing and sliding down the embankment, and threatening to send the pair tumbling if either took a misstep. H. A. didn't look back. The men had no choice but to follow or die where they stood.

He walked for an hour as the sun continued its inexorable climb into the cloudless sky. He'd tucked a smooth pebble between his teeth and tongue to try to fool his body that he wasn't severely dehydrated. When he paused to wipe the inside of his big slouch hat the heat scorched the red patch of skin on the crown of his head. He wanted to go for another hour but he could hear the men struggling behind them. They weren't yet at the point where he would consider abandoning them, so he led them to the lee of a particularly tall dune and began to erect a sunshade using the horse blankets. The men flopped to the ground, panting as he set up their meager camp.

H. A. checked on Peter Smythe. The young man's lips were nothing but raw blisters that leaked clear fluid and the tops of his cheeks were burned as if with an iron straight from the brazier. Ryder reminded him to only loosen his boot laces. All of their feet were so swollen that to remove their boots meant they'd never get them back on again. They watched him expectantly as he finally took a couple of canteens from a saddlebag. He unstoppered one of them and immediately one of the horses nickered at the scent of water. The others crowded over and his own mount brushed its head against H. A.'s shoulder.

So as not to lose even a single drop, Ryder poured a measure into a bowl and held it for the animal to drink. It slurped noisily and its stomach rumbled as water reached it for the first time in three days. He poured out a little more and again watered the horse. He did this to all of them first despite his own raging thirst and the angry glares of his companions.

"They die, you die" was all he had to say, for they knew he was right.

Having drunk only a quart of water each, the horses could still be cajoled to eat from the feed bags of oats one of them had carried. He hobbled them with leg ropes and only then did he pass around the bowl for the men to drink. He was even stricter with their ration, each receiving a single mouthful before Ryder secured the water in his pannier. There were no protests. H. A. was the only one of them to have crossed this desolate wasteland before and they deferred to him to see them through.

The shade of the horse blankets was pitiably small compared to the searing oven that was the Kalahari, one of the hottest and driest places on earth, a land where the rain might fall once a year or not for many. As the sun beat the earth with hammer strokes of heat, the men lay in torpid lethargy, shifting only when the shadows moved with the revolving sun to expose a hand or leg to the brutal onslaught. They lay with their all-consuming thirst, and they lay with their pain, but mostly they lay with their greed, for these were still motivated men, men close to becoming far wealthier than any had imagined.

When the sun reached its zenith it seemed to gain strength, making the act of breathing a battle between the need for air and the desire to keep the heat from entering their bodies. It sucked moisture from the men with each shallow breath and left their lungs aflame.

And still the heat had increased, a smothering weight that seemed to crush the men into the ground. Ryder didn't remember it being this bad when he had crossed the desert all those years ago. It was as if the sun had fallen from the heavens and now lay upon the earth, raging and angry that mere mortals were trying to defy it. It was enough to drive a man insane, and yet they endured the long afternoon, praying for the day to finally end.

As swiftly as the heat had built up it began to drop as the sun finally settled toward the western horizon, painting the sand with bands of red and purple and rose. The men slowly emerged from under the sunshade, brushing dust off their filthy clothes. Ryder scaled the dune that had protected them from the wind and panned the desert behind them with a collapsible brass telescope for signs of their pursuers. He could see nothing but shifting dunes. Their tracks had been scoured clean by the constant zephyrs, though it gave him little comfort. The men chasing them were some of the best trackers in the world. They would find them in the featureless sand sea as surely as if Ryder had left a trail of marker stones for them to follow.

What he didn't know was how much ground their stalkers had gained during the day—for they seemed superhuman in their abilities to withstand the sun and heat. H. A. had estimated that when they entered the desert they had a five-day lead on their pursuers. He felt confident that they held no more than a day's advantage now. By tomorrow that would be whittled further to half a day. And then? The next day would be when they would pay for abandoning their weapons when the packhorse went lame.

Their only chance was to find enough water tonight for the horses so they could ride them once again.

Not enough of the precious fluid remained to water the horses, and the men's ration was half of what they'd had just after dawn. For Ryder it was like adding insult to injury. The warm trickle seemed to just seep into his tongue rather than slake his thirst, which was now a gnawing ache in his stomach. He forced himself to eat some dried beef.

Looking at the raw-boned faces around him, H. A. knew that tonight's march was going to be torture. Peter Smythe couldn't stop himself from swaying where he stood. Jon Varley wasn't much better off. Only the brothers, Tim and Tom Watermen, seemed okay, but they had been in Africa longer than Smythe or Varley, working as farmhands on a big Cape cattle ranch for the past decade. Their bodies were more acclimated to Africa's brutal sun.

H. A. ran his hands through his big muttonchop sideburns, combing sand from the coarse graying hair. When he bent to tighten his boot laces he felt twice his fifty years. His back and legs ached fiercely and the vertebrae popped when he stood again.

"This is it, lads. You have my word that tonight we will drink our fill," he said to bolster their flagging morale.

"On what, sand?" Tim Watermen joked to show he still could.

"The Bushmen who call themselves the San have lived in this desert for a thousand years or more. It's said they can smell water a hundred miles off and that's not far off the mark. When I came though the Kalahari twenty years ago I had a San guide. The little bugger found water where I would have never thought to look. They scooped it from plants when there was a fog in the morning and drank from the rumen of the animals they killed with their poison arrows."

"What's a rumen?" Varley asked.

Ryder exchanged a glance with the Watermen brothers as if to say everyone should know the term. "It's the first stomach in an animal like a cow or antelope where they produce their cud. The fluid in it is mostly water and plant juice."

"I could go for some of that now," Peter Smythe managed to mumble.

A single drop of claret-red blood clung to the corner of his cracked lip. He licked it away before it could fall to the earth.

"But the San's greatest ability is to find water buried under the sand in dried-out riverbeds that haven't flowed in a generation."

"Can you find water like them?" Jon Varley asked.

"I've been looking in every streambed we've crossed for the past five days," H. A. said.

The men were startled. None of them had realized they'd crossed any dried-out rivers. To them the desert had been featureless and empty. That H. A. had known about the wadis increased their confidence that he would see them out of this nightmare.

Ryder continued, "There was a promising one day before yesterday but I couldn't be certain and we can't afford the time for me to be wrong. I estimate we're two, maybe three days from the coast, which means this part of the desert gets moisture off the ocean, plus the occasional storm. I'll find us water, lads. Of that you can be sure."

It was the most H. A. had spoken since telling the men to dump their guns and it had the desired effect. The Watermen brothers grinned, Jon Varley managed to square his shoulders, and even young Smythe stopped swaying.

A cold moon began to climb behind them as the last rays of the sun sank into the distant Atlantic, and soon the sky was carpeted with more stars than a man could count in a hundred lifetimes. The desert was as silent as a church save for the hiss of sand shifting under boots and hooves and the occasional creak of leather saddlery. Their pace was steady and measured. H. A. was well aware of their weakened condition, but never forgot the hordes that were surely on their trail.

He called the first halt at midnight. The nature of the desert had changed slightly. While they still slogged through ankle-deep sand there were patches of loose gravel in many of the valleys. H. A. had spotted old watering holes in a few of the washes, places where eland and antelope had dug into the hard pan searching for underground water. He saw no sign of humans ever using them, so he assumed they had dried out eons ago. He didn't mention his discovery to the men but it served to bolster his confidence in finding them a working well.

He allowed the men a double share of water, sure now that he could replenish the canteens and water the horses before sunup. And if he didn't, there was no use in rationing, for the desert would claim them on the morrow. Ryder gave half his ration to his horse although the others eagerly drank theirs down with little regard to the pack animals.

A rare cloud blotted the moon a half hour after they started marching again, and when it passed, the shifting illumination caused something on the desert floor to catch Ryder's eye. According to his compass and the stars, he'd been following a due-westerly direction, and none of the men commented when he suddenly turned north. He paced ahead of the others, aware of the flaky soil crunching under his boots, and when he reached the spot he dropped to his knees.

It was merely a dimple in the otherwise flat valley, no more than three feet across. He cast his gaze around the spot, smiling tightly when he found bits of broken eggshell, and one that was almost intact except for a long crack that ran like a fault line along its smooth surface. The shell was the size of his fist and had a neat hole drilled through the top. Its stopper was a tuft of dried grass mixed with native gum. It was one of the San's most prized possessions, for without these ostrich eggs they had no way to transport water. That one broke when they were refilling could have very well doomed the party of Bushmen who last used the well.

H. A. almost felt their ghosts staring down on him from the ancient riverbed's bank, tiny little spirits wearing nothing but crowns of reeds around their heads and rawhide belts festooned with pouches for their ostrich eggs and quivers for the small poisoned arrows they used to take game.

"What have you found, H. A.?" Jon Varley asked, kneeling in the dirt next to the guide. His once shining dark hair fell lank around his shoulders, but he had somehow maintained the piratical gleam in his eyes. They were the eyes of a desperate schemer, a man driven by dreams of instant wealth and one willing to risk death to see them fulfilled.

"Water, Mr. Varley." Though twenty years his senior, H. A. tried to speak deferentially to all his clients.

"What? How? I don't see anything."

The Watermen brothers sat on a nearby boulder. Peter Smythe collapsed at their feet. Tim helped the lad move upright so his back was against the water-worn rock. His head lolled against his thin chest and his breathing was unnaturally shallow.

"It's underground, like I told you."

"How do we get it out?"

"We dig."

Without another word the two men began scraping back the soil that a Bushman had laboriously used to refill the precious well so that it didn't dry out. H. A.'s hands were broad and so callused that he could use them like shovels, tearing into the friable earth with little regard to the flinty shards. Varley had the hands of a gambler, smooth and, at one point, neatly manicured, but he dug just as hard as the guide—raging thirst allowing him to ignore the cuts and scrapes and the blood that dripped from his fingertips.

They excavated two feet of earth and still no sign of water. They had to expand the hole because they were much bigger than the Bushmen warriors whose job it was to dig these wells. At three feet H. A. took out a scoopful of dirt and when he dropped it away from the hole a thin layer clung to his skin. He rolled it between his fingers until he'd produced a little ball of mud. When he squeezed it a quivering drop of water shone in the starlight.

Varley whooped and even H. A. cracked an uncommon smile.

They redoubled their efforts, slinging mud from the hole with reckless abandon. Ryder had to put a restraining hand on Varley's shoulder when he felt they'd dug deep enough.

"Now we wait."

The other men crowded around the well and they watched in expectant silence as the darkened bottom of the excavation suddenly turned white. It was the moon reflecting off water seeping into the hole from the surrounding aquifer. H. A. used a piece torn from his shirt as a filter and dipped his canteen into the muddy water. It took several minutes for it to fill halfway. Peter moaned when he heard it sloshing as H. A. lifted it from the hole.

"Here you go, lad," Ryder said, handing over the canteen. Peter reached for it eagerly but Ryder didn't let go. "Slowly, my boy. Drink it slowly."

Smythe was too far gone to listen to H. A.'s advice; his first massive gulp sent him into a paroxysm of coughing and the mouthful of water was wasted on the desert floor. When he'd recovered he took tentative sips, looking sheepish. It took four hours to recover enough water for the men to drink their fill and finally manage to eat their first meal in days.

H. A. was still watering the horses when the sun began to brush against the eastern horizon. He was careful with them so they wouldn't bloat or cramp, and fed them sparingly, but still their great bellies rumbled with contentment as they ate and managed to stale for the first time in days.

"H. A.!" Tim Watermen had gone over the riverbank to relieve himself in private. He stood silhouetted against the dawn frantically waving his hat and pointing toward the rising sun.

Ryder plucked his telescope from his saddlebag and raced from the horses, climbing the hill like a man possessed. He smashed into Watermen so both fell to the dust. Before Tim could protest, Ryder clamped a hand over his companion's mouth and hissed, "Keep your voice down. Sound travels well over the desert."

Lying flat, H. A. extended the telescope and set it against his eye.

Look at them come, he thought. *God, they are magnificent.*

WHAT had brought these five men together was Peter Smythe's utter hatred of his father, a fearsome man who claimed to have had a vision of the archangel Gabriel. The angel had told Lucas Smythe to sell everything he owned and travel to Africa to spread the word of God among the savages. While not particularly religious before his vision, Smythe devoted himself to the Bible with such urgency that when he applied to the London Missionary Society they considered denying his application because he had become a zealot. But in the end the Society accepted him if for no other reason than to get him away from their offices. They sent him and his begrudging wife and son to Bechuanaland, where he was to replace a minister who'd died of malaria.

Away from the constraints of society at a tiny mission in the heart of the Herero people, Smythe became a religious tyrant, for his was a vengeful God who demanded total self-sacrifice and severe penitence for even the most minor transgressions. It was nothing for Peter to be cane-whipped by his father because he mumbled the last words of a prayer or be denied dinner for not being able to recite a particular psalm on command.

At the time of the family's arrival, the Herero king, Samuel Maharero, who had been baptized some decades earlier, was in a bitter dispute with the colonial authorities, and thus shunned the German minister sent to his lands by the Rhenish Mission Society. Lucas Smythe and his family enjoyed the patronage of the king even if Maharero was hesitant of Smythe's rantings of hellfire and brimstone.

While young Peter enjoyed his friendships with the king's many grand-children, life as a teen near the royal kraal was tedium punctuated with moments of terror when the Spirit seized his father, and he wanted nothing more than to run away.

And so he plotted his escape, confiding in Assa Maharero, one of the king's grandsons and his best friend, what he intended to do. It was during one of their many strategy sessions that Peter Smythe made the discovery that would change his life.

He was in a storage *rondoval*, a circular hut the Herero used to store fodder when the fields were too barren for their thousands of cattle. It was the place he and Assa had chosen as their hideout, and though Peter had been there dozens of times, this was the first he noticed that the hard-packed earth along one mud-and-grass wall had been dug up. The black soil had been carefully tamped down but his sharp eye spotted the irregularity.

He used his hands to dig into the spot, and discovered that there was only a thin layer of soil laid over a dozen large earthen beer pots. The jugs were the size of his head, and a membrane of cowhide had been stretched over their tops. He lifted one from its resting place. It was heavy and he could feel something rattling around inside.

Peter carefully worked the stitches around the rim, loosening them just enough so that when he tipped the pot a few unremarkable stones dropped into his palm. He began to shake. While they looked nothing like the stylized drawings of faceted stones he'd seen, he knew by how they scattered the meager light in the hut that he was holding six uncut diamonds. The smallest was the size of his thumbnail. The largest more than twice as big.

Just then Assa ducked through the arched doorway and saw what his friend had uncovered. His eyes went wide with terror and he quickly looked over his shoulder to see if any adults were about. Across the fenced stockade a couple of boys were watching some cattle and a woman was walking a few hundred yards away with a bundle of grass perched atop her head. He leapt across the *rondoval* and took the beer pot from Peter's startled fingers.

"What have you done?" Assa hissed in his odd German-accented English.

"Nothing, Assa, I swear," Peter cried guiltily. "I saw that something had been buried and I just wanted to see what it was, is all."

Assa held out a hand and Peter dumped the loose stones into his palm. The young African prince spoke as he tucked the stones back under the leather cover. "On pain of death you must never speak of this to anyone."

"Those are diamonds, aren't they?"

Assa regarded his friend. "Yes."

"But how? There are no diamonds here. They're all down in the Cape Colony around Kimberley."

Assa sat cross-legged in front of Peter, torn between his oath to his grandfather and pride at what his tribe had accomplished. He was three years younger than Peter, just thirteen, so youthful boasting won out over his solemn promise. "I will tell you but you must never repeat it."

"I swear, Assa."

"Since diamonds were first discovered, men of the Herero tribe have traveled to Kimberley to work in the pits. They worked a one-year contract and came home with the pay the white miners gave them, but they also took something else. They stole stones."

"I heard that the men are searched before they are allowed to leave the miners' camps, even their bums."

"What our men did was cut their skin and place the stones inside the wound. When it scarred over there was no evidence. Upon their return they reopened the wounds with assegais and retrieved the stones to present to my great-grandfather, Chief Kamaharero, who had first ordered them south to Kimberley."

"Assa, some of these stones are pretty big—surely they would have been discovered," Peter protested.

Assa laughed. "And some Herero warriors are pretty big, too." He then turned serious as he continued the tale. "This went on for many years, as many as twenty, but then the white miners discovered what the Herero were doing. A hundred were arrested and even those who hadn't yet hid a stone under their skin were found guilty of stealing. They were all put to death.

"When the time is right we will use these stones to throw off the yoke of the German colonial office"—his dark eyes shone—"and we will again live as free men. Now, swear to me again, Peter, that you will tell no one that you have discovered the treasure."

Peter's gaze met that of his young friend and said, "I swear."

His oath lasted him less than a year. When he turned eighteen he left the little mission in the center of the royal compound. He told no one that he was leaving, not even his mother, and for that he felt guilty. She alone would have to bear the weight of Lucas Smythe's righteous tirades.

Peter had always felt he was a survivor. He and Assa had camped dozens of times on the veldt, but by the time he reached a trading station fifty miles from the mission, he was nearly dead from exhaustion and thirst. There he spent a couple of the precious coins he'd hoarded from birthday presents from his mother. His father never gave him anything, believing that the only birth the family should celebrate was that of Jesus Christ.

There was barely enough to pay the wagon master to take him to Kimberley on the buckboard of a twenty-oxen span returning south with a load of ivory and salted meat. The wagon master was an older man wearing a huge white hat, and had the thickest sideburns Peter had ever seen. Tagging along with H. A. Ryder were a pair of brothers who'd been promised grazing land by the Cape colonial office only to find it already occupied by Matabele. With no desire to fight an army, they had prudently chosen to return south. Also with the party was a lean, hawk-faced man named Jon Varley.

In the weeks they trudged south, Peter never did get a sense of what Varley did or what had brought him so far from the Cape Colony; all he knew was that he didn't trust the man as far as he could spit.

At camp one night following the dangerous crossing of a river where Peter saved the life of one of Ryder's oxen by actually jumping on the animal's back and riding it across like a horse, Varley revealed a cache of liquor. It was fiery cape brandy, as raw as pure spirits, but the five of them sat around a campfire digesting a meal of guinea fowl that Tim Watermen had taken with his shotgun and drank the two bottles empty.

It was Peter's first taste of alcohol and, unlike the others, the brandy went to his head after only the first tentative sips.

It was inevitable that talk would turn to prospecting since it was second nature for anyone in the bush to keep a sharp eye for minerals. It seemed every day a new diamond field or gold reef or coal mine was staked and someone became an instant millionaire.

Peter knew he shouldn't have opened his mouth. He'd made a pledge to Assa. But he wanted to fit in with these rough-and-ready men who spoke so knowledgeably about things he himself was unaware. They were worldly, especially Varley and H. A., and Peter wanted them to respect him more than anything he'd ever wanted in his life. So with lips made slack by brandy he told them of the dozen clay pots filled with uncut diamonds in the royal kraal of King Maharero.

"How do you know this, boy?" Varley had hissed like an adder.

"Because the lad's father is the preacher in Hereroland," H. A. had answered and looked at Peter. "I recognize you now. I met your old man a couple of seasons back when I went to see the king about hunting concessions on his land." His steady eyes swept the group. "He's been living with the Herero, what, five years now?"

"Almost six," Peter answered proudly. "They know me and trust me."

Before another fifteen minutes had passed they were discussing openly the possibility of stealing the beer pots. Peter went along with the scheme only after the others promised that the five of them would only take one container each and leave seven for the Herero people; otherwise he wouldn't tell them where the stones were located.

At a trading post a further hundred miles south, H. A. Ryder sold his wagon and its precious load for half of what he could have fetched for the ivory in Kimberley and outfitted the men with proper horses and gear. He'd already decided the course they would take out of the Herero empire, the one that afforded their only chance of escape once the theft was discovered. The trading post was at the end of a newly laid telegraph line. The men waited three days while Ryder made arrangements with a trader he knew in Cape Town. H. A. shrugged off the staggering cost of what he ordered, figuring he'd either be a millionaire able to pay the debt or a corpse lying in the searing Kalahari sun.

It was impossible to sneak into the royal kraal. Runners reported their presence to the king as soon as they crossed into his domain. But H. A. was known to the king, and Peter's father was surely eager to have his son returned to him, though Peter suspected he'd be given a treatment worthy of Job rather than that of the prodigal son.

It took a week to reach the kraal from the border and Samuel Maharero himself greeted the riders when they finally reached his camp. He and H. A. spoke for an hour in the king's native tongue, the guide giving him news of the outside world since the king was in exile by order of the German colonial office. The king in turn told Peter, to his great relief, that his parents had just left for the bush, where his father was baptizing a group of women and children, and wouldn't return till the following day.

The king granted them permission to spend the night but denied H. A.'s request to hunt on Herero land, as he had four years previously.

"Can't blame a man for trying, Your Highness."

"Persistence is a white man's vice."

That night they'd stolen into the *rondoval*. The hut was packed to the roof poles with hay and they had to burrow into the pile like mice to reach the spot where the diamonds were hidden. It was when John Varley plucked a second pot from the ground and dumped its contents into a saddlebag that Peter Smythe realized he'd been duped from the beginning. The Watermen brothers, too, emptied several pots into their bags. Only H. A. kept his word and took the contents of only one of the beer pots.

"If you don't take them, I will," Varley whispered in the dark.

"Your choice," Ryder drawled. "But I'm a man of my word."

As it was they didn't have enough bags for all the stones, and after stuffing pants pockets and anything else they could, four of the big pots remained unmolested. H. A. carefully reburied the cache and did everything he could to hide the theft. They left camp at dawn, thanking the king for his hospitality. Maharero asked Peter if he had any message for his mother. Peter could only mumble to tell her he was sorry.

* * *

LYING on the crest of the dune above the water hole, H. A. allowed himself just a moment to watch the king's men.

When they'd started out after the thieves there had been an entire *impi*,
an army of a thousand warriors, tracking them from the tribal lands. But
that had been five hundred miles ago, and the hardship had whittled their
numbers. H. A. estimated there were still more than a hundred of them,
the very strongest, and they ran at a ground-eating pace despite their own
hunger and thirst. The sun was just high enough to glint off the honed
blades of their assegais, the stabbing spears their people used to vanquish
any who stood in their way.

H. A. tapped Tim Watermen on the leg and together they slid to the
bottom of the dry wash where the others clustered nervously. The horses
had picked up on the sudden shift in mood. They shuffled their hooves in
the dust and their ears twitched as if they could hear the approaching
danger.

"Mount up, lads," Ryder said, accepting the reins from Peter Smythe.

"We're going to ride?" he asked. "Through the day?"

"Aye, boy. It's that or one of Maharero's warriors going to garland his
hut with your insides. Let's go. We have only a mile on them and I don't
know how long the horses are going to take the heat."

Ryder was aware that had they not found water last night, the Herero
would have been on them like a pack of wild dogs by now. As it was, only
one of his canteens was full when he threw a rangy leg over his horse's
broad back. They climbed out of the wadi abreast, and all five men turned
when they left the shadow of the depression and felt the raw sun burning
at the backs of their necks.

For the first miles, H. A. kept them at a steady trot that gained them a
mile for every three on the advancing Herero *impi*. The sun baked the
earth and dried their sweat the instant it burst from their pores. Under the
protection of his big slouch hat, H. A. had to ride with his eyes closed to
slits to protect them from the blinding reflection off the dunes.

Resting under a sunshade as the Kalahari turned into an oven was
bad enough, but trying to cross the empty waste under its brutal onslaught
was the hardest thing H. A. had ever done in his life. The heat and the
light were maddening, as if the fluid in his skull was being boiled. The

occasional sip of water did little more than scald his throat and remind him of his raging thirst.

Time lost meaning and it took all of Ryder's concentration to remember to check his compass to steer them ever westward. With so few distinctive landmarks to guide him, his navigation was more guesswork than science, but they pressed on because there was no alternative.

The wind, like the sun, was their constant companion. H. A. estimated they weren't more than twenty miles from the South Atlantic and had expected a breeze off the ocean to hit them head-on, but the wind kept at them from the rear, always pressing them onward. Ryder prayed that his compass hadn't malfunctioned and the needle that was to guide them to the west was somehow leading them deeper into the raging interior of the molten desert. He checked it constantly, relieved that the men had strung out somewhat so no one could see the consternation on his face.

The wind grew and when he looked back to check on his men he could see the tops of the dunes were being eaten away. Long plumes of sand were cast from crest to crest. Grit stung his skin and made his eyes tear. He didn't like this at all. They were heading in the right direction but the wind wasn't. If they were caught out in a sandstorm without adequate cover there was little chance they'd survive it.

He debated calling a halt to erect a shelter, juggling the odds of a major storm hitting them, their proximity to the coast, and the enraged army that wouldn't stop until every last man in their party was dead. Sunset was in an hour. He turned his back on the wind and nosed his horse onward. Despite its flagging pace, the animal was still faster than a man on foot.

With a suddenness that left H. A. reeling he reached the top of one more featureless dune and saw that there were no more. Below him spread the slag gray waters of the South Atlantic and for the first time he could smell its iodine tang. Rolling waves turned to white froth as they roared onto the broad beach.

He lowered himself from his horse, his legs and back aching from the long ride. He didn't have the strength to whoop for joy so he stood silently, a ghost of a smile on the corners of his lips as the sun retreated into the cold dark waters.

"What is it, H. A.? Why'd you stop?" Tim Watermen called when he was still twenty yards back and just coming up the final dune.

Ryder looked down on the struggling figure, saw that Tim's brother wasn't far behind. A bit further back, young Smythe clung to his horse's back as the animal followed in its brethren's footsteps. Jon Varley wasn't yet in sight. "We made it."

It was all he had to say. Tim spurred his horse for the final ascent and when he saw the ocean he let out a triumphant yell. He reached down from the saddle and squeezed H. A.'s shoulder. "Never doubted you for a second, Mr. Ryder. Not for one damned second."

H. A. allowed himself a laugh. "You should have. I sure as hell did."

The others joined them within ten minutes. Varley looked the worst of the group and H. A. suspected that rather than rationing his water, Jon had drunk most of it in the morning.

"So we've reached the ocean," Varley snarled over the crying wind. "What now? There's still a bunch of savages after us and in case you didn't know we can't drink that." He thrust a shaky finger at the Atlantic.

H. A. ignored his tone. He pulled his Baumgart half hunter from his pocket and tilted it toward the dying sun to read its face. "There's a tall hill a mile or so up the beach. We need to be on top of it in an hour."

"What happens in an hour?" Peter asked.

"We see if I'm the navigator you all hope I am."

The dune was the tallest in sight, towering two hundred feet above the beach, and on its crest the wind was a brutal constant weight that made the horses dance in circles. The air was filled with dust, and the longer they stayed on the hillock the thicker the dust seemed to get. Ryder made the Watermen brothers and Jon Varley look up the beach to the north while he and Peter kept watch to the south.

The sun was well down as seven o'clock came and went according to H. A.'s pocket watch. *They should have signaled by now.* A weight like lead settled in his stomach. It had been too much to ask: crossing hundreds of miles of empty desert and thinking he could come within a few miles of a specific spot on the coast. They could be a hundred or more miles from the rendezvous.

"There!" Peter cried and pointed.

H. A. squinted into the darkness. A tiny red ball of incandescence hung close to shore far down the coast. It stayed within sight for no more than a second before vanishing once again.

A man standing at sea level can see approximately three miles before the curvature of the earth blocks his view. By climbing the bluff, H. A. had extended their range to eighteen and a half miles in either direction. Adding the height the flare had climbed, he guessed their rendezvous was about twenty miles down the coastline. He *had* led them across the barren wastes to within sight of their target, a remarkable feat of navigation.

The men had been awake for forty-eight torturous hours, but the thought that their hardships were almost at an end, with a king's ransom for a reward, buoyed them those last miles. The bluffs sheltered the broad beach from the intensifying sandstorm, but dust was clouding the waters along the surf line as sand settled onto the ocean. The once white crests were mud brown, and it seemed the seas were sluggish under the tons of sand blowing into it.

At midnight they could see the lights of a small ship anchored a hundred yards from shore. The vessel was steel-hulled and coal-fired, a littoral cargo ship about two hundred feet long. Her superstructure was well aft, punctured by a single tall funnel while the forward part of her hull was given over to four separate hatch covers for her holds, serviced by a pair of spindly derricks. Sand blasted at the ship and H. A. couldn't tell if her boilers were still fired. The moon was mostly hidden by the storm, so he couldn't be sure if there was smoke coming from her funnel.

When they were abreast of the steamer, H. A. plucked a small flare from his saddlebag, the only item besides the stones he'd refused to leave behind. He ignited the flare and waved it over his head, yelling at the top of his lungs to be heard over the gale. The men joined him, whooping and hollering, knowing in a few minutes they would be safe.

A searchlight mounted on the ship's flying bridge snapped on, its beam cutting through the whirling sand and coming to rest on the group of men. They danced in its glow as the horses shied away. A moment later, a dory was lowered from the lifeboat mount, a pair of men working the oars with swift professional strokes that cut the distance in moments. A third figure sat in the back of the craft. The men rushed into the water to greet the boat as its keel sliced into the sand just inside the surf line.

"That you, H. A.?" a voice called out.

"You damned well better hope so, Charlie."

Charles Turnbaugh, first officer of the HMS *Rove*, leapt from the dory and stood knee deep in the surf. "So is this the biggest cock-and-bull story I've ever heard or did you actually do it?"

H. A. held up one of his saddlebags. He shook it, but the wind was too fierce for anyone to hear the stones rattling around inside. "Let's just say I've made your trip worth your while. How long have you been waiting for us?'

"We got here five days ago and have been firing a flare every night at seven just like you asked."

"Check your ship's chronometer. It's running a minute slow." Rather than make introductions H. A. said, "Listen, Charlie, there's about a hundred Herero bucks after us, and the sooner we're off the beach and over the horizon the happier I'll be."

Turnbaugh began directing the exhausted men into the dory. "We can get you off the beach but not over the horizon for a while."

Ryder put a hand on his dirty uniform jacket. "What's the matter?"

"We grounded ourselves when the tide went out. The shoals and sand-bars along the coast are always shifting. Come next high tide we'll float free. Don't worry."

"Oh, one thing," Ryder said before stepping into the little boat. "Do you have a pistol?"

"What? Why?"

H. A. twitched his head over his shoulder to where the horses huddled together, growing more terrified as the storm strengthened.

"I think the captain has an old Webley," Turnbaugh said.

"I'd be obliged if you fetched it for me."

"They're just horses," Varley said, huddled in the dory.

"Who deserve something better than dying on this forsaken beach after what they did for us."

"I'll do it," Charlie said.

H. A. helped push the little craft until she floated free and waited with the horses, talking to them soothingly and rubbing their heads and necks. Turnbaugh returned fifteen minutes later and silently handed over the weapon. A minute after that, H. A. climbed slowly into the dory and sat unmoving as he was rowed out to the tramp freighter.

He found his men in the wardroom devouring plates of food and drinking enough water to make each of them look a little green. H. A. took measured sips, allowing his body to adjust. Captain James Kirby stepped into the small room with Charlie and the ship's engineer just as H. A. took his first bite of stew left over from the officers' mess.

"H. A. Ryder, you've got more lives than a cat," the captain boomed. He was a great bear of a man with thick dark hair and a beard that reached midway down his chest. "And if it had been anyone other than you making such a damned fool request I would have told them to shove off."

The two men shook hands warmly. "At the price you're charging I knew you'd wait until hell froze over."

"Speaking of price?" One of Kirby's bushy eyebrows climbed halfway up his forehead.

Ryder placed his saddlebag on the floor and made a show of undoing its buckles, drawing out the moment until he could taste the crew's greed. He opened the flap, rummaged through the bag's contents until he found a stone he thought appropriate, and set it on the table. There was a collective gasp. The light in the wardroom was just a pair of lanterns hanging from hooks in the ceiling but they caught the diamond's fire and cast it around so it looked like they were standing inside a rainbow.

"This ought to pay you for your trouble," H. A. deadpanned.

"With a little change left over," Captain Kirby breathed, touching the stone for the first time.

A rough hand woke H. A. the following morning at six. He tried to ignore it and turned away on the tiny bunk he was using while Charlie Turnbaugh was on duty. "H. A., damnit. Get up."

"What is it?"

"We've got a problem."

The grimness in Turnbaugh's voice brought Ryder instantly awake. He swung off the bunk and reached for his clothes. Dust spilled from the cloth as he struggled into his pants and shirt. "What is it?"

"You have to see it to believe it."

Ryder was aware that the storm continued to blow stronger than ever.

The wind screamed over the ship like an animal trying to claw its way in while even stronger gusts made the entire vessel shudder. Turnbaugh led him up to the bridge. Dun light filtered though the windscreen and it was almost impossible to see the *Rove*'s bow only a hundred and fifty feet away. H. A. saw the problem immediately. The storm had dumped so much sand on the freighter's deck that the weight of it pinned her to the bottom despite the rising tide. Furthermore, where once they had a hundred yards of water between them and the beach, now less than fifty separated ship from shore.

The Kalahari and the Atlantic were locked in their eternal struggle for territory, a fight between the erosive actions of waves verses the awesome volume of sand the desert could pour onto the waters. They had fought each other since the dawn of time, constantly reshaping the coastline as sand found weaknesses in the constant scouring of current and tide and struggled to expand the desert a foot or a yard or a mile. And all this played out with little regard to the ship caught in the tumult.

"I need every available hand to start shoveling," Kirby said darkly. "If the storm doesn't abate, this ship is going to be landlocked by nightfall."

Turnbaugh and Ryder rousted their respective crews and using coal shovels from the engine room, pans from the kitchen, and a hip bath from the captain's washroom they ran into the raging storm. With scarves covering their mouths and the wind so strong that talking was impossible, they pushed mounds of loose sand off the deck and into the water. They raged against the tempest, cursing it because every shovelful they heaved over the side only seemed to come back into their faces.

It was like trying to hold back the tide. They managed to get one hatch scraped clean only to see the amount of sand piled onto the other three had doubled. Five adventurers and a ship's compliment of twenty was no match for the storm that had traveled across thousands of square miles of seared earth. Visibility was cut to almost zero, so the men worked blind, their eyes tightly closed to the stinging grit that assaulted the *Rove* from every point on the compass.

After an hour of frantic work, H. A. went to look for Charlie. "It's no use. We have to wait and hope the storm slows." Even with his lips touching Turnbaugh's ear Ryder had to repeat himself three times to be heard over the shrieking wind.

"You're right," Charlie screamed back and together they went to recall their men.

The crews staggered back into the superstructure, shedding cascades of sand with each step. H. A. and Jon Varley were the last ones through the hatch, H. A. out of duty to make sure everyone was all right, Varley because he had a rat's cunning to never give in when he was certain of a reward.

It was still difficult to hear out of the wind inside the companionway.

"Dear Jesus, please let this end." So awed by the force of nature arrayed against them, Peter was almost in tears.

"Do we have everyone?" Charlie asked.

"I think so." H. A. sagged against a bulkhead. "Did you do a head count?"

Turnbaugh started counting off his people when there was a sharp rap on the hatchway.

"Good God, someone's still out there," someone called.

Varley was closest to the hatch and undogged the latches. The wind slammed the door against its stops as the gale whipped into the ship, scouring paint from the walls with the merest touch. It appeared no one was there. It had to have been a loose piece of equipment rattling outside.

Varley lurched forward to close the door and had it almost shut when a bright silver blade emerged a hand's span from his back. Gore dripped from the spear's tip, and when it was pulled from the raw wound blood sprayed the stunned crew. Jon pirouetted as he collapsed to the deck, his mouth working soundlessly as his shirt turned crimson. A dark wraith wearing little but feathers and a cloth around his waist stepped over Varley with an assegai in his hands. Behind him more shapes were primed for the charge, their war cries rivaling even that of the storm.

"Herero," H. A. whispered with resignation as the wave of warriors burst into the ship.

THE storm was a freak of nature, a once-in-a-hundred-years occurrence that raged for over a week, forever changing the coast of southwest Africa. Once mighty dunes had been rendered flat, while others had grown to newer and even greater heights. Where once there were bays, now great peninsulas of sand thrust into the cold waters of the South Atlantic. The continent had grown five miles bigger in some places, ten in others, as the Kalahari won one of its battles against its arch foe. The map would have to be redrawn for hundreds of miles up and down the coast, that is if anyone cared to map the forlorn shore. Every sailor just knew to stay well off the treacherous seaboard.

Of the *Rove* and all those aboard her, the official report listed her as lost at sea. And that wasn't far from the truth, though she lay not under hundreds of feet of water, but under an equal amount of pure white sand, nearly eight miles inland from where the icy waves of the Benguela Current pounded against Africa's Skeleton Coast.

2

THE LABORATORIES OF MERRICK/SINGER
GENEVA, SWITZERLAND
PRESENT DAY

SUSAN Donleavy sat hunched like a vulture over the eyepiece of her microscope and watched the action unfold on the slide as though she were a god of Greek mythology being entertained by mortals. And in a sense she was, for what lay on the slide was her own creation, an engineered organism that she had breathed life into as surely as the gods had molded man out of clay.

She remained motionless for nearly an hour, enraptured by what she was seeing, amazed that the results were so positive this early in her work. Against all scientific principles, but trusting her gut, Susan Donleavy removed the slide from the scope and set it on the workbench next to her. She crossed the room to where an industrial cooler hulked against one wall and removed one of several gallon jugs of water kept at precisely sixty-eight degrees.

The water had been in storage for less than a day, having been flown to the lab as soon as it had been collected. The need to keep fresh water samples was one of the principle expenses of her experiments—nearly as costly as the detailed gene sequencing of her subjects.

She opened the jug and smelled the salty tang of ocean water. She dipped a dropper into its surface and siphoned up a small amount, which she then transferred to a slide. Once she had it centered under the microscope, she peered into the realm of the infinitely tiny. The sample teemed with life. In just a few milliliters of water there were hundreds of zooplankton and diatoms, single-celled creatures that formed the first link of the food chain for the entire ocean.

The microscopic animals and plants were similar to the ones she'd been studying earlier, only these had not been genetically modified.

Satisfied that the water sample hadn't degraded in transport, she poured some into a glass beaker. Holding it over her head, she could see some of the larger diatoms in the glare cast by the banks of fluorescent lights. Susan was so focused on her work she didn't hear the door to the lab open, and since it was so late she didn't expect anyone to be disturbing her.

"What have you got there?" The voice startled her and she nearly dropped the beaker.

"Oh, Dr. Merrick. I didn't know you were here."

"I've told you, like I tell everyone in the company, to please call me Geoff."

Susan frowned slightly. Geoffrey Merrick wasn't a bad sort, really, but she disliked his affability, as if his billions shouldn't affect the way people treated him, especially staffers at Merrick/Singer who were still working toward their doctorates. He was a year over fifty, but kept himself in shape by skiing nearly year-round, chasing the snows to South America when summer came to the Swiss Alps. He was also a bit vain about his appearance, and his skin remained too tight following a face-lift. Though a doctor in chemistry himself, Merrick had long since given up lab work and instead spent his time overseeing the research company that bore his and his ex-partner's names.

"Is this that flocculent project your supervisor ran past me a few months ago?" Merrick asked, taking the beaker from Susan and studying it himself.

Unable to lie to get him out of her lab Susan said, "Yes, Doctor, I mean, Geoff."

"It was an interesting idea when it was presented, though I have absolutely no idea what it could be used for," Merrick commented, handing back the beaker. "But I guess that's what we do here. We chase down our whims and see where they take us. How's the project coming?"

"I think okay," Susan said, anxious because no matter how nice he was, Merrick intimidated her. Though, if she were truthful with herself, most people intimidated her, from her boss down to the older women she rented her apartment from and the counterman at the café where she bought her morning coffee. "I was about to try an unscientific experiment."

"Good, we'll watch it together. Please proceed."

Susan's hands were beginning to tremble so she placed the beaker on a stand. She retrieved the first slide, the one containing her engineered phytoplankton, and sucked up the sample with a fresh dropper. She then carefully injected its contents into the beaker.

"I forget the particulars of what you're doing," Merrick said, standing over her shoulder. "What should we be seeing here?"

Susan shifted to hide the fact his proximity made her uncomfortable. "As you know, diatoms like this phytoplankton have a cell wall made of silica. What I've done is, well, what I'm trying to do, is find a way to melt that wall and ramp up the density of the cell sap within the vacuole. My engineered specimens should attack the unaltered diatoms in the water and go into a frenzy of replication and if things work out right . . ." Her voice trailed off as she reached for the beaker once again. She slid a hand into an insulated glove so she could touch the glass container. She tilted it onto its side but rather than spilling quickly, the water sloshed up the side with the viscosity of cooking oil. She righted the beaker before any dripped onto the lab table.

Merrick clapped, delighted as a child for whom she'd just performed a magic trick. "You've turned the water sort of gooey."

"Kind of, I guess. The diatoms have actually bound themselves in such a way that they capture the water within a matrix of their sap. The water's still there, it's just held in suspension."

"I'll be damned. Well done, Susan, well done."

"It's not a total success," Donleavy admitted. "The reaction is exothermic. It generates heat. Around a hundred and forty degrees in the right conditions. That's why I need this thick glove. The gel breaks down after only twenty-four hours as the engineered diatoms die off. I can't figure out the process behind the reaction. I know it's chemical, obviously, but I don't know how to stop it."

"I still think you're off to a tremendous start. Tell me, you must have some idea what we could do with such an invention. The idea of wanting to turn water into goop isn't something that struck you out of the blue. When Dan Singer and I started working on organic ways to trap sulfur we thought it might have applications in power plants to reduce emissions. There must be something behind your project."

Susan blinked, but should have known Geoffrey Merrick didn't get where he was without a keen sense of perception. "You're right," she admitted. "I thought maybe it could be used for settling ponds at mines and water-treatment plants and maybe even a way to stop oil spills from spreading."

"That's right. I remember from your personnel file, you're from Alaska."

"Seward, Alaska, yes."

"You must have been in your early teens when the *Exxon Valdez* hit that reef and dumped all that oil in Prince William Sound. That must have had quite an impact on you and your family. It must have been rough."

Susan shrugged. "Not really. My parents ran a small hotel and with all the people on the cleanup crews they did okay. But I had a lot of friends whose parents lost everything. My best friend's parents even divorced as a result of the spill because her dad lost his job at a cannery."

"Then this research is personal for you."

Susan bristled at his slightly condescending tone. "I think it's personal for anyone who cares about the environment."

He smiled. "You know what I mean. You're like the cancer researcher who lost a parent to leukemia, or the guy who becomes a fireman because his house burned down when he was a kid. You're fighting a demon out of your childhood." When she didn't reply Merrick took it to mean he was right. "There's nothing wrong with revenge as a motivation, Susan. Revenge against cancer, or a fire, or an ecological nightmare. It keeps you far more focused on your work than doing it just to get a paycheck. I applaud you and by the looks of what I've seen tonight, I think that you're on the right path."

"Thank you," Susan said shyly. "There's still a lot more work to go. Years, maybe. I don't know. A tiny sample in a test tube is a long way off from containing an oil spill."

"Run your ideas to ground, is all I can say. Go wherever they take you, and for as long as you need." From someone other than Geoffrey Merrick that would have sounded trite but he spoke it with sincerity and conviction.

Susan met his eye for the first time since he'd entered the laboratory. "Thank you . . . Geoff. That means a lot."

"And who knows. After we patented our sulpher scrubbers, I became a pariah to the environmental movement because they claimed my invention didn't do enough to stop pollution. Maybe you can finally salvage my reputation." He left with a smile.

After he'd gone Susan returned to her beakers and test tubes. Wearing protective gloves she took the one filled with her genetically modified diatoms and slowly tilted it to the side again. Ten minutes had elapsed since she'd last handled it and this time the water sample at its bottom clung to the glass as though it were glue; and only after inverting the hot beaker completely did it start to ooze downward, as slowly as chilled molasses.

Susan thought about the dying otters and seabirds she'd seen as a child and redoubled her work.

3

THE CONGO RIVER
SOUTH OF MATADI

THE jungle would eventually swallow the abandoned plantation and the three-hundred-foot wooden pier built along the river. The main house a mile inland had already succumbed to the effects of rot and encroaching vegetation, and it was only a matter of time before the dock was swept away and the metal warehouse nearby collapsed. Its roof sagged like a swaybacked horse, and its corrugated skin was scaled with rust and flecked paint. It was a haunted, forlorn place that even the soft milky glow of a three-quarter moon couldn't liven.

A large freighter was nudging closer to the pier, dwarfing even the massive warehouse. With her bow pointed downstream and her engines in reverse, the water under her fantail frothed as she fought the current to stay on station. It was a delicate balance to maintain her position, especially considering the Congo's notorious back-currents and eddies.

With a walkie-talkie held to his lips, and his other arm flailing theatrically, the captain paced the starboard wing bridge and yelled at the helmsman and engineer to make corrections. The throttles were moved in fractional increments to keep the 560-foot vessel exactly where he wanted.

A group of men wearing dark fatigues waited on the dock and watched the operation. All but one carried an assault rifle. The man without an AK-47 had a huge holster strapped to his hip. He tapped the side of his leg with a leather riding crop and despite the darkness sported mirrored aviator shades.

The captain was a large black man wearing a Greek fisherman's cap atop his shaved head. The muscles of his chest and arms strained against his white uniform blouse. Another man was with him on the bridge wing: slightly shorter and not as muscled, he was somehow a more commanding presence than the captain. He exuded authority from his watchful eyes and the loose, casual way he carried himself. With the wing bridge lofting three stories above the quay there was no chance of their conversation being overheard. The captain nudged his companion, who'd been studying the armed troops rather than paying attention to the tricky maneuvering.

"Seems our rebel leader stepped straight out of central casting, eh, Chairman?"

"Right down to the riding whip and shades," the chairman agreed. "Of course, we're not beyond giving people what they expect to see, either, *Captain* Lincoln. That was a nice little performance with the walkie-talkie."

Linc looked at the walkie-talkie in his big hand. The small device didn't even have batteries in it. He chuckled softly. As the most senior African-American member of the crew, Lincoln had been tapped by the ship's real captain, Juan Cabrillo, to act the part for the current operation. Cabrillo knew that the representative sent by Samuel Makambo, the leader of the Congolese Army of Revolution, would be more comfortable dealing with a man who shared the same skin color.

Linc looked over the rail once again, satisfied that the big freighter was holding steady. "All right," he bellowed into the night. "Let go fore and aft lines."

Deckhands at the stern and bow lowered thick ropes through the hawseholes. With a nod from their commander, two of the rebels slung their weapons over their shoulders and looped the lines over the rust-coated bollards. Windlasses took up the slack and the big freighter gently kissed the old truck tires slung along the length of the pier that acted as fenders. Water continued to foam at the ship's stern as reverse thrust was maintained to fight the current. Without it, the ship would have ripped the bollards from the decaying wooden dock and drifted downstream.

Cabrillo took just a moment to check the freighter's stations, keeping position, gauging current, windage, rudder, and power with one sweep of the eye. Satisfied, he nodded to Linc. "Let's make a deal."

The two stepped into the ship's main bridge. The room was illuminated by a pair of red night-lights, giving it a hellish appearance that made its dilapidated state all the more obvious. The floors were unwashed linoleum that was cracked and peeling in the corners. The windows were dusty on the inside while the outsides were rimmed with salt crust. The sills were the graveyards of all manner of dead insects. One needle on the tarnished brass engine telegraph had broken off long ago, and the ship's wheel was missing several spokes. The vessel carried few modern navigational aids and the radio in the shack behind the bridge could barely transmit a dozen miles.

Cabrillo nodded at the helmsman, an intense Chinese man in his early forties, who shot the Chairman a wry smile. Cabrillo and Franklin Lincoln descended a series of companionways lit only occasionally by low-watt bulbs in metal cages. They soon reached the main deck where another member of the crew waited.

"Ready to play jungle jeweler, Max?" Juan greeted.

At sixty-four Max Hanley was the second oldest member of the crew, and was only just showing the signs of age. His hair had retreated to a ginger fringe around his skull and his belt line had thickened a bit. But he could more than handle himself in a fight and had been at Cabrillo's side since the day Juan had started the Corporation, the company that owned and operated the tramp freighter. Theirs was an easy friendship of mutual respect borne of countless dangers faced and bested.

Hanley hoisted an attaché case from the pitted deck. "You know what they say—'diamonds are a mercenary's best friend.'"

"I've never heard them say that," Linc said.

"Well, they do."

The deal had been a month in the making, through countless cutouts and several clandestine meetings. It was pretty straightforward. In exchange for a quarter pound of rough diamonds, the Corporation was giving Samuel Makambo's Congolese Army of Revolution five hundred AK-47 assault rifles, two hundred rocket-propelled grenades, fifty RPG launchers, and fifty thousand rounds of Warsaw Pact 7.62 mm ammunition. Makambo hadn't asked where the crew of a tramp freighter got their hands on so much military hardware, and Cabrillo didn't want to know how the rebel leader obtained so many diamonds. Though coming from this part of the world, he was sure they were blood diamonds, mined by slaves in order to finance the revolution.

Able to recruit boys as young as thirteen for his army, Makambo needed weapons more than soldiers, so this shipment of arms would ensure that his attempt to overthrow the shaky government now stood a pretty good chance.

A crewman lowered the gangplank down to the dock and Linc led Cabrillo and Hanley onto the quay. The lone rebel officer detached himself from his Praetorian guards and approached Franklin Lincoln. He snapped Linc a crisp military salute, which Linc returned with a casual touch to the bill of his fisherman's cap.

"Captain Lincoln, I am Colonel Raif Abala of the Congolese Army of Revolution." Abala spoke English with a mixture of French and native accents. His voice was flat, without any trace of inflection or humanity. He didn't remove his sunglasses and continued to tap the riding crop against the seam of his camouflage pants.

"Colonel," Linc said, holding up his arms while a pock-faced aide de camp frisked him for weapons.

"Our supreme leader, General Samuel Makambo, sends his regards and regrets that he could not meet you in person."

Makambo had been waging his year-long insurrection from a secret base somewhere deep in the jungle. He hadn't been seen since taking up arms, and had managed to foil all government attempts to infiltrate his headquarters, murdering ten handpicked soldiers who'd tried to join the CAR with orders to assassinate him. Like bin Laden or Abimael Guzman, the former leader of Peru's Shining Path, Makambo's air of invincibility only added to his appeal, even with the blood of thousands blamed on his coup attempt.

"You have brought the weapons." It was more statement than question.

"And you will see them as soon as my associate here inspects the stones." Lincoln made a casual wave toward Max.

"As we agreed," Abala said. "Come."

A table had been set up on the dock with a light powered by a portable generator. Abala threw a leg over one of the chairs and sat, setting his whip on the tabletop. In front of him was a brown burlap bag with the name of a feed company inked in French on its side. Max sat opposite the African rebel and busied himself with the contents of his case. He took out an electronic scale, some weights to calibrate it, and a bunch of plastic graduated cylinders with a clear liquid inside. He also had notebooks, pencils, and a small calculator. Guards stood behind Abala and more were behind Max Hanley. Another pair stood close enough to Cabrillo and Linc to cut them down at the slightest indication from the rebel colonel. The prospect of violence hung low over the group and the humid night air was charged with nervous tension.

Abala rested one hand on the bag. He looked up at Linc. "Captain, I think now would be the time to show some good faith. I would like to see the container carrying my weapons."

"That wasn't part of the deal," Linc said, letting just a hint of concern into his voice. Abala's aide snickered.

"Like I said," Abala continued, his tone full of menace, "it is a show of faith. A goodwill gesture on your part." He took his hand off the bag and raised a finger. Twenty more soldiers emerged from the darkness. Abala waved them off again and just as quickly as they'd appeared they had vanished back into the gloom. "They could kill your crew and simply take the guns. That is a show of my goodwill."

Without a choice, Linc turned to face the ship. A crewman stood at the railing. Linc twirled his hand over his head. The deckhand waved, and a moment later a small diesel engine bellowed to life. The center of the three derricks on the big freighter's bow section creaked to life, heavy cables sliding through rusty pullies as a great weight was lifted from a cargo hold. It was a standard forty-foot shipping container, as innocuous as any of the hundreds of thousands used every day in maritime commerce. The crane lifted it clear of the hatch and swung it to the railing, where it was lowered to the deck. Two more crewmen opened the doors and stepped inside the container. With a shout they called to the hoistman, and the container was lifted once again, rising up over the railing as the box was moved over the side of the ship. It was lowered to within eight feet of the dock but came no lower.

The men in the box used flashlights to illuminate the container's contents. Racks of AK-47s lined the walls, oily black in the dim light. The beams also revealed dark green crates. One was opened, and a crewman slung an empty RPG tube to his shoulder, showing off the weapon like a model at a trade show. A couple of the youngest rebel soldiers cheered. Even Raif Abala couldn't keep his mouth from twitching upward at the corners.

"That's the extent of my good faith," Lincoln said after the two crewmen had leapt to the ground and returned to the ship.

Without a word Abala spilled the contents of the bag across the table. Cut and polished, diamonds are the greatest natural refractor in the world, able to split white light into a rainbow spectrum with such dazzle and flash that the stones have been coveted since time immemorial. But in their raw state there is little to distinguish the gems. The pile of stones showed no sparkle. They sat dully on the table, misshapen lumps of crystal, most fashioned like a pair of four-sided pyramids fused at the base, while others were just random pebbles with no discernible shape at all. They ranged in hue from pure white to the dingiest yellow; and while some appeared clear, many were cleaved and fractured. But Max and Juan noticed instantly that none was smaller than a carat. Their value in the diamond districts of New York, Tel Aviv, or Amsterdam was far beyond that of the contents of the container, but such was the nature of commerce. Abala could always get more diamonds. It was the weapons that were hard to procure.

Max instinctively grabbed the largest stone, a crystal of at least ten carats. Cut and polished to a four- or five-carat stone, it would fetch about forty thousand dollars depending on its color grade and clarity. He studied it through a jeweler's loupe, twisting it against the light, his mouth pursed in a sour expression. He set it aside without comment and peered at another stone, and then another. He tsked a couple of times as if disappointed by what he was seeing, then pulled a pair of reading glasses from his shirt pocket. When he had them perched on his nose, he shot Abala a disappointed look over them and opened one of his notebooks, scratching in a couple of lines with a mechanical pencil.

"What are you writing?" Abala said, suddenly unsure of himself in Max's learned presence.

"That these stones make better gravel than gems." Max said, making his voice shrill and adding an atrocious Dutch accent. Abala almost leapt to his feet at the insult, but Max waved him down. "But on preliminary review I judge them satisfactory for our transaction."

He pulled a flat piece of topaz from his pants pocket, its surfaces deeply scratched. "As you know," he said in a lecturing tone, "diamond is the hardest substance on earth. Ten on the Mohs' scale, to be exact. Quartz, which is number seven, is often used to fool the uninitiated into thinking they are getting the deal of a lifetime."

From the same pocket he plucked an octagonal shaft of crystal. Bearing down with considerable force he raked the quartz across the flat chunk of topaz. The edge slid off without making a mark. "As you can see, topaz is harder than quartz and hence can't be scratched. It is eight on the Mohs' scale, in fact." He then took one of the smaller diamonds and ran it across the topaz. With a spine-shivering squeal the edge of the gem dug a deep scratch into the blue semiprecious stone. "So what we have here is a stone harder than eight on the Mohs' scale."

"Diamond," Abala said smugly.

Max sighed as if a recalcitrant student had made a gaff. He was enjoying playing at gemologist. "Or corundum, which is nine on the Mohs' scale. The only way to be certain this is a diamond is to test its specific gravity."

Although Abala had dealt with diamonds many times before he knew little of their properties other than their value. Without realizing it, Hanley had piqued his interest and lowered his guard. "What is specific gravity?" he asked.

"The ratio of a stone's weight verses the volume of water it displaces. For diamond it is exactly three point five two." Max fiddled with his scale for a moment, calibrating it with a set of brass weights carried in a velvet-lined case. Once the scale had been zeroed he set the largest stone on the pan. "Point two two five grams. Eleven and a half carats." He opened one of the plastic graduated cylinders and dropped the stone inside, noting how much water the gem displaced in his notebook. He then tapped the numbers into the calculator. When he saw the resulting number he glared at Raif Abala.

Abala's eyes went wide with indignant anger. His troopers tightened their cordon. A gun was pressed against Juan's back.

Unperturbed by the sudden show of aggression, Max let his expression go neutral and then allowed a smile to creep across his face. "Three point five two. This, gentlemen, is a real diamond."

Colonel Abala slowly lowered himself into his seat and fingers that had been ounces away from squeezing triggers were relaxed. Juan could have killed Hanley for playing his role a little too well.

Max tested eight more random stones and each time the results were the same.

"I have held up my end of the bargain," Abala said. "A quarter pound of diamonds for the weapons."

While Hanley tested more stones, Linc led Abala to the open container, signaling to a crewman on the freighter to lower it to the quay. The wooden piers holding up the jetty creaked under the weight. Five rebel soldiers went with them. By the glare of a flashlight, Abala and his men grabbed ten AK-47s from different racks and about a hundred rounds of ammunition, using a machete to cut open the wax-coated paper blocks of bullets.

Making sure he stood close by Abala in case the troops tried something, Linc watched as the men laboriously loaded the shiny brass cartridges into the AK's distinctive banana magazines. Juan, who was wearing a lightweight flak jacket under his bulky sweatshirt, stuck to Max for the very same reason. Each assault rifle was fired ten times, two three-round bursts and four single shots aimed carefully at a target stapled to the side of the disused warehouse. The gunfire echoed across the broad reach of the river and sent dozens of birds winging into the night. A soldier ran to the warehouse to inspect the damage, shouting an encouragement. Abala grunted at Linc, "Good. Very good."

Back at the table Hanley carried on his inspection, setting the empty sack on the scale and noting its weight in his notebook. Then, under the watchful eye of one of Abala's officers, he used a long-handled spoon to coax the rough stones back into the bag. Once he had them all, he weighed the bag again. On the calculator he subtracted the bag's weight from the total. He looked over his shoulder at Cabrillo and whispered, "We are eight carats short."

Depending on the stones, those eight carats could translate into tens of thousands of dollars. Juan shrugged. "I'll just be happy to get out of here alive. Let it go." Cabrillo called over to Linc, who was going over one of the RPGs with Abala and a rebel who had the professional look of a sergeant, "Captain Lincoln, the port authorities won't hold our berth in Boma. We should get going."

Linc turned to him. "Of course, Mr. Cabrillo. Thank you." He looked back to Abala. "I wish I had more weapons to offer you, Colonel, but coming across this shipment was a surprise to me and my crew."

"If you, ah, ever get such a surprise again, you know how to contact us."

They had reached the table. Linc asked Max, "Everything all set?"

"Yes, Captain, everything's in order."

Abala's smile took on an even oilier sheen. He'd intentionally shorted them on the deal, knowing that his overwhelming number of armed men would intimidate them into accepting fewer stones than agreed. The missing diamonds were in his uniform blouse pocket and would go a long way in fattening his Swiss bank account.

"Let's go then, gentlemen." Linc took the bag of diamonds from Max and strode toward the gangplank, Cabrillo and Hanley hurrying to match his long strides. The moment before they reached the gangway Abala's men swung into action. The two closest to the ramp stepped forward to block it while dozens of rebels rushed out of the jungle firing into the air and screaming like banshees. At least a dozen men swarmed the container, trying to unhook the cargo derrick.

The effect would have been overwhelming had the Corporation team not expected a double-cross.

A second before Abala shouted his order to attack, Cabrillo and Linc had started running. They were on the two rebels at the base of the gangplank before either had time to bring their weapons to bear. Linc bodily tossed one young soldier into the space between the freighter and the quay as Juan jammed his fingers into the other's throat just hard enough to make him retch. As the rebel coughed, Juan ripped the AK-47 out of his hands and sank the butt into the soldier's stomach. He fell into a fetal ball.

Cabrillo swung around and laid down a wall of cover fire as Max and Linc mounted the gangway. Juan stepped onto the sloping ramp and pressed a button under the railing. The five feet of the gangway's leading edge snapped sharply upward. With its solid sides, and now with the tip elevated ninety degrees, the three men were shielded by the withering return fire from Abala's men. Bullets whizzed over their heads, smacking into the side of the freighter and ricocheting off the metal skin of the gangway as the trio huddled safely in their armored cocoon.

"Like we wouldn't see this coming," Max said casually over the riotous din.

An operator inside the ship worked the controls of the gangplank and it lifted off the dock, allowing the men to dash into the ship's superstructure. All pretenses aside, Juan took immediate control. He slapped the button on a wall-mounted intercom. "Sit rep, Mr. Murphy."

Deep inside the freighter, Mark Murphy, chief weapons operator, was watching a monitor showing video from a camera mounted on one of the ship's five cranes.

"With the gangway up, only a couple of guys are still firing. I think Abala is trying to organize an assault. He's rallied about a hundred of them and is giving them their orders."

"What about the container?"

"The men almost have the lines off it. Hold it. Yeah, they got it. We're free of it."

"Tell Mr. Stone to prepare to get us out of here."

"Ah, Chairman?" Murphy said hesitantly. "We're still tied to the dock bollards."

Cabrillo fingered a trickle of blood from where a fleck of paint kicked free by a bullet had nicked his ear. "Tear 'em out. I'm on my way."

While their ship looked right at home up against the disintegrating dock, she hid a secret of which only a few outside the crew was aware. Her rust-streaked hull with its mismatched paint, dilapidated derricks, stained deck, and generally grimy appearance was nothing but stage dressing to disguise the vessel's true capabilities. She was a privately funded spy ship owned by the Corporation and headed by Juan Cabrillo. The *Oregon* was his brainchild and his one true love.

Under her scabrous hide she bristled with some of the most advanced weapon systems on the planet—cruise missiles and torpedoes bought from a crooked Russian admiral, 30 mm Gatling guns, and a 120 mm cannon that employed the same targeting technology as an M1A2 Abrams tank, as well as servo-controlled .30-caliber machine guns to fend off boarders. All the weapons were mounted behind deck plates along the hull or disguised as junk littering her deck. The remotely operated .30 calibers were hidden in rusted barrels placed strategically along the ship's rail. On command the lids lifted off and the weapons emerged, aided by low-light and infrared cameras.

Several decks below the ship's bridge, where Cabrillo and Lincoln had stood when the *Oregon* docked, was the operations center, the brain of the vessel. From there, her crew of retired U.S. military and CIA operatives ran the entire ship, from her engines and dynamic positioning system to all her weapons. They also possessed a suite of radar and sonar gear that was among the best a considerable amount of money could buy.

It was from the op center that the *Oregon*'s preeminent helmsman, Eric Stone, had actually docked the vessel, using athwartship bow and stern thrusters and input from the global positioning system, all linked to a supercomputer that gauged wind speed, currents, and a dozen other factors. It was this computer that employed the exact amount of reverse thrust required to keep the *Oregon* in position against the flow of the Congo River.

Cabrillo and Max stepped into a utility closet that reeked of turpentine while Linc headed off to meet with Eddie Seng and the rest of the shore operations specialists in case they were needed to keep the rebels from gaining the deck. Juan spun the handles for the slop sink like the dials of a safe and the closet's back wall opened to reveal a hallway beyond.

Unlike the cheap linoleum and peeling paint of the bridge and other sections of the superstructure, this secret interior passage was well lit, with rich mahogany paneling and plush carpets. An original Winslow painting of a whaling ship hung from a wall and a glass-encased sixteenth-century suit of armor complete with sword and mace stood at the end of the hallway.

They strode past countless cabin doors until reaching the operations center at the heart of the freighter. It was as high-tech as NASA's mission control, with computer work stations and a wall dominated by an enormous flat panel display currently showing the chaotic scene along the pier. Mark Murphy and Eric Stone sat at the forward work stations directly below the wall monitor while Hali Kasim, the ship's chief communications specialist, was to the right. Along the back wall stood a pair of damage controllers monitoring the ship's integrated safety systems and a bank of computers where Max Hanley could watch over the *Oregon*'s revolutionary magnetohydrodynamic engines.

It was no mistake that the op center had the feel of the bridge of television's starship *Enterprise*, right down to the large seat set in the middle of the room. Juan sat in what the crew called "The Kirk Chair," looped a pin microphone over his ear, and adjusted his own small computer display.

"I've got a pair of inbounds," Hali said, his dark features made a ghastly green by his radar scope. "They must have been flying nap of the earth, suggesting choppers. ETA four minutes."

"There are no known reports that Makambo has helicopters," Mark Murphy said, turning to the chairman. "But Hali just got a bulletin about a pair of choppers stolen from an oil exploration company. Details are sketchy but it reads like the company's pilots were hijacked."

Juan nodded, not sure what to make of this development.

"I've got movement behind us," Eric Stone called out. He'd switched his personal view screen to show the view from a stern-mounted camera.

A pair of patrol boats had rounded a bend in the river. Lights atop their pilothouses made it difficult to tell how they were armed, but Mark Murphy at the weapons station called up a database of Congolese military craft.

"They're American-built Swift boats."

"You've got to be kidding me," Max said. He'd served aboard Swift boats for two tours in Vietnam.

Murph continued as if Hanley hadn't spoken. "Displaces twelve tons, has a crew of twelve, and comes armed with six fifty-caliber machine guns. Top speed is twenty-five knots. Note here says that Congo's riverine forces have also added mortars and they might be carrying shoulder-fired missiles."

With the situation worsening by the second, Cabrillo made his decisions. "Hali, get me Benjamin Isaka." Isaka was their contact in the government. "Tell him that elements of his military might have found out about our mission and don't realize we're on their side. Or that two of his Swift boats have been taken by Makambo's men. Eric, get us the hell out of here. Murph, keep an eye on, well, everything, but do not fire without my say-so. If we give away our capabilities, Abala's going to know he's being set up and will leave the guns where they are. Speaking of that. Hali?"

Hali Kasim pushed a shock of curly black hair off his forehead and typed some keystrokes into his computer. "RDF tags are activated and broadcasting five-by-five."

"Excellent." Cabrillo spun in his chair to look at Max Hanley. "How about it, old boy?"

"You know we're only on battery backup," Max Hanley told him. "I can't give you more than twenty knots."

The *Oregon* had the most sophisticated marine propulsion system ever built. Her magnetohydrodynamic engines used superconductive coils cooled by liquid helium to strip free electrons from seawater. The electricity was then used to power four massive pump jets through two vector nozzles at the ship's stern. The engines could move the eleven-thousand-ton ship at speeds approaching that of an offshore race boat, and since she used seawater for fuel she possessed an infinite range. Because of a fire two years earlier on a cruise ship powered by magnetohydrodynamics, most of the world's maritime safety boards had banned their use until they could be further tested, which was why the *Oregon* flew the flag of Iran on her jack staff, a nation with a decidedly cavalier attitude toward maritime law.

Tied to a dock eighty miles up the Congo River from the Atlantic Ocean, the *Oregon* was surrounded by freshwater and thus couldn't power up her engines. She had to rely on energy stored in ranks of silver-zinc deep cycle batteries to force water through her pump jets.

Having worked so closely with the navel architects and engineers when the ship was converted from a conventional lumber carrier, Cabrillo knew that even with the current running in their favor the batteries wouldn't last more than sixty miles at full speed, twenty miles short of where the river discharged into the sea.

"Mr. Stone, what are the tidal conditions going to be in about three hours?" Cabrillo asked his helmsman.

"Mean high tide is in two hours thirty minutes," Eric Stone replied without having to access the database. As part of his job he kept track of tidal charts and weather forecasts five days out with the diligence of an accountant chasing a penny across a spreadsheet.

"This is going to be close," Juan said to no one in particular. "Okay, Eric let's get out of here before Abala's men launch their assault."

"Aye, Chairman."

With a deft hand, Eric Stone ramped up the pulse jets. Without the whine of the cryopumps and ancillary equipment for the magnetohydro-dynamic engines, the sound of water being forced through the tubes was a deep rumble that reverberated through the entire vessel. He dialed up the bow and stern thrusters and the massive ship moved laterally away from the dock at the same time she started straining against her mooring hawsers.

Sensing their quarry was about to escape, the rebels lining the quay opened fire with long sustained bursts from their automatic weapons. Bullets raked the ship from stem to stern. Windows lining the bridge exploded under the onslaught and portholes winked out in cascades of glass. Sparks flew from the Oregon's hull as hundreds of rounds were deflected by her armored belts. While it was a spectacular sight, the rebels did nothing but mar paint and destroy a few pieces of easily replaceable glass.

From astern, the approaching patrol boats added the pounding rhythm of their fifty calibers. In order to reach the rendezvous, the Oregon rode high in the water, the special ballast tanks running along her flanks used to simulate her carrying a load of goods pumped dry. This afforded the gunners racing down the river a clear view of her rudder. They concentrated their fire on the rudder post, hoping to dislodge it from the steering gear and render the big ship helpless to the whims of the current. On a normal vessel their strategy was sound; the Oregon's rudder could turn the ship when necessary, like in a port under the watchful eye of harbor officials, but she got most of her maneuverability from the vectored nuzzles of her drive tubes, which were well protected below the waterline.

Eric Stone ignored the distraction of the assault, instead watching the iron bollards bolted to the dock through his closed-circuit television. The hawsers pulled taut as the ship edged further from the dock. A pair of enterprising terrorists rushed for the stern line and started scrambling up like rats, weapons slung over their shoulders. Stone gunned the stern thruster. With the sound of tearing rotted wood, the mushroom-shaped bollard was yanked out of the dock like a festering tooth. Its tremendous weight made it pendulum against the *Oregon*'s side with a clang like an enormous bell.

One rebel fell immediately, and was sucked into the blades of the stern thruster when Eric reversed power to correct the ship's course. All that emerged from the other side of the ship was a dark stain that tinged the waters red before fading in the current. The other gunman managed to cling to the rope as automatic capstans reeled it up. When he reached the hawsehole he tried to scramble on board the ship only to be greeted by Eddie Seng and Franklin Lincoln, who'd watched his boarding attempt from tactical view screens attached to their combat vests.

Eddie had come to the Corporation after premature retirement from the CIA, and while he didn't have the combat experience of Linc's SEAL career, he more than made up for it in single-minded determination. This was why Juan had made him chief of shore operations, the head of the gun dogs, as Max called their cadre of ex-SEALs, Force Recon, and Special Forces operators.

The rebel's eyes went wide when he tried to heave himself to the deck. Linc regarded him over the sites of a Franchi SPAS-12 combat shotgun while Eddie jammed the barrel of a Glock to the soldier's temple.

"Choice is yours, my friend," Eddie said mildly.

The terrorist let his fingers go lax and plummeted into the frothing water below.

Back in the op center, Eric watched the second bollard. Despite the tons of force, it refused to pull free from the dock. Instead, large tears appeared in the wood as the underlining timbers were wrenched from their positions. A fifteen-foot section of the quay was torn away, tossing three more soldiers into the water and causing a much larger section of the dock to sway precariously.

"We're free," he announced.

"Very good," Juan replied, checking his tactical display. The choppers were two minutes away and closing at over a hundred miles per hour. He imagined that the stolen oil company helicopters would be large and state of the art. With the weapons arrays secreted around his ship, Cabrillo knew they could gun down every soldier still on the dock, knock both helos out of the sky, and turn the pursuing patrol boats into so much flotsam—but that wasn't the point of the mission they'd been hired to perform. "Bring us up to twenty knots."

"Twenty knots, aye."

The big freighter accelerated smoothly, the extra drag of the water finally tearing away the section of dock still attached to the bollard. Soon the autofire from shore stopped, but the two patrol boats continued to pound the *Oregon* with steady streams of fifty-caliber rounds.

"RPG launch," Mark Murphy called out sharply.

Abala's men must have had vehicles hidden in the jungle, which were now pacing the *Oregon* as she fled down the Congo. The small missile arched out of the underbrush, raced across the water, and slammed into the bow. The ship's armor protected the interior spaces but the explosion was deafening as the fireball rolled across the deck. Almost immediately another RPG came out of a tube held by a gunner on one of the Swift boats. This missile came on from a low angle, passing close enough to the stern rail to scorch paint and hit the ship's funnel square on. Armored to protect the *Oregon*'s sophisticated radar dome hidden inside, the grenade still detonated with enough force to knock out the system.

"I'm on it," Hali shouted as soon as his screen went blank. He ran from the op center as fire control teams and electronics specialists were automatically dispatched by the onboard computer.

Linda Ross, an elfin woman with freckles and a high, almost girlish voice took over his work station seamlessly. "Choppers are a minute out, Chairman, and the last image from the radar showed traffic ahead coming upriver."

Juan called up higher resolution on the forward-facing cameras. The river was as black as oil, hemmed in with hills made silver by the moonlight. Just emerging from around a bend was a big river ferry. She had three decks and a blunt bow, but what caught the crew's attention was the image from the infrared cameras. Her topmost deck was a sea of humanity, and it looked like every other deck was equally full of passengers headed inland toward the port of Matadi.

"God, there must be five hundred people on her," Eric said.

"And I bet she's rated for no more than two hundred," Cabrillo replied. "Take her down our port side. I want the *Oregon* between the RPGs and that tub."

Stone edged his controls and took note of the fathometer. The riverbed was rising rapidly. "Chairman, we've got less than twenty feet under our keel. Eighteen. Fifteen. Ten feet, sir."

"Hold us steady," Juan said as a hail of fresh gunfire erupted from the jungle, AK-47s and a string of RPGs launched as fast as a Roman candle.

Explosions rocked the freighter as she raced toward the lumbering ferry, the sky lighting up with each hit. One of the missiles went errant and for a horrified moment looked like it was going to hit the ferry broadside, but at the last second its motor kicked out and it detonated just shy of her hull, drenching the passengers who were frantically rushing around in a hopeless bid to stay out of the line of fire.

"Max, give me everything you've got," Juan said angrily, sickened by the callousness of Abala's troops. "We've got to protect those people."

Max Hanley released the safeties from the battery circuits and eked a few more amps out of them and into the pump jets. The *Oregon* gained another three knots but it would cost them more miles of range, miles they couldn't afford to lose.

The ferry veered toward the middle of the river, giving the *Oregon* just enough room to pass without grounding. Moments later, the Swift boats split around the oncoming vessel, cutting frothing arcs of water across the river. A motorized skiff that had been riding in the ferry's wake emerged in the confusion, and one of the Swift boats rammed it under the waves, crushing its wooden hull and two occupants without a check in speed.

Juan watched Eric at the controls. Maneuvering such a large vessel in the tight confines of the river was bad enough, but dodging traffic while being shot at was something young Stone had never faced before. Juan had full confidence in his helmsman but in the back of his mind he knew he could override Eric's work station and take the helm himself.

A voice sounded over Cabrillo's headset. "Chairman, it's Eddie. I have visual on those two choppers. Can't tell the make but they look big enough to carry at least ten men. Now might be the time to splash them."

"Negative. The pilots are civilians for one thing, kidnapped by Makambo's rebels and forced to fly for them. And secondly, we can't let them know our capabilities. We went over this before coming upriver. We'll take a pounding, but the old girl will get us home. Just be prepared if they try to drop men onto the deck."

"We're ready."

"Then God help 'em."

For an hour they raced down the Congo, dogged by the Swift boats and taking occasional fire from shore where the road came close enough to the river for the rebels to set up an ambush. The choppers continued to hover over the *Oregon* without attempting to land or off-load troops. Juan assumed they wanted to board the ship once she'd been forced aground by the RPGs.

They cruised under the Inga Dam, a massive concrete abutment holding back a tributary of the Congo River. The dam and its twin were the main sources of electricity in this part of Africa. The ship encountered rough water where the two flows met, forcing Eric to reverse thrust on the pulse jets to keep the *Oregon* from turning broadside to the current.

"Chairman, I have Benjamin Isaka on the line," Linda Ross said. "Transferring him to your station."

"Deputy Minister Isaka, Captain Cabrillo here. I assume you've been apprised of our situation?"

"Yes, Captain. Colonel Abala wants his diamonds back." The deputy defense minister's accent was almost too thick for Juan to understand. "And he has stolen two of our river patrol boats. I have a report that ten of our men are dead on the dock in Matadi where the boats were stationed."

"He also has two helicopters from an oil company."

"I see," Isaka said noncommittally.

"We could use a little help."

"Our mutual friend at Langley who recommended you said you are more than capable of taking care of yourselves."

Juan wanted to scream at the government official. "Mr. Isaka, if I take out Abala's forces he's going to be very suspicious about the weapons he just bought. The radio direction tags embedded in them are well hidden but not undetectable. The whole plan was for him to take the guns back to Makambo's jungle headquarters, giving your military its location once and for all. You can end the insurrection in a couple of days, but not if Abala leaves the weapons on the dock back at the plantation." It was the third or fourth time he'd outlined his logic to Isaka since Langston Overholt at the CIA okayed Juan to undertake the mission.

The first part of Isaka's reply was muffled by the sound of mortar fire coming from the Swift boats. They hit close enough to throw a wall of water against the *Oregon*'s side. ". . . they leave Boma now they will reach you in an hour."

"Could you repeat that please, Minister?"

The entire crew in the op center was thrown forward as the *Oregon*'s keel slammed into the river bottom, the instant deceleration sending expensive china cascading in the mess and shattering a portable X-ray machine in the medical bay that Dr. Julia Huxley had forgotten to secure.

Juan was among the first to his feet. "Eric, what the hell happened?"

"The bottom shoaled suddenly, I never saw it coming."

"Max, how're the engines?"

As a safety precaution the computer automatically took the engines offline the instant the huge ship grounded. Max studied his computer screen, his frown deepening by the second. He worked the keyboard a moment longer.

"Max?" Juan said, drawing out his old friend's name.

"Port tube is jammed solid with mud. I can get twenty percent through the starboard, but only in reverse. We try to go forward and we'll block up that one, too."

"Eric," Juan said, "I have the helm."

"Chairman has the helm, aye."

The pulse jet tubes were milled as smooth as rifle barrels from an exotic alloy to exacting standards, eliminating the possibility of cavitation, the formation of microscopic bubbles that induce drag. Juan knew that the mud and silt had likely pitted the tubes already and to force any more muck through them might make them inoperable. He would take the responsibility for further damaging his ship himself.

He set the port tube on standby and slowly fed reverse power to the starboard jet, his eyes darting between the outside cameras showing water boiling under the ship's bow and the indicators monitoring the jet's status.

He edged the controls higher, up to twenty-five percent, knowing he was scouring the tubes as surely as if he'd gone into them himself with an impact wrench.

The *Oregon* refused to move, held tight by the grip of the mud and her own tremendous weight.

"Juan," Max said in a cautionary tone.

Cabrillo was already shutting down the pumps. At his command were cutting-edge recourses, but few viable alternatives. He had maybe fifteen seconds to come up with a plan before the choppers swooped in to disgorge the rebels they carried. A pair of five-second bursts from the 20 mm Gatling gun would blow the helicopters from the sky, but would also kill the civilian pilots and expose the deadly potential of his ship. Then they would still have to deal with the Swift boats plus any number of other vessels Abala commandeered when he realized the *Oregon* was aground. The idea of surrendering the stones or jeopardizing the mission never entered his mind.

"Max, the wind's at our back, lay down a smoke screen thick enough to hide the ship, then activate the fire suppression cannons." There were four water cannons mounted on the corners of the superstructure and each was rated for a thousand gallons per minute, the pumps powered by their own dedicated diesel engine. "They can throw water more than two hundred feet. That ought to keep the choppers from landing." He keyed his microphone. "Eddie, I'm hitting the water guns, so be prepared. If that doesn't hold off the helos your boys have permission to use shotguns and pistols only. That would be a believable arsenal on a ship in these waters."

"Roger."

"And, Eddie, I want you and Linc to meet me in the boat garage. I have a mission for you. Full kit to be on the safe side."

Cabrillo was out of his chair and halfway to the elevator that would take him down two decks to the boat garage located along the *Oregon*'s waterline when Hanley stopped him with a gesture. "I can understand the smoke and using the water cannons is a master stroke, but what the hell do you have planned for Linc and Eddie?"

"I'm going to have this old girl refloated in about thirty minutes."

Max had learned over their years together to never doubt the chairman when he made such proclamations; he just didn't know how Juan was going to pull off the impossible. "You have a plan to lighten us by a couple thousand tons?"

"I'll do you one better. I'm going to raise the river by ten feet."

4

SOUTH OF WALVIS BAY
NAMIBIA

THE sand floating across the road was as fine as dust and swirled in eddies that formed whenever the cooling desert air met the still-warm asphalt. It looked like wisps of smoke or drifting snow. The sun had long since set, so the inland dunes showed pale white in the glow of the moon.

The solitary vehicle on the road was the only thing moving save the wind and the gentle surf lapping at the beach. The four-by-four pickup was only about twenty miles south of Swakopmund and its adjoining harbor town of Walvis Bay, but it was as if this was the last car on earth.

Sitting in the driver's seat, Sloane Macintyre shivered.

"Could you grab the wheel?" she asked her companion. He did, and she shrugged into a hooded sweatshirt, needing both hands to pull her long hair from under the collar and settle it over her shoulders. It was as coppery red as the dunes at dusk and set off her luminous gray eyes.

"I still say we should have waited until morning and gotten a permit to enter Sandwich Bay," complained Tony Reardon for the third time since leaving their hotel. "You know how touchy the local authorities are about tourists entering secured areas."

"We're headed to a bird sanctuary, Tony, not one of the mining concessions leased by the diamond companies," Sloane retorted.

"It's still against the law."

"Besides, I don't like the way Luka tried to warn us off from looking for Papa Heinrick. It was almost as if he has something to hide."

"Who, Papa Heinrick?"

"No, our illustrious guide, Tuamanguluka."

"Why would you say that? Luka's been nothing but helpful since we got here."

Sloane shot him a sideways glance. In the glow of the dash lights, the Englishman looked like a petulant boy acting stubborn for stubbornness' sake. "You don't have the feeling that he's been a bit too helpful? What are the odds of a guide finding us at our hotel who happens to know every local fisherman in Walvis Bay *and* can get us a deal from one of the helicopter tour companies?"

"We just got lucky."

"I don't believe in luck." Sloane turned her attention back to the road. "When we told Luka about the old fisherman mentioning Papa Heinrick he did everything in his power to dissuade us from looking for him. Luka first said Heinrick was just a beach fisherman and didn't know anything about the waters more than a mile from shore. Then he told us he wasn't right in the head. When that didn't work he says that Heinrick is dangerous, and was rumored to have killed a man.

"Was that the impression of Papa Heinrick we got from the fisherman who first told us about him?" Sloane went on. "No. He said that Papa Heinrick had forgotten more about the waters off the Skeleton Coast than any man had ever learned. His exact words more or less. That sounds like the perfect person to interview for this project and our oh-so-helpful guide doesn't want us talking to him. Tony, that stinks and you know it."

"We could have waited until morning."

Sloane ignored his comment for a moment before saying, "You know every minute counts. Someone is going to figure out what we're looking for eventually. When that happens this coastline is going to be crawling with people. The government would probably declare the shore off limits, close down the fisheries, and impose martial law. You've never been on an expedition like this. I have."

"And did you find anything?" Tony asked testily, knowing the answer.

"No," Sloane admitted. "But that doesn't mean I don't know what I'm doing."

Unlike most of Africa, the roads in Namibia are well maintained and free of potholes. The four-wheel-drive Toyota glided through the night until they reached a turnoff that was layered in sand drifts as high as the vehicle's tires. Sloane set the transmission in low range and started down the road, plowing through hillocks of sand that would have bogged any two-wheeled drive car. After twenty minutes they reached a parking area with a large cyclone fence. Signs hanging from the fence announced that vehicles were restricted beyond this point.

They'd arrived at Sandwich Bay, an extensive wetland lagoon fed freshwater by subterranean aquifers that hosted up to fifty thousand migratory birds a year. Sloane put the truck in park but left the engine idling. Without waiting for Tony, she hopped from her seat, her boots sinking into the soft sand, and made her way to the back of the Toyota. In the open bed was an inflatable raft and an electric pump that could run off the vehicle's twelve-volt system.

She quickly had the raft inflated and her gear ready, making certain of the strength of the batteries in their flashlights. They piled their backpacks and oars into the raft and carried it down to the water. Sheltered from the open sea, the lagoon was as still as a mill pond.

"The fisherman said Papa Heinrick lives at the most southern reach of the lagoon," Sloane said when they had settled in the raft and poled it off the beach with their oars. She took a compass bearing off the night sky and dug her paddle into the smooth water.

Despite what she'd said to Tony, she knew this could either be the jackpot or a complete waste of time, with the latter being the most likely. Chasing rumors, half-truths, and innuendo led to more dead ends than anything else but that was the nature of her job. It was about steady monotony leading to that one eureka moment, a moment she had yet to enjoy, but that acted like a lure to keep her plodding on, enduring loneliness, fatigue, stress, and pessimistic jerks like Tony Reardon.

A few fish splashed in the dark lagoon as they paddled southward and an occasional bird ruffled its feathers amid the reeds. It took an hour and a half to reach the extreme southern end of the bay and it looked as unremarkable as all the rest, a wall of reeds capable of surviving in the brackish water. Sloane played the beam of her light along the shoreline as they searched the area. After twenty minutes in which her anxiety mounted she spied a small cut in the tall grasses where a stream trickled into the lagoon.

She pointed silently and she and Tony maneuvered their little inflatable into the gap.

The reeds grew over their heads and joined above them, forming a living tunnel that blocked out the silvery moon. The current from the small stream was negligible and they made good progress, cutting a hundred yards into the wetlands before coming to a little pond inside the reed forest with a small island at its center that would just barely stay free of water when the tide was at its highest. The light from the moon revealed a crude hut that had been fashioned from driftwood and bits of packing crates. The door was a blanket nailed to the lintel and just outside it sat a fire pit, embers still smoldering beneath a layer of ash. Off to the right was a fish-drying rack, rusty barrels for storing fresh water, and a wooden-hulled skiff tied to a stump with a single line. Its sail was furled tightly to the mast and the rudder and centerboards were lashed inside. The flat-bottomed boat wasn't exactly ideal for fishing the open waters, leading Sloane to consider that Luka had been right about Papa Heinrick sticking close to shore.

The camp was rough but a seasoned outdoorsman could live here indefinitely.

"What do we do?" Tony whispered when they beached the inflatable.

Sloane approached the door, confirmed the sound she heard was snoring of a single person and not the wind or surf and backed off again. She settled her backside onto the sandy beach, pulled her laptop from her bag, and started typing softly, her lower lip lightly clenched between her teeth.

"Sloane?" Tony whispered a bit more stridently.

"We wait until he wakes up," she replied.

"But what if this isn't Papa Heinrick's? What if someone else lives here? Pirates or bandits or something?"

"I told you I don't believe in luck. I also don't believe in coincidences.

Us finding a cabin exactly where we were told Papa Heinrick lives means that we've found Papa Heinrick. I'd rather talk to him in the morning than scare the old codger in the middle of the night."

The gentle snoring from inside the cabin didn't change in timbre or volume but suddenly a wizened African wearing nothing but an athletic supporter pushed aside the blanket. He stood on bandy legs and was so thin that every rib showed across his chest and there were hollows above and below his collarbones. He had a broad flat nose and large jug ears pierced through with some sort of horn earrings. His hair was pure white and his eyes shone yellow.

He continued to snore and for a moment Sloane thought he might be sleepwalking, but then he scratched at himself rudely and spat into the fire pit.

Sloane got to her feet. She was easily a foot taller than the Namibian and she realized he must have some Bushmen blood to possess such a tiny stature. "Papa Heinrick, we have come a great distance to meet with you. The other fishermen at Walvis Bay say you are the wisest among them."

Sloane had been ensured that Papa Heinrick spoke English, but the gnomelike man gave no recognition that he understood. She had to take the fact that he'd stopped pretending to snore as an encouraging sign and plowed on. "We want to ask you some questions about where you fish, places that are difficult, where you lose lines and nets. Would you answer such questions?"

Heinrick turned back into his cabin, letting the blanket flow back to drape over the entranceway. He emerged a moment later with a padded blanket over his shoulders. It was made of loosely sewn sheets and feathers escaped the seams with each movement. He went a short distance off and urinated loudly into the water, scratching his belly languidly.

He squatted down next to his fire pit, his back to Tony and Sloane. The bones of his spine looked like a string of black pearls. He blew the coals into life, feeding scraps of driftwood into the embers until he had produced a small flame. "There are many difficult places to fish these waters," he said in a surprisingly deep voice for such a small frame. He hadn't turned. "I have fished them all and dare any man to follow where Papa Heinrick goes. I have lost enough fishing line to stretch from here to Cape Cross Bay." That was more than eighty miles north. "And back," he added as if challenging them to deny his boast. "I have lost enough net to cover all the Namib Desert. I have battled seas that make other men wail and turn their bowels to water. And I have caught fish bigger than the biggest ship and I have seen things that would drive other men mad."

He turned finally. In the wavering light of his fire his eyes had taken on a demonic cast. He smiled, revealing three teeth that meshed together like gears. His smile turned into a chuckle, then a barking laugh that was cut short by a coughing fit. When he'd recovered he spat into the fire again. "Papa Heinrick does not reveal his secrets. I know things you wish to know, but you will never know them because I wish you not to know them."

"Why would you wish that?" Sloane said after she analyzed his grammar in her head to make sure she'd heard right. She squatted next to him.

"Papa Heinrick is the greatest fisherman that has ever lived. Why would I tell you and make you my rival?"

"I do not want to fish these waters. I am looking for a ship that sank a long time ago. My friend and I"—she waved at Tony, who'd stepped back after getting a whiff of Papa Heinrick's body—"want to find this ship because . . ." Sloane paused and made up a story. "Because we were hired to recover something from it belonging to a rich man who lost it when it sank. We think that you can help us."

"Does this rich man pay?" Heinrick asked slyly.

"A little, yes."

The fisherman waved a hand like a bat fluttering through the night. "Papa Heinrick has no use for money."

"What would it take for you to help us?" Tony asked suddenly. Sloane had a bad feeling about what the old man might want and shot him a scathing look.

"I will not help you," Heinrick said to Tony and looked at Sloane. "You I will help. You are a woman and do not fish so you will never be my rival."

Sloane wasn't about to tell him that she'd grown up in Fort Lauderdale and had spent her summers crewing her father's charter fishing boat and then took it out herself when he was struck by Alzheimer's at age fifty. "Thank you, Papa Heinrick." Sloane pulled a large map from her pack and spread it next to the fire. Tony edged in and added illumination with his flashlight. The map was of Namibia's coastline. There were dozens of stars penciled in just off shore. Most were clustered around Walvis Bay but others were scattered up and down the coast.

"We have spoken to many other fishermen, asking them where they lose lines and nets. We think one of these places might be a sunken ship. Can you look at this and tell me if there are any they missed?"

Heinrick studied the chart intently, his eyes darting from one spot to the next, his fingers tracing the outline of the coast. He finally looked up at Sloane. She could see there was a kernel of madness behind them, as if his reality wasn't quite her own. "I do not know this place."

Confused Sloane placed her finger on Walvis Bay and said its name. Then she drew it southward and said, "Here we are at Sandwich Bay. She tapped her finger toward the top of the map. "And here's Cape Cross."

"I do not understand. Cape Cross is there." Heinrick pointed emphatically northward. "It can not be here." He touched the spot on the map.

Sloane realized that despite a lifetime at sea, Papa Heinrick had never seen a nautical chart. She groaned inwardly.

For the next two hours Sloane laboriously talked the old fisherman through the places where he had lost nets or had lines tangled. Because the desert continued under the ocean for hundreds of miles from the coast, anything that tore lines or ripped nets was either a rock outcropping or a shipwreck. Papa Heinrick would tell her that two days sailing southwest from Sandwich Bay was such a place, or five days northwest was another. Each one he described corresponded with the map she'd made over the past days talking to the commercial fishermen and day excursion captains at Walvis.

But there was one spot that only Papa Heinrick mentioned. It was nearly seventy miles out by Sloane's estimation, well away from any other. In fact, none of the other captains had even mentioned fishing in the area. Papa Heinrick said that there was little out there to attract marine life and he'd only been there himself because a freak wind had pushed him off course.

Sloane circled the spot on her chart, noting the water depth was over a hundred and fifty feet, at the limit of her scuba abilities but still doable. However, it was too deep for even the clearest water to reveal the outline of a ship against the sandy bottom—even from the helicopter they planned to rent to investigate the other sites.

"You must not go there," Papa Heinrick warned when he saw the far-off look in Sloane's eyes.

His comment refocused her attention. "Why not?"

"The seas are alive with great metal snakes. It is bad magic, I think."

"Metal snakes?" Tony scoffed.

The old man lunged to his feet, his expression fierce. "You doubt Papa Heinrick?" he thundered, spraying Reardon with clots of saliva. "There are dozens of them, a hundred feet long or more, twisting and thrashing on the water. One nearly sank my boat when it tried to eat me. Only I could have escaped its evil mouth, for I am the greatest sailor who has ever lived. You would have pissed yourself in fear and died crying like an infant." He looked back at Sloane, the edge of madness in his eyes a bit more keen. "Papa Heinrick has warned you. Go there and you will surely be eaten alive. Now leave me." He settled back at his little smoke fire, rocking on his heels and muttering in a language Sloane didn't know.

She thanked him for his help but he didn't acknowledge her. She and Tony returned to their inflatable and slowly paddled out of Papa Heinrick's isolated camp. When they emerged from the secret cleft in the reeds Tony exhaled a long breath. "That man's utterly daft. Metal snakes? *Pleeease*."

"'There are more things in heaven and earth, Horatio, than are dreamt of in your philosophies.'"

"What's that mean?"

"It's a line from *Hamlet* that means that the world is stranger than we can possibly imagine."

"You don't believe him, do you?"

"About giant metal snakes? No, but he saw something out there that scared him."

"I bet it was a surfacing submarine. The South African Navy must have some that patrol these waters."

"That could be it," Sloane conceded. "And we have more than enough sites to investigate without looking for sea serpents or submarines. We'll meet up with Luka this afternoon and figure out how we want to proceed."

They were back in their rooms at the swanky Swakopmund Hotel just as the sun began to rise. Sloane took a long shower, washing sand and the clinging feel of salt from her skin. As much as she needed to shave her legs, she put off the chore and stood under the pounding spray, letting the hot water work at the knotted muscles of her shoulders and back.

After toweling off she slipped nude between the sheets of her bed. Her dreams were filled with the images of monstrous snakes fighting each other on the open ocean.

5

AS Juan Cabrillo jogged to the boat garage located just aft of the superstructure he listened to damage reports on his comm unit. The bilges were dry, which wasn't a surprise. The riverbed was silty mud, nothing that could breach the hull. What he was worried about were the keel doors. At the bottom of the *Oregon* were two large doors that opened outward, creating a moon pool. From here the pair of submersibles the ship carried could be launched directly into the sea. Used mostly for covert insertions and extractions, one of the minisubs had a diving capability of a thousand feet and a manipulator arm, while the smaller minisub, a Discovery 1000, was limited to shallower water.

To his immense relief, a tech on duty at the moon pool reported the two doors hadn't been damaged and the subs were safely stowed in their cradles.

Juan reached the boat garage at the ship's waterline. The large space was lit by red battle lamps, giving it a ruddy cast, and it smelled of salt water and gasoline. The large door that opened along the *Oregon*'s flank was tightly sealed as crewmen prepared a black Zodiac inflatable. The big outboard on its transom could push the craft well past forty knots, though it also had a small electric motor for silent operations. The garage also housed a deep-hulled SEAL assault boat capable of even greater speed and with the capacity to carry ten armed men.

Eddie and Linc reported in a moment later. It had been Eddie Seng who'd played the part of helmsmen when Linc was acting as captain. The two couldn't have been more physically different. Linc's body bulged with muscles hewn from hours of pumping iron in the ship's weight room while Eddie was rapier lean, his physique the result of a lifetime of martial arts training.

They wore black combat fatigues, matching belts festooned with ammo pouches, knives, and various other gear. Each carried M-4A1 assault carbines, the Special Forces version of the M-16.

"What's the op, boss?" Eddie asked.

"As you know, we're grounded and we don't have time to wait for the spring rains. You remember that dam we passed a couple miles back?"

"You want us to blow it?" Linc asked incredulously.

"No, no. Just get inside and open the floodgates. I doubt they have guards, but if they do, go nonlethal if you can." Both men nodded. "You probably won't be able to catch up with us once the water hits us so we'll link up in Boma on the coast."

"Sounds like a plan," Linc breezed, fully confident in their ability to execute the mission.

Juan hit a wall mike. "Eric, I need to know when it's clear to open the garage and launch a Zodiac. Where are those patrol boats?"

"One's standing off. I think to start in with the mortars again. The other just passed behind our stern and is coming up the port side."

"Anything from the shore?"

"Infrared shows it's clean, but you and I both know Abala won't waste any time getting here."

"Okay, thanks." Juan nodded to a crewman to open the outer door. The stench and heat of the jungle rushed into the garage as the door slid upward. The air was so humid you could almost drink it. It was also tinged with the chemical stink of the smoke screen Max had laid over the ship. The river's edge was dark and overhung with dense vegetation. Despite Eric's assurance that the shore was clear, Juan could feel eyes on them.

Because the *Oregon* rode so high in the water, the launch ramp was five feet above the river. Linc and Eddie shoved the boat down the slick ramp and dove after it when it hit the water. They emerged from the river and rolled over the craft's soft side. Eddie secured their weapons while Linc engaged the electric motor. At slow speed and under the cover of darkness the Zodiac was all but invisible.

As they pulled away from the *Oregon*, Linc had to zigzag around arcing jets of water from the fire cannons that were keeping the two helicopters from getting close. The choppers dove and buzzed but never got nearear than a hundred feet before one of the cannons fired a blasting stream of water that forced the pilots to bank away sharply.

Eddie could imagine the scene inside each of the helos as the rebels threatened the oil company pilots while at the same time knowing a direct hit from one of the fire hoses would drown the helicopter's turbines and send it plummeting into the river.

They emerged from the smoke screen and saw that the two patrol boats were far enough away for Linc to switch to the Zodiac's outboard. The big four-stroke was well muffled, but it still sounded a deep bass tone that rumbled across the water as he brought the nimble craft onto plane.

It was impossible to speak at forty knots, so they drove back upriver with their thoughts, both men keyed up on adrenaline and ready for anything. They didn't hear the high keening of an approaching boat until it shot around a small island hugging the near shore.

Link whipped the Zodiac hard to starboard as the two boats nearly collided. He recognized the scared face of Colonel Abala's aide at the same instant the rebel officer recognized him. Link twisted the throttle harder against its stop as the aide-de-camp whipped the boat around and started to chase them. The boat was sleek, with two outboards and a low hull designed to ride atop the water. There were four other men with him, all carrying AKs.

"You know him?" Eddie shouted.

"Yeah, he's Abala's right-hand man."

The rebel boat began to gain on the Zodiac, a rooster tail of water jetting from its stern.

"Linc, if he's got a radio, the jig's going to be up."

"Damn. I hadn't thought about that. Any ideas?"

"Let him catch up," Eddie said, and passed one of the M-4s to Lincoln.

"And don't fire until I see the whites of their eyes?"

"Screw that. Take 'em the second they're in range."

"Okay, hold on." Linc killed the throttles and as the Zodiac settled into the water he whipped it into a tight turn, its flat bottom skipping across the river like a stone. It came to a sudden stop, bobbing on waves of its own creation, but it was more than stable enough for Linc and Eddie.

They brought their weapons to their shoulders as the rebel's boat bore down on them at fifty miles per hour. At two hundred yards they opened fire; AKs immediately winked back at them, but the rebels' aim was off because the boat was going so fast. Tiny fountains of water shot into the air well ahead and to the left of the stationary Zodiac. The Corporation men had no such difficulty, and every second brought the boat closer and increased their accuracy.

Linc fired three round bursts that stitched the small windscreen and tore chunks of fiberglass from the boat's bow. Eddie concentrated on the driver, calmly firing single shots until the man suddenly slumped. The boat veered for a moment before another rebel got hold of the wheel while the other three continued to rip through magazine after magazine. One burst came close enough to singe the air around Eddie and Linc, but neither man ducked or even blinked. They methodically fired at the oncoming boat until only one rebel remained crouched behind the wheel, covered by the long bow.

Working in coordination, Eddie kept up a steady stream of fire as Linc moved back to the idling engine. The rebel boat was no more than fifty yards away, charging straight at them like a shark coming in for the kill. It was obvious that its driver intended to ram them. Linc let him come.

When the speedboat was no more than twenty feet away he goosed the throttle and the Zodiac dashed under its high bows. Eddie already had a grenade in his hand, the pin pulled and the spoon long gone. He flipped it into the speedboat's cockpit as it screamed by them, holding up five fingers then dropping them as the seconds ticked by. His last finger went down and the speedboat went up, the crump of the grenade followed almost immediately by the spectacular explosion of the boat's fuel tanks. The hull cartwheeled across the water, chunks of fiberglass and the remains of its crew flying free amid the blazing rain of burning gasoline.

"Strike one right-hand man," Linc said with satisfaction.

Five minutes later, the Zodiac coasted to a wooden jetty near the base of the Inga Dam. The massive structure loomed over them, a sculpted wall of ferro-concrete and steel holding back a huge reservoir above the Congo River. Because nearly all the electricity generated by the hydro-dam was used during the day in the mines of Shaba, formerly Katanga Province, there was just a trickle of water coming down the spillway. They dragged the boat well out of the river and secured it to a tree, not knowing how high the water would reach. They hefted their weapons for the long climb up a set of stairs built into the face of the dam.

Halfway up the stairs the quiet of the night was shattered by gunfire erupting from below them. Shrapnel, bits of concrete, and bullets whizzed all around them as they stood exposed on the steps. Both men dropped flat and immediately returned fire. Down below two native boats had pulled up to the jetty. While rebels fired from the dock more began racing up the stairs.

"I guess Abala's guy had a radio after all." Eddie said, dropping his spent M-4 and drawing his Glock. He fired rapidly as Linc hosed the dock with 5.56 mm rounds from his assault rifle.

The three rebels charging the stairs went down with double taps from Eddie's pistol, their bodies tumbling off the steps in a tangle of limbs and blood. By the time he'd changed out magazines for his M-4, the fire from the dock had withered to a single AK-47 and Linc silenced this gun with a sustained burst that blew the rebel off the dock. The current took him almost immediately and he vanished down the river.

Above them an alarm horn had begun to sound.

"Let's go," Linc said, and the two men raced up the stairs, taking them two and three at a time.

They reached the top of the dam. Beyond it was the large reservoir and at the far end of the structure was a squat building with light spilling from its windows.

"Control room?" Linc whispered.

"Has to be." Eddie pulled his throat mike into position. "Chairman, its Eddie. Linc and I are on the dam and about to approach the control center." There was no need to tell him their presence had already been detected.

"Copy that. Advise when you're in position to open the gates."

"Roger."

Keeping low so they didn't silhouette themselves against the starry sky, they raced silently across the top of the dam. To their left spread the reservoir, a calm lake bisected by a white slash of reflected moonlight. To their right was a hundred-foot drop to a jumble of boulders littering the base of the dam.

When they reached the blockhouse, a boxy one-story concrete building with a single door and a pair of windows, they could see that beyond it were the sluice gates and penstock that diverted water to the facility's turbines that were housed in a long building at the bottom of the dam. There was only enough water passing through the channel to provide electricity to the town of Mabati.

With Linc on the other side, Eddie reached out and tried to open the blockhouse door. It was securely locked. Eddie motioned to the keyhole as if he had the key and cocked an eyebrow at Linc. Franklin Lincoln was the Corporation's expert at lock picking and was rumored to have even broken into Juan's gun safe on a bet from Linda Ross, but all he could do was shrug at his partner and pat his pockets. He'd forgotten to bring his picks.

Eddie rolled his eyes and reached into one of the pouches hanging from his belt. He molded a small amount of Semtex plastic explosives around the handle and inserted an electronic detonator. He and Linc moved a short way off.

Just before he keyed the detonator, a guard emerged from around the blockhouse. He wore a dark uniform and carried a flashlight and a pistol. Linc aimed instinctively and was an instant from firing before adjusting his site picture. He shot the pistol out of the guard's hand. The man went down, screaming and clutching his arm to his chest. Linc ran over to him, pulling a pair of flex cuffs from his combat harness. He checked the wound quickly, relieved that it was superficial, and bound the guard's hands and feet.

"Sorry, buddy," he said and rejoined Eddie.

Eddie fired off the charge. The explosion blew the handle apart and Linc threw open the door, Eddie covering him with his M-4.

The control room was brightly lit, an open space with banks of dials and levers along the walls and counters mounted with outdated computers. The three night operators immediately thrust their hands in the air when Linc and Eddie rushed into the room shouting for everyone to get down. They gestured with their rifles and the men sank to the concrete floor, their eyes wide with fear.

"Do as we say and no one gets hurt," Eddie said, knowing how trite it sounded to the terrified workers.

Linc did a quick recon of the building, finding an empty conference room behind the control space and a closet-sized lavatory that was also empty except for a cockroach the size of his middle finger.

"Do any of you speak English?" Eddie asked as he cuffed the three Africans.

"I do," one said, the tag on his blue jumpsuit showing his name was Kofi Baako.

"Okay, Kofi, like I said we're not going to hurt you, but I want you to tell me how to open the emergency floodgates."

"You will drain the reservoir!"

Eddie pointed at a multiline telephone; four of its five lights were blinking. "You've already contacted your superiors and I'm sure they're sending additional people. The gates won't be open for more than an hour. Now show me how to open them."

Kofi Baako hesitated for another second, so Eddie yanked his pistol from its holster, making sure it was never pointed at the three men. His voice went from reasonable to savage. "You've got five seconds."

"That panel there." Baako nodded at the far wall. "The top five switches disengage the safety protocols. The next five close the circuits to the gate motors and the bottom five open the gates themselves."

"Can the gates be closed manually?"

"Yes, there is a room inside the dam with big hand cranks. They need two men to turn them."

With Linc still at the front door watching for any more guards, Eddie flipped the switches in turn, watching the jeweled lights that were built into the control panel switch from red to green with each toggle thrown. Before he started on the last row he rested his throat mike against his neck. "Chairman, it's me. Be ready for it. I'm opening the gates now."

"Not a minute too soon. Abala transferred the mortars from the Swift boats and has set them up on shore. A couple more rounds and they have us ranged."

"Stand by for the big flush," Eddie said and threw the last set of switches. With the last toggle in position a noise began to rise, low at first, but building to a rumble that shook the building. The gates were coming up and water was thundering down the face of the dam in a solid wall. It hit the bottom and exploded in a roiling cauldron that grew into a solid wave eight feet high that swept down the river, inundating the shoreline and ripping out trees and shrubs as it accelerated.

"That ought to do the trick," Eddie said and emptied his clip into the control panel. The rounds punctured the thin metal and shredded the old electronics in a blaze of smoke and sparks.

"And that ought to buy us some time," Linc added.

They left the technicians cuffed to a table and made their way back down the staircase. The sound and fury of the water pouring over the dam's face was a palpable sensation while spray soaked their partially dry clothing.

By the time they reached the bottom and dragged the Zodiac to the river's edge, the water had settled enough for them to launch the inflatable and start heading downstream for their rendezvous in Boma.

Back aboard the *Oregon*, Juan was getting concerned. Abala had realized the Swift boats were too unstable for the mortars so he'd unloaded them and now his men were dialing in the range. The last explosive had hit less than twenty feet from the starboard rail.

To add to his problems, more and more native boats were arriving from upstream, loaded to the gunwales with rebels. While the water cannons were performing flawlessly, there were only four of them—and two were needed at all times to prevent the buzzing helicopters from getting close enough for the men aboard to jump down onto the freighter. Juan had called Hali Kasim back from the radar dome to coordinate communications so Linda Ross could lead Eddie's shore operations fighters. Using only shotguns and pistols, they rushed to the side of the ship where Mark Murphy said a boat was getting too close. They fired down on the rebels while ducking blistering fire from both the shore and the pirogues.

"All right," Hali exclaimed from the comm station. "My techs have the radar back."

"Will you be able to see the wave?" Juan asked him.

"Sorry, Chairman, but with the bends in the river I won't see it until it's almost on top of us."

"Anything's better than nothing."

Another mortar dropped near the ship, this time missing the port rail by inches. The rebels had them bracketed. The next rounds would fall with impunity all over the *Oregon* and her decks were not nearly as heavily armored as her flanks.

"Damage control teams, get ready," Juan said over the shipboard net. "We're going to take some hits."

"Holy God," Hali shouted.

"What?"

"Brace yourselves!"

Juan hit the collision alarm as he saw the wave on both the radar screen in the corner of the big monitor as well as the feed from the stern cameras. The surge stretched from bank to bank. Rearing up more than ten feet and easily traveling at twenty knots, the roiling wall of water bore down on them relentlessly. One of the Swift boats tried to twist away and race ahead of the swell, but was caught midway through its turn. The wave hit the vessel broadside. The patrol craft flipped instantly, tossing men into the maelstrom where they were crushed by the rolling hull of their boat.

Pirogues simply vanished with nothing to mark their passing, and the rebels lining the shore taking potshots at the *Oregon* fled for high ground as water washed away everything in its path.

Juan took his hands away from the controls a moment before the wave slammed into the *Oregon*, flexed his fingers like a pianist about to perform an impossible overture, and lightly rested them back on the keys and joystick that would maneuver his ship.

He brought the unclogged drive tube up to twenty percent just as the swell lifted the stern of the *Oregon* out of the mud. Like being caught in a tsunami the vessel lurched from a dead stop to twenty knots in an instant as a pair of mortar shells exploded in her wake, shots that would have blown through her rear cargo hatches and destroyed the Robinson R44 helicopter stored on a retractable elevator.

Juan scanned engine readouts, pump temperatures, speed over the bottom, speed through the water, and his position and course, his gaze darting from one screen to the next in an unending cycle. The ship was actually making only three knots through the water but was racing down the river at closer to twenty-five, borne onward by the tremendous pressure of water escaping over the Inga Dam.

"Max, tell me the instant that second tube clears," he called out. "I don't have enough steerage speed."

He edged the throttle higher, fighting the current as it tried to slam the *Oregon* into an island that had reared up in the middle of the channel. His fingers danced over his keyboard. He called up the bow and stern thrusters as needed to keep the ship straight and more or less centered as the dark jungle blurred passed.

They careened around a tight bend in the river, the flow pushing them hard for the opposite shore, where a small cargo ship that had been headed upriver had been pushed into the riverbank, its stern thrust far out into the Congo. Juan slammed on full power to the thrusters, laterally shoving the *Oregon* as far to starboard as he could. The hull scraped against the coastal freighter with an ear-splitting shriek and then they were clear.

"That's going to leave a mark," Eric quipped even though he was awed by Juan's handling of the vessel. He knew he wouldn't have made the turn and avoided the ship.

With the river boiling all around them they were swept further downstream, carried along like a leaf in a gutter, barely able to control their course until Juan could eke more power out of her engines. Time and again he had to fight the river to keep the *Oregon* from grounding or plowing into the riverbank, each escape seemingly closer than the last. They did hit a shoal at one point, the ship decelerating hard as it gouged a furrow through the muddy riverbed. For a moment, Juan feared the freighter would grind to a halt again because the computer had shut off the pulse jet, but the current was strong enough to drag them over, and as soon as the bottom was free the ship picked up speed like a sprinter out of the blocks.

Despite the danger, or maybe because of it, Cabrillo found he was enjoying the challenge. It was a test of his skills and the capabilities of his ship against the vagaries of the raging flood—the epic struggle of man versus nature. He was the type of man who never backed away from anything because he knew his limitations and had yet to meet a situation he didn't think he could handle. In others this trait would come off as cockiness. In Juan Cabrillo it was simply supreme confidence.

"Scouring action has cleared the second tube," Max announced. "Just be gentle on her until I get a team into it to check for damage."

Juan dialed up the second tube and immediately felt his ship respond. She was no longer sluggish coming about and he had to use the thrusters less and less. He checked their speed—twenty-eight knots over the bottom and eight through the water. He had more than enough speed to control the freighter, and now that they'd covered several miles the once-turbulent flow had started to even out. Colonel Abala's forces were either dead on the river or left far behind and the two choppers he'd stolen had peeled off soon after the wave hit.

"Eric, I think you can take her from here on down to Boma."

"Aye, Chairman," Stone replied. "I have the helm."

Juan sat back in his chair. Max Hanley placed a hand on his shoulder. "Hell of a piece of driving if I say so myself."

"Thanks. Don't think I want to do that again anytime soon."

"I'd love to say we're out of the woods, but we aren't. Battery charge is down to thirty percent. Even with the current at our backs we're going to run out of juice a good ten miles from the sea."

"Do you have any faith in me at all?" Juan asked, pained. "Weren't you here when Eric said mean high tide is in . . ." Juan checked his watch. "An hour and a half? Ocean's going to run fifteen or twenty miles inland and turn the Congo brackish. Might be like running regular gasoline in a race car engine but there's enough salinity to spool up the magnetohydrodynamics."

Max cursed. "Why didn't I think about that?"

"For the same reason I get paid more than you. I'm smarter, more clever by half, and much better looking."

"And you wear your humility like a well-tailored suit." Max then turned serious. "Soon as we get to Boma I'll get some of my engineers into the tubes, but from what I could tell from the computer I think they're okay. May not be at hundred percent, but my gut tells me they don't need to be re-lined."

Though he carried the title of president within the Corporation and was tasked with a lot of the day-to-day affairs of running a successful company, Max most enjoyed his role as the *Oregon*'s chief engineer, and her state-of-the-art engines were his pride and joy.

"Thank God." Replacing the lining of the drive tubes was a multimillion-dollar job. "But I don't want to be in Boma any longer than necessary. Once we pick up Linc and Eddie I want us in international waters just in case Minister Isaka can't keep the heat off us for opening their dam," Juan said.

"Good thinking. We can check the tubes in the open ocean about as easily as tied to a dock."

"Anything else from the damage reports you've gotten?"

"Other than a broken X-ray machine down in medical and Maurice squawking about a whole lot of broken dishes and glassware, we came through okay." Maurice was the *Oregon*'s chief steward, the only member of the crew older than Max. Better suited to the Victorian age, Maurice was also the only non-American aboard. He'd served in the British Navy, overseeing the mess on a number of flagships before being cashiered out because of his age. In his year with the Corporation he'd quickly become a crew favorite, throwing the perfect parties for everyone's birthdays and knowing which delicacies they preferred from the ship's highly trained cooking staff.

"Tell him to go easy on what he orders this time. When we lost all those dishes racing to save Eddie a few months back Maurice replaced them with Royal Doulton to the tune of six hundred dollars a place setting."

Max arched an eyebrow. "Quibbling over a few pennies?"

"We lost forty-five thousand dollars' worth of finger bowls and sorbet cups."

"Okay, a couple of dimes, then. You forget that I've seen our latest balance sheets—we can afford it."

Which was true. The Corporation had never been in better financial shape. Juan's gamble at forming his own private security and surveillance outfit had surpassed even his most optimistic estimates, but that also meant there was a downside. The need for such organizations in the post–Cold War world was a sobering fact of life in the twenty-first century. He'd known that without the polarizing effects of two dominant superpowers, regional flare-ups and terrorism would proliferate all over the globe. Being in a position to make a profit from conflicts, provided they had a say in which side they chose to help, was both a blessing and a curse that wracked Cabrillo in the sleepless hours of the night.

"Blame my grandmother," Juan said. "She could stretch a dollar for a mile and have change left over. I used to hate going to her house because she always bought stale bread to save a couple of cents. She'd toast it, but you could tell, and toasted bologna sandwiches are about as disgusting as you can get."

"Okay, to honor your grandmother, I'll tell Maurice to stick with Limoges this time," Max said, and sauntered back to his station.

Hali Kasim approached Juan carrying a flatscreen clipboard. A frown turned down the corners of his mouth and made his gunslinger mustache droop.

"Chairman, the Sniffer caught this a couple minutes ago." The Sniffer was their name for the dedicated surveillance array that swept the electronic spectrum for miles around the ship. It was able to siphon in everything from regular radio broadcasts to encrypted cell phones. The ship's supercomputer sifted through the minutia every half second, trying to detect a grain of intelligence wheat in all that chaff. "Computer just broke the code. I'd call it high-end civilian or mid-level military encryption."

"What's the source?" Juan asked, taking the glowing clipboard from his communications expert.

"Satellite phone broadcasting from forty thousand feet."

"That means either a military aircraft or an executive plane," Juan said. "Commercial jetliners rarely fly above thirty-eight thousand."

"That's what I think, too. Sorry, we caught just the beginning of the conversation. Sniffer went down the same time as the radar and by the time it was back up the plane was out of range."

Juan read the single line aloud. ". . . not quite so soon. We'll have Merrick at the Devil's Oasis by four A.M." He read it again silently and looked at Hali, his face a mask. "Doesn't mean much to me."

"I don't know what the Devil's Oasis is, but when you were on the dock unloading the weapons Sky News broke the story that Geoffrey Merrick was kidnapped along with an associate from his company's headquarters in Geneva. Working backward given the information provided by the wire services, a fast executive jet would put Merrick and his kidnappers right over our heads at the time we intercepted this call."

"I assume we're talking about the same Geoffrey Merrick who runs Merrick/Singer?" Cabrillo asked.

"The billionaire whose inventions in the field of clean coal have opened up a world of possibilities for the industry and made him one of the most hated men on the planet by environmental groups because they still think coal's too dirty."

"Any ransom demands yet?"

"Nothing on the news."

Juan made his decision quickly. "Get Murph and Linda Ross working on this." With her background in Naval Intelligence, Ross was the perfect choice to spearhead the research and Murph was the best at finding obscure patterns in an avalanche of information. "Tell them I want to know exactly what's going on. Who took Merrick? Who's in charge of the investigation? What and where is the Devil's Oasis? The works. Plus background on Merrick/Singer."

"What's our interest in him?"

"Altruism," Cabrillo said with a piratical smirk.

"Nothing to do with the fact he's a billionaire, huh?"

"I'm shocked you'd think that of me," Juan said with convincing indignation. "His wealth never left my mind—I mean, entered it."

6

JUAN Cabrillo sat behind his desk, his feet propped up on the inlaid wood, as he read Eddie's and Linc's after-action reports off his tablet PC. Despite what had to have been a hair-raising series of events, both men made the material dull, exhorting their partner's contribution to the mission over their own and downplaying the dangers until it almost read like stereo instructions. He jotted a couple of notes using a light pen and sent the electronic reports to the computer's archive.

He then checked the weather services. The ninth major Atlantic storm of the year was forming to their north and while it wasn't a threat to the *Oregon*, he was interested because so far three storms had become hurricanes and the season was only a month old. Forecasters were predicting that this year would rival or even top the number of named storms that slammed the United States in 2005, destroying New Orleans and severely damaging Texas's Gulf Coast. The experts claimed that this was part of a normal cycle of hurricane severity and frequency; however, environmental groups were clamoring that the superstorms were the result of global warming. Juan put his stock with the forecasters, but the trend was troubling.

The weather along Africa's southwestern coast looked clear for at least the next five days.

Unlike his disheveled appearance playing at a greedy officer aboard a tramp steamer the night before, the morning found Cabrillo freshly showered and wearing a pair of English-cut blue jeans, a Turnbull and Asser shirt open at the throat, and a pair of deck shoes without socks. Because people would see his ankles, he had donned a prosthetic right leg covered in flesh-toned rubber, rather than one of his more mechanical-looking limbs. He kept his hair short, just longer than a crew cut, and despite his Latino name and heritage, his hair was bleached almost white by a California upbringing spent mostly in the sun and surf.

The armored porthole covers had been lowered so his cabin was bathed in natural light. The teak wainscoting, floors, and coffered ceiling gleamed with a fresh coat of polish. From his desk he could see through to his bedroom, which was dominated by a massive hand-carved four-poster, and beyond to the head, with its Mexican tile shower stall and copper Jacuzzi tub and sink basin. The rooms had the masculine smell of Juan's aftershave and the occasional La Troya Universales Cuban cigars he enjoyed.

The décor was simple and elegant, and showed Juan's eclectic tastes. On one wall was a painting of the *Oregon* plowing through an angry sea while another had glass-fronted shelves for some of the curios he had picked up from his travels, a clay figurine of an Egyptian *ushabti*, a stone bowl from the Aztec Empire, a prayer wheel from Tibet, a piece of scrimshaw, a Ghurka knife, a doll made of seal fur from Greenland, a piece of raw emerald from Columbia, and dozens of other items. The furniture was mostly dark and the lighting was discreet and recessed, while the throw rugs on the floor were silk Persians in bright colors.

The one telling thing in the room was the lack of photographs. Where most men at sea had pictures of their wives and children, there were no such snapshots in Juan's cabin. He had been married, but her fatal drunk driving accident eleven years ago was a pain Juan had tucked deep inside and refused to acknowledge.

He took a sip of rich Kona coffee, noted the service set, and smiled.

Two of the things that enabled him to recruit and keep some of the best from America's armed forces and intelligence services were he paid well and spared no expense on his crew, be it pricey china in the mess hall and Le Cordon Bleu–trained chefs in the galley or the decorating allowance he gave each new team member to redo their private cabins. Mark Murphy had used up most of his budget on a sound system that could shake barnacles off the hull. Linda Ross had engaged a New York City decorator in her cabin, while Linc's was as Spartan as a Navy barracks—the money instead going toward the Harley-Davidson he kept in the hold.

The *Oregon* sported a large fitness facility with saunas, and when not on an assignment one of her ballast wants could be half filled and turned into an Olympic-length swimming pool. The men and women of the Corporation lived well, but as exemplified in this most recent mission, they also lived dangerously. Every member of the crew was a stockholder and while the officers enjoyed the lion's share of the profits, Juan's favorite task at the end of an operation was signing bonus checks for the technicians and auxiliary personnel. That would total some $500,000 for the job they'd just pulled off.

He was just about to start typing his report to Langston Overholt, his old friend at the CIA who brought the Corporation a great deal of business, when someone knocked on his door.

"Come."

Linda Ross and Mark Murphy stepped into his cabin. Where Linda was perky and petite, Murph was gangly and awkward with shaggy dark hair, a goatee that a single swipe with a razor would erase, and a habit of wearing nothing but black. One of the few on the ship without a military background, Mark was a certified genius who had earned his Ph.D. by the time he was twenty. He'd gone into R&D for a defense contractor where he'd met Eric Stone, who was in the Navy then, but a short-timer with a contract to come and work for Juan. Eric had convinced Cabrillo that the young weapons expert would be a perfect fit for the Corporation, and in the three years since, and despite Murph's taste for punk music and how he would turn the ship's deck into a skateboard park, Juan couldn't have agreed more.

Cabrillo glanced at the antique chronograph across from his desk. "Either you two completely struck out or you hit a home run to get back to me this quickly."

"Let's say we're on third," Murph said, adjusting the bundle of papers in his arms. "And for the record I don't like sports metaphors because I don't get them half the time."

"So this was a slam dunk more than a Hail Mary." Juan grinned.

"If you say so."

They took seats opposite Juan who cleared a bunch of papers off his desk. "Okay, what do you have?"

"Where do you want to start?" Linda asked. "The kidnapping or the company?"

"Let's start with the background first so I know who we're dealing with." Juan laced his fingers behind his head and stared at the ceiling while Linda began her report. It might have been rude not to look her in the eye but it was one of his quirks when concentrating.

"Geoffrey Merrick, age fifty-one. Divorced with two grown children, both of whom spend their time blowing through their father's money by chasing paparazzi so they can end up in tabloids. The wife is an artist living in New Mexico and keeps a low profile.

"Merrick graduated with a Ph.D. in Chemistry from MIT exactly one day younger than Mark was when he received his, and partnered up with another alum, Daniel Singer, to form Merrick/Singer, a materials research company. The firm has applied for and received eighty patents in the past twenty-five-odd years and the company has grown from the two of them in a rented space outside Boston to a campus near Geneva, Switzerland, with a staff of a hundred and sixty.

"As you may know, their biggest patent is for an organic-based system to filter up to ninety percent of the sulfur out of the smoke emitted by coal-fired power plants. A year after it was issued Merrick/Singer went public and both men became billionaires. That isn't to say there wasn't a lot of controversy at the time, which still echoes today. Environmental groups say that even with the scrubbers, coal plants are too dirty and should be shut down. Numerous lawsuits are still pending and new ones are being filed every year."

"Could ecoterrorists have abducted Merrick?" Juan interrupted.

"The Swiss police are looking into that possibility," Linda said. "But it doesn't seem likely. What would be the point? Getting back to the story: Ten years after they hit it big with their IPO, a rift developed between

Merrick and his partner. Up until this time the two had been as close as brothers. They always appeared together at press conferences. Their families even vacationed together. Then, in the span of a couple of months, Singer seemed to have gone through a personality change. He started siding with the environmentalists in the suits brought against his own company and eventually forced Merrick to buy him out entirely. His shares were valued at two point four billion and Merrick had to scramble to come up with that kind of cash. To make it happen he had to personally buy back all the shares of Merrick/Singer. It nearly bankrupted him."

"Real Cain and Abel type stuff," Mark Murphy interjected.

"At the time it was front-page news in all the financial papers."

"What's Singer been doing since?"

"After his wife left him he's been living on the coast of Maine near where he grew up. Up until about five years ago he was using his wealth to support all kinds of environmental causes, some on the extreme side of things. Then he suddenly filed fraud claims against a number of environmental groups saying they had bilked him. Said the whole movement was just a way for the people in charge of the various charities to make money for themselves and that they did nothing to really help the planet. The suits are still pending, though Singer himself has pretty much dropped out of sight."

"So he's some kind of hermit now?"

"No. Just real low-key. While doing the research I got the sense that Merrick was the front man and Singer the brains, even though they shared the podium. Merrick glad-handed everyone and really knew his way around Capitol Hill and later in the halls of power in Bern when they moved the company to Switzerland. He wore the thousand-dollar suits while Singer sported jeans and a poorly knotted tie. Merrick loved the limelight and Singer the shadows. I think since leaving the company he's just reverted back to his introverted self."

"Doesn't sound like a criminal mastermind to me," Juan said.

"I don't think so, either. He's just a scientist with a fat wallet."

"Okay, so we're stuck with a kidnapping for ransom—or is there anyone else out there gunning for Merrick?"

"Since the showdown with Singer, the company's been running smoothly."

"What exactly do they do?"

"Now that they're privately held, it's mostly pure research funded by Merrick. They still receive a few patents a year, nothing earth-shattering, just a better molecular glue for some esoteric application or a foam that can withstand a few tenths of a degree more than something else already on the market."

"Anything someone would try to steal through industrial espionage?"

"Nothing we could find, but they could be working on something in secret."

"Okay, we'll keep that in mind. Tell me about the kidnapping itself."

Mark straightened in his chair. "Merrick and a researcher named Susan Donleavy were seen by the security guard at the main building on their campus at seven last night chatting on their way out the door. Merrick had a dinner date with reservations for eight o'clock. Donleavy lives alone and apparently didn't have plans.

"They left Merrick/Singer in separate vehicles, Merrick in his Mercedes and Donleavy in a Volkswagen. Their cars were found a half mile from the facility. By studying the tire marks the police were able to determine that a third vehicle—given the length of its wheel base most likely it was a van—forced both vehicles off the road at high speed. Airbags were deployed in the Mercedes but not in the Volkswagen. Presumably, Merrick was hit first and Susan Donleavy was slowing when the van hit her. The driver's side window on Merrick's car was smashed inward so the door could be unlocked. The Volkswagen didn't have automatic locks so she was simply pulled from the car."

"How did they know this was a kidnapping and not some Good Samaritan rescuing them and taking them to a local hospital?" Cabrillo asked.

"Because they aren't at any local hospitals, leading the police to conclude they were locked in the Good Samaritan's basement."

"Right."

"So far there have been no ransom demands and a search for the van's turned up nothing. Eventually they will find it at the airport because we know Merrick, and most likely Susan Donleavy as well, were taken out of the country by plane."

"Have you checked charter flights out of Geneva for last night?"

"Eric's on that now. There are more than fifty because an economic summit meeting just concluded and all the bigwigs were headed home."

Juan rolled his eyes. "Figures."

"Might not be bad luck on our part, but thorough planning on theirs," Linda said.

"Good point."

"So far the police don't know what to make of the situation. They're playing the wait-and-see game until the kidnappers make their demands."

"Could this have been about Susan Donleavy and not Geoffrey Merrick?" Juan suggested.

Mark shook his head. "Doubt it. I checked her on the company database. She's been with them for two years, a researcher in organic chemistry still working toward her doctorate. Like I said before, she lives alone. No husband or kids. Most employee bios give a little info about interests and hobbies. Hers only gave her professional credentials. Nothing personal at all.

"No one a kidnapper would go through the expense of hiring a private jet to grab."

"Doesn't wash no matter how you look at it," Linda said. "Merrick was the target, and I bet Donleavy was nabbed because she was a witness."

"What about this Devil's Oasis that was mentioned?" Juan asked to get them back on track.

"We couldn't find any mention of it on the Internet," Linda replied. "It has to be a code name, so it could be anyplace. Backtracking from where we intercepted the call when they said they would reach it by four in the morning, it could be in a circle big enough to encompass the eastern tip of South America. Or they could have turned northward again and gone back to Europe."

"That doesn't sound likely. Let's assume that they continued on the same straight-line course south from Switzerland that took them over our position last night. What's the most likely landing site?

"Someplace in Namibia, Botswana, Zimbabwe, or South Africa."

"And with our luck what do you bet it's Zimbabwe?" Mark muttered.

Years of corruption and poor economic planning had turned the once prosperous country into one of the poorest nations on the continent. Simmering anger against the repressive government was threatening to boil over. Reports of attacks against remote villages that spoke out against the regime were growing while malnutrition and the diseases it spawned were on the rise. All indicators pointed to a full-scale civil war erupting in months or maybe even weeks.

"Again, maybe not our bad luck, but their good planning," Linda said. "The middle of a war zone would be the last place I'd look for a kidnapped industrialist. They could easily bribe the government to look the other way when they brought him in."

"Okay, concentrate your search efforts on the Devil's Oasis being in Zimbabwe, but don't rule out anything. We'll keep steaming southward and hopefully you'll have something by the time we reach the Tropic of Capricorn. Meanwhile, I'm going to talk with Langston to see if the CIA has anything on this and maybe have him send out some feelers to the Swiss government as well as the board of Merrick/Singer. Let them know they might have options."

"This isn't our usual way of doing things, Chairman."

"I know, Linda, but we might be in the right place at the right time to make this all work out."

"Or the kidnappers are going to issue their demands today, Merrick/Singer will pay the ransom, and good old Geoffrey boy will be home in time for dinner."

"You're forgetting one critical piece." Juan didn't match her light tone. "Flying him out of the country is a risk they didn't need if this was about a cash ransom. If that's all they wanted they would have stashed him someplace within Switzerland, issued their demands, and been done with it. If their planning is as meticulous as you suspect, there has to be another level to their plot we haven't seen."

Linda Ross nodded, sensing the gravity of the situation. "Like what?"

"Find the Devil's Oasis and maybe we'll know."

7

THE headphones clamped around Sloane's ears made her so sweaty that her hair felt glued to her skin, but to take them off to cool herself meant she had to endure the pounding throb of the helicopter's engine and rotor. It was a balance of discomforts that she'd endured for two fruitless days.

The back of her shirt was also sticky. Every time she shifted position it stuck to the vinyl seat. She'd learned early on to hold the shirt when she moved or it would tighten across her chest, gaining her a leering grin from Luka, who sat next to her on the rear bench seat. She would have preferred to sit in the front next to the pilot, but he said he needed Tony's weight in the cockpit to keep the small chopper in proper trim.

They were returning to Swakopmund for the last time, for which Sloane was both grateful and frustrated. Seven times they'd flown out over the ocean and searched the spots circled on her map and seven times they'd returned to refuel, having found nothing but natural rock formations. The portable metal detector they could dip into the water on a long tether failed to find any metal source large enough to be an anchor, let alone an entire ship.

Her body ached from so many hot hours in the cramped chopper and she thought she'd never get Luka's body odor out of her nostrils. She had been so sure of her plan to use local fishermen's knowledge of the waters off the coast that she hadn't even considered failing. But now that they were returning to the little heliport in the dunes outside of Swakopmund, defeat scalded the back of her throat while the glare off the ocean below penetrated her sunglasses and made her head pound.

Tony turned in his seat to look at her and motioned for her to jack her headphones back into the helicopter's internal communications net. She had unplugged it to give her pity party some privacy.

"The pilot says that the chopper doesn't have the range to check that last spot on the map. The one we got from Papa Heinrick."

"What's this about Papa Heinrick?" Luka asked, blasting Sloane with a dose of halitosis.

Something had prevented Sloane from discussing their late-night raft trip down in Sandwich Bay to visit the crazy old fisherman, mostly because she grudgingly suspected that Luka had been right all along and just didn't want to admit it to the guide.

Wishing Tony had kept his mouth shut, Sloane shrugged. "Doesn't matter. He was nuttier than a fruitcake. We've wasted more than two thousand dollars on fuel checking possibilities from reliable sources. I can't see us wasting any more on Papa Heinrick and his giant snakes."

"Giant what?" the pilot asked. He was South African with a thick Africaans accent.

"Giant snakes," Sloane repeated, feeling foolish. "He claims he was attacked by giant metal snakes."

"Most likely it was the DTs," the pilot said. "Everyone around here knows that Papa Heinrick is the world's biggest boozer. I've seen him drink a pair of Aussie backpackers under the table and both those lads were the size of elephants. Rugby players, I think they were. If it's snakes he's seeing you can bet your last Rand he was coming off a bender when he saw 'em."

"Giant snakes." Luka giggled. "Did I not tell you that Papa Heinrick is a crazy man? You waste your time talking to him. You trust Luka. I find the spot you're looking for. You see. There are still places out here where it could be."

"Not for me," Tony said. "I have to be back home day after tomorrow and I just want to sit by the pool."

"That is okay," Luka said with a quick glance at where Sloane's leg emerged from her shorts. "I take Miss Sloane alone in a boat with greater range than this helicopter."

"I don't think so," Sloane said sharply enough to get Tony's attention. She glared at him and it took him a moment to understand what their guide was really after.

"We'll play it by ear. See how I feel in the morning, huh?" he said. "Maybe a boat trip wouldn't be too bad."

"You're wasting your time," the pilot muttered.

Sloane was sure he was right.

The chopper flared over the dusty heliport twenty minutes later. The rotor blast kicked up a cloud of grit that obscured the ground and turned the limp windsock into a rigid pink cone. The pilot gently set his helicopter on the ground and immediately cut the engines. The effect was instantaneous. The piercing whine of the moter faded and the blades began to slow. He opened his door before they stopped, exchanging the hot sweat-tainted air in the cabin with hot gritty air from outside. It was still a relief.

Sloane opened her door and stepped from the helo, ducking low instinctively as the rotor continued to whirl over her head. She grabbed her duffel bag and then walked around the chopper's nose to give Tony a hand unhooking the metal detector and cable spool from the left skid. Together they lugged the hundred-pound piece of equipment to the back of the pickup they'd rented. Luka had made no offer to help and instead sucked furiously on his first cigarette in two hours.

Tony settled up with the pilot for his day's service, depleting all but two of his traveler's checks, which he'd already vowed to lose at the casino in their hotel. The pilot shook hands with both of them, thanking them for using his charter service, and left with one last piece of advice, "I'm sure you've figured Luka's a rogue and a thief, but he's right about Papa Heinrick. That old man isn't right in the head. You two have had your bit of fun looking for a sunken ship. Enjoy the last day of your holiday. Go on a tour of the dunes or relax by the pool like Tony says."

With Luka safely out of earshot, Sloane replied, "Piet, we've come halfway around the world. What's another wasted day?"

The pilot chuckled. "That's what I love about you Yanks. You never give up."

They shook hands again and Luka scampered into the back of the four-wheel-drive pickup. They dropped him in front of a bar in his working-class neighborhood along Walvis Bay. They paid him his daily wage and, despite their protestations that they probably wouldn't be needing him again, he promised to be at the hotel at nine the next morning.

"God, he's insufferable," Sloane said.

"I don't understand your problem with him. Yeah, he could use a shower and a breath mint, but he really has been helpful."

"Try being a woman around him and you'll understand."

Swakopmund was unlike any town in Africa. Because Namibia had been a German colony, the city's architecture was pure Bavaria, with lots of gingerbread trim on the houses and solid Lutheran churches. The palm-lined streets were wide and well maintained, although sand from the desert blew across everything. With access to a deep-water port at Walvis Bay, it was becoming a cruise destination for the adventurous set.

Sloane begged off Tony's suggestion of dinner at the hotel's buffet and a night at the casino. "I think I'm going to the restaurant out by the light-house and watch the sun go down."

"Suit yourself," Tony said, and headed off for his room.

After her shower, Sloane put on floral print sundress and flats and draped a sweater over her shoulders. She let her copper hair flow free around her shoulders and used makeup to even out where the tops of her cheeks had been pinked by the sun. Although Tony had been a complete gentleman the entire trip, she had a premonition that tonight, after a couple hours of pretending to be James Bond in the casino, he would make a pass. Best to just not be around, was her attitude.

She strolled down Bahnhof Street, peering in shop windows at native carvings and painted ostrich eggs for sale to the tourists. The wind coming off the Atlantic freshened the city and scoured the air of dust. When she reached the end of the street, Palm Beach was to her right and the Mole was straight ahead. The Mole was a natural spit of land that sheltered Palm Beach and at its tip was a spindly lighthouse. She reached her destination a couple minutes later. Perched above the crashing surf, the restaurant had spectacular views; a number of tourists were there with the same idea as Sloane.

She ordered a German beer from the bar and took it to a vacant seat overlooking the sea.

Sloane Macintyre wasn't used to failure, so she was especially annoyed the trip had been a bust. True, it had been a long shot from the beginning, but she still thought they had a good chance at finding the HMS *Rove*.

But then what, she asked herself for the hundredth time, what were the chances that the rumor was true? A thousand to one? A million? And what would she get for finding it? A pat on the back and a bonus. She had to wonder if putting up with Tony's petulance and Luka's leers and Papa Heinrick's insanity was worth it. She downed the last of her beer in three angry gulps and ordered another plus a fish dinner.

She ate as the sun sank into the sea, reflecting on her life. She had a sister with a husband, a career, and three kids, while she was in her London flat so infrequently she threw away all her real plants in favor of plastic ones because they always died of neglect. She thought about her last relationship and how it, too, had petered out because she was never around. But mostly she brooded on how a woman with a business degree from Columbia ends up spending her time traipsing around Third World countries questioning fishermen about where they lose their nets.

She decided as she finished her meal that when she got home she was going to take a serious look at her life and what she wanted out of it. She'd be forty in three years, and while that didn't sound old to her now she remembered how ancient it seemed when she was twenty. She was nowhere near her career goals and felt that she wasn't going to get much higher on the corporate ladder without some drastic action.

Which she'd thought she'd taken by coming to Namibia, but now this was turning out to be a bust, and her logic came full circle to being angry at herself for being so wrong.

The air grew a bit chilly with the wind coming off the cold water. She shrugged into her sweater and paid her tab, leaving a generous tip even though her guidebook said waiters didn't expect one.

She started back to her hotel, taking a different route than before just to see more of the old town. The sidewalks were quiet except around a couple of restaurants and there was no traffic on the street. While wealthy by Africa's standards, Namibia was still a poor country, and people tended to live with the rhythms of the day. Most were asleep by eight, so there were few lights in the homes.

Sloane became aware of the footsteps when the wind died suddenly. Without its gentle hiss the tap of shoes on concrete carried easily. She turned and saw a shadow duck around a corner. Had the person kept coming she would have considered the moment a figment of paranoia. But the person didn't want her to know he was there, and Sloane realized she wasn't all that familiar with this part of the city.

She knew her hotel was to her left, four, maybe five streets over. It dominated Bahnhof Street, so if she could reach that road she'd be fine. She took off running, lost a sandal after only a couple of steps and quickly kicked off the other as her pursuer gave a startled grunt at her reaction and started after her.

Sloane ran as hard as she could, her bare feet slapping against the sidewalk. Just before she turned a corner she chanced looking back. There were two of them! She thought they might have been a pair of the fishermen she and Tony had questioned, but she could tell both men were white and it looked like one of them had a pistol.

She careened around the corner and ran even harder. They would gain on her, she knew, but if she could just reach the hotel she was sure they'd back off. Her arms pumping, wishing she'd worn a sports bra rather than the lacy thing she'd chosen, Sloane dashed across a side street. The men were momentarily out of view, so when she saw an alley she dashed down it instinctively.

She was almost at the end where it opened onto another road when she kicked a metal can she hadn't seen in the darkness. The pain of her stubbed toe was nothing compared to her fury at not seeing the can. It clanged like a rung bell, and as she emerged from the alley she knew her pursuers had heard it, too. She turned left once again and saw a car approaching. Sloane ran into the street waving her arms over her head frantically. The car slowed. She could see a man and a woman inside, children in the backseat.

The woman said something to her husband and he looked away guiltily as he accelerated past her. Sloane cursed. She'd lost precious seconds hoping they would help. She ran again, her lungs beginning to burn.

The crack of the pistol shot and the spray of concrete dust exploding

off the building next to her struck Sloane at the same instant. The gunman
had missed her head by less than a foot. She fought the instinct to duck,
which would have slowed her pace, and continued to sprint like a gazelle,
weaving right and left with sharp movements to throw off their aim.

She saw a sign for Wasserfall Street and knew she was only half a
block from her hotel. She put on a burst of speed she never thought she
was capable of and emerged onto Bahnhof Street. Her hotel was almost
directly ahead and a string of cars cruised down the wide lane. There were
plenty of lights around the old converted train station. She danced through
traffic, ignoring the honks, and finally reached the hotel's entrance. She
turned back. The two men lurked across the street, glaring at her. The
shooter had hidden his pistol under his jacket. He cupped his hands to his
mouth and shouted, "This was a warning! Leave Namibia or the next
time I won't miss."

A spark of defiance compelled Sloane to want to give him the finger,
but all she could do was slump to the ground as tears welled in her eyes
and her chest convulsed. A doorman approached her a moment later.

"Are you okay, miss?"

"I'm fine," Sloane said, getting to her feet and dusting her backside.
She knuckled the moisture from her eyes. The spot where the men had
stood was deserted. Even though her lip still quivered and her legs felt like
gel, Sloane squared her shoulders, deliberately raised her right arm, and
then extended her middle finger.

8

THE thick stone walls could not absorb her screams. The walls soaked up the heat of the sun until the rock was too hot to touch, but they let Susan Donleavy's tortured wailing echo almost as if she were in the next cell. At first Geoff Merrick had forced himself to listen, as if bearing witness to her pain could somehow give the young woman comfort. He had stoically endured her piercing shrieks for an hour, flinching each time she hit a note of agony so high it felt like his skull would shatter like a piece of crystal. Now, as he sat on the earthen floor of his cell, he held his hands clamped over his ears and hummed to drown out her cries.

They'd taken her just after dawn, when the prison had yet to become stifling and the light through the room's single glass-less window high on the east wall still held promise. The cell block measured at least fifty feet square and at least thirty feet high. It was divided into numerous jail cells with stone walls on three sides and iron bars for the fourth and the ceiling. A second and third tier of cells ringed the room above him, accessible by wrought-iron circular stairways. Despite the apparent antiquity of the facility the iron bars were as secure as a modern super-max prison.

Merrick had yet to see any of his captors' faces. They'd worn ski masks when they rammed his car off the road just outside his laboratory and on the flight to this hellhole. There were at least three of them, he knew, because of differences in their bodies. One was large and hulking, and wore nothing but sleeveless athletic T-shirts. Another was slender and had bright blue eyes, while the third was distinguishable because he wasn't the other two.

In the three days since the abduction, their jailers hadn't spoken a single word to either of them. They'd been stripped in the van that had smashed into their cars and given jumpsuits to wear. All their jewelry was removed and instead of shoes they had rubber flip-flops. They were given two meals a day and Merrick's cell had a hole in the floor for a toilet that blew hot air and sand whenever the wind picked up outside. Since being dumped into the prison the jailers had only come around to feed them.

Then this morning they came for Susan. Because her cell was on another row within the block, Merrick couldn't be sure, but it had sounded as if they'd yanked her to her feet by her hair. They had bundled her past him on their way out the room's lone door, a thick metal affair with peepholes.

Susan was pale, her eyes already sheened over with despair. He had called her name and rushed his bars in an effort to touch her, to give her a token of human compassion, but the smallest guard smashed the bars with a nightstick. Merrick fell back helpless as they dragged her away. Estimating the heat that had built in the room he believed four hours had passed since then. It had been quiet at first and then the screams came. And now Susan was well into her second hour of torture.

In the first hours of their kidnapping, Merrick had been certain this was about money—that their captors would demand cash in exchange for their release. He knew the Swiss authorities had a zero-tolerance policy when dealing with hostage takers but he also knew there were companies that specialized in negotiating with kidnappers. Because of the recent spate of abductions in Italy, Merrick had instructed his board of directors to find such negotiators if he were ever taken and secure his freedom no matter the cost.

But after being flown blindfolded for at least six hours, Merrick didn't know what was going on. He and Susan had whispered to each other late at night, speculating on their captors' intentions. While Susan insisted it had to be about his money and she was caught up in the abduction as a witness, Merrick wasn't so sure. He hadn't been asked to speak to anyone in the company about getting a ransom together or been given any indication that his people even knew he and Susan were still alive. Nothing so far fit what he knew about kidnapping. Admittedly, the rudimentary executive security course he'd taken had been years ago, but he recalled enough to know his abductors did not fit the usual profile.

And now this. They were torturing poor Susan Donleavy, a loyal, dedicated employee who knew little beyond her test tubes and beakers. Merrick recalled their conversation a few weeks back about her idea of ending oil spills with her trick plankton. He hadn't told her that while her goals were indeed lofty, her concept seemed a bit outlandish. His whole speech about revenge being a great motivator was just that, a speech, one he'd given an hundred times in a hundred variations. She'd have better luck overcoming a childhood trauma with a psychiatrist than in her laboratory.

Thinking about her project made him consider all the other research currently under way at Merrick/Singer. He'd done this many times since landing in the cell. There was nothing, absolutely nothing, they were working on that would warrant what was happening if this was a case of industrial espionage. They weren't close to patenting anything new or revolutionary. In fact, they hadn't had a really profitable patent since he and Dan Singer first marketed their sulfur scrubbers. The company was basically a vanity project for him now, a way to keep his hands in the world of research chemistry and to get invitations to speak at symposiums.

The screaming stopped. It wasn't a slow wind down, but a sudden cessation of sound that was more horrifying in its implications.

Geoff Merrick shot to his feet, wedging his face into the iron bars so he could see a sliver of the cell block door. A few minutes later the bolts shot back and the heavy slab of metal creaked open.

They had to drag her in with her arms draped over two of the guards' necks while the third held a set of large keys. As they drew near, Merrick saw blood caked in Susan Donleavy's hair. Her jumpsuit had been torn at the neck and the skin of her upper chest and shoulder was livid purple. She managed to look up as they dragged her past his cage. Merrick gasped. Her face was a pulped ruin. One eye was swollen closed while she could barely lever open the other against the weight of bruising. Blood and saliva ran in ropes from her split and slack lips.

There was just the slightest flicker of life in her eye when she glanced at him.

"Dear God, Susan. I am so sorry." He didn't try to fight his tears. She had become so pitiable a figure that he would have cried even if she were a total stranger. That she was an employee and that he was somehow responsible for what they had done to her tore at his soul.

She spat a red glob onto the stone floor and croaked, "They didn't even ask me any questions."

"You bastards!" he raged at the guards. "I will pay you anything. You didn't need to do this to her. She's innocent."

They might as well have been deaf because they gave no reaction to his outburst. They just dragged her from his view. He heard her cell door open and her dumped roughly inside. The iron door was slammed shut and the lock reengaged.

Merrick decided that when they came for him he was going to fight them with everything he had. If he was going to be beaten he wanted to inflict some punishment first. He waited in his cell for them, his fists balled, his shoulders tense and ready.

The slightest guard, the one with the bright blue eyes, appeared. He held something in his hand and before Merrick could identify it or react, the guard fired. It was a Tazer that pumped fifty thousand volts into his body and overrode his central nervous system in a blaze of pain. Merrick went rigid for a second and then collapsed. By the time he regained consciousness they had him out of the cell and almost to the main door. In such agony from the blast of electricity, he'd lost all thought of fighting them.

9

SLOANE Macintyre wore a baseball cap to tame her hair against the twenty-knot wind generated by the fishing boat's forward speed. Her eyes were protected by a pair of wraparound Oakley's on a gaily colored cord and what skin lay exposed to the sun was slathered with SPF 30. She had on a pair of khaki shorts and a loose bush shirt festooned with pockets. On her feet she wore canvas boat shoes. The glint of a gold anklet shone in the sun.

Every time she was on the water she felt like a teen again, working her father's charter boat off Florida's east coast. There had been a few bad incidences when she'd taken over for her ailing father with drunken fishermen more interested in catching her than billfish or snapper, but all in all it was the greatest time of her life. The salty tang of sea air seemed to calm her very soul while the isolation of being on a hard-charging boat helped her focus her mind.

The charter boat captain, a jovial Namibian, sensed in her a kindred spirit and when she glanced at him he threw her a knowing smile. Sloane returned it. With the twin Cummins diesels bellowing under the transom it was nearly impossible to speak, so he stood from his chair and gestured for Sloane to take the controls. Her smile turned into a grin. The captain tapped the compass to indicate their heading and stepped from the wheel. Sloane slid into his position and rested her hands lightly on the worn wheel.

He stood by her side for a couple of minutes, checking that their wake continued in a straight line. Satisfied that he was right about his passenger being able to handle the forty-six-foot cruiser, he slid down the short ladder; nodded at Tony Reardon, who was slouched in the fighting chair; and went to use the head.

Sloane would have given up on their search if those men hadn't come after her the previous night. Their actions convinced her she was on the right track to find the HMS *Rove*. Why else try to scare her off? She hadn't told Tony about the attack, but first thing this morning she'd phoned her boss and laid out the whole story. While concerned for her safety, he gave her permission to extend their stay another day so they could investigate the section of sea where Papa Heinrick had seen his giant metal snakes.

She knew she was being reckless. Any sane person would have heeded the warning and left the country on the first plane out, but that wasn't in her nature. In all her life she had never left a task unfinished. No matter how bad a book was, she'd read it to the last word. No matter how difficult a crossword, she'd work it to the last clue. No matter how difficult the job, she would see it through to the end. It was this dogged tenacity that probably kept her in doomed relationships long after she should have ended them, but it also gave her the strength to face whoever was trying to prevent her from finding her ship.

Sloane had been cautious when hiring the charter, making sure the captain wasn't one they had spoken to when she and Tony were putting together their map. Leaving their hotel, they had blended in with a large group of tourists who were headed to the waterfront for a charter fishing trip of their own and on the bus she made certain that no one was following them. Had she seen anything suspicious she would have called off the whole thing, but no one paid their vehicle any attention.

It was only when they were several miles from shore that Sloane told the captain where she really wanted to go. He'd told her that the section of the sea where she wanted to fish was devoid of any marine life but since she was paying he hadn't put up much of an argument.

That had been six uneventful hours earlier, and every mile they put behind them without incident allowed Sloane to relax that little bit more. The men who had chased her must have assumed she had taken their warning to heart and given up.

The seas were building slightly with a wind out of the south. The beamy boat rode them well, rolling to starboard with each swell and returning to an even keel smartly. The captain returned from below and stood a little behind Sloane, letting her maintain the helm. He reached for a pair of binoculars from under a bench seat and scanned the horizon. He handed them to her and pointed a bit south of due west.

Sloane adjusted the binoculars to fit her face and brought them to her eyes. A big ship coasted on the horizon, a single-funneled freighter that appeared to be heading toward Walvis Bay. At this extreme range it was impossible to see any detail other than get a vague sense of her dark hull and a small forest of booms and derricks on both her fore and aft decks.

"I never see a ship like that out here before," the charter captain said. "Only ships come to Walvis are coasters or the cruise ships. Fishermen are all closer to shore and tankers rounding the Cape run four or five hundred miles further out."

The world's oceans are divided into sea lanes that were almost as clearly marked as interstate highways. With deadlines always tight and the price of keeping a vessel at sea running into the hundreds of thousands of dollars a day for supertankers, ships invariably followed the straightest line between destinations, rarely varying a mile or two. So while some parts of the ocean teemed with marine traffic, other regions never saw a single ship in a year. The charter boat was in such a dead zone—far enough from the coast to avoid regional freighters supplying Walvis Bay but well inside established routes used for rounding the Cape of Good Hope.

"There's something else odd," Sloane said. "There's no smoke coming from her funnel. Do you think she's a derelict? Maybe she was caught in a storm and the crew had to abandon her."

Tony came up the ladder. Sloane was pondering the presence of the mystery ship and the fate of her crew and didn't hear him so when he touched her shoulder she started.

"Sorry," he said. "Look behind us. There's another boat coming this way."

Sloane whirled so fast that her hands on the wheel caused the boat to lurch to port. It was notoriously hard to judge distances at sea but she knew the boat driving hard for them could not be more than a couple of miles astern and for it to catch up to them it was running faster than the charter boat. She tossed the binoculars at the captain and eased the chrome throttle handles until they hit their stops.

"What's going on?" Tony shouted, leaning forward as the boat picked up speed.

The captain had sensed Sloane's fear and for the moment said nothing as he scoped the approaching craft with the binoculars.

"Do you recognize it?" Sloane asked him.

"Yes. She comes into Walvis every month or so. A yacht. Maybe fifty feet long. I do not know her name or her owner."

"Can you see anyone?"

"There are men on the upper bridge. White men."

"I demand to know what is going on!" Tony roared, his face flushing.

Again Sloane ignored him. Without having to see them, she knew who was in the boat behind them. She gently eased the wheel and started racing for the distant freighter, praying that her pursuers would back off if there were witnesses. Out on the open ocean she was sure they'd be killed, the fishing boat scuttled. She pressed more firmly on the throttles but the diesels were already giving her everything they had. Her lips worked as she silently prayed that she was wrong about the freighter being abandoned. If it was, they'd be dead as soon as the yacht caught up.

Tony grabbed her arm, his eyes blazing. "Damn it, Sloane, what is this all about? Who are those people?"

"I think they're the same men who chased me back to the hotel last night."

"Chased you? What do you mean, chased you?"

"What I said," she snapped. "I was chased back to the hotel by two men. One of them had a gun. They warned me to leave the country."

Tony's anger turned into fury and even the captain looked at her with an unreadable expression. "And you didn't see fit to tell me. Are you out of your mind? You get chased by men with guns and then lead us out here to the middle of nowhere? Good God, woman, what were you thinking?"

"I didn't think they would follow us," Sloane shouted back. "I messed up, all right! If we can get close enough to the freighter they won't do anything."

"What the hell would have happened if that freighter wasn't here?" Spittle popped from Tony's mouth with each word.

"Well, it is, so we'll be fine."

Tony turned to the ship's owner. "Do you have a gun?"

He nodded slowly. "I use it on sharks if they come round."

"Then I bloody well recommend you get it, mate, because we might just need it."

The boat had been taking the waves on a gentle broadside but now that Sloane had altered their course they were cutting into them, the bow sawing up and down and sea foam exploding each time they plowed through a crest. The ride was rough and Sloane kept her knees bent to absorb each impact. The captain returned from below and wordlessly handed Sloane a worn twelve-gauge and a fistful of shells, intuitively knowing she possessed a strength Tony Reardon lacked. He retook his position at the helm and made subtle corrections as each wave passed under them so as not to lose speed. The luxury yacht had gained at least a mile while the freighter looked no closer.

She scanned the big cargo ship through the binoculars and her heart sank. The vessel was in poor repair. Her hull was painted in myriad dark shades and looked like it had been patched with steel plates a dozen times over. She saw no one walking the decks or manning the bridge and while it looked like foam creamed off her bows as if she were making way it couldn't be possible because there was no smoke from her stack.

"Do you have a radio?" Sloane asked the captain.

"It is below," he replied. "But doesn't have enough range to reach Walvis if that's what you're thinking."

Sloane pointed to the freighter over the bow. "I want to alert them what's happening so they can lower a boarding ladder."

The captain glanced over his shoulder at the fast-approaching yacht. "It will be close."

Sloane slid down the steep steps using just her hands, and ran into the cabin. The radio was an old transceiver bolted to the low ceiling. She powered it up and worked the knob to channel 16, the international distress band.

"Mayday, mayday, mayday, this is the fishing vessel *Pinguin* calling the freighter en route to Walvis Bay. We are being chased by pirates, please respond."

A burst of static filled the cabin.

Sloane adjusted the radio dial and thumbed the microphone. "This is the *Pinguin* calling unidentified freighter en route to Walvis. We need assistance. Please respond."

Again she heard static, but thought she caught the ghost of a voice in the white noise. Despite the boat's violent pitching, Sloane's fingers were as delicate as a surgeon's as she moved the dial in fractional increments.

A voice suddenly boomed from the speaker. "You should have listened to me last night and left Namibia." Through the distortion Sloane was still able to recognize the voice from the previous night and her blood went cold.

Sloane mashed the microphone. "Leave us alone and we will return to shore," she pleaded. "I will be on the first plane out. I promise."

"That is no longer an option."

She looked over the transom. The yacht had cut the distance to a couple hundred yards, close enough for her to see two of the men in the bridge holding rifles of some sort. The freighter was a mile or more away.

They weren't going to make it.

"WHAT do you think, Chairman?" Hali Kasim asked from his seat at the communications station.

Cabrillo was leaning forward in his chair, an elbow on the arm of his chair, a hand cupping his unshaven chin. The forward display screen showed the view from the mast-mounted camera. The image from the gyro-stabilized video was rock solid and zoomed in on the two boats fast approaching the *Oregon*. The fishing boat was making a solid twenty knots while the motor yacht was easily closing in at thirty-five.

They'd been watching the two craft on radar for the better part of an hour and had given their presence a low priority since the waters off Namibia's coast were known fishing grounds. It was only when the first boat, which they now knew was called *Pinguin*, German for penguin, altered course to intercept the *Oregon* that Cabrillo was called from his cabin where he was just about ready to hit the showers after an hour in the gym.

"I don't have the foggiest idea," Juan said at last. "Why would pirates use a million-dollar yacht to chase an old fishing boat a hundred and fifty miles offshore? Something's hinky. Wepps, zoom in on that yacht. Let's see who's aboard her if you can."

Mark Murphy wasn't on duty, so the crewman manning the weapons station worked a joystick and trackball to bring up the image Cabrillo wanted. At such extreme zoom even the computer-assisted gyroscopes had a difficult time holding the picture steady. But it was good enough. Sunlight glinted off the expanse of sloping glass below the bridge but through the glare Juan could see four men on the sleek yacht's bridge, and two of them held assault rifles. As they watched, one of them brought the weapon to his shoulder and fired a short burst.

Anticipating the coming order, the weapons officer panned back to show the fleeing *Pinguin*. It didn't appear she had been hit but they could see a copper-haired woman crouched behind the flat transom cradling a shotgun.

"Wepps," Cabrillo said sharply. "Spool up the Gatling but don't lower the hull plate. Bring up a firing solution on that yacht and pop the starboard thirty calibers from their redoubts just in case."

"Four men with automatic weapons against a woman with a shotgun," Hali mused. "Won't be much of a fight if we don't do something."

"I'm working on it," Cabrillo said, then nodded to his communications specialist. "Patch me through to her."

Kasim hit a button on one of his three keyboards. "You're live."

Cabrillo settled his lip mike. "*Pinguin, Pinguin, Pinguin*, this is the motor ship *Oregon*." On the screen they could see the woman's head whip around as she heard him over the radio.

She scrambled back inside the cabin and a moment later her breathless voice filled the operations center. "*Oregon*, oh, thank God. For a minute I thought you were a derelict ship."

"Not far from the truth," Linda Ross deadpanned. Though not on duty, Juan had asked the elfin Ross to join him in the op center on the off chance he would need her background in intelligence.

"Please state the nature of your emergency," Juan requested, pretending they didn't have a bird's-eye view of what was happening. "You mentioned pirates."

"Yes, and they just opened fire on us with machine guns. My name is Sloane Macintyre. We're on a fishing charter and they just suddenly appeared."

"Didn't sound that way to me," Linda said, sucking her lower lip. "The guy on the yacht said he'd already warned her about something once."

"So she's lying," Juan agreed. "She was just fired at and she's lying. Interesting, don't you think?"

"She's gotta be hiding something."

"*Oregon*," Sloane called, "are you still there?"

Juan keyed the mike. "We're still here." He sized up the situation with a quick glance at the screen, projecting where each craft would be in another minute and then their locations in two. The tactical picture was grim. But worse than that was the fact he'd be acting blind. For all he knew Sloane Macintyre was the biggest drug dealer in southern Africa and was about to be greased by a rival. She and the others on the *Pinguin* might be getting everything they deserved. On the other hand she could be totally innocent.

"Then why lie?" he whispered to himself.

If he was to preserve the *Oregon*'s secrets, the margin for action would be razor tight—in fact too tight. He thought through a dozen scenarios in the time it took to scratch his chin again and made his decision.

"Helm, bring us hard to starboard; we need to cut the distance between us and the *Pinguin*. Increase speed to twenty knots. Engineering, make sure the smudge boiler is online." When alone at sea the *Oregon* produced no pollution, but when they encountered traffic a special smoke generator was switched on to create the illusion the remarkable ship was powered by conventional diesel engines.

"I fired it up a couple minutes ago," the second engineer reported from the back of the op center. "Should have done it as soon as they reached visual range but I forgot."

"No big deal. I doubt anyone noticed," Juan said before activating his mike. "Sloane, this is the master of the *Oregon*."

"Go ahead, *Oregon*."

Juan marveled at how coolly she was handling herself and thought briefly of Tory Ballinger, an Englishwoman he'd rescued a few months back in the Sea of Japan. They had the same kind of mettle. "We have turned to intercept you. Tell the *Pinguin*'s captain to take us down the port side, but don't let on that's the way you're going to go. I want to trick the yacht to pass us to starboard. Do you understand?"

"We are to pass you down your port side but only at the last minute."

"That's right. Don't cut it too close, though. The yacht won't be able to make tight turns at the speed she's doing, so avoid our bow wave as best you can. I'm going to lower our boarding stairs but don't approach them until I give you the word. Got it?"

"We won't approach until you signal," Sloane repeated.

"You're going to be fine, Sloane," Juan said, the confidence in his voice carrying over the crackling radio link. "These aren't the first pirates me and my crew have come across."

On screen he saw the gunmen try to rake the *Pinguin* again with their assault rifles but the range was still extreme from such an unstable firing platform. It didn't look like any of the rounds came close to the charter boat, yet it firmed Juan's resolve that they were doing the right thing in helping Sloane and her party.

"Hali, get some hands on deck to lower the boarding stairs and extend the ladder. Wepps, be prepared to fire the bow thirty caliber."

"I have it locked on."

The *Pinguin* was coming on gamely, now less than three hundred yards from the hulking freighter, with the yacht a scant hundred yards further back. Juan didn't want to use the machine gun but he saw there wasn't going to be any choice. The charter boat would be in range of the yacht before he could slip the *Oregon* between them. He was about to order the weapons officer to fire a short burst to slow the yacht when he noticed Sloane slithering out to the *Pinguin*'s stern. She raised her head and shoulders over the transom and let loose with the shotgun, firing the second barrel as soon as she regained her sight picture.

She had no chance of hitting the yacht but the unexpected volley forced the luxury craft to slow and make a more cautious approach. It bought her the seconds they needed to implement Cabrillo's plan.

"What's going on?" Max Hanley appeared at Cabrillo's side smelling of pipe tobacco. "I'm trying to enjoy my day off while you're up here playing chicken with what, an old fishing boat and a floating bordello?"

Juan had stopped wondering years ago how Hanley's sixth sense brought him out of his cabin when trouble was brewing. "The guys on the yacht want the people on the fishing boat dead and it doesn't look like they care if there are any witnesses."

"And you want to spoil their fun, I see."

Juan shot him a lopsided grin. "Have you ever known me to not stick my nose in other people's business?"

"Offhand? No." Max was looking at the view screen and cursed.

The yacht had put on a burst of speed and autofire raked the *Pinguin*, tearing chunks of wood from her thick stern and shattering the glass panel on the door to her belowdecks cabin. Sloane was protected by the transom, but the captain and another man on the bridge were horribly exposed.

Trading speed for protection, the Namibian skipper began to weave his boat as they careened toward the oncoming freighter, slewing it from side to side as he tried to throw off the gunmen's aim. Sloane added her own contribution by firing both barrels again. The shots were so off target that she never saw the little geysers where they hit the sea.

A fresh burst from the yacht forced her down. From her vantage on the rough plank flooring of the aft deck she couldn't see the freighter, but the boat behaved differently as it encountered waves that had been disrupted by her massive hull. Her shoulder aching from firing the gun, she knew it was now up to the *Pinguin*'s captain and the mysterious master of the *Oregon*. She lay against the transom, panting with fear tinged with exhilaration—the same sense of defiance that had put her in the predicament in the first place.

Back aboard the *Oregon* Juan and Max watched the two small craft coming closer. The *Pinguin*'s skipper was keeping her on track to race down the starboard side with the yacht actually running a bit further to the right and fast approaching the range where the gunners would have their quarry dead to rights.

"Wait for it," Max said to no one in particular. Had he been in charge of this situation he would have told Sloane to stand by the radio and given the order to turn himself. Then he realized Juan had been right to let the skipper make the call. He knew his boat's capabilities and would know when to make the cut.

The *Pinguin* was thirty yards from the *Oregon*, so close that the mast camera could no longer track her. The weapons officer switched to the gun camera on the bow thirty caliber.

The little boat was raked with yet another burst of fire from the yacht and had they been further away Juan would have abandoned his plan and blown the luxury craft out of the water with either the thirty caliber or the Gatling gun that was still tracking the target even hidden behind her steel plating.

"Now," he whispered.

Though Cabrillo hadn't activated his microphone it was as if the *Pinguin*'s captain heard him. He cut the wheel hard to the left just fifteen yards from the knife-edge prow of the *Oregon*, riding up on the swell that curled away from her hull like a surfer catching a wave.

The helmsman on the yacht jerked the wheel as if to follow, then corrected his course when he realized they were going too fast to stay on the *Pinguin*'s tail. He'd pass the freighter down her starboard side and using his superior speed reach the stern abreast of his target.

"Helm," Juan said calmly, "on my mark I want bow thrusters to starboard at full power and give me right full rudder. Increase speed to forty knots." Juan clicked through camera angles until he caught a glimpse of the *Pinguin*. He had to make sure she didn't get crushed as he made his turn. He expertly judged speeds and angles, knowing he was risking lives to preserve his ship's secrets. The yacht was almost in position, the *Pinguin* almost out of danger, but time had run out.

"Mark."

With just the click of a few keys and a subtle twist of a joystick, the eleven-thousand-ton ship did something no other vessel its size was capable of. The athwartship thrusters came to life, forcing the *Oregon*'s bow laterally through the water, fighting the inertia of her own speed and the increased thrust of her magnetohydrodynamic engines as they ramped up even faster.

One second the yacht and the freighter were running parallel if opposite courses, and the next the *Oregon* had turned forty-five degrees and rather than racing down her long flank, the yacht was headed directly for her bow at a combined closing speed of sixty knots. Like a whale protecting its young, Juan had put his ship between the yacht and the charter boat. He glanced at the screen showing the *Pinguin*. The *Oregon* had turned just past her, cutting through her wake and sending her bobbing on the rollers peeling off his ship.

As if racing to cross train tracks ahead of a locomotive, the yacht's driver tried to beat the surging bow of the *Oregon* by turning to port and outrunning what he believed to be a relatively slow ship. Had he seen the boil of water erupting under her fantail he would have cut his own engines and prayed he survived the impact with her hull.

The vectors in place were a matter of simple mathematics. The *Oregon* continued her turn, cutting across the bow of the yacht even as it desperately tried to turn a tighter circle than the freighter.

At the last moment one of the gunmen on the yacht lunged forward to yank back the throttles but the gesture was too little too late.

The gleaming prow of the yacht slammed into the *Oregon*'s scaly hull a hundred feet from her bow. Fiberglass and aluminum were no match for the old ship's tough hide and the luxury boat accordioned like a beer can hit with a sledgehammer. Her twin turbo diesels were ripped from their mounts and tore through her hull, shattering the structural ribs that held the boat together. In a burst of glass and plastic shards the vessel's upperworks came apart as if she'd exploded. The four men who were confident moments earlier that they would complete their mission died instantly, crushed into oblivion by the tremendous force of the crash.

One of her fuel tanks exploded in a rising ball of dirty orange flame that licked the *Oregon*'s rail as she continued to turn, as unaffected by the impact as if she were a shark being charged by a goldfish. A spreading pool of burning diesel coated the ocean, giving off clouds of greasy smoke that obscured the remains of the yacht in her final moments before she slipped below the waves.

"All stop," Cabrillo ordered and felt the instant deceleration as the pump jets were disengaged.

"Like swatting flies," Max said and patted Juan's shoulder.

"Let's just hope all that wasn't to protect a hornet." He hit his microphone switch. "*Oregon* calling *Pinguin*, do you copy?"

"*Oregon*, this is the *Pinguin*." They could almost hear Sloane's relieved smile over the comm. link. "I don't know how you did that, but you've got three very grateful people here."

"It would be my pleasure to have you and your shipmates aboard for a late lunch to talk about what just happened."

"Ah, wait one minute, please, *Oregon*."

Juan needed to know what had just occurred and wasn't going to give her the time to come up with a cover story. "If you don't accept my invitation I will have no choice but to file a formal report with the maritime authorities at Walvis Bay."

He had no such intention but Sloane didn't know that.

"Um, in that case we would love to accept your offer."

"Very well. My boarding ladder is extended on the port side. A crewman will escort you to the bridge." Juan looked at Max. "Well, let's go see what another fine mess I've gotten us in, Ollie."

10

FIGHTING to stay in the warm embrace of unconsciousness, Geoffrey Merrick moaned aloud as the numbing effects of the Tazer shock wore off. His extremities tingled down to his fingers and toes and the spot on his chest where the electrodes had struck burned as if he'd been splashed with acid.

"He is coming around," a disembodied voice said as if from a great distance away, but Merrick somehow knew the person was close by and it was his own addled brain that had drifted so far.

He became aware that his body was in an uncomfortable position and tried to move. His efforts proved useless. He was manacled at the wrists, and while he could barely feel the metal digging into his flesh, he couldn't move his arms more than a couple of inches. He still didn't have enough control over his legs to determine if his ankles were similarly bound.

He tentatively opened his eyes and immediately shut them. Wherever he was had to be the brightest room he'd ever been in. It was almost as if he were standing on the surface of the sun.

Merrick waited a beat and opened them again, squinting against the harsh light that scoured the room. It took a few seconds for details to come into focus. The room was roughly fifteen feet square with walls made of dressed stone exactly like the walls of his cell, so he knew he hadn't been taken from the prison. There was a large picture window along one wall. It was securely barred and the glass looked like it had been recently installed. The view outside was the most desolate he'd seen, an endless trackless sea of fine white sand baking in the glare of a remorseless sun.

He turned his attention to the people in the room with him.

There were eight men and women seated at a wooden table; unlike the guards, they weren't wearing masks. Merrick didn't recognize any of them, though he believed the big one to be one of the guards and the handsome youth with blue eyes to be another. They were all Caucasians and mostly younger than thirty-five. He had lived in Switzerland long enough to recognize the European cut of their clothes. On the table was a laptop computer turned toward the eldest of the group, a woman in her late forties judging by the silver threads shot through her hair. A web camera jacked into the computer was focused on Merrick at the foot of the table.

"Geoffrey Michael Merrick," an electronically filtered voice intoned from the computer's speakers. "You have been tried in absentia by this court and have been found guilty of crimes against the planet." Several heads nodded grimly. "The product your company patented, your so-called sulfur scrubbers, has pacified governments and individuals into believing the continued burning of fossil fuels is a sustainable option—especially the burning of so-called clean coal. No such thing exists, and while this court admits that power plants so fitted with your devices have made a slight reduction in sulfur emissions, that in no way mitigates the billions of tons of other noxious chemicals and gases poured into the atmosphere.

"Your tactical victory in producing these devices is in reality a strategic defeat for those of us who truly strive to save our world for future generations. The environmental movement cannot allow itself to be swayed by the parlor tricks of individuals like yourself or energy companies who profess to be green while continuing to peddle their poisons. Global warming is the single greatest threat this planet has ever faced and every time people like you develop a slightly cleaner technology the public believes the threat is being diminished when in fact it grows worse every year.

"It is the same with hybrid cars. True, they burn less gasoline, but the pollution expended in their development and production far outpaces what the consumer saves by driving such a vehicle. They are merely a ploy to give a handful of conscientious people a sense that they are doing their share to help the environment, when in fact they are doing the opposite. They believe the misguided notion that technology can somehow save the planet when it was technology that doomed it in the first place."

Merrick heard the words but couldn't get his mind around what they meant. He opened his mouth to speak but his vocal cords were still paralyzed so he gave a sort of croak. He cleared his throat and tried again. "Who—who are you people?"

"People who see through your charade."

"Charade?" He paused, trying to gather his wits, knowing the next few minutes would determine if he walked out of here on his own or was dragged like poor Susan. "My technology has proven itself time and again. Thanks to me there is less sulfur being produced now than since the beginning of the Industrial Revolution."

"And thanks to you"—even through the electronic filter the voice from the computer managed to impart sarcasm—"levels of carbon dioxide, carbon monoxide, particulate ash, mercury, and other heavy metals have never been higher. Nor has the sea level. The power companies hold your scrubbers as proof of their environmental concern when sulfur is only one small component of the filth they produce. The world must be shown that the environmental threat comes from all sides."

"And to show them you kidnap me and beat an innocent woman half to death?" Merrick said without thinking through his predicament. He had debated this issue hundreds of times. Yes, his work had reduced sulfur levels but as a result more power plants were being built and more pollution was pumped into the atmosphere. It was a classic catch-22. But he was familiar with the arguments and felt a surge of confidence that he could talk his way out of this.

"She works for you. She is not innocent."

"How can you possibly say that? You didn't even ask her name or what she does."

"The specifics of her job are unimportant. That she is willing to work for you is proof enough of her complicity and culpability."

Merrick took a breath. He had to find a way to convince them he wasn't their enemy if he was going to get out of this alive. "Listen, you can't hold me responsible for the world's continued demand for more energy. You want to clean up the environment, convince people to have fewer children. China will soon pass the United States as the world's biggest polluter because they have a population of one point two billion. India, with its billion citizens, isn't too far behind. That is the real threat to the planet. And no matter how clean Europe and America become—God, we could go back to horse-drawn carriages and plowshares—we would never be able to counteract the pollution produced in Asia. This is a global problem, I totally agree, and a global solution is what is needed."

The men and women at the far end of the table sat unmoved by his speech and the computer's silence stretched ominously. Merrick fought to remain strong, to not give in to the fear sliding like oil through his gut. In the end he couldn't do it—his voice turned strident and fresh tears came to his eyes.

"Please, you don't need to do this to me," he pleaded. "Is it money you want? I can give you all the money your organization will ever need. Please, just let us go."

"It is too late for that," the computer said. Then the electronic filter was switched off and the person on the other end of the link spoke in his own voice. "You have been tried, Geoff, and found guilty."

Merrick knew that voice all too well, though he hadn't heard it in years. And he also knew it meant he was going to die.

11

CABRILLO didn't have time for his shower and only barely managed to change out of his workout clothes and get to the *Oregon*'s bridge before Sloane and her group were escorted in by Frank Lincoln. He glanced around quickly as he heard them mounting the outside stairs. The bridge was in its normal state of disrepair and neglect; no one had left any of their high-tech toys lying around to belie the true nature of the vessel. Eddie Seng was again playing helmsman, wearing a battered one-piece utility suit and a baseball cap as he stood casually behind the old-fashioned wheel. Seng was perhaps the most meticulous planner on the Corporation payroll, someone for which no detail was too minute. Had his temperament not been one that thrived on danger he would have made a great accountant. Juan noted Eddie had set the fake telegraph handles to All Stop and had even changed over the unused carts to show the coast of southwestern Africa.

Juan tapped the faded and stained map. "Nice touch."

"Thought you'd like that."

Juan had given no thought to what Sloane Macintyre would look like until the moment she walked through the door. Her hair was coppery red and in a tangled bush from so much wind and sun, giving her a wild and untamed look. Her mouth was a bit too wide and her nose too long, but she had such an open look to her face that these minor flaws were nearly indistinguishable. With her sunglasses dangling at her throat he could see she didn't have the green eyes of a romance novel redhead but wide-set gray ones that seemed to take in her surroundings with a quick glance. She carried a little extra weight that made her body more curvy than angular, but the flesh under her arms remained taut, which made Juan think she was a swimmer.

With her were two men, a Namibian who Cabrillo assumed owned the *Pinguin*, and another Caucasian with a prominent Adam's apple and a sour look on his face. Juan couldn't imagine many scenarios that would place an attractive woman like Sloane in his company. And by their body language he could tell that while Sloane might be in charge, her partner was extremely angry with her.

Cabrillo stepped forward, extending a hand. "Juan Cabrillo, captain of the *Oregon*. Welcome aboard."

"Sloane Macintyre." Her grip was sure and firm and her gaze was level. Juan saw no trace of the fear she must have felt when they were being fired on. "This is Tony Reardon and Justus Ulenga, master of the *Pinguin*."

"How do you do?" Reardon surprised Juan with a crisp British accent.

"By the looks of you no one appears to need medical attention. Am I right?"

"No," Sloane said. "We're all fine, but thank you for asking."

"Good, I'm relieved," Juan said, and meant it. "I'd take you to my cabin to talk about what just happened out here but it's a bit of a mess. Let's go down to the galley. I think I can get the cook to whip up a little something." Juan asked Linc to find the steward.

The truth was, the master's cabin he used to greet inspectors and harbor officials who came aboard was a disaster zone, and had been designed to make visitors want to get off the ship as quickly as possible. The walls and carpet had been chemically infused with a stench of cheap cigarettes that was guaranteed to leave even a chain-smoker gasping; and the sorrowful gaze of the velvet clown paintings made most people extremely uncomfortable, as they were supposed to. It simply wasn't the proper setting for an interview. Although the topside galley and adjoining mess hall couldn't be held to a much higher standard, at least they were reasonably clean.

Juan led them down a flight of internal stairs with treads of chipped linoleum and cautioned them about a handrail that was kept purposefully loosened. He ushered them into the mess, flicking one of two light switches to snap on the banks of fluorescents. The other switch only turned on a couple of the lights and two of them would constantly flicker and emit an annoying buzzing sound. Most Customs inspectors going over manifests preferred sitting on the bridge floor rather than working in the dining room. There were four mismatched tables in the spacious mess hall, and of the sixteen chairs only two looked even remotely similar. The walls were painted in a color Juan called Soviet Green, a dull mint hue that never failed to depress.

Two decks below this room was the *Oregon*'s real mess, as elegant a dining area as any five-star restaurant.

He indicated where he'd like them to sit, placing them so they faced a pinhole camera hidden in a picture on one wall. Linda Ross and Max Hanley were in the op center to monitor the interview. If they had any questions they wanted Juan to pose they would be passed to him by Maurice, the steward.

Cabrillo folded his hands on the tabletop, glanced at his guests but let his eyes settle on Sloane Macintyre. She returned his gaze without blinking and he believed he saw a hint of a smile at the corner of her lips. Juan expected fear or anger after what they'd been through, but she almost appeared amused by the whole thing; unlike Reardon, who was clearly rattled, or the *Pinguin*'s captain, who was pensive, most likely hoping Juan wouldn't call the authorities.

"So, why don't you tell me who those people were and why they wanted you all dead?" Sloane leaned forward brightly and was about to speak, but Juan added, "And don't forget I heard what they said on the radio about warning you off last night."

She sat back again, clearly rethinking her response.

"Just tell him, for God's sake," Tony sputtered when Sloane didn't immediately respond. "It doesn't matter now anyway."

She shot him a scathing look, recognizing that if she didn't talk openly Tony was going to tell Cabrillo everything. She let out a breath. "We are looking for a ship that sank in these waters in the late 1800s."

"And let me guess, you think there's treasure aboard?" Juan asked indulgently.

Sloane refused to let his sarcasm pass. "I am so certain I was willing to bet our lives on it. And someone else seems to think its worth killing for."

"Touché." Juan looked from Sloane to Reardon. They didn't look like treasure hunters, but it was a fever that could infect anyone. "How did you two hook up?"

"In an Internet chat room devoted to lost treasures," Sloane said. "We've been planning and saving for this since last year."

"And tell me what happened last night."

"I had gone out to dinner by myself and when I was walking back to the hotel, two men started following me. I ran and they chased me. At one point one of them fired a handgun at me. I made it back to the hotel, which was crowded, and they stopped. One of them shouted that the shot was a warning and I was to leave Namibia."

"You recognized them as two of the guys on that yacht."

"Yeah, the two with the machine guns."

"And who knew you were in Namibia?"

"What do you mean, like friends back home and stuff?"

"No, I mean who knew what you were doing here? Did you talk to anyone about your project?"

"We interviewed a great number of local fisherman," Tony said.

Sloane overrode him. "The idea was to search areas where fishermen lost nets. The seafloor around here is basically an extension of the desert, so I figured anything that could snag a net must be man-made, ergo a shipwreck."

"Not necessarily," Juan said.

"We know that now." Sloane's voice was laced with defeat. "We flew over a bunch of possibilities with a metal detector and found nothing."

"Doesn't surprise me. The currents have had a few million years to expose bedrock projections that could easily catch a net," Juan said and Sloane nodded. "So you talked to fishermen. Anyone else?"

Her mouth turned downward as she said, "Luka. He acted as a guide but I never much cared for him. And there was the South African chopper pilot. Pieter DeWitt's his name. But no one knew why we were asking about nets and we never told Piet or Luka what ship we were looking for."

"Don't forget Papa Heinrick and his giant metal snakes," Tony said tartly. He was trying to further embarrass Sloane.

One of Juan's eyebrows lifted. "Giant snakes?"

"It's nothing," Sloane said. "Just a story we heard from a crazy old fisherman."

There came a gentle knock on the door. Maurice appeared bearing a plastic tray. Juan had to suppress a smile at the repulsed look on the chief steward's face.

In a word, Maurice was fastidious, a man who shaved twice a day, polished his shoes each morning, and would change a shirt if he found a crease. He was right at home in the opulent confines of the *Oregon*, but get him on the public parts of the vessel and he had the look of a Muslim walking into a pigsty.

In deference to the ruse they were playing on their guests he'd removed his suit jacket and tie and had actually rolled up the cuffs of his dress shirt. Although Juan had a complete dossier on every member of the Corporation, the one piece of information even he didn't know was Maurice's age. Speculation ran anywhere from sixty-five to eighty. Yet he held the tray aloft on an arm as steady as one of the *Oregon*'s derricks and set dishes and glasses down without spilling a drop.

"Green tea," he announced, his English accent catching Tony's attention. "Dim sum, pot stickers, and lo mein noodles with chicken." He plucked a folded piece of paper from his apron and handed it to Juan. "Mr. Hanley asked me to give you this."

Juan unfolded the note while Maurice set out plates, napkins, and silverware, none of which matched but as least the linens were clean.

Max had written: *She's lying through her teeth.*

Juan looked toward the hidden camera. "That's obvious."

"What's obvious?" Sloane asked after taking an approving sip of tea.

"Hmm? My first officer is reminding me that the longer we're here the later we're going to be at our next port of call."

"And where's that, if you don't mind me asking?"

"Thank you, Maurice, that will be all." The steward bowed out and Cabrillo answered Sloane's question. "Cape Town. We're carrying lumber from Brazil en route to Japan, but we're picking up a couple of containers in Cape Town headed for Mumbai."

"This really is a tramp steamer, isn't it?" Sloane asked. It was evident in her voice she was impressed. "I didn't think any still existed."

"Not many. Containerization has all but taken over, but there are a few of us picking up crumbs." He gestured around the dingy dining room. "Unfortunately, the crumbs are getting smaller so we don't have the money to put back into the *Oregon*. I'm afraid the old girl's disintegrating around us."

"Still," Sloane persisted, "it must be a romantic life."

The sincerity of how she said it took Juan aback. He had always felt the vagabond existence of a tramp ship roaming from port to port, living almost hand-to-mouth rather than being a cog in the industrial machine that maritime commerce had become was indeed a romantic notion, a way of unhurried life that was virtually gone forever. He smiled and saluted her with his tea. "Yeah, sometimes it is."

The warmth of her return smile told him they had shared something intimate.

He roused himself to get on with the interview. "Captain Ulenga, do you know anything about metal snakes?"

"No, Cap'ain," the Namibian said and touched his temple. "Papa Heinrick isn't right in the head. And when he gets a bottle, well, you don't want to know him."

Juan turned his attention back to Sloane. "What was the name of the ship you were looking for?"

It was obvious she was reluctant to give it so he let it pass. "Doesn't matter. I have no interest in looking for sunken treasure." He chuckled. "Or giant metal snakes. Is that where you were headed today, the place where this Heinrick fellow saw his snakes?"

Even Sloane realized how ridiculous she had to look in Cabrillo's eyes because she flushed a little. "It was our last lead. I figured we'd come this far, we might as well see it through. Sounds kinda dumb now."

"Kinda?" Juan mocked.

Linc knocked on the mess hall's door frame. "She's clean, Captain."

"Thank you, Mr. Lincoln." He'd asked Linc to search the *Pinguin* for contraband, like drugs or weapons, just to be safe. "Captain Ulenga, can you tell me anything about the yacht that attacked you?"

"I've seen it at Walvis a couple of times. She comes maybe every month for a year or two. I think she's from South Africa 'cause only the folks down there can afford such a boat."

"Never talked to her crew or anyone who knew them?"

"No, sir. They come in, fuel up, and go again."

Juan leaned back in his chair, cocking an elbow over the seat back. He tried to link the facts together and come up with a coherent explanation but nothing really fit. Certain that Sloane had left out crucial elements from her story, he knew he'd never piece the puzzle together and had to decide how much he wanted to pursue this. Rescuing Geoffrey Merrick remained their top priority, and on that front they had enough problems without adding Sloane Macintyre's. Still, something nagged him.

Tony Reardon suddenly spoke up. "We've told you everything we can, Captain Cabrillo. I would really like to get off your ship. We have a long trip back to port."

"Yes," Juan muttered distractedly and refocused his attention. "Yes, of course, Mr. Reardon. I don't understand why you were attacked. It's possible that there is a lost ship out here loaded with treasure and you got too close to someone's operation. If they are working without government permission they very well might have resorted to violence." He gave Tony and Sloane a frank stare. "If that's the case, I advise you both to leave Namibia as quickly as you can. You're both in over your heads."

Reardon nodded at that advice but Sloane looked like she was going to ignore it. Juan let it go. It wasn't his concern.

"Mr. Lincoln," he said, "would you please escort our guests back to their boat. If they need fuel please see that it is taken care of."

"Yes, Captain."

The group stood as if on cue. Juan leaned across the table to shake hands with Justus Ulenga and Tony Reardon. When he grasped Sloane's she pulled him forward slightly and said, "May I speak to you in private?"

"Of course." Cabrillo looked at Linc. "Take them to the *Pinguin*. I'll escort Ms. Macintyre myself."

They took their seats as soon as the group left. Sloane studied him the way a jeweler inspects a diamond that he is about to cut, looking for the tiniest flaw that could ruin the gem. She came to some sort of decision, leaned forward, and rested her elbows on the table.

"I think you're a fraud."

Juan had to suppress a guffaw. "Excuse me," he finally stammered.

"You. This ship. Your crew. None of it is what it appears to be."

Cabrillo fought to keep his expression neutral and the blood from draining from his face. In the years since he'd founded the Corporation and started traipsing around the globe on a succession of ships all named *Oregon*, no one had ever thought they were anything but what they appeared to be. They'd had harbor officials, inspectors of every kind, even a canal pilot on their transits of Panama, and no one had shown the slightest suspicion about the ship or its crew.

She doesn't know, he thought. *She's fishing.* He had to admit to himself that they hadn't pulled out all the tricks they utilized when they were in port and about to be inspected, but there was no way an untrained person who'd been aboard for all of thirty minutes could see through their carefully laid deception. His heart slowed as he came to this realization.

"Care to explain?" he invited casually.

"The little things, for one. Your helmsman was wearing a Rolex exactly like the one my father had. That's a two-thousand-dollar watch. A bit too nice if you guys are as poor as you say."

"It's a fake," Juan replied.

"A knock-off wouldn't last five minutes in the salt air. I know because I had one when I was a teenager and working on my father's fishing boat after he retired from the merchant marines."

Okay, Juan said to himself, *she's not completely untrained when it comes to ships.* "Maybe it is real but he got it from a fence who stole it. You'd have to ask him."

"That's a possibility," Sloane said. "But what about your steward? I've been working in London for the past five years and recognize English tailoring when I see it. Between his Church's dress shoes, custom suit pants, and handmade shirt, Maurice was sporting about four thousand dollars' worth of duds. I doubt he bought them off a fence."

Juan chuckled, imagining Maurice wearing anything secondhand. "He's actually richer than Croesus but is—how would the English put it—dotty. He's the black sheep of an old-money family who has been knocking around the globe since he turned eighteen and got his inheritance. He approached me last year when we were in Mombassa, asked to be our steward, and said we wouldn't have to pay him. Who was I to turn him down?"

"Right," Sloane said drawing out the word.

"It's true, honest."

"I'll leave that for now. But what about you and Mr. Lincoln? There aren't a whole lot of Americans working aboard ships because Asians are willing to do the jobs at a fraction of the wage. If the company who owns this vessel is as tight as you claim, the crew would be Pakistanis or Indonesians." Juan made to reply but she cut him off. "Let me guess, you work for a pittance, too?"

"My mattress isn't exactly stuffed with cash, Ms. Macintyre."

"I bet." She raked her hand through her hair. "Those are the little things I figured you would explain away. How about this? When I first saw your ship there wasn't any smoke coming from the funnel."

Uh-oh, Juan thought, recalling how the engineer had forgotten to turn on the smoke generator until after the *Pinguin* was in visible range. At the time Juan hadn't thought it a big deal, but that oversight was coming back to haunt them.

"I first thought that the ship had been abandoned but then I saw you were making headway. A few minutes later, smoke starts pouring from the stack, a good amount of it, in fact. Interestingly, the exact same amount when you were charging toward us at twenty knots as when I was on the bridge and noticed the telegraph was set to all stop. And speaking of your charge, there is no way a vessel this size could turn that fast unless you have isopod directional thrusters, which is a technology developed long after this ship was built. Care to explain that away?"

"I'm just curious why you even care," Juan hedged.

"Because someone tried to kill me today and I want to know why and I think you can help."

"I'm sorry, Sloane, but I'm just the captain of a rust bucket not long for the breakers yard. I can't help you."

"So you're not denying what I saw."

"I don't know what you saw but there's nothing special about the *Oregon* or her crew."

She stood up and walked unerringly to where the tiny camera had been mounted in the frame of an old picture of an Indian actress who'd been famous fifteen years ago. She pulled the picture from the wall and the camera popped free to dangle by its wire. "Oh, really?"

This time blood did drain from Juan's face.

"I noticed it when you said 'that's obvious' after getting the note from Maurice. I assume someone is monitoring us right now." She didn't wait for Juan to reply. "I'll make a deal with you, Captain Cabrillo. You stop lying to me and I'll stop lying to you. I'll even go first." She sat back across from him. "Tony and I didn't hook up through an Internet chat room. We work together in the security division of DeBeers and we really are looking for a sunken ship that might be loaded with about a billion dollars' worth of diamonds. Do you know anything about diamonds?"

"Only that they're rare, expensive, and if you give one to a woman you damned well better mean it."

That made her smile. "Two out of three."

"Two out of three, huh? I know they're expensive and I know they're rare so you must have men casually giving you diamonds all the time. You're certainly attractive enough."

Her smile turned into a little laugh. "Ah, no. They are expensive and you should mean it, but diamonds aren't rare. They're not as common as semiprecious stones but they're not as scarce as you're led to believe. The price is kept artificially inflated because one company controls about ninety-five percent of the market. They control all the mines so they can set any price they wish. Every time a new diamond field is discovered they are there to buy it up and eliminate any chance of competition. It's a cartel so tight it makes OPEC look like amateurs. It's so controlling that several executives would be arrested for antitrust violations if they ever set foot in the United States.

"They dribble out stones from their vaults at a very selective pace in order to keep prices at a constant. If inventories dwindle they increase production and when there is an excess of stones they hoard them in their London vaults. Bearing all this in mind, what do you think would happen if a billion dollars in diamonds were ever to be dumped in the marketplace?"

"Prices would drop."

"And we lose our monopoly and the whole system comes crashing down. All those women out there would realize the rocks on their fingers aren't forever after all. It would also ripple through the world's economy, destabilizing gold prices and currencies."

That was something Juan knew a little about since it was only a couple months ago that he and the crew thwarted an attempt to flood the world's gold market. "I see your point," he said.

"If such a treasure-laden ship existed, there are two ways our office would prevent this from happening. Number one is wait to see if someone else finds the diamonds and simply buy them all outright. Obviously this would be expensive, so we would want to take the second route."

"Check to see if the rumor of a sunken treasure is true and find it for yourselves."

Sloane touched the tip of her nose. "Bingo. I was the person who first pieced together the story behind the treasure so I was given the lead on this trip. Tony's ostensibly my assistant but he's absolutely worthless. This is a big deal for me and my career. If I could find the stones I would probably be named VP."

"Where did the diamonds come from?" Juan asked, interested in what she had to say despite himself.

"Fascinating story there. They were originally mined in Kimberley by members of a tribe called the Herero. The Herero king knew there was a battle coming with the German occupiers of his homeland and thought if he had the diamonds he could use them to buy English protection. For a decade or so his men worked in Kimberley and snuck stones back to Hereroland when their contracts ended. From what I was able to learn, workers would cut themselves in the arm or leg a couple of months before starting their contracts. When they arrived at Kimberley charts of their bodies were made noting all the old scars they had. Once they were in the workers' compound a tribesman who had been there for a while and had already pilfered a suitable stone from the pit would reopen the wound and slip it inside. When it came time to leave a year later, the guards at the workers compound would check the chart made when the Herero first showed up. They would often surgically reopen fresh scars to check for hidden stones, a popular smuggling system after the more obvious down-the-throat technique, which was literally voided with laxatives. But the old scar was on their chart and wouldn't be checked."

"Damned clever," Juan remarked.

"According to what I was able to discover they had sacks and sacks of only the largest and clearest stones when the tribe was robbed."

"Robbed?"

"By five Englishmen, one just a teen whose parents were missionaries in Hereroland. I was able to put the story together from the father's journal because after the robbery he went to track his son. His journal reads like a torturer's checklist of things he wanted to do once he caught the boy.

"I won't bore you with the details, but the teenager, Peter Smythe, hooked up with an adventurer of the old school named H. A. Ryder as well as three other men. As part of their plan they cabled Cape Town to have a steamship, the HMS *Rove*, wait for them off the coast of what was then called German South West Africa. They planned to cross the Kalahari and Namib deserts on horseback and meet up with the ship."

"And I take it the *Rove* was never heard from again?"

"She left Cape Town right after receiving the telegram from Ryder and was later reported lost at sea."

"Say all this is true and not another myth like King Solomon's mines. What makes you think it would be in this area?"

"I drew a straight line west from where the diamonds were stolen to the coast. They were crossing perhaps the worst stretch of desert on the planet and would have taken the most direct route. That puts the rendezvous with the *Rove* about seventy miles north of Walvis Bay."

Juan found another hole in her logic. "Who's to say the *Rove* sank after steaming back to Cape Town for a week, or what if the men never made it and the stones are someplace in the middle of the desert?"

"Those are the same two points my boss threw at me when I brought this to him. And to that I said: If I was able to figure all this out, then someone else could, too, and a billion dollars' worth of diamonds could be sitting a couple miles offshore where anyone with scuba tanks and a flashlight could find them."

"To which he said?"

" 'I'll give you a week and Tony Reardon to help you. And no matter what, destroy all the evidence you've gathered.' "

"That isn't anywhere near enough time to check an area that must be a couple hundred square miles," Juan said. "To do it properly you'd need a ship able to tow a side-scan sonar unit as well as metal detection gear. And even that isn't guaranteed."

Sloane shrugged. "They didn't put much credence in my idea. Giving me a week, a little money, and Tony was more than I could hope and why I wanted to tap local sources for information."

"I'm curious—why did you take this to your superiors? Why not just search for the ship yourself and keep the diamonds if you found them?"

Her mouth turned downward in a deep frown as if he'd just insulted her, which he had. "Captain, the thought never crossed my mind. Those diamonds were mined at a DeBeers facility and rightfully belong to the company. I would no more keep them for myself than I would walk into the vault and load my pockets with loose stones."

"I'm sorry I said that." Juan was charmed by her integrity. "That was way out of line."

Sloane said, "Thank you. Apology accepted. Now that I've told you the truth, will you help? I can't promise you anything but I'm sure the company will reimburse you for your time if we do find the *Rove*. It's only a couple hours of your time to check the coordinates Papa Heinrick gave me."

Juan said nothing for a moment, his blue eyes cast toward the ceiling as he thought through his next moves. He suddenly got to his feet and started for the door. "Would you excuse me a moment," he said to Sloane, then addressed the hidden microphones. "Max, meet me at my cabin." He meant the faux cabin they used for Customs inspectors. It was the midway point between the elevator up from the op center and the mess hall.

Hanley was waiting outside the filthy cabin when Juan rounded the corner. He was leaning against a bulkhead tapping his pipe stem against his teeth, a sure sign something was on his mind. He straightened when the Chairman approached. Even with the door closed Juan's nose wrinkled at the stale smoke smell emanating from the cabin.

"What do you think?" Juan asked without preamble.

"I think we need to stop messing around and get to Cape Town to pick up the equipment we're going to need if we want to rescue Merrick before he dies of old age."

"Besides that."

"The whole thing sounds like a crock to me."

"I'd agree totally if we hadn't seen the attack on the *Pinguin* for ourselves." Juan paused, marshaling his thoughts.

"You think we've stumbled onto something?" Max asked to prod his friend.

"Guys on million-dollar yachts don't go blasting away at someone without a damned good reason. In this case, I believe they're protecting something. Sloane says no one knew what vessel they were looking for so it's possible they're guarding something other than a purported treasure ship."

"You don't seriously believe in Papa Heinrick's giant metal snakes?"

"Max, there's something here. I can feel it." Juan turned to his friend, catching his eye so there would be no misunderstanding. "Do you remember what I told you just before we took on those two guys from NUMA headed for Hong Kong harbor?"

"They were checking out the old SS *United States*. That was the mission you lost your leg," Max said, his voice matching Cabrillo's introspective tone.

Juan unconsciously shifted, placing his weight on the limb made of carbon fiber and titanium. "The mission that cost me my leg," he echoed.

Max stuck his pipe in his mouth. "It's been a couple of years but I believe your exact words were 'Max, I hate to quote an overused cliché, but I've got a bad feeling about this.'"

Juan didn't blink and held Hanley's appraising stare. "Max, I've got the same damn feeling."

Max held the gaze a second longer, and then nodded. A decade together had taught him to trust the chairman no matter how irrational the request and no matter how long the odds. "What's your play?"

"I don't want to delay the *Oregon* any more than we already have. As soon as I'm away make for Cape Town and pick up the equipment we need. But on the way I want you to send up George to have a look where the snakes were spotted." George Adams was the pilot of the Robinson R44 Clipper helicopter secreted inside one of the holds. "I'll get the coordinates from Sloane."

"You're headed for Walvis Bay?"

"I want to talk to Papa Heinrick for myself and also to Sloane's guide and her chopper jockey. I'll take one of the lifeboats off the topside davits so Sloane won't know about the boat garage or anything else." Though they looked as dilapidated as the rest of the *Oregon*, the two lifeboats were as high-tech as their mother ship. If they had the range Juan would feel more than comfortable crossing the Atlantic during hurricane season in one of them.

He continued. "This shouldn't take more than a day or two. I'll link back up with the *Oregon* when you return to Namibia. That reminds me, I've been in the gym for the past hour and haven't been updated. What's the latest?"

Max crossed his arms. "Tiny Gunderson's rented us a suitable plane, so that's taken care of. As you know, the ATVs are waiting for us at Duncan Dock in Cape Town and Murph's got a librarian in Berlin pulling out everything they have about the Devil's Oasis or, as we now know, the *Oase des Teufels*."

Their break at finding the location where Geoffrey Merrick was being held had come when Linda Ross guessed that the Devil's Oasis might be in Namibia, and checked for references using its German name. But after gathering preliminary data their break seemed short-lived.

At the turn of the twentieth century the Imperial German government decided to copy the notorious French penal colony in Guiana called Devil's Island, a remote, escape-proof penitentiary for the nation's most hardened criminals. The German government constructed a maximum-security prison in the middle of the desert in what was their most isolated colonial outpost. Built of native stone and surrounded by hundreds of miles of sand dunes, even if a prisoner were to escape there was no place to go. They would die in the desert long before they reached the coast. Unlike Devil's Island or even San Francisco's infamous Alcatraz, there wasn't even a hint of rumor that any prisoners successfully escaped from the jail until its closure in 1916 because of the drain the remote facility caused to Germany's wartime economy.

A rail line that once serviced the Devil's Oasis had been removed when the prison was abandoned, so there was no reliable access except by air or all-terrain vehicles. Both options posed their own challenges and obstacles because even a small contingent of captives holding Merrick prisoner would detect either a helicopter or a truck long before Cabrillo could get his forces into attack position.

By trolling archived databases and using commercially available satellite images, they were well on their way to finalizing an audacious plan to rescue the billionaire.

"Anything from the kidnappers or Merrick's company?"

"Nothing from the kidnappers and Merrick/Singer is talking with a couple different HRTs." While normally the job of the military or police, there were private companies who handled kidnappings. Though it was not the usual kind of job they undertook, Hanley was presenting the Corporation as a hostage rescue team and while they intended to rescue Merrick/Singer's founder no matter what, it wouldn't hurt if they could get a little something for their efforts.

"How about Overholt at Langley?"

"He likes the idea of us being here so long as it doesn't interfere with any upcoming missions. Also, he confided that Merrick has been a big contributor to the president in the past and that the two of them had skied together a few times. We do this right and our stock in Washington's on the rise."

Cabrillo grinned wryly. "For what we do it doesn't matter where our stock is. When it comes to ops so far off the books they're actually out of the library, Uncle Sam doesn't have many options. And what do you bet if we pull this off there will be a flurry of diplomatic messages between the Administration and the Namibian government and in the end everyone will claim it was an American commando team working with local forces that saved Merrick?"

Max feigned a hurt expression. "I can't believe you'd say that about the slipperiest agent at the CIA."

"And if we fail," Juan added, "he disavows all knowledge blah, blah, blah. Escort Sloane down to the *Pinguin* so she can explain to Reardon that she's remaining aboard, and get someone to unlimber the portside lifeboat. I need to shower and pack."

"I wasn't going to say anything," Max said as he started down the hallway, "but even standing upwind you're pretty gamey."

Juan peeled off the graying uniform shirt he'd worn for Sloane's benefit as soon as he was through the door to his real cabin and had his shoes kicked off by the time he reached his bathroom. He turned the gold taps in the shower stall to a comfortably cool temperature and removed the rest of his clothing. He leaned against the glass enclosure to pull his leg from his prosthetic limb's suction socket.

The powerful multihead sprays of water cascaded over him and while he'd like time to think through his decision to help Sloane Macintyre, he knew enough to trust his instincts. He doubted there was a treasure ship in these waters as much as he doubted the seas were infested with monstrous steel snakes. But, there was no denying the fact that someone wanted Sloane to suspend her investigation. That was what he wanted to discover for himself—who they were and what they were protecting.

After toweling off and refitting his artificial leg, Juan threw some toiletries into a leather dopp kit. From the wardrobe in his bedroom he tossed a couple changes of clothes into a leather bag, and some sturdy boots. Next he went back to his office. He sat at his desk and spun the chair around to face an antique safe that had once sat in a train depot in New Mexico. His fingers on the dial were well practiced and fast. When the final pin clicked in place he spun the handle and heaved open the heavy door. Besides bundles of hundred-dollar bills, twenty-pound notes, and stacks of a dozen other currencies, the safe contained his personal arsenal. There was enough firepower in the big safe to start a small war. Three machine pistols, a couple assault rifles, a combat shotgun, a Remington 700 sniper rifle, plus drawers containing smoke, fragmentary, and flash-bang grenades as well as a dozen pistols. He gauged the possible situations he could be facing and grabbed a Micro Uzi submachine gun and a Glock 19. He would have preferred the FN Five-SeveN pistol, which had quickly become his favorite handgun, but he wanted interchangeability of ammunition. Both the Glock and the Uzi used 9mm.

The four magazines were stored empty to preserve their springs, so he took a moment to load them. He stuffed the weapons, magazines, and a spare box of ammo under the clothes in his bag and finally dressed in lightweight duck trousers and an open-collared shirt.

He caught his reflection in the glass covering a picture on one wall. His jaw was firmly set and behind his eyes he could almost see the embers of anger stoking into a fire. He owed Sloane Macintyre nothing, nor did he owe anything to Geoffrey Merrick, but he would no more abandon them to an unknown fate than he'd strand a little old lady at a busy intersection.

Cabrillo snatched the bag off his bed and started topside, his body already responding to the first tingle of adrenaline.

12

IT was inevitable that sand fleas would learn that the once abandoned prison deep in the desert was occupied again. Drawn by the scent of warm bodies, they had returned to the prison to act as a natural torture to the man-made ones meted out there over the years. Capable of laying sixty eggs a day, the first few that had entered the penitentiary had quickly grown to an infestation. The guards had been prepared with chemical sprays to keep the loathsome insects at bay. Their prisoners weren't so lucky.

Merrick lay with his back propped against the hard stone wall of his cell scratching furiously at the bites that seemed to cover every inch of his body. In a perverse way it was good they had found him because the painful welts and constant new stings kept his mind focused on something other than the horror that had already taken place and the even greater calamity to come.

He cursed as a flea bit deep into the back of his ear. He caught the insect and crushed its body between his fingernails, grunting with satisfaction when he heard the carapace snap. A small victory in a war he was losing.

Without the moon, the darkness in the cell block was a tangible presence, a spectral ether that seemed to rush down Merrick's throat whenever he opened his mouth and filled his ears so he couldn't hear the whisper of wind he knew had to be blowing. The prison was slowly robbing him of his senses. The pervasive sand had choked his nose so he could no longer smell the food he'd been given, and without smell his sense of taste was but a dull suspicion that the meals were something other than dust. He was left only with his hearing and sense of touch. And with nothing to listen to and his body aching from so many days spent on a stone floor and now sting-ing with flea bites, they did him little good.

"Susan?" he called. He'd said her name every few minutes since being returned to his cell. She hadn't once responded and he suspected she might have been dead but he continued anyway for no other reason than calling her name was more rational than giving in to the overwhelming urge to scream.

To his amazement he thought he heard her stir, a mewling sound like a newborn kitten and the rasp of cloth against stone.

"Susan!" he said more sharply. "Susan, can you hear me?"

He distinctly heard her moan.

"Susan, it's Geoff Merrick." *Who else would it be?* he thought. "Can you speak?"

"Dr. Merrick?"

Her voice was ragged and weak and yet it was the most glorious sound he had ever heard. "Oh, thank God, Susan. I thought you were dead."

"I—um." She faltered and coughed and that made her moan all the more loudly. "What happened? My face, it's numb, and my body, I think my ribs are broken."

"You don't remember? You were beaten up, tortured. You said they never asked you any questions."

"Did they hit you, too?"

Merrick's heart squeezed. Through her pain and confusion, Susan Donleavy could still care about his condition. Most people never would have asked and just gone on about their own injuries. He wished, God how he wished, that she hadn't been dragged into this nightmare. "No, Susan," he said gently. "They didn't."

"I'm glad about that," she replied.

"I learned who kidnapped us, and why."

"Who?" There was hope in her voice when she asked, as if putting a name and face to their captors would make their situation better.

"My former business partner."

"Dr. Singer?"

"Yes, Dan Singer."

"Why? Why would he do this to you?"

"To us, you mean. Because he's sick, Susan, a twisted, bitter man who wants to show the world his warped vision of the future."

"I don't understand."

Neither did Merrick. He couldn't get his mind around what Singer had already accomplished and what he was about to carry out. It was all just too much. Singer had already killed thousands of people and no one knew it. Now he was preparing to kill tens of thousands more. And for what? To teach the United States a lesson about environmental control and global warming. That was part of it, but Merrick knew his former best friend all too well.

This was personal to Dan, a way for him to prove to Merrick that he had been the brains behind their success. They had been like brothers in the beginning, but Merrick was the charmer, the one who could turn a good phrase in an interview, so it was inevitable that the media singled him out as the face of Merrick/Singer and marginalized Dan to the shadows. Merrick had never thought this had bothered his partner. He'd been an introvert at MIT so why would it be any different in the real world? He now knew that it had, that Singer had fostered a hatred toward him that bordered on the pathological.

It had changed everything about Singer's personality, driving him from the company he'd helped build and sending him to the fringes of the environmental movement, where he used his wealth to do everything he could to ruin Merrick/Singer. But when that failed he turned his back on his new-found eco-friends and returned to his home in Maine to lick his wounds.

If only that were true, Merrick thought. But Singer had used his time to let his hatred grow and fester. And now he was back, with an incredibly audacious and horrifying plan. A plan that had already been taken so far that there wasn't any way it could be stopped. He hadn't abandoned his environmental crusade, but had taken it in a new and twisted direction.

"We have to get out of here, Susan."

"What's going on?"

"We have to stop him. He's out of his mind, and the people he's gathered together are environmental fanatics who don't give a damn about humanity. And if that's not enough he claims to have hired a bunch of mercenaries, too." Merrick buried his face in his hands.

It was his fault. He should have seen Dan's anger in the beginning and insisted that he get a share of the limelight. He should have recognized the fragility of Dan's ego and how the attention paid to Merrick tore it to pieces. If he had, then none of this would be taking place. The sting of tears turned into sobs, and all thoughts of his own discomfort vanished as he was overcome by what was happening. He just kept repeating, "I'm sorry, I'm sorry" without really understanding who he was apologizing to, Dan or his intended victims.

"Dr. Merrick? Dr. Merrick, please, why is Dr. Singer doing this to us?"

Merrick heard the agony in her voice but couldn't reply. He was crying so hard it sounded as though his soul was being shredded. The wracking convulsions went on for twenty minutes until he'd cried his tear ducts dry.

"I'm sorry, Susan," he gasped when he'd finally gained enough control to speak. "It's just—" He didn't have the words. "Dan Singer blames me because I was the public face of our company. He's doing this because he's jealous. Can you believe that? Thousands of people are already dead and he's doing it all because I was more popular than him."

Susan Donleavy didn't respond.

"Susan?" he called and then louder, "Susan! Susan!"

Her name boomed and echoed, then faded. Silence once again filled the cell block. Merrick was certain that Daniel Singer had just claimed another victim.

13

"YOU can rest down below if you want," Juan offered when Sloane yawned.

"No thanks, I'm fine," she said and yawned again. "But I will take some more coffee."

Cabrillo pulled the silver thermos from the holder at his knee and handed it across, his eyes automatically scanning the lifeboat's rudimentary gauges. The engine was running fine and they had more than three quarters of a tank of fuel and only another hour to go to reach Walvis Bay.

When Max had called an hour after they departed the *Oregon* to tell him that George Adams's helicopter reconnoiter of the area where the crazy old fisherman had seen his metal snakes had turned up nothing but glass-smooth empty ocean, Juan briefly considered simply returning Sloane to her hotel and catching a flight to Cape Town to rejoin his ship. It would have been the logical thing to do. But now, hours later and having a better sense of what made Sloane Macintyre tick, he was sure helping her was the right decision.

She was as driven as he was, someone who couldn't leave a job half-finished and someone who didn't back down from a challenge. There was something mysterious taking place in these waters and neither would be satisfied until they learned what it was, even if it had nothing to do with their respective jobs. He admired her curiosity and tenacity; two traits he also prized in himself.

Sloane poured some of the black coffee into the thermos lid, her body swaying to the rhythms of the waves passing under the hull so she didn't spill a drop. Still wearing her shorts, Sloane had accepted Juan's offer of a Windbreaker, one of the two safety orange nylon pullovers that he'd retrieved from a storage bin. He had his tied around his waist.

The vessel was stocked with enough provisions to last forty people for a week and a miniature desalinator to provide potable, albeit still a little salty, water. The bench seats inside the enclosed cabin looked like cracked vinyl, but were in fact soft kid leather that had been distressed to make it look shabby. A panel mounted on the ceiling could be lowered to reveal a thirty-inch plasma TV with an extensive DVD library and surround sound. It had been Max's perverse idea to cue up the movie *Titanic* first if the crew ever actually had to man the lifeboats.

Every nook and cranny had been carefully designed to maximize the comfort and convenience of anyone forced into the boat. It was more like a luxury motor yacht than a life-saving vessel. She was also built for safety. When her hatches were sealed the boat could turn completely over and still right herself, and with three-point harnesses for every seat, the passengers wouldn't be tossed around. And because she was owned by the Corporation there were a few tricks built into her that Juan had no intention of showing his guest.

There were two positions where the boat could be commanded: inside near the bow protected by the boat's fiberglass and composite cabin, or on a slightly elevated platform at the stern where Juan and Sloane stood so they could enjoy the spectacular sunset earlier and now the star-smeared night sky. A small windscreen protected them from the worst of the salt air, but the cold waters of the Benguela Current flowing north from Antarctica had dropped the temperature into the sixties.

Sloane cradled the coffee in her hands and studied Cabrillo's face in the muted glow of the dashboard lights. He was traditionally handsome, with strong, well-defined features and clear blue eyes. But it was what lay under the surface that really intrigued her. He had an easy command of his crew, a natural leadership that any woman would find attractive, but she also got the impression he was a loner. Not the walk into a post office and open fire with a rifle loner, or the geek living in cyberspace type, but someone comfortable in their own company, someone who knew exactly who he was, what he was capable of, and found what he saw to his liking.

She could tell he made decisions quickly and apparently never second-guessed himself. That level of confidence only came from being right more often than wrong. She wondered if he had military training and decided he did. She imagined he'd been in the Navy, an officer, but one who couldn't put up with the incompetence of those above him so he quit. He had traded in the structured life of the armed forces to live like a drifter on the high seas, clinging to an old way of doing things because he was really born a couple of centuries too late. She could easily see him on the bridge of a clipper ship crossing the Pacific with a load of spices and silk.

"What are you smiling at?" Juan asked.

"Just thinking you're a man living in the wrong time."

"How so?"

"Not only do you rescue damsels in distress, you also take up their causes."

Cabrillo puffed out his chest and struck a heroic pose. "And now, fair lady, I gird myself for battle against metallic sea serpents."

Sloane laughed. "May I ask you a question?"

"Fire away."

"If you weren't the captain of the *Oregon* what would you do?"

The question didn't veer into any dangerous territory so Juan gave her an honest answer. "I think I'd be a paramedic."

"Really? Not a doctor?"

"Most doctors I know treat patients like a commodity—something they have to work on if they want to get paid before returning to the golf course. And they're backed by a huge staff of nurses and technicians and millions of dollars' worth of equipment. But paramedics are different. They are out there working in pairs with just their wits and a minimum of gear. They have to make the first critical assessments and often perform the first life-saving acts. They're there to tell you everything is going to be all right and make damn sure it is. And once you get the person to the hospital you simply fade away. No glory, no God complex, no 'gee, doc, you saved my life.' You just do your job and go on to the next."

"I like that," Sloane said after a beat. "And you're right. My father cut his leg really badly on a charter once and we had to radio for an ambulance and I had to take the boat back in. I still remember it was Dr. Jankowski who stitched up the leg in the hospital but I have no idea of the name of the guy who first dressed the wound on the dock. Without him my dad would have probably bled out."

"Unsung heroes," Juan remarked quietly. "Those are the ones I like." For a moment his mind flashed to the wall of stars in the entrance to CIA headquarters at Langley. Each one represented an agent who had been killed in the field. Of the eighty-three agents represented thirty-five remained nameless, still keeping the Company's secrets long after their deaths. Unsung heroes, each and every one. "What about you? What would you do if you weren't a security specialist for a diamond company?"

She threw him a saucy grin. "Why, I'd be captain of the *Oregon*."

"Oh, Max would love that."

"Max?"

"My chief engineer and first officer," Juan said fondly. "Let's just say Max put the rump in grumpy."

"Sounds like I'd like him."

"He's a piece of work, my Mr. Hanley. In truth, I've never met a more loyal man or had a better friend."

Sloane finished her coffee and handed the lid back to Juan. He screwed the cap back onto the thermos and checked the time. It was nearly midnight.

"I was thinking," he said, "rather than tie up in Swakopmund at oh dark thirty and possibly arouse suspicion, why don't we head south to where you met Papa Heinrick? That way we can catch him first thing in the morning before he goes out fishing. Do you think you could find his camp again?"

"No problem. Sandwich Bay is about twenty-five miles south of Swakopmund."

Juan checked their GPS, estimated the new coordinates, and punched them into the automatic navigator. Servos moved the wheel a few degrees to port.

A little over forty minutes later Africa emerged from the darkness with bluffs of sand shimmering in the moonlight and occasionally the brighter white of waves curling onto the beach. The long peninsula that protected Sandwich Bay was a quarter mile to their south.

"Nice bit of navigating," Sloane said.

Juan tapped the GPS receiver with a knuckle. "Gladys here gets the credit. GPS has made lazy navigators of us all. I don't think I could compute my position with a sextant and watch if my life depended on it."

"Somehow I doubt that."

Juan backed off the throttle to reduce their wake as they entered the fragile ecosystem. They motored for twenty minutes until reaching the southernmost edge of the bay. Sloane panned the dense wall of reeds with a flashlight as they tracked along the shore looking for the cut in the grass that led to Papa Heinrick's private little lagoon.

"There," she said, pointing.

Juan slowed the boat to a crawl and edged its bow into the reeds. He kept a sharp eye on the depth gauge and constantly checked that floating chunks of vegetation didn't foul the props. The lifeboat cut through the tall grass and the blades made a hissing sound as they scraped the hull and sides of the cabin.

They had covered seventy yards when Juan caught the scent of smoke. He raised his face and sniffed the air like a dog but couldn't detect it again. Then it came back, stronger, the sooty smell of burning wood. He grabbed Sloane's wrist so he could cover the lens of her flashlight with his hand.

Ahead he could see the orange glow of a fire, but not the contained fire pit Sloane had described. This was something altogether different.

"Damn." He gunned the throttles and prayed the water maintained its depth as the boat leapt forward, knocking Sloane into his arms. He steadied her quickly and tried to peer through the curtain of grass that blocked their way.

They suddenly burst into the clearing that surrounded Papa Heinrick's island. Juan glanced at the depth gauge. There was less than a foot of water under the keel. He jammed the throttles into full reverse, causing a torrent of water to erupt at the stern, and hit the release for the anchor. They hadn't yet picked up a great deal of speed, so he managed to stop the lifeboat before she grounded.

He idled the engines and only then did he take in the scene around them. The shack perched at the center of the island was a pyre, with flames and embers leaping twenty feet from its thatch and driftwood roof. Papa Heinrick's overturned fishing boat was also ablaze, but the craft was so waterlogged that the fire hadn't really caught. Banks of thick white smoke coiled from under the skiff and wafted from the seams of its wooden hull.

Over the roar of the burning cabin Juan heard the unmistakable scream of a man in mortal agony.

"Oh, my God!" Sloane cried.

Cabrillo reacted instantly. He launched himself onto the roof of the lifeboat's cabin and raced down its length. The cabin ended five feet shy of the boat's sharp bow. Cabrillo measured his steps perfectly, jumping off with his artificial leg so his left foot landed on the aluminum railing that ringed the bows and then kicking off from that in a long graceful dive. He knifed into the water, kicking strongly, and came up swimming.

When his feet touched bottom he charged out of the water like a rampaging animal and ran up the beach. That was when he heard another sound, the deep bass rumble of a marine engine.

A white bow runner circled around the far side of the little isle and one of the two men in its open cockpit opened fire with an automatic weapon. Sprays of sand erupted all around Cabrillo as he dove for cover, his hand reaching instinctively for the small of his back. He hit the ground, rolled twice, and came up into a kneeling firing position, the Glock he'd stuck in his pants when he had gotten the Windbreakers held steady in a two-handed grip. The range was thirty yards and widening, and he was firing into the darkness while the gunman had Juan backlit by the burning hut.

Cabrillo didn't even get a shot off before more autofire poured onto the island, forcing him to roll back into the lagoon. He drew a deep breath at the moment a round blasted into the beach inches from his head, forcing him to inhale the gritty sand.

Ducking underwater and fighting the uncontrollable urge to cough his lungs out, Juan swam about thirty feet, making sure his hands were in contact with the bottom so he didn't reveal himself. He sensed through the water that the powerboat was coming around, hunting him. He approximated their location and swam a little further, gagging silently as his chest tried to convulse. When he thought he knew where they were he planted his feet firmly on the bottom and raised himself quickly, continuing to hold his breath for a fraction longer.

The boat was ten yards away and the two men aboard were looking in the wrong direction. With water streaming down his face and his lungs ready to explode, Juan raised the Glock and fired. The pistol's recoil broke the lock he'd maintained on his breathing and he began to cough violently. He didn't know if he hit anything or not. But he must have been close because the low burbling engine suddenly ramped up and the bow runner made for the channel back out to the open bay, kicking up a rooster tail as she ran.

Juan bent double, his hands on his knees, and coughed until he vomited. He wiped at his lips and looked across the lagoon at the lifeboat. "Sloane," he croaked. "Are you okay?"

Her head emerged from behind the cockpit coaming. The fire's shifting light couldn't hide the roundness of her eyes or give hue to the pallor of her skin. "Yeah," she said and then firmed her voice. "Yes, I'm fine. Are you?"

"Yeah," Juan replied then turned his attention to the flaming ruins. He could no longer hear Papa Heinrick's cries but he forced himself closer. The roof was moments from collapsing and the heat thrown off by the blaze forced Juan to shield his face with an arm as he moved closer. The smoke burned his eyes and sent him into another paroxysm of coughing. His lungs felt like they were filled with ground glass.

Cabrillo used a length of wood to rip down the burning flap of cloth that Heinrick had used for a door. He could see nothing because of the smoke, and was about to edge into the burning structure when a gust came up and parted the soot like a curtain. For a moment Juan had a clear view of the bed and he knew at that instant the sight would haunt him for the rest of his life.

What remained of Heinrick's arms were still manacled to a bed frame, and despite the ravages of the flames on the corpse, Juan could tell the old man had been tortured before his shack had been set on fire. His gap-toothed mouth remained open in his final scream of life while the blood pooled under the bed sizzled.

The roof collapsed in an explosion of flames and sparks that licked at

Cabrillo before he could turn away. None of the embers could burn through his wet clothes but the sudden surge of adrenaline galvanized him.

He sprinted back to the water's edge and dove in, striking out for the idling lifeboat. Because it rode high in the water, he made for the vessel's bow and used the anchor chain to heave himself up to the deck. Sloane was there to help him slide under the railing. She said nothing about the pistol shoved into the waistband of Juan's trousers.

"Come on." He took her hand and together they jogged down the length of the boat and jumped into the cockpit. Juan hit the switch to raise the anchor. He firewalled the throttle as soon as it lifted from the bottom, and used his palm to spin the wheel furiously.

"What are you doing?" Sloane shouted over the roar of the engine. "That was a ski boat. They've got a five-minute head start and can outrun us by twenty knots or more."

"Like hell they can," Cabrillo said without looking at her, his rage barely in check. He straightened their course when the lifeboat's prow was facing the little channel out of the lagoon.

"Juan, we'll never catch them. Besides, they had machine guns. You've only got a pistol."

Reeds whipped at them like switches as they rocketed down the channel. Juan steered with one eye on the depth gauge and a moment after bursting out of the grass he grunted with savage satisfaction.

"Hold on," he said and hit a switch hidden under the dash.

The forward part of the lifeboat's hull began to rise out of the water as hydraulics under the boat activated and extended a series of fins and underwater wings. Sloane was a second late to react. She staggered and would have fallen overboard had Juan not clutched for the front of her jacket and held her tight. The hydrofoils began to generate more lift and raised the hull even higher until just the wings and telescoping propeller shaft were dragging through the water. It took just seconds but their speed more than doubled to forty knots.

Sloane looked at Juan incredulously, unsure what to say or how to react to the plodding lifeboat becoming a streaking high-performance hydrofoil. She finally blurted, "Who in the hell are you?"

He glanced at her. He normally would have come up with a pithy remark but his anger at Papa Heinrick's murder was all-consuming.

"Someone you don't want to piss off." His eyes were as hard as agate. "And they just pissed me off." He pointed ahead. "Do you see how the sea is glowing a little bit?" Sloane nodded. "Their boat's motion through the water caused bioluminescent organisms to fluoresce. We never would have found them in daylight but at night Mother Nature's giving us some help. Can you take the helm and keep us on that trail?"

"I've never driven a boat like this."

"Not many people have. It's just like your father's charter only faster. Just keep the wheel straight and if you have to turn do it gently. I'll be back in a second."

He watched her for a moment to make certain she would be all right, then ducked through the entrance to the cabin. He strode down the central aisle to where he'd tossed his leather duffel. He rummaged through the clothes and came up with the mini-Uzi and spare magazines. After reloading the Glock he jammed it back into his waistband and slid the magazines into his rear pocket. He stepped over to another one of the benches and activated a hidden button under the cushion. A catch released and the seat pivoted forward. Most of the space under the seats was given over to food and other provisions, but this one was different. He threw aside rolls of toilet paper until the bin was empty then touched another hidden lever. The false bottom sprang open and Juan lifted the lid.

Inside the bilge space the snarl of the engines and the shriek of the foils through the water were deafening. Juan groped for a tube secured in the bilge with metal clips. He got it free and lifted it out. Made of tough plastic with a waterproof cap, the tube was nearly four feet long and ten inches around. He unscrewed the cap and slid an FN-FAL assault rifle onto an adjacent seat. The venerable Belgian weapon could trace its roots back to the Second World War but was still one of the best all-around guns in the world.

Juan quickly loaded a pair of magazines with the 7.62 mm ammunition stored in the tube, racked a round into the chamber, and double-checked that the weapon was safed. He recalled Max questioning the need for such a gun on a lifeboat; his reply had been, "Teach a man to fish and he eats for a day, give him an assault rifle and some sharks and he can feed his crew for a lifetime."

He climbed back out onto the rear deck. Sloane had kept the boat dead center on the feebly glowing wake but Juan could tell they'd cut the distance to the fleeing bow runner. The microorganisms had had less time to settle down so the bioluminescence was brighter than it had been just moments before.

Juan set the FN onto the dash, tossed the thermos down into the cabin, and slipped the mini-Uzi into its place.

"Are you always prepared for World War Three or did I catch you at a particularly paranoid moment?"

Sloane was using humor to try to get him to relax and he was grateful. Cabrillo knew all too well that going into combat without first controlling your emotions was a deadly mistake. He grinned at her as he took her place behind the wheel. "Don't knock it. It just so happens I was paranoid enough."

Moments later they could make out the low-slung speedboat arrowing down the bay. And no sooner did they spot the bow runner then the men aboard saw them, too; the boat cut a nimble turn and started edging closer to the marshy shore.

Juan eased the wheel over to stay on their stern, leaning far over to keep his balance as the hydrofoil canted sharply in the water. In just a couple of minutes they had cut the gap to thirty yards. While the bow runner's driver concentrated on their route, the second man laid himself over the rear bench seats to steady his automatic rifle.

"Get down," Juan shouted.

Bullets pinged off the bow and whizzed by the cockpit. The hydrofoil was riding too high for him to hit them so the gunman shifted his aim to one of the struts supporting the foils. He managed to slam a few rounds into it but the struts were made of high-tensile steel and the rounds ricocheted harmlessly.

Juan pulled the mini-Uzi from the cup holder, juked the hydrofoil to give himself a clear firing lane around her bows, and greased the trigger. The little weapon bucked in his hand and a shining arc of spent brass rose into the hydrofoil's slipstream and vanished over the stern. Juan couldn't risk killing both men so he aimed a bit to the side of the fleeing ski boat. The water exploded along its port side as twenty rounds raked the sea.

He had hoped that would have ended the chase because the men had to realize their former prey was bigger, faster, and equally armed. However, the bow runner kept up its speed and curved even closer to the swampy shore.

Juan had no choice but to stay on them as they zipped by clots of reeds and spindly trees. He soon found himself dancing the hydrofoil around stands of grass and little islands that dotted the coastline. What the ski boat lacked in speed it made up for in maneuverability, and as they weaved around obstacles in the water it widened the distance to fifty yards, then sixty.

Cabrillo could have turned to open water and closed in again, but he was afraid if he lost sight of his quarry they would escape into the towering sea grass where their shallower draft was the ultimate advantage. And to go in to find them invited walking into an ambush. He knew the best way to end this was to keep on their tail.

They slashed past stands of trees, sending birds shrieking for the sky, and their wakes sloshing through the marsh caused the mats of grass to undulate as though the bay were breathing.

Ever mindful that the foils were vulnerable to underwater obstructions, Juan had to make easier turns than the ski boat, allowing them to continue to widen the gap. Something ahead caught Cabrillo's eye. He had just a second to realize it was a partially submerged log. Hitting it would tear the wings right off the boat, so with a deft hand on the throttle and wheel, he snaked the hydrofoil around the log. The quick move avoided the log but forced them into a gap between two low mud-covered islands.

Juan glanced at the depth gauge and saw it was pegged at zero. There was perhaps six inches of water between the wings and the bottom. He leaned against the throttle to eke out a bit more power and hopefully raise the boat a few more inches. If they grounded at this speed he and Sloane would be tossed from the hydrofoil like rag dolls; the impact with the water would be like hitting pavement after a fifty-foot fall.

The channel between the islands grew narrower. Juan turned to look astern. The normally white wake kicked up by the foils and propeller was a deep chocolate brown as their passage roiled silt from the seafloor. The boat staggered for an instant as a wing brushed bottom. He couldn't slow down because the hydrofoil would drop off plane and she'd auger into the mud and he had the engine keening at well above red line.

The channel seemed to grow narrower still.

"Brace yourself," he shouted over the engine because he knew he'd gambled and lost.

They raced through the narrowest spot on the channel, losing a bit of speed when the forward wings kissed the bottom a second time before the channel widened and the depth began to increase.

Juan blew out a long breath.

"Was that as close as I think it was?" Sloane asked.

"Closer."

But the maneuver had halved the distance to the bow runner because it had been forced to slalom through a stand of mangroves. The gunman braced himself at the ski boat's stern. Juan eased off the throttle and cut across the marsh to once again place the hydrofoil directly in their wake, using his craft's superior size as a shield just as a fresh fusillade poured from the nimble little boat. The rounds peppered the sea and blew out two panes of safety glass that ran along the lifeboat's cabin.

A straight section of marsh allowed Cabrillo to firewall the engine again. In just seconds the big hydrofoil loomed over the bow runner. In the turbulence of her wake the hydrofoil began to ventilate, to draw air under the water wings and lose lift. Her bow sawed up and down, which is what Juan had anticipated. The ski boat's driver tried to dance out from under the crushing bow, but Juan matched him turn for turn. The bow slammed down on the bow runner's stern but the blow wasn't hard enough to slow it, and Cabrillo had to back off slightly to regain lift.

He glanced at the dash to check the RPMs and as soon as he did Sloane screamed.

He looked up. When the hydrofoil's bow hit the rear of the ski boat the gunman had jumped for the railing. He now stood at the hydrofoil's prow, clutching the railing with one hand while the other held an AK-47, its barrel aimed directly between Juan's eyes. There wasn't time to draw his own weapon so Juan did the only thing he could.

His hand lashed out and chopped the throttle an instant before the AK blazed. He and Sloane were slammed into the dashboard as the hydrofoil slowed from forty miles per hour to almost nothing in an instant, a wild burst from the assault rifle stitching a ragged line across the top of the cabin. The boat came off plane hard, and while the gunman managed to keep his grip on the railing his chest was crushed against the aluminum struts by the massive wall of water that exploded over the bow with the force to douse Juan and Sloane all the way at the vessel's stern. The hydrofoil's forward momentum was enough that he slid under the hull and when Cabrillo pressed on the throttle again her wake frothed pink.

"Are you okay?" Juan asked quickly.

Sloane was massaging her upper chest were it had impacted with the dash. "I think so," she replied and raked wet hair from her forehead. She pointed to his arm. "You're bleeding."

Cabrillo made sure the boat was gaining on the bow runner before looking at the wound. A shard of fiberglass torn off the boat by the spray of bullets was partially embedded in his upper arm.

"Ow," he exclaimed when he felt the first flicker of pain.

"I thought tough guys could ignore a little thing like that."

"Like hell. It hurts." He gently worked the postcard-sized piece of fiberglass from his flesh. The shard had cut cleanly and there was little blood. Juan dug out the small medical kit from a bin next to the dash. He handed it to Sloane, who rummaged through it and found a roll of sterile gauze. He held still as she wrapped his arm with the bandage and tied it off tightly.

"That should hold you," she pronounced. "When was your last tetanus?"

"February twentieth two years ago."

"You remember the exact date?"

"There's a fifteen-inch scar on my back. Days you get a gash that big tend to stick with you."

In a minute they had regained all the ground they had lost to the ski boat. Juan noted that the marsh to their right was giving way to a boulder-strewn beach that would afford no protection to his quarry. It was time to end this. "Can you take the helm again?"

"Yes, sure."

"Watch for my signal, then ease back on the throttle. Be prepared to turn. I'll point which way."

Unlike before he didn't wait to see if she was comfortable at the controls. He hefted the FN assault rifle and spare magazine and clambered up the length of the boat.

The bow runner was no more than five yards in front of him. He steadied himself against the railing and brought the FN to his shoulder. He fired controlled three-round bursts. When the first bullets slammed into the bow runner's engine cowling, the driver sheared away, trying to find shallow water close to shore. Juan raised his arm and pointed to port, and Sloane followed his lead. Her turn was a little steep, but she seemed to have a handle on the hydrofoil's drive characteristics.

As soon as he regained the sight picture he wanted he loosened another three-round burst into the bow runner's engine. And a third. The driver tried to throw off Cabrillo's aim but the chairman anticipated every juke and twist and slammed another half dozen bullets into the boat.

The wisp of white smoke that suddenly appeared from under the engine cowling quickly turned into a black cloud. The engine would seize any second, and Juan readied his signal to Sloane for them to slow so they wouldn't ram the bow runner.

Between the bow lights on the hydrofoil and the ski boat's dash lights, Cabrillo could just discern the driver's features when he turned to look back at him. They locked eyes for just an instant but Juan could feel the hatred across the distance like the heat from a fire. Rather than fear, he read defiance in the man's expression.

The man cranked the wheel hard over. Juan raised his hand to stop Sloane from pursuing because the bow runner was heading directly for the rocky shore. Cabrillo had wanted to take one of the men prisoner from the very start of the chase, but he felt the chance slipping from his grasp. He fired again, raking the ski boat's stern, not sure of what he was hitting because of the smoke, but desperate to prevent what he knew the driver intended.

The bow runner had picked up most of the speed it had lost in the turn when it was still twenty feet from the coast. The engine's shriek stuttered for a moment, but it was too late. The boat hit the shoaling bottom at thirty-plus knots and shot out of the water like a javelin. It arced high through the night air before nosing into the ground and came apart as if a bomb had gone off inside its fiberglass shell. The hull splintered into hundreds of pieces and her engine was torn from its mount as the craft cartwheeled up the beach. The impact burst the fuel tank and the gasoline became an aerosol cloud. The body of the driver was flung twenty feet before the fuel/air mixture detonated into a mushrooming fireball that consumed what remained of the ski boat.

Sloane had had the presence of mind to ease the hydrofoil off plane then slow it to a crawl by the time Juan had scurried back to the cockpit. He double-checked that the FN-FAL was safe and set it back on the dash. After raising the retractable foils he eased the boat as close to the wreckage as he could, idled the engine, and dropped the small anchor.

"He killed himself, didn't he?"

Cabrillo couldn't take his eyes off the burning boat. "Yup."

"What does that mean?"

He glanced at her as he processed her question and all the implications his answer meant. "He knew we weren't the authorities, so he was willing to die rather than risk capture and interrogation. It means we're dealing with fanatics."

"Like Muslim fundamentalists?"

"I don't think he was an Arab jihadi. This is something else."

"But what?"

Juan didn't reply because he had no answer. His clothes were still drenched from his earlier swim, so he simply stepped off the back of the hydrofoil and into water that came up to his neck. He was almost to shore when he heard Sloane hit the water behind him. He waited for her at the surf line and together they approached the body. There was no sense checking out the boat since all that remained was melted fiberglass and scorched metal.

The damage done to the corpse by the impact and subsequent roll up the beach was horrifying. Like the vision of a demented artist, his neck and every limb were set at obtuse angles. Cabrillo checked there was no pulse before slipping the Glock into the waistband of his pants. There was nothing in the man's rear pockets so Juan rolled the corpse, shaken by the boneless way the body moved. The man's face was severely abraded.

Sloane gasped.

"Sorry," Juan said. "You might want to stand back."

"No, it's not that. I know him. That's the South African chopper pilot Tony and I hired. His name's Pieter DeWitt. Damn, how could I be so stupid? He knew we were going to investigate Papa Heinrick's snakes because I told him. He sent that boat to follow us yesterday and then came here to make sure no one ever questioned the old man again."

The repercussions of her presence in Namibia hit Sloane fast and hard. She looked like she was about to be ill. "If I hadn't come here looking for the *Rove* Papa Heinrick would still be alive." Her eyes were wet when she looked at Juan. "Luka, our guide, I bet they've already killed him, too. Oh God, what about Tony?"

Cabrillo knew intuitively that she didn't want to be hugged nor did she want him to speak. They stood in the night as the ski boat burned and Sloane cried.

"They were totally innocent," she sobbed, "and now they're all dead and it's my fault."

How many times had Juan felt the same way, taking responsibility for the actions of others just because he was involved? Sloane was no more at fault for Papa Heinrick's death than the wife who asked her husband to run an errand was responsible if he's killed en route. But God how that guilt was there, corroding the soul as surely as acid eats away steel.

The tears flowed for five minutes, maybe longer. Juan stood at her side with his head bowed and only looked at her when she sniffled back the last of it.

"Thank you," she muttered softly.

"For what?"

"Most men hate to see a woman crying and will do or say anything to make it stop."

He gave her his warmest smile. "I hate it as much as the next guy, but I also knew if you didn't do it now you'd just do it later and it would be a hell of a lot worse."

"That's why I thanked you. You understood."

"I've been there a few times myself. Do you want to talk about it?"

"Not really."

"But you do know you're not responsible, right?"

"I know. They would be alive if I hadn't come but I didn't kill them."

"That's right. You're just one link in the chain of events that led to their murders. You're probably right about your guide, but don't worry about Tony. No one onshore knows that the attack against you failed.

They already think you and Tony are dead. But to be on the safe side we'll head for Walvis. The *Pinguin* didn't look like she had the speed to reach her home port yet. If we hurry we can warn them off."

Sloane wiped at her face with the sleeve of her Windbreaker. "Do you really think so?"

"Yeah, I do. Come on."

Thirty seconds after clambering aboard the hydrofoil, Juan had them rocketing down the bay while Sloane changed into dry clothing from the craft's stores. She took the wheel while Cabrillo changed and broke out some rations.

"Sorry, all I have are MREs," he said, holding up two brown foil packets. "It's either spaghetti with meatballs or chicken and biscuits."

"I'll take the spaghetti and give you the meatballs. I'm a vegetarian."

"Really?"

"Why do you look so surprised?"

"I don't know. I always picture vegetarians wearing Birkenstocks and living on organic farms."

"Those are vegans. In my opinion they're extremists."

Her statement got Juan thinking about fanaticism and what drove people to it. Religion was the first thing that sprang to mind, but what else were people so passionate about they would mold their entire lives around it? The environmental and animal rights movements were the next groups he considered. Activists were willing to break into laboratories to release research animals or burn subdivisions at ski resorts to get their message across. Were some willing to kill for it, too?

He wondered if the polarity of opinion had been so sharpened in the past few years that societal norms of restraint and respect no longer applied. East, West. Muslim, Christian. Socialist, capitalist. Rich, poor. It seemed every issue could drive a wedge deep enough to cause one side or the other to consider violence.

Of course, it was into this very divide that he sailed the *Oregon*. With the world no longer cowering under the threat of nuclear annihilation from a war between the old Soviet Union and the United States, regional flare-ups had proliferated to the point that conventional means could no longer contain them.

Cabrillo had known this was coming and had formed the Corporation to combat these new threats. It was disheartening to think it, but he knew they would have more work than they could ever handle.

With no ransom demands from Geoffrey Merrick's kidnappers it appeared more and more likely that his abduction was politically motivated; and given the nature of Merrick's work, the politics most likely involved were the extreme environmental fringe.

Then he wondered if his kidnapping was somehow connected to whatever Sloane Macintyre had stumbled into. The odds were dead against it despite the coincidental fact that both were connected to Namibia. The Skeleton Coast was far from the world consciousness when it came to the environment. Brazilian rain forests or polluted waterways, those were what people were familiar with, not a remote strip of desert in a country that many couldn't find on a map.

Then he thought of another scenario. Diamond mining was one of Namibia's biggest industries. And considering how tightly controlled the market was, according to Sloane, the likely possibility was that they had stumbled into an illegal mining operation. People were more than willing to risk their lives for the idea of immeasurable wealth. And people committed murders for a lot less. But did that explain Pieter DeWitt's apparent suicide?

It would if he considered the consequences of being caught worse than a quick death.

"What would happen to a man like DeWitt if he was caught in some sort of illegal diamond mining activity?" Cabrillo asked Sloane.

"It varies from country to country. In Sierra Leone he'd be shot on sight. Here in Namibia it's a twenty-thousand-dollar fine and five years in prison." He looked at her askance for knowing the answer so readily. "I'm a security specialist, remember? I have to know the laws pertaining to the diamond trade in a dozen countries. Just like you have to know the Customs laws of the ports you visit."

"Well, I'm still impressed," Juan said, then went on, "Five years doesn't sound too bad, certainly not enough of a sentence for someone to commit suicide rather than doing the time."

"You don't know African prisons."

"I can't imagine they rate many stars in the *Michelin Guide*."

"It's not just the conditions. Tuberculosis and HIV infection rates in

African jails are among the highest in the world. Some human rights groups believe any jail time is tantamount to a death sentence. Why are you asking about all this?"

"I'm trying to get a handle on why DeWitt killed himself rather than risk capture."

"You're thinking maybe he's not a fanatic or something?"

"I don't know what I'm thinking," Juan admitted. "There's something else going on that I can't tell you about, and I thought for a second they could be linked. I'm just making sure they're not. Understanding motivations is the key to seeing these aren't two pieces of the same puzzle but two different puzzles altogether. It's just that there's a coincidence involved—"

"And you hate coincidences," Sloane finished for him.

"Exactly."

"If you want to tell me what else is happening maybe I can help."

"Sorry, Sloane, that wouldn't be a good idea."

"Loose lips sink ships and all that."

Sloane was just being flippant and didn't know how her words would soon prove to be prophetic.

THE de Havilland Twin Otter approached the rough landing strip so slowly it appeared to be hovering. Although her design dated back to the 1960s, the high-winged, two-engined aircraft continued to be a favorite among bush pilots the world over. She could land on just about any surface and in about a thousand feet. Her takeoff runs were even shorter.

The hard pan abutting the Devil's Oasis had been marked with orange flags and the pilot set the plane down dead center in a whirl of dust. The blast of her turboprops kicked up more dirt so when she slowed she was enveloped momentarily in a dark cloud. Power was taken off the propellers and in moments they'd juddered to a stop. An open-topped four-wheel drive reached the aircraft just as the rear door creaked open.

Daniel Singer unlimbered his lanky six-foot-seven-inch frame from the aircraft and knuckled his spine to work out the kinks of being confined for the seven-hundred-mile flight from Zimbabwe's capital, Harare. He'd flown there from the States because enough money in the right hands ensured there was no record of his arrival in Africa. For all anyone knew he was still at his home in Maine.

The truck's driver was a woman named Nina Visser. She had been with Singer from the beginning of his quest and had been instrumental in recruiting other members to their cause, like-minded men and women who recognized that the nations of the world needed to be jolted out of their complacency when it came to environmental issues.

"About time you showed up to share in our misery," she said by way of greeting, but there was a smile on her face and a spark of affection in her nearly black eyes. Born in Holland, like many of her countrymen, she spoke English with little accent.

Singer stooped to kiss her cheek and quipped, "Nina, my dear, don't you know we evil geniuses need a remote lair?"

"Did you have to pick one that's a hundred kilometers from the nearest flush toilet and overrun by sand fleas?"

"What can I say, all the hollowed-out volcanoes were taken. I rented this place through a dummy company from the Namibian government on the pretext we're going to film a movie here." He turned to accept a bag from the pilot who'd appeared at the door. "Get the plane refueled. We're only going to be here for a short while."

Nina was surprised. "You're not going to stay?"

"Sorry, no. I have to get to Cabinda earlier than I'd planned."

"Problems?"

"A slight glitch with the equipment has delayed the mercenaries," he said. "And I want to make sure the boats we are going to use for the assault are ready. Besides, Mother Nature is being more than cooperative. Another tropical storm is brewing on the heels of the one that dissipated a couple of days ago. I don't think we'll need to wait more than a week or so."

Nina stopped suddenly, her face showing joy. "So soon? I can't believe it."

"Five years of work are about to pay off. When we're done there won't be a person on the planet who can sanely deny the dangers of global warming." Singer settled himself into the truck's passenger seat for the short drive to the old prison.

The penitentiary was a three-story stone monstrosity as large as a warehouse with a crenellated rampart on the roof for guards to watch out over the desert. There was just a single window on each wall of the outside façade, which made the structure appear even more solid and foreboding. The shadow it cast was a midnight stain on the white sand.

A set of towering wooden doors with iron hinges mortared into the stone and broad enough to admit a much larger truck gave access to the central courtyard. The bottom floor of the prison was given over to administrative spaces and dormitories for the guards who'd once lived here while the second and third stories were for the cell blocks that ringed the courtyard.

The sun beat onto the exercise yard, reflecting and rebounding so the air was as heavy as molten lead.

"So how are our guests doing?" Singer asked when Nina braked in front of the entrance to the main administration area.

"The men from Zimbabwe arrived yesterday with their prisoner," Nina said and turned to her mentor. "I still don't understand why they're here."

"A tactical necessity, I'm afraid. Part of the bargain to allow me to enter Africa without having to get visas and all that other junk was that we let them use a portion of the prison for a short while. Their prisoner heads the main opposition party and he goes on trial for treason soon. The government is rightly justified in thinking that his followers would break him out and smuggle him to some other country. They just need someplace to keep him until the trial starts and then he'll be returned to Harare."

"Won't his people just stage their breakout when he goes back?"

"The trial will last less than an hour and sentence will be carried out immediately."

"I don't like this, Danny. Zimbabwe's government is one of the most corrupt in Africa. I think anyone who opposes them is probably in the right."

"I agree with you, but this is the bargain I got stuck with." His tone made it clear he didn't want to be questioned further. "How about my illustrious former business partner? How's he doing?"

Nina smirked. "I think he's finally beginning to understand the ramifications of his success."

"Good. I can't wait to see the look on that smug bastard's face when we pull this off and he finally understands he's at fault."

They entered the prison and Singer greeted his people by name. While he would never have Merrick's charisma, among the activists he'd gathered together he was already a hero. He handed out three bottles of red wine he'd brought with him and they drank them down over the course of the next half hour. One woman in particular received special attention, and when he called for a toast in her honor, the others cheered.

He then took the office once occupied by the warden and asked that Merrick be brought down from his cell. He spent several minutes trying to find the right pose for when Merrick entered. He tried sitting behind the desk but didn't want the height disadvantage so instead he stood by the office's window with his head bowed as if he alone shouldered the weight of the world.

A moment later, two of Singer's men led Merrick into the office with his hands bound behind his back. The two hadn't physically seen each other since the split, but Merrick had been on enough television interviews for Singer to recognize the physical toll the past days of captivity had taken on his former partner. He was especially gratified at how his once bright eyes had sunken into his skull and gazed at him with a haunted look. But incredibly, he saw them begin to brighten, and once again he felt the mesmerizing intensity that Merrick had always possessed and Singer had secretly coveted. Singer had to fight the urge to sit.

"Danny," Merrick started in a sincere tone, "I can't begin to under-stand why you've done what you've done other than to get back at me. I just want to say you've won. Whatever you want is yours so long as you stop right now. You want the company back, I will sign it away right now. You want all my money, just give me an account number to transfer it into. I will issue any statement you prepare and take any responsibility you believe I deserve."

God, he was good, Daniel Singer thought. *No wonder he could al-ways beat me.* For a moment he was tempted to take him up on his offer but he wouldn't let himself be swayed. He thrust aside the momentary doubt. "This isn't a negotiation table, Geoff. Having you as a witness is only a bonus I'm giving myself. You are the sideshow, my old friend, not the main attraction."

"It doesn't have to be this way."

"Of course it does!" Singer roared. "Why do you think I'm giving the world a taste now?" He took a deep breath and continued a bit more calmly, but with an equal amount of passion. "If we continue on the path we've set my demonstration will be nothing compared to natural events. We have to change, only the fools that run the world refuse to see it. Damnit, Geoff, you're a scientist, surely you understand. Within the next century global warming is going to destroy everything mankind has accomplished.

"An increase of just a degree of surface temperatures will have untold ripple effects on the environment—and it's already happening. The planet isn't hot enough yet to melt all the glaciers, but in Greenland the ice is flowing into the sea quicker than ever because meltwater is acting as a lubricant when it scrapes over the ground. In some places they are advancing twice as fast as normal. This is taking place today. Right now."

"I'm not going to deny what you're saying—"

"You can't," Singer snapped. "No rational person can, but still nothing is being done about it. People have to see the effects for themselves, in their homes, not on some glacier in Greenland. They have to be galvanized into action or we're doomed."

"All the deaths, Dan—"

"Pale in comparison to what's coming. They have to be sacrificed in order to save untold billions of others. You have to cut off a gangrenous limb in order to save the patient."

"But we're talking about innocent lives, not infected tissue!"

"Okay, so it was a bad analogy, but my point still stands. And besides, the death toll won't be as high as you think. Forecasting has come a long way. There'll be plenty of warning."

"Yeah? Ask the people living in New Orleans when Katrina hit," Merrick spat.

"Exactly. Local, state, and federal authorities had ample time to evacuate and yet more than a thousand perished needlessly. This is what I'm saying. We've had two decades of scientific fact as to the effects we're having on the environment and only token action has been taken. Can't you see I have to go forward? I have to do this to save humanity."

Geoffrey Merrick knew his former partner and best friend was insane. Sure, Dan had always been a little odd, they both had been, otherwise they wouldn't have thrived at MIT. But what had once been quirky behavior had turned into full-blown mania. He also knew he'd never find an argument to get Singer to give up. You couldn't rationalize with a fanatic.

He still wanted to try one more tack. "If you care so much for humanity, then why did you have to kill poor Susan Donleavy?"

Singer's expression was unreadable as he broke eye contact. "The people helping me lacked certain, ah, skills, so I had to hire outsiders."

"Mercenaries?"

"Yes. They went beyond, ah, what was strictly called for. Susan's not dead, but I'm afraid her condition is grave."

Merrick gave no outward sign of what he intended. He merely shook off the men who held his arms loosely and launched himself across the room. He vaulted onto the desk and managed to smash a knee into Singer's jaw before the guards reacted. One yanked at the cuff of his jumpsuit hard enough to topple the industrialist. With his hands bound behind his back he couldn't cushion the blow and landed on his face. There was no momentarily flicker, no slow fade to black. He was unconscious as soon as his head hit the floor.

"I'm sorry, Dan," one of the guards said, crossing behind the desk to help Singer to his feet. Blood trickled from the corner of his mouth.

He smeared the blood with a finger, inspecting it as though he couldn't believe it had come from his body. "Is he alive?"

The second guard checked Merrick's pulse at his wrist and throat. "Heart's beating fine. He'll probably have a concussion when he wakes."

"Good." Singer stooped over Merrick's prone form. "Geoff, I hope that cheap shot was worth it, because it was the last act of free will you will ever experience. Lock him back up."

Twenty minutes later the Twin Otter took to the skies once again, heading northward to the Angolan province of Cabinda.

15

As soon as the harbor pilot had climbed down the rope ladder to his waiting tender, Max Hanley and Linda Ross took the secret elevator from the wheelhouse down to the operations center. It was like stepping from a junkyard into NASA's mission control. They'd played the roles of captain and helmsman for the benefit of the South African pilot, but Max was officially off duty. The watch belonged to Linda.

"You going back to your cabin?" she asked, settling herself in the command seat and slipping on her headset.

"No," Max said sourly. "Doc Huxley's still worried about my blood pressure so she and I are heading for the gym. She plans on introducing me to power yoga, whatever the hell that is."

Linda chuckled. "Oh, I would love to see that."

"If she tries to bend me into a pretzel I'm going to tell Juan to start searching for a new chief medical officer."

"It'll be good for you. Cleanse your aura, and all that."

"My aura is fine," he said with good-natured gruffness and headed off to his cabin.

The watch was quiet as they cleared the shipping lanes and started to ramp up the speed. An unexpected storm was brewing to their north but would likely blow itself westward by the time they reached Swakopmund late the next day. Linda used the idle hours to go over the mission briefing Eddie and Linc had written about their upcoming assault on the Devil's Oasis.

"Linda," Hali Kasim called from his communication's station. "I just got something off the wire service. You're not going to believe it. I'm sending it to your display."

She scanned the news item and immediately sent out a ship wide page for Max to come to the op center. He arrived a minute later from the engine room where he'd been performing an unnecessary inspection. The yoga had taken a toll on him: his gait was noticeably hampered by muscles not used to so much stretching.

"You wanted to see me?"

Linda swiveled her flat-panel display so Max could read the news for himself. The tension in the room had risen as though an electric current had passed between the two.

"Will someone please tell us what's happened?" Eric Stone asked from the helmsman's position.

"Benjamin Isaka has been implicated in a coup plot," Linda replied. "He was arrested a couple of hours ago."

"Isaka. Why does that name sound familiar?"

Max answered, "He was our government contact in the Congo for that weapons deal."

"Oh, man, that is seriously not good," Mark Murphy said. Though there was no need to man the *Oregon*'s offensive systems he usually took his position whenever the senior staff had the watch.

"Hali, any word on the weapons we delivered?" Linda asked. She didn't care about Congo's local politics, but the Corporation had a responsibility for those arms.

"Sorry, I haven't checked. That report just came through the AP wire service a minute ago."

Linda looked to Max. "What do you think?"

"I have to agree with Mr. Murphy. This could be a potential disaster. If Isaka told the rebels about the radio tags and they disabled them, then we just handed five hundred assault rifles and a couple hundred grenade launchers to one of the most dangerous group of thugs in Africa."

"I can't find anything about weapons being seized," Hali said. "The story's still breaking so maybe it will come through later."

"Don't count on it." Max had his pipe in his hand and was tapping the stem against his teeth. "Isaka had to have told them. Hali, is there any way we can check the signals from the radio tags?"

The Lebanese-American frowned. "I don't think so. Their range is pretty limited. The whole idea was for Congolese army forces to follow the arms back to the rebel base using handheld detectors that could pick up the tags' signals. They only needed to broadcast for a couple of miles."

"So we're screwed," Linda said, her anger putting a hard edge in her girlish voice. "Those guns could be anywhere and we have no way of finding them."

"Ye of little faith," Murph said with a broad grin.

She turned to him. "What have you got?"

"Will you guys ever stop underestimating the chairman's cunning? Before we sold the guns he asked me and the chief armorer to replace a couple of tags the CIA gave us with some of my own design. Their range is nearly a hundred miles."

"Range isn't the issue," Hali said. "Isaka knew where we hid the tags on the weapons. He's bound to have told the rebels, and they could disable ours just as easily as the ones we got from the CIA."

Mark's smile never faltered. "The CIA tags were hidden in the butt stocks of the AKs and forward grip assembly of the RPGs. I put our tags in the grips of the AKs and modified the sling swivels to hide them on the grenade launchers."

"Oh, bloody brilliant," Linda said with true admiration. "Once they find the CIA tags they wouldn't look for any more. Ours are still in place."

"And transmitting on a different frequency, I might add." Mark crossed his arms over his chest and leaned far back into his seat.

"Why didn't Juan tell us about this?" Max asked.

"He sort of thought he was straying from prudence into paranoia with his idea," Murph replied. "So he didn't want to mention it because more than likely our tags would never be needed."

"How close did you say we need to be to pick up the signals?" Linda asked.

"About a hundred miles."

"That still leaves us searching for a needle in a haystack without some idea where the rebels were headed."

Mark wiped the smug look from his face. "Actually, there's another problem, too. To give the tags that kind of range I had to sacrifice battery life. They'll start failing in another forty-eight to seventy-two hours. After that there really is no way to find them again."

Linda looked to Max Hanley. "The decision to find those weapons has to come from Juan."

"I agree," Max said. "But you and I both know he'll want us to track them down and alert the Congolese army so they can get 'em back."

"As I see it we have two options," Linda said.

"Hold on a sec," Max interrupted. "Hali, call the Chairman on his satellite phone. Okay, two options?"

"One is we turn back and send a team from Cape Town up to the Congo with whatever detection gear they need. Mark, this stuff is man portable, right?"

"The receiver's not much bigger than a boom box," the technical wizard told her.

Normally someone would have commented on the size of the boom box he played when he turned part of the *Oregon*'s cargo deck into a makeshift skateboard park complete with ramps, jumps, and a half pipe made from an old section of ship's funnel.

Max said, "Going back to Cape Town will cost us the five hours we've steamed so far, another couple messing around in port, and a further five to return to this exact same spot of ocean."

"Or we keep going and send a team in from Namibia. Tiny's got the jump plane waiting at the airport in Swakopmund and will have one of our jets there by tomorrow afternoon for when we have Geoffrey Merrick. We can chopper them directly to the airport, Tiny can fly them up to the Congo, and be back in time for the raid."

"I can't get the Chairman on his sat phone," Hali told the group.

"Did you try the radio on the lifeboat?"

"Nada."

"Damn." Unlike Cabrillo, who could think through a dozen scenarios at a time and intuitively pick the right one, Hanley was more deliberative. "How much time do you think we'd save for the search team by turning back right now?"

"About twelve hours."

"Less," Mark said without turning from his computer screen. "I'm checking flights right now between Cape Town and Kinshasa. There isn't much."

"So we'd have to charter a plane."

"That's what I'm checking," Eric Stone said. "I'm finding only one company in Cape Town with jet aircraft. Hold on. No, there's a note on their website saying both their Learjets are grounded." He looked over at his shipmates. "If it's any consolation they do apologize for the inconvenience."

"So we're looking at saving maybe eight hours," Mark concluded.

"And costing us twelve and pushing back the rescue attempt by another full day. Okay, there's our answer then. We keep heading north." Max focused on Hali. "Keep trying Juan. Call him every five minutes and let me know the instant you reach him."

"Aye, Mr. Hanley."

Max didn't like that Juan wasn't replying. Knowing how close they were to launching their attack on the Devil's Oasis there was no way he wouldn't be carrying his sat phone. The chairman was a stickler about communications.

There were a hundred possibilities why he couldn't be reached and Hanley didn't like any of them.

16

CABRILLO squinted into the distance, not caring for how dark clouds were building to the east. When he and Sloane had motored out of Walvis in the lifeboat there hadn't been any weather advisories, but that didn't mean much in this part of the world. A sandstorm could whip up in a matter of minutes and blot the sky from horizon to horizon. Which was exactly what looked like was happening.

He glanced at his watch. Sunset was still hours away. But at least Tony Reardon's plane from Namibia's capital, Windhoek, to Nairobi and on to London had left the ground four minutes ago.

The night before they had intercepted the *Pinguin* a mile from the harbor entrance. After explaining what had happened to Papa Heinrick, Justus Ulenga agreed to take his boat north to another town and fish up there for a week or two. Cabrillo took Tony Reardon onto the lifeboat.

The British executive had complained bitterly about the situation, railing against Sloane, Cabrillo, DeBeers, Namibia, and anything else that came into his head. Juan gave him twenty minutes to vent while they waited offshore. When it seemed he would go on for hours more Cabrillo gave him an ultimatum: Either shut up or he'd knock him unconscious.

"You wouldn't dare!" the Englishman had shouted.

"Mr. Reardon, I haven't slept in twenty-four hours," Juan replied, moving closer so their faces were inches apart. "I just saw the body of a man who was horribly tortured before being murdered and I was shot at about fifty times. To top it off I have the beginning of a headache, so you will go below, sit on one of the benches, and keep your damned mouth shut."

"You can't ord—"

Juan pulled the punch at the last second so he didn't break Reardon's nose but the blow had enough power to send him crashing through the hatch to the lifeboat's passenger compartment, where he sprawled on the floor in an untidy heap. "I warned you," Cabrillo said and turned his attention back to keeping the craft facing into the wind as they waited for dawn.

They stayed a couple miles offshore as the Walvis fishing fleet paraded out for their daily catch and only turned to enter the port after Juan had made arrangements over his satellite phone. Reardon remained below, massaging his swelling jaw and even more bruised ego.

A taxi was waiting at the wharf when Cabrillo eased the lifeboat into a berth. He made sure that Sloane and Tony stayed below while he presented his passport to a customs official. Without the need for a visa and with a cursory inspection of the lifeboat and the Britons' already stamped passports, Juan's own passport was stamped and they were free to leave the docks.

He paid to have the boat's fuel tanks refilled, giving the attendant a large enough tip to ensure he did the job properly. He retrieved the Glock from where he'd stashed it in the bilges and made sure nothing looked suspicious before calling over the car and bundling his two companions into the rear seat.

They crossed the Swakop River and raced through Swakopmund on their way to the airport. Being that one of the gunmen from the previous night was the helicopter charter pilot, Cabrillo couldn't take the risk of hiring a private aircraft to spirit Reardon out of the country. But today was one of the four days a week that Air Namibia had a flight from the coastal city to the capital. He'd timed their arrival in town so Reardon would spend only a couple of minutes at the airport before his flight, and his connection to Nairobi was the next flight out of Kenya.

Juan noted a twin-engine plane sitting idle on the tarmac well away from other aircraft. It was the one Tiny Gunderson, the Corporation's chief pilot, had rented for their assault. If everything went according to plan the big Swede was en route with their Gulfstream IV. Juan had considered waiting and using their own plane to get Reardon out of Namibia, but he didn't think he could spend that much time in the man's company.

The three entered the small terminal together, Cabrillo's senses tuned to any detail that seemed out of place, though their opposition should still be assuming that their quarry was already dead. While the Englishman checked in for his flight, Sloane promised that she would pack up his belongings still at the hotel and bring them back to London with her once she and Cabrillo finished their investigation.

Reardon muttered something unintelligible.

She knew he was beyond reasoning with and honestly couldn't blame him. Tony went through security without a backward glance and was quickly gone from their view.

"*Bon voyage*, Mr. Chuckles," Juan quipped and the two of them left the airport and rode back to town.

They went straight for the neighborhood where Sloan's guide, Tuamanguluka, lived. Even in broad daylight Juan was thankful to have the automatic stuffed into the waist of his pants and hidden by the tails of his shirt. The buildings were mostly two-story and lacked the Germanic influence found in the better parts of town. What little pavement remained was potholed and faded almost white. Even at this early hour men loitered in the entrances of apartment blocks. The few children on the streets watched them with haunted eyes. The air was laden with the smell of processed fish and the omnipresent dust of the Namib Desert.

"I'm not exactly sure which building he lived in," Sloane confessed. "We used to drop him in front of a bar."

"Who are you looking for?" the cabbie asked.

"He goes by the name Luka. He's a sort of guide."

The taxi stopped in front of a decrepit building that housed a hole in the wall restaurant and a used clothing store on the first floor and, judging by the laundry billowing out the windows, had apartments on the second. After a beat, a scrawny man stepped from the restaurant and leaned into the cab. The two Namibians exchanged a few words and the man pointed up the street.

"He says Luka lives two blocks that way."

A minute later they stopped in front of another building, this one more run-down than most. The clapboard siding was bleached and split and the building's sole door hung from a hinge. A mangy dog lifted his leg against the corner of the structure then took off after a rat that had emerged from a crack in the foundation. From inside they could hear a child wailing like a siren.

Cabrillo opened the taxi door and stepped onto the sidewalk. Sloane slid across the seat and emerged from his door, not wanting to be separated from him by even the width of a car.

"You'll wait here," Cabrillo told the cabbie and handed him a hundred dollar bill, making sure he saw the other two in his hand.

"No problem."

"How will we know which apartment's his?" Sloane asked.

"Don't worry, if we're right, we'll know."

Cabrillo led her into the apartment building. The interior was dim but the heat remained oppressive and the smells were nauseating—the stink of poverty that was the same the world over. There were four apartments on the first floor; one of them housed the crying child. Juan paused outside each door for a moment to inspect the cheap locks. Without comment, he took the stairs to the second floor.

At the landing he heard what he'd most feared, the incessant buzz of flies. The drone rose and fell like a tuneless song. The smell hit a second later, something that carried above the background stench. It was an odor he'd know on a primordial level even if he'd never smelled it before. It was as if the human brain could discern the decomposition of one of its own kind.

His ears and nose led him to a back apartment. The door was closed and the lock didn't look damaged. "He let his killer in, which means he knew him."

"The pilot?"

"Probably."

Juan kicked the door. The wood around the handle was so brittle that it shattered. The flies hummed angrily at being disturbed and the smell was thick enough to coat the back of their throats. Sloane gagged but refused to shy away.

The room was filled with pale light diffused by the grime covering the only window. There was little furniture—a chair, a table, a single bed, and a packing crate used as a night table. The overflowing ashtray on top of it was made from a car's hubcap. The walls had been whitewashed thirty years before decades of smoke had turned them a murky brown and they were spotted with dark stains from innumerable insects being slapped against the plaster.

Luka lay on an unmade bed wearing a pair of dingy boxer shorts and unlaced boots. His chest was soaked in blood.

Quashing his own distaste, Juan inspected the wound. "Small caliber, twenty-two or twenty-five, and at close range. I can see powder burns." He looked at the floorboards between the bed and the door. Drops of blood formed an easily recognizable trail. "His killer knocked at the door and fired as soon as Luka answered it, then pushed him back on the bed so the body wouldn't make any sound when it fell."

"Do you think anyone in this building would care if they heard it?"

"Probably not, but our guy was careful. I bet if we'd stuck around and inspected the bow runner last night we would have found a pistol with a silencer."

Juan checked every inch of the apartment, looking for anything that might give him an insight into what was behind the murder. He found a stash of marijuana under the kitchen sink and some dirty magazines under the bed but that was about it. There was nothing hidden in the few boxes of food, and nothing in the trash can but rancid cigarette butts and Styrofoam coffee cups. He patted down the clothes lying on the floor next to the bed and turned up a few local coins, an empty wallet, and a pocketknife. The clothing hanging from nails on one wall was empty. He tried raising the window but it was painted shut.

"At least we confirmed he's dead," he remarked grimly as they headed out of the apartment. He closed the door behind them. Before leaving the floor Cabrillo took a detour to lift the tank lid on the communal toilet at the end of the hall, just to be thorough.

"What now?"

"I suppose we could check out the chopper pilot's office," Juan said with little enthusiasm. He was confident that the South African had covered his tracks well and they'd find nothing.

"What I'd really like to do is go back to my hotel, take the longest bath in history, and sleep for twenty-four hours."

Juan was at the top of the stairs and saw the light coming in through the wrecked front door flicker for a second as if something or someone had just entered the building. He pushed Sloane back a pace and drew the Glock.

How could I be so stupid, he thought. *They must have figured out something went wrong with their attack on the* Pinguin *and on their murder of Papa Heinrick*. Anyone investigating what was going on would certainly show up at Luka's apartment eventually, so they staked it out.

A pair of men came into view, both carrying wicked little machine pistols. They were immediately followed by a third also carrying a Czech-made Skorpion. Juan knew he'd get one with the first shot but he'd never get the other two without the stairway turning into a slaughterhouse.

He backpedaled silently, keeping a hand on Sloane's wrist. She must have felt the tension in his grip because she didn't speak and made sure her footfalls were as quiet as possible.

The hallway was a dead end and in about five seconds the assassins would have them trapped. Juan turned and made for Luka's apartment once again. He crashed through the door. "Don't think about it," he said. "Just follow me."

He ran for the window and dove headlong into the glass. The pane exploded around him, daggers ripping at his clothes. Just outside Luka's apartment was a corrugated metal shed roof he'd noted when he first tried to open the window. He crashed onto it, smearing the skin of his palms and nearly losing the Glock. The steel was scalding hot and his flesh burned. As he slid he rolled himself over onto his back; when he reached the edge he kicked his legs over his head and did a tight backflip. His landing wouldn't earn any Olympic medals, but he managed to stay on his feet as shards of glass cascaded off the roof like icicles.

He paid no attention to the old man mending a fishing net in the shade of the roof. A moment later he heard Sloane scrabbling across the metal. Her body was launched off the edge and Juan was ready to catch her. The impact drove him to his knees.

At the same instant dime-sized holes were punched through the roof, the sound of a machine pistol shattered the malaise of the street. Bits of hemp were thrown into the air as the big net absorbed a dozen rounds. The fisherman was well back from the roof's edge so Juan didn't have to worry about him. He took Sloane's hand and together they raced to their left to what looked like a busier street.

When they broke out from under the porch bullets stitched the ground all around them. The Skorpion was designed for close-in work and the gunman was too hopped on adrenaline to tame the notoriously inaccurate weapon. Juan and Sloane found temporary cover behind a ten-wheeled truck.

"Are you okay?" he panted.

"Yeah, just sorry for you that I've been eating like a pig since I arrived here."

Cabrillo chanced a peek around the back of the MANN truck. One of the gunmen was inching his way down the roof, covered by his comrades crowding Luka's apartment window. They spotted Juan and raked the truck with autofire. He and Sloane raced toward the cab. The tall cargo box hid them from the window, allowing Juan to step from the front tire onto the long hood and then onto the cab. He had his pistol ready and took the shot before the gunmen upstairs could see him in this unexpected position. The range was only twenty-five yards and Juan compensated for the difference in height. The bullet slammed into the gunman on the roof, tearing a chunk out of his right hand. The Skorpion went flying as he lost his grip on both it and the corrugated sheeting. He tumbled down the roof, slamming into the ground hard enough for his breaking bones to be heard across the street.

Juan ducked out of sight before the other assassins could pinpoint his location.

"What now?" Sloane asked, wide-eyed.

"One of them will stay in the window to make sure we don't make a break for it while the other takes the stairs down." Juan looked around.

While this was never a busy part of town, the road was utterly deserted now and in a way looked like it hadn't been occupied for years. Trash fluttered in the gutters and he expected to see tumbleweeds blowing by at any second.

He wrenched open the truck's passenger door and saw the keys weren't in the ignition. Franklin Lincoln could hot-wire it in under a minute but

Juan wasn't as skilled. The gunman would be on them long before he got the diesel fired. He took another quick look up at the apartment. The assassin was well back from the window frame but maintained an uninterrupted view of the truck.

"Think, damn it, think."

The building next to them had once been a grocery store but its windows were shuttered with sheets of plywood. Up the block was an open park with dirt rather than grass while behind them were more apartments and small single-family homes that seemed to lean on one another to stay upright.

He rapped a knuckle against the truck's exposed fuel tank. It rang hollow: almost, but not quite, empty. He unscrewed the filler cap and saw waves of diesel fumes rise in the hot air.

There were a few things Juan carried with him at all times: a small compass, a pocketknife, a tiny flashlight with a xenon bulb, and a Zippo lighter that would remain lit once the flint wheel was turned. He used the knife to cut a strip from the bottom of his shirt and lit it with the Zippo. He moved Sloane toward the front of the truck and dropped the burning rag into the tank.

"Step onto the bumper but stay low and keep your mouth open," he warned and made certain Sloane plugged her ears.

Had the tank been full the explosion would have blown the truck apart. As it was, when the rag ignited the puddle of fuel pooled in the bottom of the tank the detonation was more powerful than Juan anticipated. And even though he was protected from its effects by the cab, and more important, the engine block, he could still feel its searing heat. The truck rocked on its suspension as if struck by a cannon, and Juan's head rang as if he'd been hit with a hammer.

He jumped back to the ground and looked at what he'd accomplished. As he'd hoped the explosion had shredded the plywood protecting the supermarket's windows and blown the glass halfway down the denuded aisles. "Come on, Sloane."

Hand-in-hand they fled into the dark interior of the grocery store while outside the truck burned. At the back of the store was a door leading to a storage area and loading docks. Juan turned on his penlight and spied an exterior door. He assumed that the assassins knew where they'd gone, so he didn't bother being stealthy. Cabrillo blew the lock off the chain securing the door with his pistol. The chain rattled to the concrete floor and he shoved the door open.

Across the street from the rear of the grocery store was the wharf where they'd docked the lifeboat. It looked right at home tied up amid the broken-down fishing boats and sagging docks. Running flat out they crossed the road and raced along the maze of interconnected jetties while behind them one of the gunmen emerged from the back of the grocery store and continued the pursuit.

Fishermen working on their boats and kids casting lines off the dock were still looking at the smoke rising over the abandoned grocery store as Sloane and Juan ran by. The wooden docks were slick with mold and fish slime, but they pushed their pace even harder.

The buzz-saw screech of a Skorpion on full automatic raked the air. Juan and Sloane both fell flat, sliding across the slippery wood and falling off the dock and into a small skiff with an outboard motor mounted to its transom. Juan recovered in an instant but stayed low as wood splinters and lead danced along the edge of the dock.

"Start the engine," he ordered Sloane, and peered over the edge of the jetty. The gunman was fifteen yards away but would need to walk at least fifty to reach the outboard because of the peculiar layout of the piers. He tried to fire when he saw the top of Cabrillo's head, but the machine pistol was empty.

Sloane yanked on the starter cord and to their relief the engine fired on the second pull. Juan cut the painter and Sloane torqued the throttle. The little boat raced away from the dock and across to where the lifeboat waited. The assassin must have realized his targets were escaping and that he was too exposed to keep after them. Namibia still had a police force, and after the past few minutes of gunplay every cop in Walvis and Swakopmund would be descending on the harbor. He threw his gun into the water to hide any evidence and ran back the way he'd come.

The prow of the little outboard kissed the side of the lifeboat. Juan held their craft steady while Sloane climbed aboard. He followed her onto his own boat, reached over, and gunned the outboard's throttle, sending the little boat arrowing back across the marina.

He had the lines cast off and the engine fired in record time. In minutes they had cleared the outer buoy and were racing into open water. He kept a straight course to get them into international waters as quickly as possible in case Harbor Patrol came after them, not that they could catch them once Juan engaged the hydrofoils and the boat lifted from the sea.

"How are you doing?" Juan asked when he had the boat in trim.

"My ears are still ringing," she said. "That was about the most insane thing I've ever seen anyone do."

"Crazier than helping a woman being pursued by God knows how many assassins?" he teased.

"Okay, second craziest." Her mouth turned upward into a smile. "So are you going to tell me who you really are?"

"I'll make you a deal. Once we check out the area where Papa Heinrick saw his metal snakes and determine for ourselves what's going on, I'll tell you my whole life story."

"You're on."

They soon crossed Namibia's twelve-mile territorial border, according to the boat's GPS and Juan throttled down the engine to take the hydrofoil off plane.

"This old girl drinks fuel at an awful rate when she's up on her wings," he explained. "If we're going to make it out and back we have to keep her to about fifteen knots. I'll stand the first watch, why don't you head below? I can't offer you a bath but we have plenty of water to freshen up and you can get some sleep. I'll wake you in six hours."

She lightly brushed her lips against his cheek. "Thank you. For everything."

TWELVE hours later, they were approaching the region where the metal snakes reportedly lurked. The wind was picking up as a storm swept across the desert and slammed into the moist, cold air above the ocean. Cabrillo wasn't concerned about weathering a storm in the lifeboat. What bothered him was a reduction in visibility making their search that much more difficult. And to top it off, static electricity building in the atmosphere was playing havoc on the craft's electronics. He couldn't get a tone on his sat phone and the radio received nothing but static across all the bands. And the last time he checked the GPS it wasn't receiving enough signals from the orbiting satellites to properly fix their position. The depth meter was reading zero feet, which was impossible, and even the compass was acting up, slowly revolving in its liquid gimbals as though magnetic north was swirling all around them.

"How bad do you think it's going to get?" Sloane asked, jerking her chin in the direction of the storm.

"Hard to tell. It doesn't look like any rain is falling, but that could change."

Cabrillo settled a pair of binoculars to his eyes and slowly scanned the horizon, timing his movements with the slow undulation of the waves so he had maximum height as he scouted each direction. "Nothing but empty water," he reported. "I hate to say this but without the GPS I can't set up a proper search grid, so we're just blundering around out here."

"What do you want to do?"

"The wind's holding steady from due east. I can use it to keep my bearings so we can hold a course. I guess we can search until it gets dark. Hopefully the storm will blow over by dawn and the GPS will come back online."

By rough estimate, Juan piloted the lifeboat in mile-wide lanes, tracking back and forth across the vast ocean like he was mowing a lawn. The seas built steadily as they searched, so the waves were topping seven feet while the wind freshened, carrying the taste of the desert so far from land.

With each lane searched both became more convinced that everyone had been right about crazy old Papa Heinrick and that his metal snakes were nothing more than a raging bout of the DTs.

When Cabrillo saw a glint of white in the distance he dismissed it as the spume riding atop a wave. But he kept his eye on the spot and when they crested another swell, the speck was still there. He snatched the binoculars from their holder. His sudden movements after so many monotonous hours grabbed Sloane's attention.

"What is it?"

"I'm not sure. Maybe nothing."

He waited until another surge bore the lifeboat up the face of a wave before putting the glass on the distant glimmer. It took him long seconds to fully comprehend what he was seeing. The scope of it defied belief.

"I will be damned," he muttered, drawing out each word.

"What?" Sloane cried excitedly.

He handed her the binoculars. "Look for yourself."

As she adjusted the eyepieces to fit to her smaller face, Juan kept an eye on the object. He was trying to judge scale and found it next to impossible. With nothing to compare it to it could easily be a thousand feet long. He wondered how George Adams could have missed it during his aerial reconnaissance of the area.

Then from the white object came an intense burst of light that flashed against the scudding clouds. The range was two kilometers, perhaps a little more, but at a thousand miles per hour the Israeli-made Rafael Spike-MR antitank missile ate the distance so fast it gave Juan just seconds to react.

"Incoming!" he roared.

17

JUAN'S Glock was still secured at the small of his back, so he grabbed the satellite phone in its waterproof bag and tackled Sloane around the waist, throwing them bodily over the rail and into the dark water. They began to swim frantically from the lifeboat, trying to put as much distance between themselves and the impending explosion.

The rocket's dual electro-optic and infrared seeker stayed homed in on its target as it streaked across the sea, arrowing in on the plume of scorching exhaust from the lifeboat's engine. It slammed into the hull moments after being launched, punching a hole through the side and detonating just fore of the engine block. Designed to core through a foot of armor, the shaped charge sliced the keel, breaking the lifeboat's back as debris was blown thirty feet into the air.

The smoking, smoldering ruin folded almost in half as she sank, a gout of steam erupting when the sea made contact with the red-hot engine and manifolds.

The overpressure wave was magnitudes greater than when Cabrillo blew up the truck's tank back at Walvis Bay and had he not tossed himself and Sloane off the boat they would have been crushed by its force. They floundered in the chaotic waves radiating from the blast site, spitting and sputtering water that they had inadvertently swallowed.

Bicycling his feet to stay afloat, he reached for her to make sure she wasn't injured.

"Don't ask me if I'm okay," she managed to say. "You've already asked me that a dozen times since yesterday."

"It has been an exciting twenty-four hours," Juan admitted, toeing off his shoes. "We have to get as far away from the boat as possible. They will almost certainly send someone out to investigate."

"We headed where I think we're headed?"

"Time to catch a ride on Papa Heinrick's snake."

Though swimming a mile wasn't a difficult feat for two people in shape, battling the waves that crashed into them hampered every movement. It grew more difficult when a white luxury yacht identical to the one that had chased the *Pinguin* nosed its way into their area, the cyclopean eye of a searchlight cutting through the gathering dusk. It was the boat that had first caught Juan's eye, but it was what that boat had been tied to that commanded his attention.

"Must have gotten a buy-one-get-one deal on those babies," Juan said.

"Only BOGOs I get are at the supermarket for potato chips," Sloane quipped back.

After fifteen minutes of them swimming around to avoid the searchlight's powerful beam, the big yacht roared off into the darkness, giving Juan a bearing on which way to head, not that he thought he could miss their target.

The cool water had begun to sap their strength. To make their job easier, Juan handed his Glock and the satellite phone to Sloane and shucked off his pants. He tied the legs closed at the cuffs and held the open waist into the wind so the pants filled with air. He quickly cinched them closed with the belt. He traded the makeshift flotation device to Sloane for his gun and phone. "Just make sure you keep one hand on the waistband so it doesn't leak air."

"I've heard about doing that but I've never seen it done."

Sloane's teeth hadn't begun to chatter but he could hear the strain in her voice. Juan said, "It was a lot easier practicing in a swimming pool."

Now wasn't the time to tell her that the maneuver had saved his life on more than one occasion.

Buoyed by the air-filled pants Sloane swam much more strongly. And as they got closer to their destination, its massive size was acting like a damper for the waves.

"Do you feel that?" Sloane asked.

"What?"

"The water, it's warmer."

For a moment Juan was afraid that Sloane's body was no longer fighting the cold but rather succumbing to its icy tentacles. But then he felt it, too. The water was warmer and not just a degree or two but as much as ten or fifteen. He wondered if an active geothermal vent was causing such a temperature increase. Could that also explain the massive structure floating atop the waves? Did it somehow harness its power?

What Papa Heinrick had called a metal snake was in fact a dull green pipe that Juan judged to be at least thirty feet in diameter with all but the top six submerged. The pipe wasn't solid, however; it flexed along its length with each wave that passed under it. He judged his earlier estimate that the structure was a thousand feet long to be accurate.

The water was nearly eighty degrees when they finally reached the pipe. Juan placed his hand against the metal and felt it was warm to the touch. He could also feel the vibration of machinery from within the structure, massive pistons sawing back and forth with each thrust of the sea.

They swam along its flank, keeping enough distance so a wave wouldn't smash them into it, and found one of the hinge points after a couple hundred feet. The sound of machinery was louder as the mechanism converted the action of the waves into potential energy of some kind. Rungs were welded to the side of the pipe to allow workers access to the massive hinge. Juan had Sloane climb up first. She had his pants deflated and untied by the time he joined her.

She gasped. There was just enough light for her to see that below his knee his right leg was a prosthesis. "I'm sorry, that was rude," she whispered. "I had no idea. You don't limp or anything."

"Gotten used to it over the years," Juan replied, tapping the titanium strut that acted as his shin. "Parting shot from the Chinese Navy a few years back."

"I *have* to hear your life story."

Juan thrust aside thoughts about how George Adams could have missed the pipe when he reconnoitered the area from the *Oregon*'s chopper. Instead, he steeled himself to the practicalities of their situation. He and Sloane were vulnerable as long as the men remained on the yacht tied up on the far end of the structure. There was no other option.

He slipped into his pants and found an access hatch on top of the pipe. He opened it and saw there was a second hatch below. They'd explore later. He wedged the bag containing the satellite phone in the space between the two doors and locked the outer hatch closed.

He took Sloane's hand so she would look him in the eye. "I can't afford to take prisoners because I don't know how long we're going to be stuck out here. Do you understand?"

"Yes."

"You can stay here if you want, but I'm not ordering you to."

"I'll come with you and see how I feel when we get closer."

"Honest enough. Let's go."

For the first five hundred feet they could walk in a crouch to keep from being seen from the yacht, but as they got closer Juan ordered Sloane flat, and together they crawled across the undulating pipe, clutching at its smooth surface whenever a particularly large wave caused it to snap like a whip.

Juan, who'd never suffered seasickness in his life, found the odd lurching motion nauseating. Sloane, too, looked a little worse for wear.

Fifty feet from the yacht, he had them slither forward so the crest of the pipe hid them from the boat until they were just a dozen or so feet away. They could see the yacht clearly where it was tied to a dock that itself was secured to the side of a pipe segment. Heavy duty rubber fenders flexed and creaked to keep everything separated. Lights blazed from the yacht's windows while up on the bridge a lookout was silhouetted against the green glow of a radar monitor. They could see a tripod-mounted rocket launcher secured to the long foredeck.

Had the Corporation been running this operation Juan would have fired the entire crew for poor light discipline. The yacht could be seen from a mile away and an observer in a small boat could easily hide from the radar in the back clutter of the storm.

Though he was forced to admit they had gotten a damned good bead on him and Sloane when they approached.

They clung to the side of the pipe for nearly an hour, their bodies able to withstand their wet clothes and the cold wind because of the warm metal. Juan determined there were four men aboard the yacht and that they took turns monitoring the radar display on the bridge. For a while they took to carrying weapons with them, still hyped up after blowing apart the *Oregon*'s lifeboat, but soon boredom dulled their vigilance and Juan could see they no longer had their machine pistols slung across their shoulders.

With nothing but the element of surprise to overcome the four-to-one odds, Juan knew his best approach was stealth and then overwhelming savagery.

"I'd better do this alone," he told Sloane and slowly eased himself over the top of the pipe.

The hard-edged timbre in his voice made her shudder.

Cabrillo slid across the pipe and dropped nimbly to the floating dock, all the while never taking his eyes off the bridge watch stander who was distracting himself by peering into the storm through a pair of night vision goggles. He padded across the dock and lightly stepped over the gunwale and onto the yacht's aft deck. A sliding glass door led into the cabin while a set of stairs integrated into the boat's fiberglass shell rose up to the bridge.

The door was tightly sealed against the wind.

Juan crouched low as he took the steps, twisting his head horizontal when he reached the top so only a sliver of his face could be seen from the bridge. The watch stander was still looking out at the sea. Moving so slowly that he appeared to be standing still Juan inched up the rest of the way. A pistol was sitting on the dash, less than a foot from the man, who Juan noted had him by a good three inches and thirty pounds. The size difference meant strangling him silently was out of the question. He'd fight like a bull.

Cabrillo crossed the ten feet separating them when a strong gust hit the boat. The man was just reaching up to remove the goggles from around his head when Juan yanked his jaw with one hand and used the power of his shoulder to slam his forearm into the side of his skull. The paired forces torqued his spinal column past the breaking point and vertebrae separated with a discreet crack. He laid the corpse gently onto the deck.

"Three to one," he mouthed silently, feeling nothing for the killing because two hours earlier they had blown his boat out of the water without warning.

He eased himself over the side of the bridge to a narrow catwalk that allowed access to the long forward deck from the aft section of the yacht. There were windows to his right and left. One was dark while the flicker of a television from the second cast an electric hue. He snuck a quick glance into the area where the TV was playing. One of the guards was sitting on a leather sofa watching a martial arts DVD while another stood in the dimly lit kitchenette tending a teapot on one of the gas burners. He had a pistol in a shoulder holster. Juan couldn't tell if the other man was carrying.

He could tell from their placement in the room that he wouldn't have a clear shot at either of them from the aft deck, and he had no idea where the fourth guard was. Presumably he was asleep, but Juan knew how easily presuming could get you killed.

Cabrillo leaned back over the polished aluminum railing to give himself a little room on the narrow walkway and opened fire. He put two rounds into the guy at the stove, the impact lifting his body up onto the lit burners. His shirt caught fire instantly.

The guard on the couch had reflexes like a cat. By the time Juan swiveled the barrel and triggered off two more rounds he was off the couch and rolling across the plush carpet. The bullets tore through the sofa and blew wads of ticking into the air.

Juan adjusted his aim, but the guard had found cover behind a wet bar set against the far wall. He didn't have enough ammunition to blast away randomly and was already angry at himself for the two bullets he wasted on the couch. When the second guard emerged from behind the bar he had his machine pistol ready and triggered off half a magazine in an uncontrolled burst.

Cabrillo dove flat as glass shattered and bullets screamed above him. The spray of rounds ricocheted off the massive steel pipe behind him, zinging harmlessly into the night. He scrambled aft and fought the natural urge to roll off the boat and onto the dock. Instead he gripped a stanchion that supported a retractable awning and whipped his body around it so that he was on the stairs again. He climbed as quickly as he could and leaned over the railing above the shattered window.

The stubby barrel of the guard's machine pistol appeared, tracking back and forth as he sought his prey. When he couldn't see Cabrillo's body lying dead on the catwalk, his head and upper back emerged. He looked fore and aft and when he still didn't see Cabrillo he leaned out further so he could look down on the dock.

"Wrong direction, pal."

The guard twisted his shoulders, trying to raise the Skorpion. Juan stopped him with one round through the temple. The machine pistol dropped into the gap between the boat and the dock.

The Glock's sharp report gave his position away to the final guard. The bridge floor erupted with ragged holes as the gunman below sprayed the cabin ceiling.

Juan tried to throw himself onto the dash but staggered when a bullet blew his artificial foot in half. The kinetic force of the impact, plus his own momentum, vaulted him over the low windscreen and he rolled down the sloping wall of glass that fronted the lower cabin spaces.

His back slammed into the foredeck, forcing the air from his lungs in an explosive whoosh. He levered himself onto his knees, but when he tried to stand the mechanisms that controlled his foot refused to respond. His state-of-the-art prosthesis was now no more than a wooden peg leg.

Inside one of the yacht's beautifully appointed cabins he could see the fourth gunman silhouetted against the raging fire burning in the main salon. The propane line that fed the stove had burned through and a roaring jet of liquid fire blasted upward, spreading flames across the ceiling from corner to corner. Molten plastic dripped onto the carpet, starting numerous smaller blazes.

The guard had heard Juan's tumble over the roar of the inferno. He shifted his aim from his cabin's ceiling to the main window and stitched the safety glass with bullets. A dozen crazed spiderwebs appeared in the wide pane and chips rained down on Cabrillo like fistfuls of diamonds.

Juan waited a beat and started to rise in order to fire back, and as he did the guard burst through the weakened glass, slamming into his chest and knocking him flat once again. He managed to wrap an arm around the man's leg as they tumbled across the deck. The guard ended up on top of Cabrillo but couldn't maneuver his machine pistol for a shot. He had Juan's gun hand pinned. The guard tried to smash his forehead against Juan's nose but Cabrillo ducked his chin at the last second and their skulls collided hard enough to make Juan's eyelids flutter.

The guard then tried to ram his knee into Cabrillo's groin. He deflected the blow by twisting his lower body and absorbing the impact on his thigh. When the guard tried it again, Juan wedged a knee between the two of them and thrust upward with every ounce of his strength. He managed to lift the man off of him momentarily, but the guard was just as strong and tried to crush Cabrillo as he came back down.

Juan had managed to lever his prosthetic limb up just enough so the dagger-sharp remains of his carbon fiber foot sliced into the taut muscles of his opponent's abdomen. Juan grabbed his attacker's shoulders, drawing the guard toward him at the same time he kicked hard with the leg.

The sensation of the artificial limb sinking into the guard's stomach would haunt the chairman's nightmares for years to come. Juan pushed the guard aside as his screams gave way to wet gurgles, and finally silence.

He staggered to his feet. The back half of the yacht was engulfed in fire, flames torn almost horizontal by the powerful wind. There was no way to battle the conflagration so Juan stepped to the side of the boat. He eased over the railing and lowered himself to the deck. He knelt and quickly rinsed his prosthesis in the sea.

"Sloane," he shouted into the night. "You can come out now."

Her face emerged over the top of the immense pipe, a pale oval against the dark night. Slowly, she rose from a crouch and came toward him. Juan hobbled across the deck to meet her. They were two feet apart when he saw her eyes go wide. Her mouth began to open but Juan had already anticipated her warning. He whirled, his damaged leg kicking out from under him on the slick dock yet still he raised the Glock as a fifth guard appeared on the yacht's foredeck, carrying a pistol in one hand and a briefcase in the other. He was also a second faster than Cabrillo.

His weapon cracked once as Juan continued to lose his balance, falling as if in slow motion. Juan triggered off two rounds as his backside connected with the dock. The first missed but the second impacted center mass. The guard's gun flew from his lifeless fingers and the case clattered onto the floating pier.

He turned to look at Sloane.

She was on her knees, her hand pressed into her underarm. Her face was a mask of silent agony.

Juan slithered to her side.

"Hold on, Sloane, hold on," he soothed. "Let me see."

He gently raised her arm, causing her to suck air through her teeth. Tears leaked from her eyes. Her blood was hot and slick as Juan felt for the wound and when he accidentally touched the torn flesh Sloane cried out.

"Sorry."

He pulled her blouse away from her skin, wedged his fingers into the rent torn by the bullet, and ripped the fabric apart so he could see the entry point. He used a flap of cloth to softly wipe away some of the blood. The light from the burning yacht was wavering and erratic but he could see that the bullet had gouged a two-inch trench along the rib cage under her arm.

He looked into her eyes. "You're going to be okay. I don't think it penetrated. It just grazed you."

"It hurts, Juan, oh sweet God, it hurts."

He held her awkwardly, mindful of her wound. "I know it does. I know."

"I bet you do," she said, stifling her pain. "I'm crying like baby over this when you had a leg shot off by the Chinese Navy."

"According to Max, when the shock finally wore off I sounded like a whole nursery full of colicky infants. Wait here for a second."

"Not like I'm going to go for a swim or anything."

Juan went back to the yacht. The fire was too advanced for him to recover anything from the cabins but he managed to strip the guard he hadn't expected of a sports coat. The fact that he was wearing a thousand-dollar Armani blazer told him this guy wasn't a guard but was most likely the head of this operation. A suspicion confirmed when the briefcase turned out to be a laptop computer.

"If it was important enough to save," Juan said, holding up the ThinkPad when he returned to Sloane's side, "it's important enough to retrieve. We have to put some distance between us and that boat. When its twin exploded against the side of the *Oregon* she made one hell of a fireworks show."

It was almost as if they needed each other to move, Juan with his damaged prosthesis and Sloan with her wounded chest, but somehow they managed to stagger back to where Juan had stashed the satellite phone. He laid Slone down onto the warm metal pipe and sat next to her so she could rest her head on his thigh. He covered her with the sports coat and stroked her hair until her body overcame the pain and she slipped into unconsciousness.

Cabrillo opened the laptop and began to scan the files. It took him an hour to figure out what the thousand-foot-long machine did and another to discover that there were thirty-nine more just like it nearby arranged in four long rows. Although he still had no idea as to its purpose, dawn was an hour away when he finally figured out how to shut it down by plugging the laptop into a service portal under the access hatch where he'd hidden the phone.

When the indicator light on the slim monitor showed that the machine was no longer generating electricity even though its mechanisms were still responding to the action of the waves passing down its length Juan checked his sat phone. He got a signal immediately.

It was the massive electrical field created by the wave-driven generator and its clones that had played havoc with the electronics on the lifeboat, knocked out the phone, and made the compass needle spin out of control. With the generators off-line the field collapsed, and his telephone worked fine. He assumed the laptop had been hardened against the powerful EM pulses.

He dialed a number and the phone on the other end was picked up after the fourth ring.

"This is the front desk, Mr. Hanley. You wanted a four-thirty wake-up call."

"Juan? Juan!"

"Hiya, Max."

"Where the hell are you? We couldn't reach you on the lifeboat. You wouldn't pick up your phone. Even your transdermal locator wasn't broadcasting."

"We will wait for your signal," Mafana said and shook Cabrillo's hand. "Tonight you will help save a nation."

The African rebels jogged back to their vehicles a quarter mile distant. The sound of their engine's firing came a few moments later. Juan double-checked the knots as he waited and leaned back slightly in preparation for the jolt.

To his credit, the driver of the tow vehicle went easy on the acceleration. The two thousand feet of nylon line they'd cobbled together came taut as the truck inched forward. Cabrillo leaned back even further when the rope tied around his chest began to pull. The plastic insert he'd used to para-ski across the desert started hissing over the sand as the tow truck picked up speed. The parachute pulled clear of the dirt that had been piled on it and when they reached ten miles per hour air began to fill the foil. It shot off the desert floor and yanked at Cabrillo's risers but they weren't going fast enough to generate the lift needed to get him airborne.

Because the line was so long, Juan knew if he fell now the driver would never see he was down. He'd be dragged across the ground until he could somehow untie the rope. To keep his balance he had to bend deeply as the truck continued to accelerate, the tension on his risers increasing by the second.

Juan juked left to avoid a rock, almost hit another, and nearly fell backward when the plate skidded out from under him. He lifted both legs from the ground to get the ski back under him, relying on the partially inflated chute to give him a second's reprieve. His actions nearly collapsed it, but he managed to stay on his feet and find his center of balance once again.

The truck hit twenty miles per hour, then twenty-five. Juan's legs and knees were burning and then suddenly he felt nothing. He was airborne.

Enough air was flowing across the air foil to overcome his weight and the weight of his gear. The truck continued to pick up speed and Juan sailed ever higher. Soon the altimeter strapped to his wrist read nineteen hundred feet. The ride was exhilarating.

"Parachuting, para-skiing, para-sailing." He laughed. "All in a day's work."

He used his pocket knife to cut away the ropes binding the plate he'd used to ski on his artificial leg. He wished he could have kept the olive-drab piece of plastic as a souvenir but he had no choice if he wanted to make a safe landing.

There was enough slack and give to the rope that his ride was relatively smooth, although not as steady had he been behind a boat where the sport of para-sailing had become popular at resorts all over the globe. The truck down below him would occasionally dip into a valley, jerking Juan like a kite at the end of a string, but it wasn't too bad.

It was up to Cabrillo to decide when he'd detach himself from the tow line. Behind him the first molten blush of the coming dawn spread like cobalt-hued ink. He knew from their combat briefing on the *Oregon* that sunrise was in fifteen minutes. But as colors spread across the desert he could just make out the blockhouse design of the Devil's Oasis about a mile away. Without another thought, he untied the rope connected to a D ring on his combat harness. The line whipped out of his hands as the chute rose another hundred or more feet, no longer tethered to the truck.

One of Mafana's men would be watching for it to tumble out of the sky and the convoy would come to a halt before it could be spotted by a sentry at the prison. The men had scant minutes to get into position.

Juan heaved down on the toggles to give himself the maximum amount of time aloft as the wind carried him toward the old penitentiary. It wasn't the first occasion tonight that luck remained on his side. Provided the wind held, he had more than enough height to glide to the prison's roof.

If anything, the breeze freshened, bearing him along like a leaf. He worked the toggles, changing direction slightly to keep the prison centered between his dangling boots. The sky was still a deep indigo when he crossed over the top of the Devil's Oasis and no alarms had been sounded. He spilled air from the chute in a controlled descent and touched down so lightly that it felt as if he'd just taken the last step of a flight of stairs.

Turning, he quickly bundled the chute into his arms to keep it from blowing into the prison's inner courtyard. He shucked off the harness and the backpack of rocket shells and temporarily used them as dead weight to keep the chute in check. He hefted the MP-5 and did a fast reconnoiter of the parapet. He noted where his team had earlier secured lines to descend into the prison. The ropes had been cut away, but the eyebolts were still drilled into the thick wooden roof. Peering over the outside wall he saw that the sand had been scratched up and he recognized the trails where the bikes had been ridden off. Two of them looped around toward the main gate while the third, Linc's, vanished into the wasteland. There was another set of tracks, a truck's, judging by their size, that disappeared into the east.

After tying his parachute to one of the eyebolts, Cabrillo quickly designated his targets and found the best vantage point for his attack. He had seven rockets for the RPG-7 and four targets, but he figured that after so many years a couple of the projectiles would be duds. Still, he liked his odds.

He called the *Oregon*. Though Hali Kasim was the ship's communications director, Linda Ross was coordinating the assault. She answered the call before the first ring had ended. "Linda's house of pleasure and pain," she said by way of greeting.

"Put me down for some of the former," Juan whispered. "I'm in."

"We expected nothing less. Of course, I've seen seventy-year-old grandmothers para-sailing at Cabo, so I'm not all that impressed." Her light tone vanished. "Tiny took off about fifteen minutes ago. He'll stay out of range until fifteen minutes after sunup. After that you should be able to talk to Linc over your tactical net."

There was no need for Cabrillo to further compromise his location by speaking so he said nothing.

"Just want to say good luck," Linda added, "and get our boys out of there. *Oregon* out."

Juan clicked off the phone and settled it in its hard case at his hip.

The three guards lazing by the front gate suddenly came, if not to attention, at least a bit more alert as a door opened directly under where Juan was perched. Ringed by stone crenellations like a medieval castle, Juan had ample cover as he watched a lone figure cross the courtyard, a flashlight clutched in his hand. He spoke to one of the guards for a moment, then retreated the way he'd come.

The full glare of the sun struck Juan's back as it finally climbed over the horizon. Despite the long shadows he could see three wooden stakes had been driven into the ground against the wall to the left of the main gate. Before light could bathe the enclosed quad Juan plucked his little buck knife from his pocket and with an easy toss threw it toward the execution stakes. It landed and skidded right up against the middle post. It had been the grandfather who'd given him that first knife who'd also taught him horseshoes.

As Juan readied the rocket launcher, men began to trickle onto the parade ground, in ones and twos at first, but soon there were dozens streaming in. He could tell by body language and how they horsed around that the soldiers were eager for the execution. He estimated there were about a hundred. And unfortunately, more than half of them had kept their weapons with them. The buzz of conversation and rough laughter drifted up from below until another door was slammed open.

Juan had to crane his neck to see a pair of escorts leading Eddie, Mike, and Ski from within the prison. He felt a squeeze of pride in his chest. His crew walked with their shoulders back and heads high, and had their hands not been bound behind their backs he knew their arms would be swinging in step. They were going to their deaths as men.

He clicked on his machine pistol's laser sight.

EDDIE Seng had seen more than a few executions while under deep cover in China and while those had been carried out with quiet efficiency, the guard commander here was turning this into a show for his men, inspired no doubt by some movie he'd seen on how such things were done.

If he hadn't been the one trussed up and about to face the firing squad he would have chuckled at the absurdity.

He was a brave man, braver than most, but he also didn't want to die, not like this—powerless. His thoughts turned to his family. Although his parents had been dead for a couple of years, there were dozens of aunts and uncles in New York, and more cousins than he could count. None of them knew what he did for a living nor would any ask on his infrequent trips home. They simply welcomed him into the fold for as long as he stayed, plied him with more food than he could possibly eat, and made sure he met the children born since his last visit.

He would miss them more than he realized. But they wouldn't know he was gone, not until Juan showed up with a seven- or eight-digit check, the value of Eddie's share of the Corporation. No matter what the chairman said to explain how Eddie had amassed such a fortune, he knew they wouldn't believe him. They were simple, hardworking people and would assume Eddie had been into something illegal. The check would be thrown away and his name would never be mentioned again.

Eddie clenched his jaw a little tighter and blinked tears from his eyes for bringing his family shame.

He didn't pay attention to the tiny speck of light flickering at the base of Ski's neck until his subconscious mind realized the random pattern wasn't random at all. It was Morse code.

"—au Geste has your back." Eddie willed himself not to look around as they neared the execution ground. The chairman was here, using a laser, probably the sight from his gun, to send him a message. The crafty son of a bitch was going to get them out.

"RPG B 4 U tied. Knife base centr pol."

Eddie understood that Cabrillo was going to use a rocket-propelled-grenade attack to cover them and that there was a knife lying on the ground at the base of the center pole, the one they would likely tie him to since he was sandwiched between Mike and Ski. The plan was brilliant because with guards getting ready to tie them to the stakes their comrades would be less likely to open fire on them.

"Chairman's here," Seng told his comrades over the din of jeering soldiers flanking their route. There was no need to say more. They would react to whatever Cabrillo did and adapt to the changing circumstances accordingly. Ski's only acknowledgment that he'd heard was a slight nod.

"About damn time," Mike said and a guard slammed the heel of his hand into the back of his head.

A couple of soldiers spat at the prisoners as they passed or tried to trip them up. Eddie barely noticed. He was focusing on how he would get the knife and mentally ran through the moves he would have to make in order to slice through Ski's plastic ties.

The phalanx of soldiers opened up as they neared the wooden stakes. Three guards stood behind the poles with lengths of rope to tie them. One of the men leading the parade happened to be looking down when they reached the stakes. He spotted the knife and before anyone else could jump in and take it he snatched it from the ground and jammed it in the pocket of his fatigues.

When he turned to face the condemned he startled at the murderous look Eddie was giving him.

Biggest mistake of your life, pal, Eddie thought and modified his attack plan.

CABRILLO waited with only the corner of his face exposed to the men below, not that any of them were looking anywhere other than at the prisoners. His hand was on the RPG-7's pistol grip and it would take only a second to swing the weapon onto his shoulder and fire.

The guard commandant stepped through the throng of cheering soldiers, waving and returning casual salutes. He had provided them with some unexpected entertainment and wanted to bask in the glow. He stood in front of his prisoners and held his arms aloft to silence the rowdy crowd.

Juan hoped he could personally take the man down, but in combat there were few guarantees.

The commander started speaking in an African language, his deep voice booming off the confining wall of the parade ground. The men listened and occasionally cheered when he said something particularly inciting.

Cabrillo could imagine what he was saying. Captured three CIA spies, blah, blah, blah. Long live the revolution, etc. etc. etc. Aren't I the greatest officer you've ever had, yada, yada, yada.

Get on with it already.

The commandant finished his ten-minute speech, turned, and nodded to the three men positioned to tie the captives.

Juan twisted around the stone block he was hiding behind and brought the RPG up. As soon as he had one of the doors leading back inside the prison in the rocket launcher's crude sight he squeezed the trigger and was in motion the instant the missile cleared the tube. The rocket ignited, singing the back of his hand as he raced to where he'd cached the next projectile.

Trailed by a line of white vapor, the five-pound warhead shot across the courtyard and exploded just above the door leading to the former prison's barracks. The explosion of the shaped charge blew apart the lintel and caused the wall above to partially collapse. Loose rock tumbled across the opening until it was completely blocked.

*   *   *

THE instant Eddie heard the whoosh of the rocket motor igniting he spun around and kicked the guard set to tie him in the side of the head hard enough to send him flying back a half dozen feet. He then stepped to the soldier who'd found the pocketknife. Eddie got one foot behind the man's legs and continued forward. Though the guard had him by a few inches, Eddie still had the element of surprise and had no trouble tripping him.

They crashed to the ground at the moment the missile detonated against the prison wall. With his hands bound behind him, Eddie used the momentum of the fall to slam his chin into the guard's throat with enough force to crush his larynx. With his airway closed the soldier began to gag and thrash, clawing at his throat as if he could open it again.

Eddie rolled off him and reached for his pocket, but couldn't get a hand inside because of the soldier's spastic dance. He could feel the outline of Cabrillo's little pocket knife through the fatigues and in a fit of concentration and strength he tore the knife free, coming away with a handful of cloth.

A second RPG arced across the open patch of sky above the courtyard and while Eddie wasn't paying attention to where it hit, he suspected the chairman was systematically sealing off all entrances into the prison proper. He worked the knife open. Ski obviously figured what was up because he was on the ground less than a foot away with his back toward Eddie. Seng rolled over to him so they were back-to-back and cut the plastic tie binding the big Pole's hands.

Ski took the knife and sliced through Eddie's tie. So as not to waste even a fraction of a second Seng rolled away from Ski, knowing the ex-Marine would free Mike Trono. Now able to fight with his hands, Eddie procured an AK-47 from one of the confused guards with a strike to the back of his head. Unlike when he'd knocked Susan Donleavy unconscious, he didn't hold back. The soldier was dead before his body crumpled into the dirt.

He whirled and saw a guard aiming at where Ski was cutting through Mike's flex cuffs. Eddie put him down with a double tap that sent him sprawling into several of his comrades. The sound of his shots had been overwhelmed by the volley of autofire now being directed along the prison ramparts. Twenty guns or more were blasting away at the jagged stone crenellations, wreathing the low wall with a cloud of stone chips and dust. Eddie raced toward his teammates, covering them with his assault rifle until they could find cover under one of the trucks parked in the courtyard.

WITH soldiers blasting away along the east and west walls, Cabrillo stayed low and circled the prison. He loaded another round into the RPG as he ran. He came up hard against the wall opposite the last door that led into the prison. So far none of the guards had recognized his strategy of locking them inside the parade ground, but all it took was one sharp officer to understand what was happening and order men back inside. He knew their first job would be to execute Moses Ndebele. His whole plan hinged on every guard being outside to witness the execution and him being able to prevent them from retreating.

He popped up between two stone blocks and fired, ducking back as a dozen automatic weapons backtracked the RPG's contrail and peppered his cover position. The air was alive with grit and shattered bullet fragments. The rocket motor didn't burn evenly, causing the missile to shoot skyward in a complete misfire. He slithered out of the worst of the fusillade and crawled thirty feet, pausing to let the undisciplined fire die down. He slipped the MP-5 over the wall and triggered off half a clip, aiming across to the second floor so as not to accidentally hit his men down below.

In response, the guards redoubled their counterfire, raking the stone as if sheer volume of rounds would bore through the rock. Juan ignored the scream and whine of bullets passing inches over his head and calmly reloaded the RPG. He crawled farther along the roof, coming to the point where he would need to fire at the most oblique possible angle and still hit the last remaining door, but he was at least fifty feet from where the guards were still hammering with their AKs.

The distance he'd covered would buy him perhaps a second before he was spotted again. Then he thought of a better strategy and rolled away from the wall lining the courtyard. He backed from the edge until when he got to his knees he couldn't see the men down on the ground. And more important, they couldn't see him. He shuffled forward a couple of inches and could see a little farther into the prison, a little farther down the far wall. He took another couple of tentative steps on his knees.

There! He could just make out the Roman-like arch above the distant door but couldn't see any of the guards milling around.

Cabrillo brought the RPG to his shoulder, aimed carefully, and touched the trigger.

What he couldn't see and couldn't know was that a sergeant of the guards had recognized Juan's tactic and was leading a small squad to the door when the rocket streaked across the courtyard. One of the soldiers was directly under the door's arch when the shaped charge slammed into the wall. As the explosion blew chunks of rock across the parade ground and cut the squad apart, the concussion from the blast shattered every bone in the lead soldier's body before he was crushed under an avalanche of debris.

Juan rushed forward so he could see the results of his attack. Though badly damaged, he could still see the dark confines of the prison through the ruined doorway. There were gaps in the rubble large enough for a man to crawl through. He spied a soldier making a break for the door. Cabrillo tripped his machine pistol's laser sight and when the tiny speck of light appeared between the guard's shoulders he fired one-handed, forgetting the weapon was on full auto. It didn't matter that his second, third, and fourth rounds went wild. The first one drilled the guard exactly where he'd aimed. He crashed into the pile of loose stones and lay still.

Cabrillo reloaded the rocket launcher a fifth time, taking a new position to better center the door. A solid sheet of lead rose from the angered soldiers and seemed to fill the sky where he'd been standing moments earlier. He inched forward again so he could see the crown of the door opening and fired off his next round, ducking when he knew the shot to be true. He loaded the Russian antique yet again, hearing the sound of an avalanche over the frenzied fire. When he peeked over the wall he saw the doorway was now a mountain of jumbled stone blocks obscured by a cloud of dust.

The guards could no longer enter the prison proper. It was time to call in the cavalry.

DOWN in the courtyard the commanding officer screamed at the top of his lungs to get his men's attention. The ambush had set them off like berserkers and, apart from the one sergeant who'd realized the attack was meant to trap them on the parade ground, the men seemed blithely unaware that they were standing in a potential killing field. At any moment he expected gunners on the roof to open up and cut down his command like lambs at the slaughter.

He singled out three of the smallest of his men, slender youths who had a chance to slither through the destroyed doorways and execute Moses Ndebele before the assault force could spirit him away. He also directed some men to open the prison's main gate, but to do so carefully in case there were more troops waiting outside. With so many weapons firing it was impossible to hear if any of the perimeter alarms had been tripped.

He grunted in satisfaction when he saw one of his officers attempting to erect a long piece of pipe against the eaves so men could scale it and gain access to the roof. As soon as the top of the pipe touched in a notch between two of the stone crenellations, a soldier with an AK-47 slung across his back and no shoes on his feet shimmied up the rusted piece of steel with the agility of a spider.

EDDIE Seng saw the soldier climbing the length of pipe too late. He had scant seconds to aim before the man reached the top of the wall and vanished. With his vantage limited by the truck's undercarriage, he flipped onto his back to get a better view, raising the assault rifle's barrel so he had an approximate shot. He was within a hair's breath of pulling the trigger when the man disappeared and angrily moved his finger away. There was no sense in firing and giving away their position. Juan would have to deal with this new threat on his own. Eddie slid deeper into the shadow cast by the truck. Mike laid a hand on his shoulder, a reassuring gesture meant to tell him there was nothing he could have done.

It did little good.

CABRILLO was hunched over the RPG, loading his second-to-last round. All he had to do was blow the main gates open and Mafana and his men would charge into the prison, freeing him to find Ndebele and Geoffrey Merrick. He clicked the round home and stood.

The sun was still low on the horizon and the shadows it cast were elongated to the point that it was impossible to tell what cast them. The shadow that suddenly emerged next to where he stood hadn't been there a second ago. Juan whirled and just had time to see one of the guards standing with his back to the courtyard when the man's AK opened up, its muzzle flash like a strobe light aimed into his eyes.

Juan dove left, hit the wooden roof with his shoulder, and before the guard could adjust to the fact his quarry had avoided the ambush, he had the RPG tucked against his flank. He pulled the trigger, aiming by instinct rather than sight.

The rocket leapt from the barrel in a cloud of stinging gas. The guard's body didn't provide enough resistance to set off the explosive head when it slammed into his chest, but the kinetic energy of a five-pound projectile traveling at a thousand feet per second did more than enough damage. With his ribs crushed back against his spine the guard was flung off the roof like a limp doll. He landed amid a throng of his comrades thirty feet from the wall where he'd been standing, and this time the force of the impact was enough to detonate the shaped charge. The explosion tore through flesh and bone, leaving a smoking crater rimmed with the dead and injured.

Juan had just one last round for the RPG and if it failed so would the assault. He fitted it hastily, rushed forward to get a bead on the thick slabs of wood that protected the main entrance into the prison, and fired, dimly aware that there were a cluster of men about to open the doors.

The rocket ran true and hit the gate dead center, but the projectile failed to detonate. The guards who'd dropped flat when the missile flashed over their heads got to their feet slowly, nervous laughter turning into cheers when they realized they'd been spared.

Seeing what happened, Cabrillo flipped his machine pistol off his back. As soon as the laser sight speared out in the area around the embedded rocket he opened fire. Splinters erupted from the door as the hot-loaded 9-mm rounds chewed into the wood. Just before the magazine ran dry a bullet struck the dormant projectile. The resulting explosion scythed down the men who'd been celebrating their good fortune moments earlier and blew the door apart in a shower of smoldering boards.

Just beyond the sensor range of the perimeter alarms, four trucks idled, their occupants all battle-hardened veterans of one of Africa's bloodiest civil wars and all ready to lay down their lives for the one man they thought could pull their nation back from the brink of ruin.

22

"LAWRENCE of Arabia calling Beau Geste. Come in, Beau."
So exhausted by the past forty-eight hours—and especially the past twelve—Cabrillo had forgotten all about the tactical radio he was wearing and for a moment thought he was hearing voices. Then he remembered that Lawrence of Arabia was Linc's call sign.

"Damn, Larry," Juan radioed back. "Am I glad to hear you."

"Just saw an explosion at the main gates and looks like our new allies are sweeping in."

"Affirmative. What's your position?"

"We're about three miles out at five thousand feet. Eagle-eye Gunderson saw the blast. Are you ready for us to land yet?"

"That's a negative," Cabrillo replied. "I still have to secure our passengers and we need to make sure Mafana's men can keep the guards bottled up long enough for you to come in."

"No problem, we'll keep circling," Linc said, then added with humor in his deep baritone, "Danger pays by the hour, anyway."

Juan slammed a fresh magazine into the receiver of his MP-5 and racked the bolt to chamber a round. Before anyone else tried to outflank him by climbing onto the roof he dashed to where his parachute billowed over the outside wall of the prison, one end held fast by one of the eyebolts his men had installed earlier—when this was supposed to have been a simple clandestine hostage rescue from a bunch of long-haired ecoterrorists.

The battle in the courtyard now sounded like World War Three as the Zimbabweans fought each other in such close quarters that their assault rifles were used as clubs as much as guns.

Clutching the fabric of the chute, Juan slipped over the edge of the roof so his feet dangled three stories above the desert floor. He lowered himself slowly and carefully. The nylon was as slick as silk. When he reached the end of the writhing mass of parachute cloth he was still a good three feet above the window opening. He planted his boots against the wall, tucked his knees against his chest, and kicked off as hard as he could.

His body pendulumed away from the prison for nearly ten feet before gravity took hold of him and sent him careening back toward the building. It felt like his knees would explode when he slammed into the rough stone, but the experiment told him he could make the attempt, but his timing would have to be perfect.

Again he flexed his legs and launched himself into space, his grip on the chute like iron. When he reached the apex of his swing, he focused on nothing but the dark opening that gave entry into the prison. He started arcing down, building up speed, and more importantly angular momentum. Like a stone released from a sling, Juan let go when his feet were pointed at the window.

He flew through the window, clearing the bottom sill by inches and smashed onto the floor, rolling until he came up hard against the iron railing that overlooked the floors below. The sound of his body slamming into the loose railing echoed in the cavernous cell block.

He groaned as he got to his feet, knowing that in a couple of hours his back was going to be zebra-striped with evenly spaced purple bruises.

Feeling no need to be stealthy in this block of cells after such a loud entrance, Cabrillo rushed down the stairs. He already knew from Eddie's reports to Linc that this particular section of the prison was empty. On the ground floor he paused at the open door, checking the hallway in both directions, thankful that the generator was still powering the lights. When he started off to the right he took the precaution of smashing the exposed bulbs as he went. He had no intention of leaving the prison the way he had come in and he didn't want to make it any easier for a guard who managed to enter through the blown-up doorways.

He peered around a corner, saw a chair outside a large door, exactly how Eddie had described the scene where they were holding Merrick. Although their original mission had been to rescue the scientist, Cabrillo's first obligation now rested with getting Moses Ndebele to safety. He trotted past the door, imagining that Merrick's kidnappers were holed up inside, not knowing how to react to the unfolding situation.

The prison never really shed the heat it absorbed during the torturous days, and now that the dawn had arrived the passageway was growing hotter. Sweat ran from Cabrillo's pores as he jogged. He was halfway down the long hall when motion ahead caught his eye. Two slightly built guards ran toward him from the opposite direction. They were much closer to the entrance to the next cell block than Cabrillo, and their presence told him that this was where they were holding their prize prisoner.

Juan dove flat, his elbows scraping against the stone floor as he aimed his machine pistol. He fired a wild spray that forced the soldiers back the way they'd come and around another bend.

They must have climbed through the debris piled outside the doors, he thought absently and tried to ignore the fact he was too exposed and outgunned. He slithered back to where the hallway was much darker and rolled to the opposite wall to confuse them. He fired every time one of the guards tried to check the hallway, filling the air with the stench of burned gunpowder. The area around the Chairman was littered with stumpy brass shell casings.

He slid across the hall again a moment before one of the soldiers laid down a blistering barrage of cover fire. Bits of stone and hot copper bullets seemed to fill the corridor. Juan tried to suppress the burst of autofire with a return volley, but the guard hung tough and continued to shoot.

His partner dashed from around the corner to add his gun. While neither of them could see Cabrillo in the darkened passage, the chance of a lucky shot doubled. The first guard broke from his position and raced for the entrance to the cell block. Either the door hadn't been locked or he'd shot away the mechanism because he disappeared inside before Juan could take him down.

Cabrillo had seconds before the guard assassinated Moses Ndebele. In what must have seemed like reckless rage, he launched himself from the floor and out of the murky shadows. His gun spit flame as he ran, firing from the hip. The beam from his laser sight was a ruby line cutting through the smoke. It finally settled on the guard's torso; the next three rounds hit center mass and tossed him off his feet.

Cabrillo kept sprinting. Rather than slow to enter through the open door to the cell block, he careened off the stout jamb, absorbing the blow on his shoulder with barely a check in speed.

A line of cells was directly in front of him, each enclosure fronted by iron bars. They all appeared empty. For all he knew Ndebele could be on the second or third floor and the guard had too much of a head start to find him. Then, over the sounds of his ragged breathing and hammering heart, he heard voices coming from behind the cells. The voice was melodious, soothing, not the plaintive cries of the condemned, but rather the fatherly understanding of a priest granting absolution.

He raced around the corner. The guard was just outside of one of the cells while a man wearing a filthy prison uniform stood next to the bars, not two feet away from the soldier aiming at his head with an AK-47. Moses Ndebele stood calmly, with his arms at his side as if he weren't facing his executioner but rather talking with a friend he hadn't seen in while.

Juan raised his gun to his shoulder, the laser never wavering from the guard's shiny forehead as the African turned at the sound of Cabrillo coming to a halt thirty feet away. The soldier started to draw down on his weapon in order to engage but wouldn't have the time before Juan pulled the trigger. The bolt crashed against an empty chamber. The click of metal on metal was loud but at the same time nothing compared to what was supposed to happen.

The guard had his weapon aimed halfway between Juan and Moses Ndebele. He wasted a half second of thought between his sworn duty and the need to eliminate Cabrillo. He must have figured he could riddle the main rival of his nation's dictator and still gun down Juan before Cabrillo could reload the machine pistol or draw a handgun because he started to turn back toward Ndebele.

Juan let the Heckler & Koch drop from his hands and kicked his artificial limb up into his chest so he could wrap his hands around his calf, his knee braced against his shoulder as though he were holding a gun.

The barrel of the soldier's AK was just a couple of arc degrees from pointing at Ndebele when Juan's fingers found a button recessed into the touch plastic exterior of his combat leg. It was a safety device that allowed him to depress another button on the opposite side of the limb.

Integrated within the prosthesis was one more trick Kevin Nixon in the *Oregon*'s Magic Shop had devised—an eighteen-inch-long, nickel-pipe in .44-caliber. The dual triggers guaranteed the weapon would never discharge accidentally. When Juan hit the second one the single-shot gun went off with an explosion that shook dirt from the rafters and blew a nearly half-inch hole through the bottom of his boot.

The recoil sent him tumbling. He picked himself up quickly, yanking at his pants cuff so he could draw the Kel-Tec .380 automatic pistol. He needn't have bothered. The hollow-point .44-caliber slug had hit the guard in the right arm as he stood in profile to Cabrillo and transited his entire body through his chest cavity, shredding his internal organs. The exit wound in his opposite shoulder was the size of a dinner plate.

Moses Ndebele looked at Juan in stunned silence as the chairman rammed a fresh magazine into his machine pistol and returned the Kel-Tec to its hiding place inside his leg. There were blood splatters on his prison uniform and a trickle of crimson on one cheek. Juan noticed the burn marks on Ndebele's bare arms, the swelling around his eyes and mouth, and how he stood with all his weight on one leg. Juan looked down at Ndebele's bare feet. One was normal, the other was so swollen it resembled a football. He guessed every bone from ankle to toe had been broken.

"Mr. Ndebele, I am here with an army of your followers headed by a man named Mafana. We're getting you out of here."

The African leader shook his head. "The damned fool. I told him when they first imprisoned me not to try something like this, but I should have known he wouldn't listen. My old friend Mafana chooses the orders he wishes to obey."

Juan motioned him away from the cell door so he could shoot the lock open. Ndebele had to hop to keep his damaged foot from touching the ground. "I've got a friend named Max who pulls the same thing on me." Juan glanced up to catch Ndebele's eye. "And more often than not he's right about which ones to disregard."

He popped two rounds into the old iron lock and gave the door a heave. It slid open on protesting hinges. Ndebele made to hobble out of the cell but Juan held up a hand.

"We're going out another way."

When researching the Devil's Oasis, Linda Ross had come across the account of a prisoner who tried to widen the six-inch sewer holes inside the lower-tier cells. A prison trustee checked them every other day and when he found that the man had used a spoon or other implement to scrape away at the foot-thick stone in order to make the hole big enough to escape through he immediately reported it to the guards. They systematically crammed the prisoner down the small opening, breaking whatever bones necessary until only his head remained inside the cell.

No one else ever tried to escape that way again.

Juan handed the MP-5 to Ndebele asking him to cover them and sat next to the hole. He hurriedly took off his boot and retrieved the remainder of his cache of plastic explosives. He molded the plastique into a long strand that he affixed in a ring at the bottom of the hole. He plucked the detonator from behind his leg's ankle joint and set the timer for one minute, enough time to lead Ndebele safely away.

With his boot in hand he stuck the timer into the soft explosive and left the cell with Moses draped over his shoulder in order to protect the man's foot. The bomb went off like a volcano, sending a geyser of flame, smoke, and chunks of stone high enough to ricochet off the ceiling. Cabrillo had his boot back on, but didn't bother to lace it when he returned to the cell. As he'd anticipated, the charge had been more than enough for the job. The hole was now five feet wide, its jagged edges blackened by the blast.

He dropped through the opening, and helped Ndebele descend. The man sucked air through his teeth when his broken foot brushed against the ground under the prison.

"You okay?"

"I think maybe when the time comes I will ask you where you got your artificial leg. I don't think I will have this foot much longer."

"Don't worry, I know a pretty good doctor."

"He can't be that good if you lost your leg."

"Believe me, she is—she only started working for me after my original was blown off."

Together they struggled through the tunnel that allowed the constant desert winds to desiccate the human waste that once fell from above and eliminate the need for emptying slop buckets.

The confines were tight and they had to crawl on elbows and knees in the dirt. Juan led them to the eastern side of the prison, closest to the airstrip. Fortunately, the wind was at their backs so the blowing sand didn't scour their faces. It took five minutes to reach the perimeter of the building. The sunlight glaring through the opening was especially bright after the dim confines of the penitentiary. The two men lay side by side just short of the opening.

Cabrillo keyed his radio. "Beau Geste to Lawrence of Arabia. Can you hear me, Larry?"

"Five by five, Beau," Linc answered back. "What's your situation?"

"I have the native guest with me now. We've made it to the exterior wall. I'm looking at the airstrip. Give me fifteen minutes to secure the primary target and come pick us up. Our boys will know to make a break for it when they see the plane."

"Negative, Beau. From the looks of it our allies are taking a hell of a pounding in there. They won't last fifteen minutes. I'm coming in now."

"Then give me ten minutes."

"Chairman, I ain't foolin'. You don't have it. If we don't come in now there won't be enough of Mafana's men left to count on one finger. This wasn't a suicide operation. We owe it to them to cover their retreat." Even as Linc spoke, the big cargo plane arrowed out of the sky. "I've also just gotten word from Max that our situation has changed somewhat."

By landing now, Linc had forced Cabrillo's hand. Moses would never make it to the airstrip unaided. Juan would have to carry him. The plane was too vulnerable on the ground to wait for him to return to the prison and rescue Geoffrey Merrick. And as soon as Mafana and his men began their retreat from the prison, the guards would swarm after them in hot pursuit. Without aerial cover they would be slaughtered out on the open desert.

As for whatever change Max Hanley was talking about, Juan would have to trust that his second in command had a much better grasp of the overall operational picture.

The old de Havilland Caribou was an awkward-looking aircraft, with a rudder that was as tall as a three-story building and a cockpit hunched over a blunt nose. The high wings allowed for it to carry a large payload for its size and also to make incredibly short takeoff and landing runs. The particular aircraft Tiny Gunderson had rented was painted white, with a faded blue strip running the length of the fuselage.

Juan saw that his chief pilot had lined up on the runway for his final approach. It was time to go.

"Come on," he said to Moses Ndebele and crept out from their position under the prison. The sound of gunfire in the courtyard was muted by the building's thick walls, but it still sounded as though a thousand men were in a fight for their lives.

When both men were on their feet Juan transferred his H&K to his left hand and stooped to lift the African leader over his shoulder. Ndebele was a tall man, but years of imprisonment had shrunk him to little more than skin and bones. He couldn't have weighed more than a hundred and twenty pounds. Normally Cabrillo wouldn't have had a problem carrying such a burden, however, his body was exhausted by hours of unrelenting abuse.

Juan straightened his legs, his mouth a tight, grim line. Once he had Ndebele settled on his shoulder he took off in a loping gait. His boots sank into the sand as he jogged, taxing his quivering legs and aching back with every pace. He kept a wary eye on the side of the prison where the entrance doors were located but so far none of Mafana's men had tried to flee. They remained engaged with the guards, knowing that the longer they gutted it out the better chance their leader had of escaping.

The seventy-foot-long twin-engine cargo plane touched down when Cabrillo was halfway to the landing strip. Tiny reversed the pitch of the propellers and gunned the motors, kicking up a veritable sandstorm with the prop wash that completely obscured the aircraft. The maneuver cut the distance he needed to land to less than six hundred feet, leaving more than enough room to take off into the wind without backtracking to the end of the runway. Gunderson feathered the props so they no longer bit into the air but barely cut power to the 1,500-horsepower engines. The airframe shuddered with unreleased energy.

Motion to Juan's left caught his eye. He glanced over to see one of Mafana's trucks emerge from the prison. Men in the back continued to fire into the courtyard, while the driver raced for the plane. Moments later the other three trucks appeared. They weren't going anywhere near as fast. The rescuers were trying to further delay the guards from breaking out.

Juan turned his attention back to the Caribou. The cargo ramp was coming down, Franklin Lincoln standing at its very tip with an assault carbine in his hands. He waved Juan on but kept his attention focused on the approaching truck. There was another black man with him, one of Mafana's men whom Juan had sent to rendezvous with the plane the night before.

The ground under Cabrillo's feet firmed as he reached the gravel runway and he put on a burst of speed, adrenaline allowing him to ignore the pain for a few minutes more.

Juan reached the plane and lurched drunkenly up the ramp a few seconds before the lead truck braked just beyond the edge of the ramp. Doc Huxley was waiting with her medical cases. She'd strung saline drip bags to a wire running along the ceiling, the cannulas ready to replace any blood the fighters had lost. Juan laid Ndebele on one of the nylon mesh bench seats and turned to see what he could do to help.

Linc already had the truck's rear gate open. There were a dozen wounded men strewn on the floor and over the sound of the roaring engines Juan could hear their agony. Blood drizzled from the tailgate.

Lincoln lifted the first man out and carried him into the aircraft's hold. Ski was right behind him, lugging another of the wounded. Mike and Eddie carried a third between them, a great bear of a man with blood saturating his pants from the thighs down. Juan helped an ambulatory man step to the ground. He cradled his arm to his chest. It was Mafana, and his face was ashen, but when he saw Moses Ndebele sitting up against a bulkhead he cried out in joy. The two wounded men greeted each other as best they could.

Back at the prison, the remaining trucks from the original convoy took off into the desert, their wheels kicking up spiraling columns of dust.

Moments later, two other vehicles emerged. One of them started after the fleeing four-wheel drives while the second turned for the airstrip.

"Chairman," Linc shouted over the noise as he stepped onto the ramp carrying another of the injured. "Last one. Tell Tiny to get us out of here."

Juan waved in acknowledgment and threaded his way forward. Tiny was leaning out of his seat, and when he saw Cabrillo give him a thumbs-up he turned his attention back to the controls. He slowly changed the propellers' angle of attack and the big aircraft began to roll.

Cabrillo headed aft again. Julia was cutting away one man's bush jacket to expose a pair of bullet holes in his chest. The wounds bubbled. His lungs had been punctured. Undaunted by the unsanitary conditions or the bumpiness of the takeoff, she got to work on triage.

"Did you have to leave it to the last second?" Eddie asked when Juan approached. He was grinning.

Cabrillo shook his outstretched hand. "You know what a procrastinator I can be. You guys okay?"

"Couple more gray hairs, but none the worse. One of these days you're going to have to tell me how you rustled up an army in the middle of nowhere."

"Great magicians never divulge their secrets."

The plane continued to pick up speed and was soon outpacing the guards' truck. Through the open ramp Juan could see them fire off a few rounds in frustration before the driver braked hard and turned to give chase to the rest of Mafana's men. A third and then fourth truck roared out of the prison gate after them.

Tiny hauled back on the yoke and the old Caribou lifted off the rough field. The vibrations that had built until Juan was sure he'd lose a filling finally evened out. Mindful that the ramp would have to remain open, the patients were moved to the front of the aircraft, leaving the area at the rear open. Linc stood on the ramp, a safety line stretching from a D ring on the floor to the rear of his combat vest. He wore a helmet with a microphone so he could talk with Tiny in the cockpit. There was a long crate at his feet.

Juan clipped himself in, too, and cautiously approached the big SEAL. Hot wind whipped through the cabin as Tiny banked the plane to come in behind the guards' vehicles. With their newer trucks they had already eaten away half the lead Mafana's troops had managed to gain on them.

The trucks were approaching a deep valley between towering dunes when the plane hurtled over the two sets of vehicles. There was less than a half mile separating them. Tiny kept them at a thousand feet as he flew along the length of the valley, but in an instant the valley came to a sudden end. Rather than opening up again onto open desert, the valley was only three miles long, a dead end. Its head was a sloping dune so steep that the trucks would have to slow to a walking pace to reach the summit.

"Bring us around again," Linc shouted into his mike. "Come up behind them."

He motioned for Mike and Eddie to join them. The two men quickly got themselves secured, leaning over to maintain their balance as the plane banked around. Linc opened the crate. Inside were four of Mafana's RPGs. They were the reason Juan had sent one of Mafana's men to hook up with Linc.

Linc handed one of the rocket-propelled grenade launchers to each of them.

"This is going to have to be some pretty fancy shooting," Mike shouted dubiously. "Four trucks. Four RPGs. We're doing a hundred and twenty miles an hour and they must be close to fifty."

"Ye of little faith," Linc yelled back.

The plane evened out again at the entrance to the valley. Tiny took them lower, fighting updrafts of hot air lofting off the desert floor. The dunes flashed by no more than a hundred feet from the wing tips. Linc was listening to the pilot as he counted down how long it would be before they shot over the guards' convoy. When he lifted the RPG to his shoulder the other three did likewise.

He pointed at Juan and Ski. "Aim at the base of the dune to the left of the convoy. Mike and I will take the right. Drop the grenades about twenty yards in front of the lead vehicle."

Tiny took them lower still, and then gained elevation quickly when the plane came under fire from below. He steadied the Caribou just as they passed the last truck in line. For a fleeting second, Juan and the others were looking down at the convoy and it appeared that every gun the guards had was blazing away at them.

"Now!"

They triggered the RPGs simultaneously. The four rockets popped from their tubes and ignited, their white contrails corkscrewing through the clear air. The plane had overshot Mafana's trucks by the time the warheads slammed into the base of the dunes. The shaped charges went off in blinding eruptions of sand. And while they seemed puny compared to the massive scale of the dunes, the explosions had their desired effect.

The equilibrium of angle and height that held the dunes in place was thrown off by the blasts. A trickle of sand began to slide down each face, accelerating and growing until it looked like both sides of the canyon were racing for each other. And caught in the middle was the guards' convoy.

The twin landslides crashed onto the valley floor. The right-side avalanche had been going a bit faster than its partner so when it slammed into the convoy, the four vehicles were blown onto their sides. Men and weapons were tossed from the beds of the trucks only to be struck by the second wall of sand as it careened into them, burying everything under thirty or more feet of earth.

A cloud of dust was all that marked their grave.

Linc hit the button to close the ramp and all four men stepped back.

"What did I tell you?" Linc grinned at Mike. "Piece of cake."

"Lucky thing this valley was here," Mike retorted.

"Lucky, my butt. I saw it when I hightailed it out last night. Juan had Mafana's men drive here specifically so we could take out all the guards in one fell swoop."

"Pretty slick, Chairman," Trono conceded.

Juan didn't try to hide his self-satisfied smile. "That it was. That it was." He turned his attention back to Lincoln. "Does Max have everything set?"

"The *Oregon*'s tied to the dock in Swakopmund. Max will meet us at the airport with a flatbed truck carrying an empty shipping container. We load the wounded in and hop aboard ourselves. Max will then drive down to the wharf, where a Customs inspector with a pocket bulging with baksheesh will sign off on the bill of lading and we get hoisted onto the ship."

"And Mafana's men are going to drive through to Windhoek," Juan concluded, "where they can fly out to wherever we can find Ndebele a safe haven." His tone soured. "All well and good, except we didn't rescue

Geoffrey Merrick and have lost any chance to find him again. I'm sure his kidnappers left the Devil's Oasis five seconds after the guards."

"Ye of so little faith," Linc said for the second time with a sad shake of his head.

NINA Visser was sitting in the shade of a tarp anchored to the bed of their truck when she heard a buzzing sound. She had been writing in her journal, a habit she'd kept up since her early teens. She'd filled volumes of notebooks over the years, knowing someday it would be an important resource for her biographer. That she would be important enough to need a book written about her life was something she'd never doubted. She was going to be one of the great champions of the environmental movement, like Robert Hunter and Paul Watson, Greenpeace's cofounders.

Of course the current operation wouldn't be included. This was one blow she would strike from the shadows. She was only writing out of habit and knew she would have to destroy this journal and any others that mentioned her involvement with Dan Singer's scheme.

She closed the notebook and slid her pen into the spiral binding. Crawling out from under the tarp was like opening the door of an oven. The afternoon sun beat down mercilessly. She stood, dusted off the seat of her pants, and shielded her eyes from the sun, searching the sky for the plane Danny had promised. Even with dark sunglasses it took her a few seconds to spot the little jewel glinting in the sky. A couple of her friends crawled out from the tarp to join her, including Susan. They were all tired from the drive, and thirsty because they hadn't packed enough water.

Merrick was faring the worst since he was bound and gagged and left leaning against the side of the truck, where there was only a sliver of shadow. He hadn't gained consciousness since being injected with the heroin and his sunburned face was rimmed with dried sweat. Flies buzzed around his wound.

The plane made a pass of the dirt runway and everyone waved as it overshot them. The pilot wagged the aircraft's wings and circled back. It floated along the runway for a hundred feet before the pilot could finally get it down. He quickly throttled back and taxied to where the truck was parked on the edge of the field. The deserted town was a few hundred yards behind them, a clutch of crumbling buildings that the desert was slowly consuming.

A ramp at the rear of the aircraft slowly lowered, reminding Nina of a medieval drawbridge. A man she didn't recognize emerged and approached the group. "Nina?" he asked, yelling over the engines noise.

Nina stepped toward him. "I'm Nina Visser."

"Hi," he said in a friendly tone. "Dan Singer wanted me to tell you that the United States' government has a program called Echelon. With it they can listen to just about any electronic conversation in the world."

"So?"

"You should be more careful what you say over a satellite phone, 'cause someone was listening last night." Even as his words were sinking in, Cabrillo dropped his easy demeanor and whipped a pistol from behind his back, aiming it at Nina Visser's tall forehead. Three more men charged down the Caribou's ramp, led by Linc. Each was armed with an MP-5 machine pistol and they swept their guns from person to person. "Hope you guys like it out here," Juan continued. "We're on a rather tight schedule and don't have time to haul you in to the police."

One of the environmentalist fanatics shifted his weight to lean closer to their truck. Juan fired a bullet close enough to his foot to gouge the edge of his rubber-soled boot. "Think again."

Linc kept the environmentalists covered, clearing the way for Juan to cut Geoff Merrick free while the other two Corporation men bound each of the kidnappers with plastic flex cuffs. Merrick was unconscious and his shirt was caked with dried blood. Julia was aboard the *Oregon* tending to the wounded freedom fighters from Zimbabwe, but one of her orderlies had made the flight. Juan turned Merrick over to the medico and stepped back out into the sunlight carrying two jerry cans of water.

"If you ration this it should last a week or so." He tossed the cans into the back of the truck.

He searched the vehicle and found Nina's satellite phone in the glove compartment. He also came away with a couple of assault rifles and a pistol.

"Kids shouldn't play with guns," he said over his shoulder as he returned to the plane. Then he paused and came back to the group. "I almost forgot something."

He scanned their faces and spotted the person he wanted trying to hide behind a large bearded kid. Juan walked over and yanked Susan Donleavy's arm. The guy protecting her made to swing at Cabrillo's head. The effort was clumsy, and Juan easily ducked the blow, coming up with his nine millimeter pressed firmly between the collegian's startled eyes. "Care to try that again?"

The kid stepped back. Juan cinched Susan Donleavy's cuffs tight enough to let her know there was going to be worse to come, and frog-marched her to the plane. At the ramp he paused and addressed the two team members who were going to remain behind. They had manhandled a rubber bladder of fuel for the truck off the plane. "You know the drill?"

"We'll drive about thirty miles deeper into the desert and dump them."

"That way the plane Singer sent will never find them," Juan said. "Just don't forget to get the GPS coordinates so we can get them later."

"Then we drive back to Windhoek, stash the truck someplace, and get a hotel room."

"Check in with the ship as soon as you arrive," Juan said and shook their hands. "Maybe we can get you out before we go after the guns up north in the Congo."

Just as Cabrillo was about to disappear inside the Caribou with his prisoner, he shouted at the environmentalists, "See you in a week."

Linc trotted after him, and as soon as he was aboard Tiny gunned the engines. Ninety seconds after touching down they were aloft again, leaving behind eight slack-jawed, would-be ecoterrorists who never knew what hit them.

23

"WELCOME back, Chairman," Max Hanley said when Juan reached the top of the *Oregon*'s boarding ladder.

The two shook hands. "Good to be back," Cabrillo said, fighting to keep his eyes open. "The past twelve hours have been about the worst of my life." He turned to wave down at Justus Ulenga, the Namibian captain of the *Pinguin*, the boat Sloane Macintyre and Tony Reardon had been aboard when they had been chased. Juan had contracted the fisherman at Terrace Bay, where he'd been lying low following the attack on his boat.

The affable captain tipped his baseball cap back at Cabrillo, grinning broadly because of the thick sheaf of money he'd been paid for the simple job of ferrying Juan's party to where the freighter loitered just outside Namibia's twelve-mile limit. As soon as his boat had motored a good distance from the *Oregon*, the massive freighter began accelerating northward, ersatz smoke pouring from her single funnel.

Geoffrey Merrick had been hoisted onto the deck in a medical basket. Julia Huxley was already hunched over him, her lab coat dragging in a hardened pool of oil. Under it she wore blood-smeared scrubs. She'd been patching together wounded men since the first moment the container Max had used to transfer the soldiers to the ship had been opened. With her were two orderlies standing by to bring Merrick down to surgery, but she wanted to do an assessment as quickly as possible.

A blindfolded Susan Donleavy had been escorted to the ship's brig by Mike, Ski, and Eddie as soon as she'd set foot on the *Oregon*. It was plain to see that the fact that no one had said a word to her since Juan had nabbed her in the desert was wearing on her mind. Though not yet defeated, her façade was cracking.

"What do you think, Doc?" Juan asked when Julia pulled her stethoscope from Merrick's bare chest.

"Lungs are clear but his heartbeat's weak." She glanced at the saline drip bag one of her people was holding above Merrick's prone form. "That's the third unit of saline he's taken. I want to get some blood in him to get his pressure up before I go after the bullet that's still in the wound. I don't like that he's unconscious."

"Could it be the heroin they gave him back at the Devil's Oasis?"

"It should be out of his system by now. It's something else. He's also spiking a fever and the wound looks infected. I need to get him on antibiotics."

"What about the others? Moses Ndebele?"

Her eyes clouded over. "I lost two of them. I've got one more that's touch-and-go. The others were mainly flesh wounds. So long as no one shows an infection they should be fine. Moses is a bloody mess. The human foot has twenty-six bones. I counted fifty-eight separate pieces of bone on his X-ray before I gave up. If he's going to keep it we need to get him to an orthopedic specialist within a couple of days."

Cabrillo nodded, but said nothing.

"How are you doing?" Hux asked him.

"I feel worse than I look," Juan said with a tired smile.

"Then you must feel like crap, because you look like hell."

"Is that your official medical diagnosis?"

Julia pressed her palm to his forehead like a mother checking a child for a fever. "Yup." She motioned for her people to lift Merrick's stretcher and started for the nearest hatch. "I'll be below if you need me."

Cabrillo suddenly called out to her, having remembered something he couldn't believe he'd forgotten. "Julia, how's Sloane doing?"

"She's great. I kicked her out of medical, and then out of the guest cabin because I needed it as a recovery room. I even put her to work as a candy striper. She's bunking with Linda. She wanted to be up here to meet you but I ordered her to bed. We've had a busy few hours and she's still weak."

"Thanks," Juan said with relief as Julia and her team vanished into the ship.

Max sidled up next to him, his pipe emitting a fragrant blend of apple and cedar. "That was a hell of a premonition, getting me to contact Langston and tapping into Echelon."

One of Juan's first acts when he learned that Geoffrey Merrick's rescue had fallen apart was to get Max to lean on Overholt in order to utilize the NSA's Echelon program. At any given second there were hundreds of millions of electronic data transfers taking place over the globe: cell phones, regular phones, faxes, sat phones, radios, e-mails, and Web postings. There were acres of linked computers at the NSA's Fort Meade headquarters that trawled the bandwidths looking for specific phrases or words that might be of interest to American intelligence. Though not designed to be a real-time eavesdropping tool, with the right parameters programmed into the system—like a call originating at the Devil's Oasis' geographic location and containing such terms as *Merrick*, *Singer*, *hostage*, *rescue*, *Donleavy*—Echelon could find that needle in the cyber haystack. A transcript of Nina Visser's conversation to Daniel Singer was e-mailed to Max aboard the *Oregon* three minutes after the call had ended.

"I had a feeling that after our boys were caught whoever Singer had left in charge at the prison would want to let him know what was going on and get some new marching orders." Juan ground the heels of his hands into his eyes to try to relieve some of the fatigue. "They're a bunch of amateurs. They wouldn't have contingency plans in place."

"What did you do with the rest of the kidnappers?" Max asked. His pipe had gone out and there was too much of a breeze to relight it.

Juan started walking toward a hatchway, his mind already in his glass-enclosed shower with the heat cranked as high as he could stand it. Max kept pace. "Left them out there with enough water to last a week. I'll have Lang contact Interpol. They can coordinate with Namibian authorities to pick them up and return them to Switzerland to face kidnap charges, with a charge of attempted murder for Susan Donleavy."

"Why bring her back here? Why not let her rot with the rest of them?"

Cabrillo stopped walking and turned to his old friend. "Because the NSA couldn't pinpoint Singer's location and I know she has it and because this isn't over yet. Not by a long shot. Kidnapping Merrick was only the opening gambit to whatever his former partner has planned. She and I are going to have a nice long talk."

A moment later they reached Juan's cabin and kept talking as Juan stripped out of his filthy uniform and tossed the clothes in a hamper. He threw his boots into the trash but first poured out a quarter cup of sand that had entered the shoe through the .44 caliber bullet hole. "Good thing I couldn't feel that," he remarked casually. He unhooked his combat leg and set it aside, planning on giving it to the Magic Shop staff so they could reload the gun and clean the grit out of the mechanicals.

"Mark and Eric checked in about an hour ago," Max said. He sat on the edge of the copper Jacuzzi tub while Juan climbed though the banks of steam erupting from the shower. "They've covered about a thousand square miles, but there's still no sign of the guns or Samuel Makambo's Congolese Army of Revolution."

"What about the CIA?" Juan called over the sound of water beating against his skin. "Any of their assets in the Congo have a bead on Makambo?"

"Nothing. It's like the guy vanishes into thin air whenever he wants to."

"One guy can vanish. Not five or six hundred of his followers. How did Murph set up his search?"

"They started from the dock and have been flying wider and wider circles, overlapping the radio tag's range by about twenty miles just to be safe."

"The river is the border between the Republic of the Congo and the Democratic Republic of the Congo," Juan said. "Are they staying south of it?"

"Similarities to their names aside, relations between the two countries are a mess. They couldn't get permission to cross into the R of C, so yeah, they're staying south of the border."

"What do you bet Makambo took the weapons north?"

"It's possible," Max agreed. "If Congo's northern neighbors are shielding his army it could explain why he's never been caught."

"We've only got a few more hours until the tags run out of their batteries." Juan shut off the water and opened the door. He was clean but scantly refreshed. Max handed him a thick Brazilian cotton towel. "Call Mark and have him do whatever he has to in order to get across that border and take a listen. Those guns aren't more than a hundred and fifty miles from the river. I'm sure of it."

"I'll call him now," Max said and levered himself from his perch.

Juan kept his hair short enough so he didn't need to brush it. He put on deodorant and decided he looked more dangerous with thirty hours of beard so he left his straight razor on the bathroom counter. The dark circles under his eyes and their red rims gave him a demonic cast. He dressed in black cargo pants and a black T-shirt. He called down to the Magic Shop for a tech to get his combat leg and on the way to the ship's hold he stopped in to grab a sandwich from the galley.

Linda Ross was waiting outside the hold. She was holding a Black-Berry that was receiving signals from the shipboard Wi-Fi network.

"How's our guest?" Juan asked as he approached.

"Take a look yourself." She tilted the small device so he could see the screen. "Oh, and I want to congratulate you on pulling off the rescue."

"I had a lot of help."

Susan Donleavy was strapped to a stainless-steel embalmer's table in the center of the cavernous hold where Juan had packed his parachute the day before. The only light came from a single high-intensity halogen lamp that formed a focused cone around the table so she could see nothing beyond. The feed to the BlackBerry came from a camera placed just above the lamp.

Susan's hair was lank from so long in the desert without enough water for personal hygiene, and the skin on her arms was blotchy from insect bites. Blood had drained from her face, leaving her washed out, and her lower lip quivered. She was covered in sweat.

"If she wasn't tied down she would have bitten her fingernails to the quick," Linda said.

"You ready?" Juan asked her.

"Just going over some notes. I haven't done an interrogation in a while."

"Like Max always says, it's like falling off a bike. Do it once and you never forget."

"I hope to God he didn't put a sense of humor down on his job application." Linda thumbed off the BlackBerry. "Let's go."

Juan opened the door into the hold. A wall of heat blasted him. They'd set the thermostat for a hundred degrees. Like the lighting, the temperature was part of the interrogation technique Linda had settled on to crack Susan Donleavy. They stepped silently into the room, but remained just beyond the circle of light.

He had to give Susan high marks because she didn't call out for nearly a minute. "Who's there?" she asked, a manic edge in her voice.

Cabrillo and Ross remained silent.

"Who's there?" Susan repeated a bit more stridently. "You can't hold me like this. I have rights."

There was a fine line between panic and anger—the trick was to never cross it during an interrogation. Never let your subject turn their fear into rage. Linda timed it perfectly. She could see the fury building in Susan's face, the way the muscles in her neck tensed. She stepped into the light a moment before Donleavy started to scream. Her eyes went wide when she saw that it was another woman with her in the hold.

"Miss Donleavy, right from the outset I want you to understand you have no rights. You are aboard an Iranian-flagged ship in international waters. There is no one here to represent you in any way. You have two choices and two choices only. You can tell me what I want to know or I will turn you over to a professional interrogator."

"Who are you people? You were hired to rescue Geoffrey Merrick, right? Well, you've got him so turn me over to the police or whatever."

"We are taking the 'whatever' route," Linda said. "That includes you telling me where Daniel Singer is at this moment and what his plans are."

"I don't know where he is," Susan said quickly.

Too quickly, Linda noticed. She shook her head as though she were disappointed. "I had hoped you would be more cooperative. Mr. Smith, would you please join us?" Juan came forward. "This is Mr. Smith. Up until recently he was employed by the United States government to extract information from terrorists. You might have heard rumors about how the

U.S. moved prisoners to countries with, how shall I say it, more lenient laws concerning torture. He was the man they used to get intelligence through any means necessary."

Susan Donleavy's lip started trembling again as she stared at Juan.

"He got anything he wanted from some of the most hardened men in the world, men who fought the Russians in Afghanistan for a decade and then our forces for years, men who swore an oath to die rather than submit to an infidel."

Juan lightly traced the outside of Susan's arm. It was an intimate gesture, the caress of a lover rather than a torturer, and it made her stiffen and try to shy away, but the ties holding her down prevented her from moving more than a couple inches. The threat of pain was far more effective than inflicting it. Already Susan's mind was conjuring images that were far worse than Linda or Cabrillo could conceive. They were letting her torture herself.

Again Linda's timing was spot on. Susan was struggling to rein in her imagination, to banish whatever she'd envisioned. She was finding within herself the courage to face whatever would come. It was Linda's job to keep her offguard.

"What he will do to a woman I have no idea," Linda said softly, "but I know I won't be around to watch it." She leaned down so her face was inches from Susan's, making sure that Juan was still in her field of view. "Tell me what I want to know and nothing will happen to you. I promise."

Juan had to fight not to smile because suddenly Susan Donleavy looked at Linda with such trust that he knew they'd get everything they wanted and more.

"Where is Daniel Singer, Susan?" Linda whispered. "Tell me where he is."

Susan's mouth worked as she fought the sense of betrayal she must be feeling toward divulging what she knew. Then she spit a glob of saliva into Linda's face. "Screw you, bitch. I'll never tell you."

Linda's only reaction was to wipe her cheek. She stayed close to Susan and continued to whisper. "You must understand that I don't want to have to do this. I really don't. I know that saving the environment is important to you. Perhaps you're even willing to die for your cause. But you have no idea what's coming. You can't comprehend the pain you are about to endure."

Straightening, Linda motioned to Juan. "Mr. Smith, I apologize for asking you to leave your tools behind. I thought she would be more cooperative. I'll give you a hand with the drills and the other equipment you need and then I'll leave you two alone." She looked back at Susan. "You realize that after today you will recoil in horror every time you look in a mirror."

"There is nothing I won't sacrifice for Dan Singer," Susan said defiantly.

"Ask yourself this question—what is he willing to sacrifice for you?"

"This isn't about me. This is about protecting the planet."

Linda looked around the darkened hold as if searching for something. "I don't see anyone else with us, Susan, so this is most definitely about you. Singer is off someplace safe while you are strapped to a table. Think about that for a moment. And then think about how long you will live with the consequences of your choice today. You are facing years in prison. You can serve them in a Namibian jail or a nice cushy cell in Europe with running water and a bunk that isn't infested with fleas. We haven't decided who to turn you over to."

"If you hurt me I will make sure you pay," Susan spat.

Linda arched an eyebrow. "Excuse me? Make us pay?" She chuckled. "You have no idea who we are, so how are you going to make us pay? You don't get it yet. We own you, body and soul. We can do anything we want with total impunity. You no longer have free will. We took that from you the moment we picked you up, and the sooner you understand that the quicker all this is going to end."

Susan Donleavy had no reply to that.

"How's this? Tell me what Dan Singer has planned and I will make sure you are turned over to Swiss authorities on accessory to kidnapping charges. I will convince Geoffrey Merrick to forgo an attempted murder rap." Linda had been hitting her with the stick, now it was time to show her the carrot. "You don't even need to tell me where he is, all right? Just lay out the bare outline of what he intends to do and your life is going to be unimaginably easier."

Linda made a hand gesture like an out-of-balance scale and said, "Two or three years in a Swiss prison or decades rotting in a Third World jail. Come on, Susan, make it easier on yourself. Tell me what he's planning."

As part of her technique Linda kept hammering home the point about how easy it would be, how Susan had everything to gain and nothing to lose by telling her. Had Juan not wanted the information so quickly Linda would have chosen a different question, one that really had no consequences, just to get the dialogue open. Still, she was making progress. The defiance that had hardened Susan Donleavy's features moments before was giving way to uncertainty.

"No one will ever know," Linda persisted. "Tell me what he wants to do. I assume it's going to be a demonstration of some kind, something he wants Merrick to witness. Is that it, Susan? Just nod your head if I'm right."

Susan's head remained immobile but her eyes dipped slightly.

"See, that wasn't so hard," Linda cooed, as if to a child who'd just swallowed her medicine. "What kind of demonstration? We know it has something to do with warming the Benguela Current."

A look of shock ran across Susan's face and her mouth gaped.

"That's right. We found the wave-powered generators and the undersea heaters. They were shut down some time ago. Part of Singer's plan has already unraveled but that isn't important right now. All that's important is you tell me the rest."

When Susan didn't say anything, Linda threw up her hands. "This is a waste of my time! I'm trying to do you a favor and you won't help yourself. Fine. If that's the way you want it then that's the way it's going to be. Mr. Smith." With that Linda strode from the hold with Juan right behind. He closed the hold's door and spun the lock.

"Jesus, you can be scary," Juan said.

Linda was checking the camera feed on her BlackBerry and didn't look up when she said, "Apparently not scary enough. I thought she'd crack."

"What's she doing?"

"Trying not to wet herself."

"So now we wait her out?"

"I'll go back in a half hour," Linda said. "That'll give her enough time to think about what's coming."

"And if she still won't talk?"

"Without enough time to properly soften her up I have no choice but to use drugs, which I hate by the way. It's too easy to get the subject to tell you what you want to hear rather than the truth." Linda looked back at the little screen. "On second thought . . ." She held up a hand with her fingers splayed and ticked them off silently. When the last digit curled into her palm Susan Donleavy began screaming from the other side of the closed hatch.

"Come back! Please! I'll tell you what he's going to try to do!"

A shadow crossed Linda's eyes. Rather than satisfied with her work she appeared sad.

"What is it?" Juan asked.

"Nothing."

"Talk to me. What's the matter?"

She looked up at him. "I hate doing this. Breaking people, I mean. Lying to them to get what I want. It leaves me, I don't know, dead inside. I climb into someone else's mind to ferret out information and in the end I end up knowing everything about them—how they think, what their hopes and dreams are, every secret they thought they'd never tell. In a couple of hours I will know more about Susan Donleavy than anyone else in the world. But it's not like having a friend confide in you. It's like I'm stealing that information. I hate doing it, Juan."

"I had no idea," he said softly. "If I did I wouldn't have asked you to do this."

"That's why I've never told you. You hired me because I have a certain background, and skills that no one in the crew possesses. Just because I hate part of my job doesn't mean I don't have to do it."

Juan gave her shoulder a gentle squeeze. "You going to be okay?"

"Yeah. I'm going to let her scream for a few more minutes and then go back in. I'll find you when I'm done. Then I'm going to have a glass of wine too many and try to get Susan Donleavy out of my head. Go get some rest. You look terrible."

"Best suggestion I've heard all day."

He turned to go, wondering how much each of them was sacrificing of themselves to the Corporation. They were always mindful of the physical dangers they faced when they accepted a mission, but there was a hidden cost, too. To fight from the shadows meant the justifications for their actions had to come from within each person. They weren't soldiers who could merely say they were taking orders. They'd chosen to be here and do the things necessary to guarantee a free society even if they themselves operated outside of societal boundaries.

Juan himself had felt that burden on more than one occasion. And while the Corporation regularly flouted international law in order to achieve their perfect record of success, there were gray areas that they had skirted that made him more than a little uncomfortable.

As he walked back toward his cabin, he knew there were no alternatives. The enemies he'd faced when he'd been with the CIA played by the rules for the most part. But the rulebook went out the window when slamming airplanes into skyscrapers became a legitimate form of attack. Wars were no longer fought between armies in the field. They were being fought in subways and mosques, nightclubs and market squares. It seemed that in today's world anyone and anything was fair game.

He reached his suite of rooms and pulled the curtains over his cabin portholes. Now, with his bed no more than a couple of feet away, the wave of fatigue that hit Cabrillo made him stagger. He undressed and slid between a set of cool sheets.

Despite his exhaustion sleep was a long time coming.

24

JUAN knew by how the diffused sunlight seeping around the drapes was the color of blood that he'd been asleep for only a couple of hours when the phone rang. He shimmied up against the headboard, feeling as if he'd just gone fifteen rounds with the heavyweight champion of the world. And lost.

"Hello," he said, working his tongue around his mouth to loosen the gummy saliva.

"Sorry to disturb your beauty sleep." It was Max. If anything, he sounded as though he was enjoying waking the chairman. "We've got some major developments. I've called a meeting in the boardroom. Fifteen minutes."

"Whet my appetite." Juan threw aside his sheets. The skin around his stump was red and swollen. One of Julia's orderlies was a professional masseuse, and he knew he'd need the leg tended to if he was going to function.

"Daniel Singer plans to cause the biggest oil slick in history and helping him is a mercenary army that we provided the weapons to."

The news shocked any vestiges of sleep from Cabrillo's brain.

He reached the boardroom in fourteen minutes, his hair still wet from the shower. Maurice had coffee waiting for him and an omelet bursting with sausage and onions. His first thought was for Linda Ross. The diminutive intelligence officer was at her customary seat with a laptop opened in front of her. Her face had the pale brittle look of a porcelain doll, and her normally bright eyes were as dull as old coins. Though only a few hours had passed since she began interrogating Susan Donleavy, Linda seemed to have aged a decade. She tried to smile at Juan but it died on her lips. He gave her a nod of understanding.

Franklin Lincoln and Mike Trono were also present, to make up for Eric Stone's and Mark Murphy's absence.

Max was the last to arrive and he was talking on a phone when he entered the room. "That's right. A coastal oil facility. I don't know exactly where, but your pilot must have some ideas." He paused a beat while he listened. "I know some of the radio tags must have failed by now. I also know that you overbuilt them enough so a couple are still transmitting. You'll just have to get closer to find them."

"Murph?" Juan asked after hastily swallowing a bite of his omelet.

"I want him focusing on the coast. I did a little research and found there's a long string of offshore oil production platforms at the mouth of the Congo River that arc north to Angola's Cabinda province."

"Angola's to the south of the Congo," Eddie said.

"That's what I thought, too." Max eased himself into his chair. "But there is an enclave north of the river and it's sitting on a couple billion barrels of oil. For what it's worth, I actually found out the U.S. gets more crude from Angola than it does from Kuwait, which pretty much negates the war for oil rant of a couple years ago."

Juan turned to Linda. "Want to fill us in?"

She straightened her shoulders. "As you all know, Daniel Singer forced Geoffrey Merrick to buy him out of the company. Since then Singer's used his money to fund environmental groups—rain-forest preservation in South America, antipoaching efforts in Africa, and a lot of the best lobbyists money could buy in capitals all over the world. Then he began to realize that all the money he'd spent had done very little to change people's attitudes. Yes, he was saving a couple of animals and some tracts of land, but he hadn't made an impact on the fundamental problem. That problem being that while people say they care about the environment, when it comes down to dollars and cents no one is willing to sacrifice their lifestyle in order to effect change."

"So Singer decided to get more radical?" Juan asked.

"Fanatical is more like it." Linda checked her computer for a second. "According to Susan he became active with groups that burned down luxury homes under construction in Colorado, Utah, and Vermont, as well as destroying SUVs sitting on dealers' lots. She claims he used to put golf balls in the fuel tanks of logging trucks as well as sand in the oil filler tubes."

"Golf balls?" Linc asked.

"Apparently the diesel will dissolve them, allowing the rubber strings inside to unravel. Does more damage than sugar or salt. Singer bragged that he'd caused at least fifty million dollars' worth of damage, but that still wasn't enough. He thought about sending bombs through the mail to top executives in the oil industry but knew they would just end up killing some poor mailroom clerk. He also knew that it wouldn't change anyone's life.

"That's when he heard how the hurricane seasons over the next couple of years are going to be particularly brutal. While it's part of a natural cycle, he figured the media would try to link it with global warming and he wondered if he could make the storms even worse."

"So we were right about the undersea heaters installed off the coast of Namibia." It was more a question than a statement from Cabrillo.

"He cut off all ties with the environmental movement and set his plan in motion. He hired some top-flight climatologists and oceanographers to lay out the heaters' size and location, though Susan says they were led to believe it was purely a research question and not something that would actually be built. They are designed to shift the Benguela Current just enough so the temperature of the waters off West Africa rises a couple of degrees. And as we talked about before, more heat means more evaporation and a bigger and more powerful storm.

"It's impossible to change a hurricane once it's formed," Linda went on. "Even a nuclear detonation wouldn't alter the eye structure, wind speed, or the storm's direction. However, by affecting what causes the storms in the first place, Singer believes he can create what he calls hypercanes, storms that register above Category Five on the Saffir-Simpson Scale."

"What's this have to do with blowing up oil facilities?" Eddie asked, helping himself to a cup of coffee from Juan's service.

"Here's where he's playing into media fears in a big way. The crude that's pumped from the waters near the Congo River has the highest percentage of benzene in the world. Alaska crude runs roughly one part per thousand. Oil from some of the newest fields off Angola and the Congo is a hundred times that and higher. The crude is also contaminated with arsenic. This is removed at refineries, but when it comes out of the ground it's a fairly caustic blend of oil and something called benzene arsonic acid, a known and tightly controlled carcinogen."

"He wants to sicken a bunch of West Africans?" Linc asked, disgusted by the idea.

"Not exactly, although there will be some injuries here. No, what he's after is to get the slick to disperse long enough so some of the oil evaporates."

"And once it becomes airborne," Juan concluded, "the westerly winds will carry the toxic vapors across the ocean to the Eastern Seaboard."

"The levels won't be high enough to sicken people in the United States," Linda said. "But Singer's banking on the panic caused by a toxic hurricane bearing down on the coast to get his point across."

"Say he succeeds in dumping a lot of oil," Mike interjected. "Can't it just get cleaned up before it becomes a hazard?"

"Two things would make that difficult," Juan said. "Number one is that regulations concerning oil spills are pretty lax in this part of the world. They wouldn't have enough oil skimmer ships or containment boom. The second thing, and correct me if I'm wrong, is that Singer plans on causing enough damage to enough rigs that even with sufficient equipment, cleanup crews would simply be overwhelmed."

"That's it in a nutshell," Linda agreed. "Local workers can contain an accidental spill from a tanker being improperly loaded and maybe even if a ship was holed, but with Singer's army there preventing them from getting to work and oil continually flowing from damaged rigs and pipelines there's nothing they could do."

"How long after the oil is spilled would it take for the vapors to enter the atmosphere?" Max asked.

"Immediately," Linda said. "But it would be a week or so before it could potentially get carried across the Atlantic. It's Singer's mercenaries' job to hold those rigs for as long as they can. If they can hold out for a couple of days we're talking a spill a hundred times the size of the *Exxon Valdez* disaster."

Juan's eyes scanned the faces around him and said, "So then it's going to be our job to prevent them from storming the rigs, and if we're too late then we're going to take the damn things back again."

"There might be a problem with that," Eddie said. He folded his hands on the table. "Linda, you told Max that Singer has hired Samuel Makambo to storm the oil facilities?"

"Susan Donleavy mentioned him by name as well as his Congolese Army of Revolution. It's a straight pay-to-fight deal. Makambo has no political stake in any of this. For few million of Singer's dollars Makambo's willing to send in some cannon fodder."

"Nice guy," Linc said sarcastically. "His men follow him because of their political beliefs and he hires them out to die for someone else's. I hate Africa."

"I don't blame you," Eddie agreed. "But can you see our problem? We supplied him with enough AK-47s, RPGs, and ammunition to outfit a couple hundred men."

Juan understood immediately. "The *Oregon* has the firepower to take on half the navies in the world, but it won't do us much good against individual terrorists aboard oil rigs who are using workers as shields."

"Precisely." Eddie leaned forward. "Retaking the production platforms is going to require individual combat. Everyone on this crew is a capable fighter, but if Makambo takes over just five rigs and puts a hundred men on each we're not going to take them back without losing at least two thirds to three quarters of our own people.

"And don't think Angola's army or police force is going to be much help," he added. "It'll take them a couple of days just to get organized. By that time Singer will have turned the entire Congo Delta into a stinking oil slick and sabotaged the rigs so the flow may never be shut off. If we can't prevent him from storming the platforms then we have a day at most to take them back."

Eddie's sober assessment hung in the air because no one in the boardroom could refute it.

There came a quiet knock on the open boardroom door. Juan turned and was delighted to see Sloane Macintyre standing at the entrance. She wore a pair of baggy shorts and a plain white T-shirt. Her arm was in a sling across her abdomen. Her coppery hair fell in waves past her shoulders. It was the first time he had seen her wearing makeup. The mascara and shadow brought out the depths of her gray eyes and the artful strokes of blush hid the pallor of her still-recovering body. Her lips were full and shining.

"Hope I'm not interrupting," she said with a smile that said she knew she was.

Juan got to his feet. "No, not at all. How are you feeling?"

"Fine, thanks. Doctor Huxley says I'll be good as new in a couple of weeks if I stick to the physical therapy regimen she laid out. The whole crew's talking about the rescue you pulled off and how you not only saved your men and rescued Geoffrey Merrick but also freed some leader from Zimbabwe."

"Believe me, it was a team effort."

"I just heard voices and wanted to say hello." She gave Juan a look. "You still owe me an explanation about what it is you all do and where you got this incredible ship."

"And I'll tell you everything. I promise."

"You'd better." She glanced over at Linda. "I'll see you back in your cabin."

"See you, Sloane."

"So what the hell are we going to do?" Max asked bluntly to get the conversation back on track.

"Obviously, we can contact Langston," Linda said. "If he can't clear the way for a rapid reaction force to be sent here, at least he can warn the governments of Angola and the Congo about a credible terrorist threat."

"What are our relations like with those countries?" Linc asked.

"No idea."

"What about getting in touch with some of our people who've left the Corporation, like Dick Truitt, Carl Gannon, and Bob Meadows," Mike suggested. "I know Tom Reyes runs a bodyguard service in California."

"Do the oil companies have their own security forces?" Max asked. "I assume they do. Juan?"

"Huh?"

"Are we boring you?"

"No." Cabrillo got to his feet. "I'll be right back."

He was out the door before anyone could ask him where he was going. He stalked down the hallway, his broad shoulders bowed and his head down. Decisions had always come easy to him and this one was no different but he had to ask a question before he committed himself. He caught up to Sloane as she reached Linda Ross's cabin.

"Juan," she said, startled by his sudden appearance and his deadly serious look.

"How sure are you about the diamonds being aboard the *Rove?*" he asked brusquely. For what he intended even the considerable financial resources of the Corporation weren't enough, and he doubted he could get the CIA to fund his plan appropriately.

"I'm sorry?"

"The *Rove*. How sure are you that the diamonds are aboard her?"

"I'm not sure what you—"

"If you were placing a bet what would be the odds? A hundred to one? A thousand to one? What?"

She composed herself for a second. "H. A. Ryder was the best guide in Africa at the time and he knew the desert better than anyone. I know as sure as I'm standing here that he got those men across the Kalahari. They had the stones when they reached the coast."

"So they are on the *Rove*, then."

"Yes."

"You're sure."

"Positive."

"Okay. Thanks."

He turned to go but Sloane placed a hand on his arm to stop him. "What's this all about? Why are you asking about the diamonds?"

"Because I'm going to promise them to someone if he helps me out."

"You don't know where the *Rove* is. It might take years to find her."

Juan gave her a wolfish grin. "I've got someone who owes me a favor who's going to find her for me."

"Who are you giving the diamonds to and why?" Caught up by Juan's determination Sloane had forgotten for a moment who she worked for and what had brought her to Namibia in the first place. "Wait just a second. Those stones don't belong to you. They belong to my company."

"According to maritime law they belong to whoever finds them. As for why I want them, come with me."

Juan stopped first at his cabin to get an item out of his safe. When they reached the guest suite, Juan knocked and entered. Moses Ndebele was sitting on the floor in the living room talking with four of his men. All of them were heavily bandaged. Canes and crutches littered the floor like a giant version of a children's game of pickup sticks. But none of it mattered. They were all smiling that their leader was back.

Moses made to get to his feet but Juan waved him down. "Your Doctor Huxley tells me that there is no need for me to be shopping for a new leg," Ndebele said.

"I'm glad to hear it. I can function with one but I sure as hell wish I still had 'em both." Juan said as they shook hands. "May I speak to you in private?"

"Of course, Captain." He said a few words to his followers and they slowly got up from the floor and hobbled to the bedroom.

Juan waited until the door was closed before speaking.

"What are the chances of you ever overthrowing your government and returning prosperity to Zimbabwe?"

"You are a man, so we will speak as men. I have eager fighters but few weapons, and if the people rise up to support a poorly armed revolt they will be gunned down. My government is ruthless. Its leaders are willing to commit any atrocity to remain in power."

"What would it take to topple them?"

"It is the same for any problem. Money and time."

"I can't do anything about the time, but what if I could fund your movement?"

"Captain, I know you are a brave and honorable man but you are talking about tens of millions of dollars."

"Mr. Ndebele, I'm talking about hundreds of millions of dollars, actually." Juan paused a beat to let that sink in, and then added, "And it's yours but I'm going to need something from you in return."

"For now I will not ask about the money," Moses said. "Friends do not discuss such matters. What is the favor you seek?"

"I need a hundred of your best fighters," Cabrillo told him. He then explained the situation. Ndebele listened wordlessly, although Sloane gasped when he described a hurricane laden with poison bearing down on the United States, most likely gunning for her native Florida.

"My people are willing to sacrifice themselves for their children and the future of our country," Ndebele said when Juan had finished. "You are asking me to send them into a battle for which they reap nothing and risk all. For what you have done for me I would fight by your side anywhere you asked. But I cannot ask my men to do this thing."

"But they are fighting for their country," Juan countered. "By doing this you will secure the financial resources to oust your government and return Zimbabwe to the democracy you all fought for when you first gained independence. I'm not going to lie to you and say that all of them will be coming back. Because they won't. But their sacrifice will be the rally cry for your followers. Explain to them what they will achieve and they will do it for you, for your country, and, most important, for themselves."

Ndebele said nothing for a few moments as he looked into Cabrillo's eyes.

"I will take this to an *indaba*, a council of my men." He waved at the closed bedroom door. "And I will let them decide."

"I can ask for nothing more," Juan said and shook Ndebele's hand again. He withdrew a pouch from his pocket and turned Ndebele's hand flat. Onto his open palm he poured the rough diamonds they had received in exchange for the weapons. "Consider this a good-faith gesture. They're yours no matter the decision. There's an intercom on the desk. The communications officer who answers will be able to find me."

Out in the hall Sloane grabbed Juan's hand. "Is that all true? And where did you get those diamonds."

"Unfortunately, it is. Daniel Singer has had years to plan this and we only have a couple of days to stop it. As to where those diamonds come from, it's a rather long story that brings this whole mess full circle."

"I guess I'll have to wait to hear that one, too."

"Sorry, yes. I have to get back to the meeting. There's a lot we have to go over."

Sloane released his hand. "I want you to know that I'll help you in any way I can."

"Good, because once we find the *Rove* you're going to help me black-mail your bosses into buying those diamonds."

"That," she said with a grin, "will be my pleasure."

Before returning to the boardroom Cabrillo went back to his cabin to place a ship-to-shore call. It was early morning on the East Coast, but he suspected the man he wanted to reach would be in his office.

Juan had the direct number and when the phone was picked up he said without preamble, "You owe me a leg but I'll call us even if you lend me a hand."

"It's been awhile, Chairman Cabrillo," Dirk Pitt replied from his office high atop the NUMA building overlooking Washington, D.C. "What can I do for you?"

25

THE *Oregon* coursed northward like a greyhound, driven by her phenomenal engines and the impatience of her crew. There was activity in nearly every section of the ship. There were five men in the armory unpacking the weapons that would be carried by Moses Ndebele's men, cleaning them of Cosmoline and loading hundreds of magazines. Other armorers were checking over the vessel's defensive systems, making certain that ammunition bins were fully stocked and that the salt air hadn't corroded the machine guns, Gatlings, and autocannons.

Down in the moon pool technicians were inspecting the *Oregon*'s two submersibles. Gear was being stripped out of both and extra CO_2 scrubbers installed to increase the number of people each could carry. They also touched up the anechoic coating that made the two craft almost undetectable when submerged. Over the sound of their work roared an air compressor filling dozens of scuba tanks in case they were needed.

In the kitchen every chef and assistant was on duty preparing combat rations while the dining staff sealed the food in airtight packages as soon as it came out of the galley. In medical, Julia Huxley and her staff were setting up the OR for an influx of casualties.

Juan Cabrillo was in his customary seat in the op center while around him his staff worked at a dizzying pace prepping the vessel, and themselves, for the upcoming battle. He read over every report as it came in concerning the vessel's status; no detail was too trivial to overlook.

"Max," he called without looking up from his computer monitor, "I've got something here that says the pressure in the fire suppression system is down by fifteen pounds."

"I ordered a test trip in the hold. The system should be back up to full pressure in about an hour."

"Okay. Hali, what's George's ETA?"

Hali Kasim pulled down one side of his headphones. "He just took off from Cabinda, Angola, with Eric and Murph. We should be able to rendezvous in about two and a half hours. He'll call ten minutes out so we can slow the ship and prep the hangar."

"And Tiny? Where's he?"

"Thirty thousand feet over Zambia."

Juan was relieved. The plan, like so many recently, had been hastily put together. One of the biggest obstacles was getting a hundred of Moses' best men out of their refugee camp near the industrial town of Francistown, Botswana. Unlike a lot of sub-Saharan Africa, there was very little corruption in Botswana, so getting the men onto a plane without passports had been more expensive than Cabrillo would have liked. Tiny's bush pilot friend had cleared the way for them on the other end, and ensured that they would have no difficulty landing in Cabinda. The *Oregon* would tie up to the city's main pier about five hours after they landed and would stay just long enough to get them aboard.

From there they would proceed north to the oil fields off the coast where Murph and Eric had detected three of the ten AK-47s with the Corporation's radio tags. The weapons were grouped in a swamp less than five miles from a massive new tanker terminal and within a ten-minute boat ride of a dozen offshore oil rigs.

Juan had contacted Langston Overholt as soon as Murph had reported in. Lang had then alerted the State Department so they could issue a warning to Angola's government. However, the wheels of diplomacy turn slowly and so far Juan's information was languishing in Foggy Bottom while the policy wonks hashed out a statement.

Because of the low-grade civil war being waged all across Cabinda

Province, the petroleum companies who leased the oil fields had their own security apparatus in place. The tanker terminal and workers' compounds were fenced off and patrolled by armed guards. Cabrillo had considered calling the companies directly but knew he would be ignored. He also knew that whatever force they had in place was a deterrent for theft and trespassing and wasn't capable of holding off an army. Any warning he did issue would likely only get more of their guards killed.

Also, he had learned from Murph's aerial reconnaissance that there were hundreds of people living in shantytowns around the oil concessions. There would be far fewer civilian casualties if the fighting took place well inside the facilities.

Linda Ross entered the op center with Sloane Macintyre in tow. Sloane stopped as soon as she stepped through the door. Her mouth hung a little loose as she looked around the futuristic command center. The main view screen on the forward bulkhead was split into dozens of camera angles showing activity all around the ship as well as a clear shot of the *Oregon*'s bow as she powered through the sea.

"Linda said I'd get a better idea of what you all do if I came with her," Sloane finally said as she approached Juan. "I think I'm more confused now than I was five seconds ago. What is all this?"

"The heart and soul of the *Oregon*," Juan said. "From here we can control the helm, the engines, communications, safety teams as well as the ship's integrated weapons systems."

"So you are with the CIA or something?"

"Like I told you before, I used to be. We're private citizens running a for-profit company that does freelance security work. Though I will admit the CIA has thrown us a lot of business over the years, usually with missions best left off their blackest books.

"Originally, our contract was to sell some arms to a group of African revolutionaries. The arms had been modified so the rebels could be tracked. Unfortunately we were double-crossed but we only learned about it after committing ourselves to rescue Geoffrey Merrick. So now we're back to get the weapons, only it turns out Merrick's ex-partner has other plans for them."

"Who paid you to supply the guns in the first place?"

"It was a deal worked out between our government and the Congo's.

Most of the money came from the CIA; the rest was going to come from selling the blood diamonds we were given in exchange for the arms."

"The diamonds you gave to Moses Ndebele for his help?"

"You got it. Hey, I guess the story wasn't so long after all," Juan quipped.

"And you make a living doing this?" she asked and then answered her own question. "Of course you do. I saw the clothes in Linda's closet. It's like Rodeo Drive in there."

"Chairman, can I talk to you privately?" Linda asked.

Juan didn't like the tone in her voice. He got up from his chair and offered it to Sloane with a flourish. "The ship's yours." He guided Linda to the far corner of the op center. "What's up?"

"I was going over my interrogation notes and, while I'm not positive, I think Susan Donleavy withheld something."

"Something?"

"Not about what Singer's attempting here. I got everything out of her about this that I could. It's something else. I just can't put my finger on it."

"It's about the timing of this whole operation," Juan stated.

"It could be. I don't know. Why would you say that?"

"It kept me up for most of the night," he admitted. He laid out his concern. "Singer's had this in motion for years, with the generators and the heaters, and suddenly he's striking at an oil facility in order to release a couple million tons of toxic sludge. Why? Why now? He's expecting hurricanes to carry the vapors across the Atlantic but he can't predict when and where a storm will form."

"Do you think maybe he can?"

"What I think is that *he* thinks he can."

"But that's impossible. At least with any degree of accuracy. Hurricanes grow randomly. Some never get stronger than a tropical depression and simply blow themselves out at sea."

"Exactly, and that wouldn't work for his grand demonstration."

"You think he knows there's a major storm coming and that it will carry the oil vapors across the ocean?"

"I'll do you one better," Juan said. "I think he knows the storm's track will slam it into the United States."

"How could he know that?"

Juan brushed a hand through his crew cut. It was the only outward sign of his frustration. "That's what kept me awake. I know it's not possible for him to predict a hurricane, much less its path, but Singer's actions can only lead us to that conclusion. Even without us here Makambo's men will eventually be overrun and the oil shut off. So Singer can't guarantee the fumes would drift far enough and remain airborne long enough to be sucked into a forming hurricane, or that if they do that the storm wouldn't dissipate on its own. Not unless there's another element to all this we don't know about."

"I can try again with Susan," Linda offered. "I ended the interrogation after I learned what I needed to know about the attack on the oil terminal."

Juan regarded her with pride. She was giving up even more of her soul. And as much as he wanted to protect her from the toll questioning Susan Donleavy had on her, he knew that she would have to do it again.

"There's something there," he said. "And I know you can find it."

"I'll do my best." Linda turned to go.

"Keep me posted."

TEN miles north of where Tiny Gunderson sat in his plane at the Cabinda airport with a hundred eager soldiers, Daniel Singer was talking with General Samuel Makambo of the Congolese Army of Revolution. Dawn was two hours away and the jungle was finally quieting as the nocturnal insects and animals bedded down for the day. Though, with the glare of so many oil rigs burning off natural gas both offshore and along the coastline, it was a wonder how the creatures maintained their circadian rhythms. Around them in the lean-to were the most senior soldiers Makambo was willing to sacrifice for this mission. Leading the four-hundred-man expeditionary force was Colonel Raif Abala. He was here for two reasons: punishment for the debacle on the Congo River when he let the arms merchants get away with the diamonds, and because Makambo suspected the colonel was skimming stones from their blood diamond trade. He wouldn't be too put out if Abala didn't return.

The rebels had been hiding in plain sight near the squatters' camps that had sprung up around the facility belonging to the oil giant Petromax. They wore regular, albeit ragged, clothing and acted as though they were here seeking employment. Their weapons and outboard boats had been easily concealed in the mangroves, with guards posted nearby to dissuade fishermen or people looking for bush meat to stray too close.

"Colonel," Makambo said, "you know your duty."

With his sheer size, Samuel Makambo was a commanding presence. And while what had once been battle-hardened muscle was slowly jelling into fat, he still possessed incredible strength. He favored mirrored sunglasses like his mentor, Idi Amin, and carried a swagger stick called a *sjambok* made of plaited hippo hide. The pistols in his twin holsters were custom-made by Beretta; their gold inlays alone were worth a small fortune.

"Yes, sir," Abala replied at once. "A hundred men will use the boats to launch attacks on the offshore loading terminal and the rigs themselves while the bulk of my force will concentrate on securing the compound."

"It's essential that you take control of the generating station as well as the pump control rooms," Dan Singer, the architect of the attack, said. "And they must not be damaged."

"The attack on those two parts of the terminal will be carried out by my best men. They will take them as soon as we break through the perimeter fences."

"And your men are clear on how to work the controls?" Singer demanded.

"Many of them were employed at this very facility until our government forbade members of our tribe from working in Congo's oil industry," Abala said. "As soon as the tanker that's currently loading has been decoupled from the terminal they know to turn the pumps on full force and dump the oil into the sea."

"And on the rigs?"

"They will destroy the undersea pipes that send crude to the storage tanks onshore."

Singer wished they could blow out the sides of the massive storage tanks, but they were situated in an earthen redoubt that would keep the oil contained. For the oil to properly evaporate he needed it spread over as large an area as possible. He turned to Makambo. "For every hour they hold the terminal and oil's pouring into the sea, one million dollars will be automatically transferred into your Swiss bank account."

"That money will go a long way to funding my revolution and improving the quality of life of our people," the guerilla leader said with a straight face. Singer knew the lion's share of the cash would remain in Makambo's account. "I made this bargain and call upon our soldiers to fight for the greater good of us all."

When searching for his mercenary force Singer had thoroughly investigated Makambo and his Congolese Army of Revolution. They were nothing more than savage butchers who used torture and the intimidation of defenseless civilians to keep themselves supplied. While there was a tribal element to the conflict, human rights groups estimated that the CAR had killed more of their own people than the government they opposed. Makambo was just another example of the despotic nature of African politics.

"Very well," Singer said. "Then it's time for me to leave."

He had planned on leaving Cabinda a day before the attack, but he'd remained as long as he dared, hoping against hope that he'd get word from Nina Visser. She and the others hadn't been at the rendezvous site when the plane arrived, although tire tracks next to the runway indicated someone had been there recently. The pilot managed to follow them from the air, but only for only a couple of miles. The relentless wind had scoured the desert floor. He'd circled the area until he had just enough fuel to return to Windhoek, failing to find any sign of them.

Singer had ordered him back to Cabinda so they could fly to the port city of Nouakchott, Mauritania, where the aged hundred-thousand-ton tanker he'd secretly purchased from a Libyan company waited. She was named the *Gulf of Sidra* and had spent her career plying the Mediterranean, ferrying Libyan oil to Yugoslavia and Albania.

When he'd toured her with Susan Donleavy she said the vessel's tanks would make perfect incubators for her organic flocculent. The marine engineering firm Singer hired to inspect the ship signed off on her hull being able to withstand a sustained thermal load of a hundred and forty degrees, although they said in their report they were unaware of any oil terminals in the world where crude retained that much of the earth's heat. Singer had closed the deal, obtained a Liberian registration for the ship, by far the easiest to get in the world, and hadn't bothered to change her name.

Susan had then overseen the initial seeding of her heat-generating goo and had checked in on it from time to time before her "abduction." Her reports showed that everything was working perfectly, so Singer knew she didn't need to be there when he released it. Still, something could come up that might require her expertise. The loss of Nina and her group was of little concern, he just wished Susan was with him. The flocculent had been her brainchild and when she'd contacted him about her discovery and its potential application she had wanted to be a part of the final act.

And then there was Merrick. Singer had so wanted to see his smug face collapse when he witnessed the creation of the most destructive hurricane ever to hit the United States and realized he and polluters like him were at fault. Singer had told Merrick of his plan, so he was left with the hope his former partner was still alive and would know the truth about what was transpiring.

Because of the specialized nature of running a supertanker, he couldn't rely on a bunch of long-haired environmentalists, so he'd been forced to hire a professional crew, men whose silence could be bought. The captain was a Greek alcoholic who'd lost his master's license after running a tanker aground in the Persian Gulf. The chief engineer was another Greek who couldn't stay away from the bottle. He hadn't worked since a steam pipe explosion in an engine room had killed four of his assistants. A board of inquiry cleared him, but rumors of negligence ruined his career.

Those two made the rest of the crew look like saints.

"You'll make your attack at dawn?" Singer asked.

"Yes. You have more than enough time to get to your plane," Makambo said with a hint of derision. Not that he was going to be here for the fight. He had a fast boat waiting to whisk him down the coast and back up the Congo River.

Singer let his tone pass. He stood. "Remember, every hour is a million dollars. If your men can hold off the security forces and Angola's police when they get organized for forty-eight hours I'll throw in a five-million-dollar bonus." He was looking at Abala. "And another five for you, colonel."

"Then, cry havoc," Makambo said using his favorite quote, "and let slip the dogs of war."

26

JUAN stood on the bridge wing and watched the old school buses crawl across the causeway that led to Cabinda's only pier, each painted in garish colors and belching oily exhaust as their old engines labored. They threaded their way around a string of shipping containers and some donated farm equipment that had just been unloaded from a Russian freighter berthed ahead of the *Oregon*.

Because his ship was pumped dry of ballast in order to reach the relatively shallow anchorage, he had a good view of the city and the hills beyond. With dawn just breaking he noted that little of Angola's oil wealth had been spent in the city nearest the fields.

Down on the quay Max Hanley and Franklin Lincoln waited with a Customs official. Both were dressed like a couple of wharf rats in keeping with the *Oregon*'s decrepit appearance. Tiny Gunderson's bush pilot friend was with them, too, to make sure everything went smoothly, as well as Mafana, Ndebele's old sergeant. The Customs man had already given a briefcase to his wife, who'd come down to the docks for the specific reason of taking the bribe money back home with her.

The elevator from the op center suddenly rose up from the bridge floor. Linda Ross didn't wait until it had come even with the deck before jumping off and rushing toward Cabrillo.

"Juan, you don't have your phone on," she said hotly. "The attack's started. Hali's intercepting calls from the Petromax facility to their headquarters in Delaware. They estimate at least four hundred armed men have stormed the gates. And the platforms are reporting a large number of small boats are heading their way. Security is being completely overrun."

He had hoped and prayed that they'd have a day at least to work with Moses Ndebele's troops, but somehow he'd known he wasn't going to get it. He would have to trust that time hadn't dulled the skills they'd honed in their bitter civil war nearly three decades ago.

Cabrillo cupped his hands around his mouth and shouted Max's name. When Hanley glanced up Juan made a motion with his arm to hurry things along. Max said something to Mafana just as the first of the buses screeched to a halt at the foot of the gangplank. The side door opened and a string of men emerged. The first went to give Mafana a congratulatory hug for rescuing Moses Ndebele, but the African rebel must have told him to get aboard quickly. The men started up to the main deck as the other buses pulled alongside the ship.

Juan activated his phone and dialed down to the hangar where he knew George "Gomez" Adams would be with his chopper. The pilot answered on the second ring.

"Fly By Night Airlines."

"George, Juan."

"What's up, Chairman?"

"Singer's men have launched their attack. As soon as we clear the harbor I want to send up one of our UAVs." The unmanned aerial vehicles were essentially commercial model airplanes outfitted with miniature cameras and infrared detectors.

"I'll get it prepped," Adams said. "But I can't fly both if you need the chopper."

"Tiny's coming aboard with Ndebele's men. He'll fly it. I just want you to get it ready."

"I'm on it."

Cabrillo glanced over the rail again. Two lines of men were marching up the gangway. None of them were overweight, which didn't surprise him since they lived in a refugee camp, but there were a few giants among them. He saw more gray hair than he had hoped, but the former freedom fighters looked capable. These weren't bowed old men, but lean, hungry soldiers who knew their duty.

He called Eddie Seng to tell him to meet the new arrivals, but his Shore Operations Director was already at the head of the gangway directing the soldiers to one of the ship's holds where Moses Ndebele was waiting to address them. It was there that they would be outfitted with assault rifles, ammunition, and other gear.

Pressed by the urgency of the attack being under way, Juan's people seemed to have found new heights of efficiency. He expected no less.

Eric Stone had been watching the procession over the closed circuit television system from the op center; as soon as Max and Linc followed the last soldier up the gangplank it immediately began to rise. Juan looked up to see a dense cloud of smoke boil from the *Oregon*'s funnel. The busted looking intercom mounted just inside the bridge wing door chimed.

"We're ready," Eric said when Juan answered. He looked down the length of the ship where a stevedore was waiting by the aft line. He threw the man a signal and he heaved the heavy rope off the bollard and let it slide into the water. A capstan immediately started reeling it into the ship. Juan repeated the motion to the longshoremen waiting near the bows. Before he could tell Stone they were free he saw water boil between the *Oregon* and the dock as the athwartship thrusters came online. When they cleared the stern of the Russian freighter Eric powered up the magnetohydrodynamics, keeping the speed down so her forward momentum wouldn't cause the hull to squat, or settle deeper in the water. It was only when they were a mile from the shallow harbor that he started pouring on the power.

Juan waited on the flying bridge for another couple of moments, knowing it would be his last seconds of peace until the mission was over. The slide of dread he'd felt when Linda told him the attack had begun was giving way to a new sensation, one he knew too well. It was the first feeling of adrenaline being pumped into his body. It was almost as though he could detect each time his adrenal glands secreted a dose into his bloodstream.

His stump was still sore, but he no longer felt it. His back still ached, but it no longer bothered him. He no longer missed the sleep he hadn't gotten. His mind became focused on the task at hand and his body responded, willing to do whatever he asked of it.

He turned to Linda. "Ready?"

"Aye."

On the elevator down to the op center he asked her about Susan Donleavy.

"I had planned on talking to her today, but, well . . ."

"No problem," Juan said. The elevator doors whisked open. "Hali? What's the latest?"

"Petromax is trying to reach the provisional authorities to tell them about the attack, but so far the government hasn't responded. Nothing's happening in the workers' compound. The assault is focused solely on the terminal and the offshore rigs. It seems two platforms are under terrorist control while two more are trying to defend themselves using firefighting water cannons. One of the rig's tool pushers radioed that he's lost a couple of men to small arms fire and that he doesn't think they can hold out much longer."

"Eric, what's our ETA?"

"An hour."

"Murph, weapons status?"

Mark Murphy craned around to look at Juan. "We're loaded for bear, Chairman."

"Okay, good. Oh, and guys, nice job finding the radio tagged guns. God knows how much worse things would get if we'd been floundering around the Congo River."

Cabrillo turned to head for his cabin and noted Chuck "Tiny" Gunderson seated at a work station at the back of the room. In front of him was a computer monitor. On-screen was an image of George Adams cleaning the lens of the camera mounted in the nose of the aerial drone.

"Looks good," Tiny said into his mike. He moved his hands over the computer keyboard. "Step back; I'm firing the engine now."

The camera began to vibrate as the plane's little motor caught.

"Okay, green across the board. Up, up, and away."

The image began to move as the plane sped down a launch ramp, past the *Oregon*'s forward derricks and then over the railing. Tiny brought its nose down with a joystick, exchanging altitude for speed and then eased back on the stick to send it into the sky.

Juan went to his cabin to get ready. Before changing into his newly refurbished combat leg and dark fatigues, he turned on his computer to get the live feed from the UAV's cameras. He kept one eye on the monitor as he readied his arsenal of weapons.

The four-foot-long airplane was at about a thousand feet and flying over the large peninsula that the *Oregon* had to go around in order to reach the Petromax oil terminal. A more powerful transmitter aboard had allowed them to expand the drone's range from fifteen miles up to forty so it no longer had to stay so close to the ship. It flashed over farmland and jungle and finally the area of mangrove swamps that effectively cut off the port from the rest of Cabinda save for a single road.

Tiny dropped the plane down so it was five hundred feet off the haul road. A few miles from the entrance to the terminal a line of trucks sat idle. Juan guessed why, and in a moment the camera revealed the road had been blocked by felled trees. Because the ground just off the road was so soft the big tanker trucks couldn't turn around. It would take giant earthmovers or a week of chain-sawing to remove the obstacle. If the Angolan government did send troops they would have to abandon any fighting vehicles well short of their target.

Having studied satellite pictures of the remote port, Cabrillo had anticipated this move because it was exactly what he would have done had he been in charge of the assault.

He watched as Tiny made the model plane gain altitude again as it neared the terminal. From a thousand feet everything looked normal at first. The two-hundred-acre facility sprawled along the coast, with a massive tank farm at its southernmost point and a separate compound for workers' dormitories and recreational facilities to the north. Between them were miles of pipes in a hundred different sizes twisting and bending together in a maze only its designers could understand. There were warehouses as large as anything Cabrillo had ever seen, as well as a harbor for the tenders and workboats that took personnel to and from the offshore rigs. Shooting off from the facility was a mile-long causeway that led to the loading berths for the supertankers that took the crude to markets all over the globe. A thousand-foot tanker was tied to one, her tanks empty if

Juan were to judge by the amount of red antifouling paint he could see above her waterline.

He spotted a large building constructed on an specially hardened pad near one of the terminal's tallest vent towers. Juan knew from the research his people had done there were three General Electric jet engines inside the structure that provided electricity to the whole instillation. High-tension power lines ran from it to every corner of the port.

Three miles off the coast sat a string of dozens of oil rigs running northward like a man-made archipelago, each connected back to the port by undersea pipelines. Though not as large as rigs Juan had seen in the North Sea or the Gulf of Mexico, each was at least two hundred feet tall, their superstructures held above the waves on massive support piers.

It all appeared normal except when he started looking more carefully. Some of the flames he saw weren't from natural gas being intentionally burned off. Several trucks had been set ablaze, and more than one building was wreathed in sooty smoke. The tiny stick figures lying randomly around the yard were the corpses of workers and members of the security force who'd been gunned down by Makambo's soldiers. What Juan first took to be shadows around them were actually pools of blood.

Tiny Gunderson then swept the drone over the shoreline and out along the causeway. The pipes that fed the floating dock looked as big around as railcars. Juan cursed when he saw the men swarming around the loading gantries. They had removed them from the tanker and now crude oil was being dumped into the sea in four thick streams. The spill already surrounded the pier and was spreading by the second. One of the men must have seen the drone because suddenly several of them looked up. Some pointed with their arms while others opened fire at the little plane.

The chance of hitting the UAV was remote, but Tiny juked the aircraft and headed for the nearest offshore platform. From a half mile away Juan could see it was ringed with oil. The crude weighed enough to crush the waves that tried to pass under it. All the ocean could do was to make the slick undulate like a lazy ripple of black silk. The prevailing current was already stretching the spill northward even as the slick grew in size from the oil gushing off the rig in a black rain. When the drone approached the second platform under the terrorists' control, Cabrillo saw that this slick was even larger than the first.

Although it was impossible, Juan felt like he could smell the sharp chemical stench of the crude as it poured into the sea. It scalded the back of his throat and made his eyes water. Then he realized that what he was sensing was his own revulsion to the willful act of environmental destruction and the mindless waste of human life. Singer's demonstration was the greatest act of ecoterrorism in history, and as much as he professed wanting to save the planet his actions would see the earth pay in a heavy coin.

And if the Corporation failed, the effects could spread half a world away.

He gathered up his gear and headed for the hold. When he arrived, he saw that the room was crowded with more than a hundred men, a few of them his own, the rest belonging to Moses Ndebele. The Africans had already been issued weapons and ammunition as well as clothing to make up for anything they lacked, sturdy boots mostly. They all sat on the floor and listened raptly as their leader addressed them from a dais made of pallets. His foot was swathed in surgical gauze and a pair of crutches rested against the bulkhead behind him. Juan didn't enter the hold, but rather leaned on the doorjamb and listened. He couldn't understand the language but it didn't matter. He could feel the passion in Ndebele's words and how they affected his followers. It was palpable. He spoke clearly, his eyes sweeping the room, giving each man a moment's attention before moving on. When they settled on Juan, he felt a tug in his chest as if Ndebele had touched his heart. Juan nodded and Moses returned the gesture.

When he finished his speech the men gave him a thunderous applause that made the hold echo. A full two minutes passed before the cheering started to subside.

"Captain Cabrillo," Moses called over the din. The men quieted instantly. "I told my people that to fight at your side is to fight at mine. That you and I are now brothers because of what you did for me. I told them you have the strength of a bull elephant, the cunning of a leopard, and the fierceness of a lion. I said that even though today we fight in a different land, this is the day we start to take back our country."

"I couldn't have said it any better," Juan replied. He wondered if he should address the men but he could see in their eyes, in the way they held themselves, that nothing he could say would inspire them more than

Moses' words. He said simply, "I just want to thank you all for making my fight yours. You honor me and you honor your homeland."

He caught Eddie Seng's attention to get him to come over. "Do you have the duty roster figured out?"

"I have it here." He tapped an electronic clipboard. "Mafana helped me sort through the men before their arrival so I have a pretty good idea of their skills. I also have seat assignments for all the vessels involved in the assault."

"Any last refinements to the plan we came up with?"

"Nothing, Chairman."

"Okay, then. Let's get this show on the road."

Juan would be leading the assault on one of the oil platforms that had already been taken over and Eddie would head up the other, so both men gathered up the handful of Zimbabweans coming with them and left the hold for the moon pool. Others would be using the ship's lifeboat and her fleet of other watercraft to hit the loading pier and the facility itself in a coordinated attack with the *Oregon*, under Max's command, acting as fire support.

On their way down Max called from the op center. "Just want you to know we'll be in position to launch the submersibles in another ten minutes."

Juan checked his watch. Eric had gotten them here quicker than promised. "Once we clear the doors it'll take us another twenty to get to the rigs, so don't approach the coast until we call."

"I was paying attention at last night's briefing," Max said archly. "Just before you launch your counterattack we'll make a dash for the terminal and send out the lifeboat. We'll take out any of the terrorists hitting the other two rigs, then move into position off the dock. When we're close enough and can cover for them, Ski and Linc will head out in the SEAL assault boat to cover the retaking of the loading pier."

"Let's just hope that Linda's right and Makambo's men aren't willing to die to hold the terminal. Hopefully if we hit them hard enough and fast enough they will surrender quickly."

"And if she's wrong and these guys really believe in their mission?"

"Then this is going to be a long, bloody day."

With the ship still under way, the hull doors under the moon pool remained closed, but the metal grating over the hole had been removed and the larger of the *Oregon*'s two submersibles, the sixty-five-foot No-mad 1000, was hanging above the opening on its lifting cradle. Capable of diving to more than a thousand feet, the Nomad sported a cluster of lights around its blunt nose and a manipulator arm as flexible and delicate as a human's but capable of ripping steel. The smaller Discovery 1000 was suspended above the Nomad and would be launched as soon as its big sis-ter was away.

Linda would accompany Juan while Jerry Pulaski was ready to mount up with Eddie. The shore attack would be commanded by Franklin Lin-coln and Mike Trono, who were already getting their forces together in the lifeboat as well as in the amidships boat garage. Technicians had gone over the submersibles, so there was nothing for Juan to do but give the hull a slap for luck and mount the ladder a crewman held steady. The sub swayed slightly as he reached the top. He threw Eddie a quick salute and dropped through the hatch.

Juan climbed down into the sub and made his way to the cockpit, a claustrophobic pair of reclined seats surrounded by dozens of computer screens, control panels, and a trio of small portholes. Though she was big-ger than the Discovery, the interior of the Nomad was actually smaller be-cause of her hull thickness, the massive batteries she carried to give her a sixty-hour range, and the fact she was outfitted with a saturation dive chamber. Juan's crew had stripped out enough gear to increase her pas-senger load from six to eight, the same number as the Disco could carry. It would be a small force to attack the rigs and only the cream of Ndebele's fighters would accompany the two subs.

Linda crawled in after him, but didn't take her seat. She showed the men how to strap themselves in while Juan went through the pre-dive checklist.

Cabrillo jacked a pair of lightweight headphones into the communica-tions panel. "Nomad to *Oregon*. This is a comm test. How do you read?"

"Five by five, Nomad," Hali answered immediately. "We're nearly finished decelerating, Juan. Moon pool doors can be opened in about a minute."

"Roger."

He looked over his shoulder as Linda crawled into her seat, setting her silenced machine pistol next to Juan's. "Everybody set back there?" A couple of the men didn't look too keen on being confined, especially when the hatch was dogged tight, but they all managed to mirror his thumbs-up. "Mafana? You okay?"

Though injured slightly during Moses' rescue, the former sergeant had insisted on accompanying Cabrillo. "I now have a better understanding of the Bible." Juan's face showed his confusion so Mafana added, "Jonah and the whale."

"It'll be a short ride and we won't be more than fifty or so feet under-water."

A series of strobe lights mounted throughout the three-deck-high room began to flash and a horn would be sounding, although Juan couldn't hear it from inside the minisub. He looked down through the porthole as the large doors at the very keel of the ship began to open. Water sluiced across the metal as the sea was carefully allowed to enter the ship, quickly filling the moon pool to the *Oregon*'s waterline.

With a mechanical clank, the cradle supporting the submarine began to lower it into the sea. The water climbed over the portholes and the Nomad's interior grew noticeably darker, lit now only by the computer screens and a low-voltage system in the crew's area. Once the sub was floating free the cradle decoupled.

"You're free," a crewman called over Juan's headset.

"Affirmative." Juan hit the ballast controls to flood the tanks and in seconds the minisub submerged down through the moon pool and out into open ocean. "Nomad's away. You can launch the Disco."

He powered up the motors, listening to the mechanical whine as the props bit in, and set the computer to level them out at fifty feet, deep enough that an observer on the surface wouldn't see the matte-black hull cruising by. The *Oregon*'s master computer had already calculated the course and downloaded it to the minisub, so there was nothing for Juan to do but enjoy the ride.

Five minutes later Eddie announced they had successfully launched the Discovery and they were en route to the second oil rig.

Capable of only ten knots, the ride toward the coast seemed to take forever, though Juan knew what was frustrating him was that every minute that elapsed meant more oil was being pumped into the sea. If he thought it would make a difference he would have gotten out and pushed.

"*Oregon,* this is the Disco," Eddie called over the acoustical link. "We've arrived at the rig and are hovering just below the surface. The oil slick must be three miles across by now."

"Disco, this is the Nomad," Juan said. "Computer puts us under our platform in three minutes." He knew by how dark the ocean had become that his minisub was traveling under an identical oil slick and had been for some time.

The Nomad's GPS system guided the sub between two of the oil rig's tall support legs and brought the craft to a halt mere feet from a third column, one they'd identified from the UAV overflight as having a ladder that went up to the top of the platform.

"Houston, the Nomad has landed."

"Roger that, Nomad," Hali replied. "Give us one minute so Tiny can double-check that you don't have company down there and you're free to surface and pop the hatches."

Juan connected his headset back to his personal radio, levered himself out of the padded seat, and stepped carefully to the hatch, his MP-5 slung over his shoulder. Mafana and his men undid their lap belts.

"Juan," Linda called down the length of the vessel. "Hali says we're clear. There isn't anyone down here, but Tiny estimates there are at least thirty terrorists milling around the platform."

"Not for long," he muttered, then ordered Linda to gently blow the ballast tanks.

Like a creature from a horror movie, the Nomad's broad back slowly emerged through the reeking mat of crude pooled under the oil platform. It oozed off the hull as more of the sub broached the surface, but was sticky enough to cling to anything protruding off the craft. Clots of oil stuck to the hatch coaming and rudder.

"Masks," Juan said and fitted a surgical mask over his nose and mouth. Julia had researched the toxic crude and its effects on the human body, and as long as they kept their exposure down to a couple of hours and remained in well-ventilated areas there was no need to wear more cumbersome gas masks.

He hit the button to open the hatch and recoiled at the harsh chemical smell that assaulted his senses. Being this close to the slick made his eyes water.

He climbed out of the minisub and clipped a line to the eyehole welded to the hull. There was a barnacle-encrusted platform ringing the nearby support leg and he leapt over to it, tying off the line to the integrated ladder. Set equidistant between the four towering legs, the riser pipe dropped down off the platform and into the ocean. Inside it would be the drill string for when the rig was exploring for oil and pipes to allow oil to flow back up to be pumped to shore. Unlike some other fields, the crude was under enough pressure that it didn't need to be coaxed out of the earth. It gushed freely. And now that the terrorists had either destroyed pipeworks on the platform or opened some valves, it came tumbling back down in a waterfall of shimmering obsidian that twisted and scintillated in the clear morning sunlight. The sound of it striking the slick was like thunder.

Juan tore his eyes away from the mesmerizing sight and glanced out to sea as the men started emerging from the Nomad. The *Oregon* was driving toward the coastline. Though she was an ugly industrial ship, more function than form, with a deck resembling a denuded forest of cranes and her hull a patchwork of mismatched paint, she had never looked better to him. Max was headed for the third platform, where Petromax employees were still holding off the terrorists but were reporting that they were getting ready to abandon the rig in her lifeboats. The men defending the fourth platform were calling over the airwaves that they would never give up.

After sealing the minisub's hatch, Linda was the last to jump from the Nomad to the platform. "Let's go," she shouted over the tumbling oil. "The air down here is going to play havoc with my skin. I can already feel oil clogging my pores." She then added with a saucy grin, "You can best believe the Corporation is going to pay for whatever spa I go to."

27

WHEN the *Oregon* emerged over the horizon none of the rebels in the swift outboard boats dancing around the legs of the third platform paid it any attention. Their sole focus was clambering up the ladder to take over the rig. So far their efforts had been thwarted by the workers above training water cannons down the column and blowing the terrorists back into the sea. But it wasn't so one-sided. The men in the boats poured a constant stream of fire up the forty-foot leg; occasionally they hit their marks and a Petromax employee would go down. Sometimes they merely fell to the deck but occasionally one would tumble off the platform and slam into the water. The attackers would cheer. It was a war of attrition between squirt guns and automatic rifles with an outcome that was inevitable.

Seated at the weapons station in the op center, Mark Murphy simultaneously watched a half dozen camera feeds as well as the status boards for the *Oregon*'s integrated arsenal. Eric Stone sat in the next station over, one hand on the joystick that controlled the rudder and directional pump jets, the other resting lightly on the throttles.

"Mr. Stone, lay us in five hundred yards off the platform," Max said from the master's chair. "And clear the bow to bring the Gatling to bear.

Wepps, open the hull plates covering the Gatling's redoubt and prepare to fire on my order."

Tiny Gunderson flew the UAV in a loose circle around the rig so Mark could pick his targets. Murph designated the four boats swarming under the rig as Tangos One through Four and once they were entered into the computer the ship's electronic brain kept them under constant surveillance. High in the bow, the six-barreled GE M61A1 spun up, its rotating barrels dipping and turning as the computer compensated for the *Oregon*'s motion through the water, the waves that gently shook her hull, and the speed of the distant outboard.

"Nomad to *Oregon*, we've reached the platform." Juan's voice filled the room from hidden speakers.

"About time, Nomad," Max teased. "Discovery's been waiting for two minutes."

"We stopped for coffee and Danish on the way up. Are you in position?"

"Just waiting for your word and we'll launch the lifeboat. Then it's go time."

"We're ready."

Max changed channels on his communication console. "Op center to lifeboat. Mike, you there?"

"We're ready," Trono replied. His voice had the emotionless timbre of total concentration.

"Lifeboat away and good luck."

Out on deck and hidden from the oil platform by the ship's hull, the lifeboat carrying sixty freedom fighters practically sitting on one another's laps was lifted off its cradle and swung over the rail. The davits slowly lowered the boat to the sea and as soon as it had settled Mike had the lines released and the engine spooled up.

When Trono had left the Air Force after six years as a para-rescue jumper, with five successful downed pilot rescues to his credit, he'd done a stint as a professional power boat racer. The thrill of flying across the water at more than a hundred miles an hour had tempered some of his adrenaline addiction, but he had jumped at the chance to join the Corporation, bringing with him the experience of being one of the elite boat drivers in the world.

He had the lifeboat on plane in no time. Then he extended the foils and poured on the power. The ugly looking craft skimmed across the water like a flying fish, keeping well out of any terrorist's range as he waited for the order to turn east and make landfall near the Petromax terminal's tank farm. From there he'd lead the counterattack to wrest control back from Makambo's men.

There was an unexpected explosion on the rig the *Oregon* had targeted. Tiny zoomed in with the camera to show a pair of rebels in one of the aluminum outboards reloading a rocket launcher. Flames and dense smoke coiled from a catwalk where moments before two oil employees had been shooting hundreds of gallons of seawater at the attackers. The men were gone and the water cannon was a twisted ruin.

"I'm getting another call from the rig to Petromax headquarters in Delaware," Hali said, holding up a finger as he listened. "They're abandoning the platform."

"No they're not," Max said savagely. "Wepps?"

"I got 'em."

Mark loosened the safeties on the Gatling and gave the computer permission to fire. Capable of throwing a stream of 20-mm depleted uranium slugs at six thousand rounds per minute, Murph had dialed back the barrels' rotation speed, so in the two seconds that ammunition blurred through the loading feeds, only eighty rounds erupted from the weapon with a sound like an industrial buzz saw.

Under the platform the cheering terrorists never knew what hit them. One moment the four boats jinked and juked and the next two of them had vanished in a pall of shredded aluminum and vaporized flesh.

The Gatling had destroyed Tangos Two and Four. The driver of Tango One must have seen where the fire had originated because he shot his boat around the far side of one of the columns and didn't reemerge into the *Oregon*'s sights. The computer waited for the boat a moment longer than Murph would have liked, so as he flipped a toggle to override the Gatling's automatic fire controls he made a mental note to check the system's programming.

On his main flat panel display a reticle appeared where the barrel was currently aiming, the curved gray side of the support leg. He tracked back the camera's zoom and found the fourth outboard speeding off for the next oil rig. A tiny movement of a joystick centered the sight on the flee-ing craft and a second's long touch of the trigger blew it to oblivion.

He reset the weapon to automatic and the multibarrel gun pivoted back to the platform for the last boat. A sliver of the outboard's stern ap-peared from around the column, a target that was less than a square foot. Even at five hundred yards from an unstable ship it was more than enough. The Gatling shrieked again. The outboard's motor exploded, blowing the boat out of the water, sending its eight occupants flying in every direction. Some were launched into the sea, others were slammed into the column, and two of them seemed to have simply vanished in the blast.

"Platform three secure," Mark said, exhaling a long breath.

"Helm, get us to the last rig under attack," Max grunted, knowing the two submersible teams wouldn't have it so easy.

CABRILLO was thinking the exact same thing as he crouched on an ex-posed stairwell hanging over the side of the platform. Below him the oil slick pulsed like a living thing even as it killed the surrounding ocean. It had stretched in an inky bloom as far as he could see and had probably al-ready reached the concrete breakwater running along the front of the Petromax terminal. With a freshening wind out of the south the smell wasn't as bad as it had been down below, but the petrochemical taint still hung in the air.

Unlike the mammoth oil rigs of the North Sea or the Gulf of Mexico that could house hundreds of workers for months at a time and stood taller than many skyscrapers, this platform was no more than four hun-dred feet square, dominated by the spidery drill tower and a brightly painted mobile crane used to raise and lower supplies from tenders.

There were several metal-sided buildings clinging to the deck and can-tilevered over the edges of the structure. One would be a control center; the others housed machinery to regulate the flow of crude from the well head on the sea floor. The deck was also crisscrossed with a maze of pipes and littered with equipment—broken auger bits, lengths of drill string, and a couple of small cargo containers for storage. Though only a few years old, the platform was streaked with grime and showed signs of neglect.

He thought it was a good sign that he didn't see any bodies of dead workers.

At the base of the drill tower was an ever-erupting volcano of oil gushing from deep within the earth. The ebony fountain reached a height of fifteen feet before collapsing under its own weight, only to be replenished with fresh crude. The flow poured through openings around the rotary table and drained into the Atlantic. With that much oil bursting up the riser it was impossible to tell if the pipes had been permanently sabotaged or if the safety valves had been cracked open.

Cabrillo was ever mindful that a stray spark could ignite the oil. The resulting explosion would probably level trees along the coast.

When he and his team had first arrived at the top of the platform the terrorists had been milling around. A few peered disinterestedly over the sides of the structure just to make sure no one was approaching, but on the whole they seemed certain they had the situation well in hand.

It wasn't until the *Oregon* approached the third rig and blew away their comrades like so much chaff that they found their discipline once again. The leader of the thirty-man contingent organized lookouts to watch for any approaching ships and had others prep their RPGs in case the freighter came within range. Juan had hidden himself and his people in a chain locker when a four-man patrol circled the catwalk ringing the lower of the platform's two decks.

Now that the *Oregon* was moving farther down the string of offshore rigs, the terrorists seemed to be losing their vigilance somewhat. The lookouts' attention wandered and men lined the far rail, watching to see what effects the ship would have on their compatriots attacking the final platform. Juan had recalled that many of Makambo's forces were little more than teenagers, and he doubted the rebel general would supply Daniel Singer with his best troops no matter what he was being paid. He wouldn't let himself dwell on how poverty and hopelessness had brought these men here, only that they were now perpetrating a terrorist act and had to be stopped.

He tapped Mafana to take his position at the top of the stair and retreated downward to confer with Linda Ross. "This was the first rig attacked so I think they probably took it without meeting any resistance," he whispered, though his voice couldn't carry over the sound of the spilling oil. "It was when they hit the second rig that the crew put up a fight."

"You think they rounded them up and locked them away?"

"I know these guys are ruthless, but it would be more practical than executing a hundred workers."

"Want me to go find them?"

Juan nodded. "Once we take over the rig we're going to need them to shut off the oil, and if there are no survivors on Eddie's platform we'll need to transport them over to work on that one, too. Take three men and scout out the interior spaces. There has to be a rec room or dining hall, something big enough to hold the entire crew."

"I'm on it."

Cabrillo had to smile at the sight of Linda leading three men more than twice her size through a doorway into the rig. It reminded him of Goldilocks with the three bears in tow, only Baby Bear tipped the scales at one eighty. He climbed back up the steps and lay next to Mafana. He scanned the scene once again, calculating firing angles, cover positions, and areas they could fall back to if necessary. He could feel Mafana's eyes on him.

"You just want to charge them, don't you?" Cabrillo asked.

"It is the best plan I have," he admitted with a wide grin. "And it has always worked for me before."

Juan shook his head and gave Mafana his orders. The sergeant relayed them to his men. Wordlessly, the Africans crested the stairs; Cabrillo had designated the ambush sites with the finesse of a chess master moving his pieces for the final gambit.

Though used to jungle fighting, the men moved well in the unfamiliar environs, stalking across the deck with the patience of seasoned hunters—hunters who had spent their youth chasing the most dangerous prey of all: other men. It took ten minutes for them to deploy, and Juan studied the deck again, making sure everyone was where he intended them to be. The last thing he wanted on his conscience was a friendly fire incident.

Satisfied, he launched himself up the last couple of steps and raced to the corner of a nearby container, pressing himself flat against the wall and triple-checking that his assault rifle's safety was off. The terrorist commander was a hundred yards away and talking on a large radio, presumably with the overall leader of the attack, who was probably still onshore. Juan hefted the MP-5 to his shoulder and put the laser sight on the man's chest, just left of center.

An instant later, the laser's red dot was replaced with a dime-sized bullet hole. The man simply collapsed as though his bones had vanished. The silencer prevented anyone from hearing the shot, but a handful of men had seen their leader go down. It was as if the rebels were a single entity with a single mind because it seemed that everyone came alert at once. Guns were gripped tighter as men sought cover.

When one of Cabrillo's soldiers opened up with the unsilenced AK-47 he'd been issued from the ship's stores, thirty guns replied. Swarms of rounds crisscrossed the deck in every direction but one. Cabrillo had made sure that none of his people were close enough to the drilling derrick to cause the rebels to fire anywhere near the volatile upsurge of oil.

Six rebels were felled in the opening seconds of the attack, and Juan took out two more with a hip shot on automatic as they appeared around the container, but if anything the ferocity and intensity of the battle increased. One of his men dashed for his secondary cover position and took a bullet to the leg. He rolled flat on the hard deck ten feet from Cabrillo. Without giving it a moment's thought, Juan laid down a wall of suppression fire, dashed into the open, and dragged the man to cover by his collar.

"*Ngeyabongo,*" he gasped, clutching his bloody thigh.

"You're welcome," Juan said, understanding the sentiment if not the word. An instant later his world turned upside down as an RPG exploded on the far side of the container.

LINDA wished the lights inside the platform were off so she could switch on her night vision goggles to give her an edge, but the utilitarian corridors were brightly lit.

The rig's lower level was mostly machinery housed in four large rooms, but when they climbed to the upper deck they found themselves in a maze of passageways and interconnected rooms. They found several small dormitories for men who spent more than their shift on the platform as well as a suite of offices for the administrative staff.

It was slow going checking each room, but there was no other way. She could feel the press of time. The longer it took, the longer the Chairman was fighting without almost half his force. She didn't disagree with his tactics, but she wanted to be more involved in the fight.

She peered around another corner and saw two rebels leaning on either side of a door, their AKs slung from their shoulders. She withdrew her head quickly, her unexpected motion drawing her men's attention. Linda pointed at her eyes, made a gesture of around the bend and held up two fingers. The sign language was nearly universal to anyone who'd fought in a war and her men nodded. She pointed at one of them and made a motion for him to get down on the floor. He shook his head, pointed at a comrade, made a gesture like firing a gun, and flashed a thumbs-up. No, he was saying, this man is a better shot. Linda acknowledged the sniper and he got into position.

Her H&K's laser sight cut random patterns across the ceiling as she inched closer to the corner. She carefully drew down on the weapon as she peeked around the wall again. She double-tapped the farthest guard in the chest at the same time the sniper put a single round into the closer one, the crack of his AK masking the whisper of her silenced machine pistol.

Her entire team rushed around the corner and ran for the door. A third guard appeared around a far bend and all four of them opened up, the kinetic impact of so many bullets tossing the corpse against a bulkhead. When the firing stopped Linda could hear autofire coming from beyond the door and the screams of men in panic and pain.

She was the first to reach the door and blew off the handle with a three-round burst. She hit the door without slowing, exploding into the room, her lithe body sailing a few yards before she landed on her shoulder, letting her momentum carry her back onto her knees, the MP-5 pulled tight to her shoulder. Alerted by the gunfire outside the mess hall two rebels were firing indiscriminately into the throng of terrified oilmen.

The scene was utter chaos, with men running and screaming, falling over one another in their rush to get away from the onslaught, while others went down with horrifying wounds. Linda was jostled by a pair of men making a break for the door the instant she pulled the trigger and her three rounds passed through the opening leading to the kitchen and punched a tight group of holes in a stainless-steel vent duct. Another two workers were gunned down before she could adjust her aim and kill the first rebel with a head shot.

Her three men had pushed their way into the dining room shouting for the workers to get down as they sought the second terrorist. He had stopped firing as soon as Linda had killed his comrade and was trying to blend in with the workers as they rushed for the exit.

"No one leaves," she shouted, her high-pitched voice almost lost in the tumult. But the sniper had heard her. He and the others moved back to block the door and no matter how the workers tried to force their way through they held fast.

Linda got to her feet, scanning faces. She'd caught the barest glimpse of the second rebel but didn't see him now. Then there was movement to her left. The kitchen door had moved slightly on its two-way hinges. She rushed across the room, the men moving out of her way because of the gun in her hands and the murderous look in her eye.

When she reached the solid door she rammed it inward with her foot. It slammed against something solid after opening halfway then recoiled back. When there was no reaction from inside the kitchen she hunkered low and slowly eased her way inside. She could see a dishwashing station to her left and a hallway that seemed to lead to either a storage area or maybe out of the kitchen entirely, but her view of the rest of the kitchen was blocked by the door.

Just as she turned to check to the right of the door a strong hand clutched the back of her neck. She was pulled to her feet, the hot barrel of an assault rifle pressed into her kidney. The rebel spoke in his native language, panting out the words that Linda couldn't understand but knew nevertheless. She was now his prisoner and if anyone tried to attack him he'd blow her spine out of her body before he went down.

IT had taken less than ten minutes for the *Oregon* to reach the fourth platform and sweep the seas of the rebel boats. Only one had remained at the rig following the destruction of the first set of outboards, but Tiny Gunderson's eye in the sky found three of them fleeing toward the tanker loading pier. Rather than let them reinforce the land-based attack, Max Hanley had ordered Murph to take them out. The range was growing extreme by the time Murph targeted the last boat so it took a five-second burst before eight of the Gatling's rounds found their mark amid the explosions of water from shells impacting around the craft. The final outboard pinwheeled atop the waves after it had been cut nearly in two.

In a maneuver that made the hull plates moan in protest Eric had the *Oregon* torqued around using her thrusters and drive tubes and was accelerating for the dock by the time the little boat sank.

"*Oregon* to *Liberty*," Max radioed. Though never given official names, *Liberty* was what they called the primary lifeboat. The one Juan had had blown out from under him off the coast of Namibia had been nicknamed *Or Death*.

"This is *Liberty*," Mike Trono replied.

"We've secured the fourth rig and are now getting into position to cover your assault." Approaching a well-defended dock in the unarmed lifeboat was suicide, but under the protection of the *Oregon*'s weapons, Cabrillo and the senior staff who'd come up with the plan were more than confident they'd land safely.

"Roger that, *Oregon*. I have you in sight. Looks like you need five more minutes before we can turn for shore."

"Don't wait for me," Eric said from the helm, bumping the throttles even more. "I'll be on station before you're a mile from the beach."

Max flicked his monitor to show the status of his beloved engines and saw Stone had them wavering just below redline. Any misgivings he'd had about damaging them when they had grounded in the Congo River faded. The old girl was giving them everything she had and more.

"We're headed in."

Mike had kept the hydrofoil two miles from shore, carving lazy circles until it was time to strike. He cranked the wheel eastward, aiming for the collection of huge storage tanks at the terminal's southern edge. The UAV's overflight had shown this to be the area of least rebel activity, but they were bound to be spotted as they approached, and men would certainly be shifted to repel the attack.

He had to steer around the oil slicks that were slowly coalescing into one massive spill. He had no way of estimating its size, but from what he could see it already looked frighteningly like Prince William Sound after the *Exxon Valdez* holed herself on Bligh Reef.

He was standing in the rear cockpit to give himself 360-degree vision and didn't hear the approaching UAV over the hydrofoil's engine. Tiny buzzed him at no more than twenty feet, waggling the drone's wings as he arrowed it in toward the seawall.

"Crazy SOB," he muttered with a smirk and glanced at the flatscreen display that had been hastily installed the night before.

Everything looked the same as it had when the model plane made its first pass over the facility. There were no rebel soldiers around the tank farm or the power plant. It was only when Tiny guided the UAV north-ward that he could see any insurgents. Some were guarding the entrance gates while others were draining a fleet of eighteen-wheeler tanker trucks. Thick ropes of oil snaked from the rear of each trailer and slithered over the seawall. Another contingent was on the floating pier getting the sec-ond set of loading gantries ready to begin pumping crude into the sea. Linc would be leading the attack there once Mike and his men were in po-sition to back them.

Then, when they were a mile from the quay closest to the tank farm, he saw from the digital uplink that he had been spotted. Men were racing off the causeway and getting into Petromax vehicles in order to rush across the facility. They came in trucks, forklifts, even a large crane, anything their commander could get running. Others came on foot, swarming across the terminal like berserkers.

"*Oregon*, you seeing what I'm seeing?"

"We see it," Max replied.

Mark Murphy retracted the hull plates shielding the ship's 40 mm Bo-fors automatic cannon and activated the hydraulics that moved the weapon into firing position. His computer screen automatically split into two halves, one showing the targeting camera for the Gatling, the second for the pom-pom gun. He started designating targets as fast as he could, mov-ing the reticle around the screen with a pair of joysticks and designating vehicles in the sight as soon as the computer told him he had a lock. The Bofors began to pound out high explosive shells and the Gatling spit a tongue of fire fifteen feet from the *Oregon*'s side. The weapons were seek-ing new targets before the first salvos struck home.

The Gatling rounds raked the side of a dump truck, the near hyperve-locity slugs tearing the engine off its mount, shredding everything in the cab, and punching fist-sized holes through the inch-thick dump bed. The force of the impacts sent the twelve-ton vehicle careening onto its right-side wheels for an instant before it tipped completely.

A pair of 40-mm rounds blew twin craters in the asphalt in front of an SUV with armed men standing on the running boards and hanging on the doors. The driver veered sharply but the left front tire dropped into one of the smoking gouges just as a third round impacted behind the right front wheel. The blast tossed the truck through the air, rebels flying from its hurtling carcass like dolls thrown by a spoiled child.

"Eric," Murph said without looking up from his computer, "turn us side on. We're in range to deploy the deck .30 calibers."

Controlled from other weapons stations, each of the .30-caliber M-60s could be individually targeted. While they were used primarily for defense against boarders the six heavy machine guns were more than capable of engaging individuals onshore. They were disguised in oil drums on deck, and on a command from Murph the lids swung free and the guns popped up, their barrels swinging down to horizontal and pivoting outward. Each gun emplacement had its own camera with low light and infrared capabilities. Once they were deployed, Mark turned his attention back to his own weapons systems and let his gunners do their job. In moments the machine guns added their chattering tones to the symphony he was conducting.

It took another five minutes to check the headlong rush of men to the tank farm pier where Mike was bringing the hydrofoil off plane in preparation to dock. Yet rebels still managed to cross the yard in twos and threes, leaping from cover to cover when the M-60s were engaged elsewhere, and a vanload of gunmen had circled along the outer perimeter fence, using the entire terminal to hide their advance.

Murph had done his job of clearing most of Mike's LZ, but they were still in for a fight. And until Trono and his African troops had swept the yard of rebels, Linc and Ski couldn't attack the tanker pier and prevent the insurgents from continuing to dump four hundred tons of toxic crude per minute into the sea.

28

EDDIE Seng looked at the oil gushing up from the well drilled deep below the platform and wanted to shoot the fifteen rebels who'd surrendered five minutes into the gun battle. The Petromax workers trying to staunch the flow looked puny and ineffective compared to this awesome demonstration of man's attempt to tame nature.

He glanced again at the kneeling terrorists lined against the edge of the platform, their arms bound behind them with the flex cuffs he'd brought and electrical wire the workers had provided. None were older than twenty-five, and as his eyes swept the line none of them could meet his cold stare. The bullet-ridden bodies of the six fighters taken out in Eddie's lightning attack had been laid together and covered with an old piece of tarp.

Only one of Eddie's men had been injured during the minute-long assault and that was just a flesh wound in the leg from a ricochet. As soon as the remaining rebels realized the ferocity of the attack they dropped their weapons and threw up their hands. A few of them had even begun to cry. Eddie had gone below and found the rig's crew unguarded in the mess hall and learned eight of their coworkers had been gunned down when the platform was first assaulted.

The rig's tool pusher had been killed when the rebels swarmed the platform, so it was his second in command who was in charge of shutting off the flow. He detached himself from the men gathered around the well head and approached Eddie. His coveralls and gloves were black with oil and his ebony face was streaked with the grease.

"We can fix it," he said in accented English. "They replaced the topside Christmas tree with a twelve-inch shunt valve. They opened that valve to let the oil come out and broke off the handle. I think they dropped the Christmas tree over the side."

Eddie imagined a Christmas tree was what the oilman called the well cap that diverted oil to pipelines connected to shore. "How long?"

"We have another tree in the stores. It's not as strong as the one we lost, but it will take the pressure. Maybe three hours."

"Then don't waste time talking to me."

Though it was a mile away, and the crude belching out of the well made a sound like a train roaring past, Eddie could still hear the sustained gunfire from the Chairman's rig and knew Juan was having a much harder time of it.

FOR a stunned moment Cabrillo had no idea where he was or even who he was. It was only when the constant bark of distant automatic weapons finally cut through the ringing in his head that he remembered what was happening. He opened his eyes and nearly cried out. He hung forty feet over the bubbling mass of oil lapping against the platform's legs and would have been blown off the rig entirely if he hadn't gotten tangled in the safety nets encircling the upper deck. The container he'd been hiding behind bobbed on the sea of crude but there was no sign of the wounded man who'd been next to him when the RPG detonated.

He flipped onto his back and spider-crawled across the shaky net, keeping one eye on the deck perimeter to make sure none of the rebels saw his vulnerable position. When he reached the platform he cautiously peered over the edge. Terrorists still had control of the rig and return fire from his own men was diminished. He could tell only a couple were still in the fight, and by the way they fired only single shots he knew they were low on ammunition. The rebels didn't seem to have such a shortage and blasted away indiscriminately.

When Juan was sure no one was looking in his direction he rolled off the net and under the crawler treads of the mobile crane. He checked over his weapon and changed out the half-depleted magazine. He didn't have a good enough view of the battle to start sniping the rebels without risking another blast from an RPG. He scooted around and wriggled to the back of the crane, cautiously looking around for better cover.

An insurgent suddenly sprang up from behind a crate and was about to toss a grenade across the deck at where a wounded Zimbabwean cowered behind a huge valve. Juan drilled the terrorist with a single shot and a moment later the grenade went off, lifting his corpse and the mangled body of a comrade on a column of smoky flame.

Before anyone could pinpoint where the shot had originated, Juan rushed out from under the crane, running doubled over across the deck, and threw himself behind a pile of six-inch-thick drill pipes. He edged around the pipes so he could look down their lengths. The effect was disorientating, like a rendition of a fly's prismatic eyes, but he could see one of the rebels moving across the ironworks tower a few feet from where the oil fountained from the well head.

Juan thrust the barrel of his MP-5 into a pipe and triggered off a three-round burst. Two of the bullets struck the interior of the pipe and went wild, but one hit the terrorist low in the abdomen. He staggered back and was caught in the avalanche of oil. One second he seemed to be leaning against the surging mass and the next he'd been pulled in, like he'd been absorbed, and vanished in the cascade draining down to the ocean.

Cabrillo circled back around the pile of pipes when a half dozen rebels raked it with autofire, the impacts making the steel pipes sing. He was beginning to realize the attack might fail. If Linda didn't finish up below and add her team as reinforcements, Juan had to seriously consider calling retreat. There was nothing the Oregon could do to help, not without risking setting the rig ablaze.

With so many rebels still fighting he knew that the climb down to the minisub would be suicide. They'd be picked off before they were a quarter of the way down the ladder. Juan had to think of an alternative and considered taking the platform's lifeboat, a reinforced fiberglass escape pod that could be automatically lowered. The only problem was the lifeboat's davits were on an isolated spot on the far side of the deck, surrounded by open space—a killing field if Juan had ever seen one.

He tapped his radio to get Linda's frequency as another fusillade slammed into the drill string. "Linda, its Cabrillo. Forget about the workers and get your butts up here double time." When she didn't respond Juan repeated her name. "Where in the hell is she?"

SHE'D spent five hours a week every week for two straight years. More than five hundred hours training on the mats Eddie Seng had brought into the *Oregon*'s fitness center dojo. He'd learned from a master who no longer bothered with rankings because there were few people on the planet capable enough to certify him.

Hearing Juan's voice was enough to get Linda Ross over her moment of panic and into action. She stepped out and back so quickly that the killer didn't realize the receiver of his gun was now against her hip. Slamming her elbow into his sternum sent a wave of rancid breath across her face. She then smashed her fist between his legs, recalling Eddie's words at this point in the oft-practiced counterattack: "If you feel his weight on your back, toss him. If not, grab on until he goes down."

But she felt the man deflate against her. She reached for his arm, cocked her hip, and threw him over her shoulder, holding on to him so their combined weight crushed him against the deck. Unable to get air into his deflated lungs the terrorist gasped like a fish. Linda chopped him at a pressure point on the side of his exposed throat and his eyes fluttered and rolled back into his head. He'd be out for hours.

She got to her feet to see the man she thought of as "the sniper" peering at her through the open counter to the dining hall. He was just lowering his AK for a shot he hadn't dared to take. She gave him a little curtsy and was rewarded with a broad smile.

Linda threw a pair of flex cuffs around the nearby stove's leg and secured the terrorist's wrists as a precaution. Returning to the mess hall, she saw her other two men still guarding the door to make sure none of the workers left to face another slaughter on the deck.

Bodies littered the floor. A few of them were dead but most had just been wounded in the mindless melee. Some of their coworkers were already trying to help get them into more comfortable positions and pressing rags and wads of napkins into their wounds. One man in particular seemed to be leading the medical efforts. He was a white man with a fringe of sandy hair around his red scalp and the biggest hands she had ever seen. He was also one of the most ruggedly handsome men she'd ever seen. When he got up from examining a crewman leaning against an overturned table he noticed her and came across the room in five long strides.

"Little lady, I don't know who you are or where in all get all you came from, but damn, darlin', am I glad to see you." He towered over her and his voice was pure west Texas. "I'm Jim Gibson, this here rig's tool pusher."

Linda knew that was the title given to the boss on an offshore platform. "Ross, my name is Linda Ross. Hold on a second." She resettled her radio earpiece, which had been dislodged during the fight. "Juan, it's Linda."

"Thank God. I need you and your men up here *now*. We're taking a pounding. Worry about the workers later." The sound of a firefight raging in the background underscored his urgent words.

"They're secure and I'm on my way." She looked back up at the big Texan. "Mr. Gibson."

"Jim."

"Jim, I need you to keep your people here. There's still terrorists topside. They've done something to the platform so oil's pouring into the ocean. When we take care of the rebels, can you guys stop the crude?"

"Hell yeah we can. What's going on?"

Linda put a fresh magazine into her machine pistol as she answered. "A group of rebels from the Congo were hired to take over several platforms and the main tanker terminal."

"Is this some political thing?"

"Jim, I promise when this is over I'll explain it all, but right now I've got to go."

"You can tell me over dinner. I know a great Portuguese restaurant in Cabinda City."

"I know a better one in Lisbon," Linda called over her shoulder, "But you're still buying."

MIKE kept the *Liberty* driving straight for the seawall before cranking the wheel and chopping the throttles at the very last second. Though already off her foils, the boat settled deeper in the water as her side kissed the concrete so lightly that it didn't disturb any of the mussels clinging to its side.

The forward hatch was open and men began streaming out of the boat and onto the quay, seeking whatever cover they could find. A smattering of small-arms fire came from the direction of the terminal, but between Mark Murphy's efforts and Trono's deft abilities with a boat, only a few of the rebels were yet in range.

Mike gathered up his gear and jumped for the wall. There was nothing to tie off the boat to so he unholstered a special gun from behind his back. Actuated by a .22-caliber cartridge, the gun fired a six-inch steel rod into the cement. He jacked the gun to reset it and fired a second bolt, then tied off a line dangling over the *Liberty*'s side.

The freedom fighters hadn't forgotten their hard-won lessons in the years since their civil war. They were properly fanned out with each man able to cover the soldier to either side. Their first objective was less than a hundred yards away. Mike glanced at the metallic patch of cloth on the inside of his left sleeve and cursed. The feed was down.

With no choice, he led the charge, leapfrogging from position to position, always with men firing from behind to keep the terrorists at bay. Though there were only a handful of rebels at the moment, each passing minute saw more arriving in the area, having evaded the *Oregon*'s sophisticated array of sensors.

The sixty-man contingent took their first casualty when a gunman suddenly emerged from behind a small utility shed and opened fire Hollywood-style, his AK held low at the hip and his finger never leaving the trigger as he sprayed bullets. It was a suicide attack and the counterfire obliged him, but four of Mike's men were down, one of them obviously dead.

Undeterred they ran on, dashing and weaving, holding up where they had protection so they could cover the skirmish line's advance. It was urban street fighting at its worse, with enemies able to pop up almost anywhere.

Mike's radio crackled so he skidded behind a shot-up tow truck to listen. "*Liberty*, this is Eagle Eye, sorry about the delay but I've got you patched back in." It was Tiny Gunderson flying the UAV.

Trono again glanced at the odd square embedded on the sleeve of his black battle jacket. The silvery material had morphed to reveal a picture of the tanker terminal beamed to the E-paper screen from the drone. The flexible monitor's resolution was as clear as the big flat panel in the *Oregon*'s op center, though power constraints allowed for only snapshots to be sent from the UAV on ten-second intervals rather than a continuous feed. The technology was state of the art, and still prone to bugs, so it was still years away from deployment with the U.S. Army.

The image changed as Tiny zeroed in on Mike's location. He saw there were three rebels on the far side of a warehouse who were about to outflank his men. Rather than explain how he knew, he leapt from behind the tow truck and dashed back so he could get a bead on the corner of the building where they huddled. A knob on the grenade launcher slung under his machine pistol constricted the barrel a fraction of a millimeter and thus slowed the projectile, allowing him to set any range he wanted. He estimated the corner of the building was forty yards away and dialed it in. The weapon made a funny, hollow *bloop* sound when it fired but the results were anything but comical. The grenade landed a foot from the edge of the building and detonated, shrapnel tearing through the thin corrugated metal and flesh.

The next time he looked at his sleeve the image showed him the three rebels prone in a cloud of explosive gas.

Now with their guardian angel looking out from above, their pace doubled since Mike was able to show his men where an ambush was coming long before the terrorists could spring it.

They reached the terminal's power plant without losing another man. Despite its soundproofing, the building shook with the roar of the jet engines it used to produce electricity. Mike had already selected the five soldiers who'd accompany him and ordered the rest to keep crossing the yard so they could support Linc's attack on the tanker pier.

He entered the power plant by shooting the lock off a side door. The sound of the jets intensified; without ear protection they'd only be able to remain inside for a few minutes. He raced in, his H&K's laser sight sweeping the massive space. Lined up in a row on concrete and steel supports were the three General Electric jet engines, their intakes fed air through gleaming ducts, their exhaust vented out the back of the building through conduits blackened by the tremendous heat.

Only one of the engines was in operation. Max had explained during their briefing that a facility like this would alternate between two of the engines and have a third as backup for times of peak load. Rather than level the powerhouse with the *Oregon*'s 120 mm cannon, they decided to take just the one operational engine offline, knowing the men dealing with the cleanup would need electricity.

Mike ran for the control room near the front of the building, protected by his phalanx of men. They could see a pair of workers through the triple-layer sliding glass doors overlooking the power station with a trio of guards watching over them. The Petromax employees were studying a tall display board festooned with lights. The guards and workers stood too close together to risk a shot, so as Mike approached he fired over their heads, blowing out the glass in a hail of scintillating chips. The shock alone of the engine noise penetrating the insulated room was disorientating enough, but Mike also heaved a concussion grenade called a flash/bang through the ruined pane.

He ducked so the detonative force rolled over him and was in the room before anyone could get to their feet. He clipped one of the rebels with his weapon's stock and his men covered the other two with their AKs. Mike tossed one of them a handful of flex cuffs and went to check on the engineers. One had been cut by flying glass, but it didn't look too bad. The others were just dazed.

He looked the least shaken man in the eye and had to shout at the top of his lungs to be heard over the banshee scream of the nearby jet. "Can you shut that down?" he asked, jerking a thumb over his shoulder.

The man looked at him blankly. Mike pointed at the engine again and made a cutting motion across his throat. The universal gesture sank in. The engineer nodded and went to a control station. He used a mouse to scroll through a number of screens on a computer, clicking icons as he went. It seemed like nothing was working until suddenly the piercing whine began to fade past the point of pain to the merely uncomfortable. It continued to wind down as the compressor blades slowed until finally it fell silent, although Mike's ears continued to ring.

He turned to the leader of his scout party. "Stay here and don't let anyone refire that engine." He'd already given him a walkie-talkie. "Call me if any rebels do show up."

"Yes, *Nkosi.*" By his tone it was obvious he didn't like being left out of the fight. "What about them?" He waved the barrel of his assault rifle toward the bound rebels.

Mike started jogging for the exit. "If they give you any trouble, shoot them."

"Yes, *Nkosi.*" The reply came with a bit more enthusiasm.

AS Linda led her men toward the platform's main deck she was in communication with Juan, getting situational reports about the fluid gun battle. Rather then head to the nearest hatch leading out to the open, Cabrillo ordered her to thread her way through the lower floor so she would emerge on the rig's far side, behind the greatest concentration of gunmen.

He had her pause just out of view as he made hand gestures to his remaining fighters, coordinating what he hoped would be a final push to either break the rebels' will to fight or overwhelm them altogether. With only two magazines left in his ammo pouches, this was his last gambit.

"Okay, Juan, we're in position," Linda said. "I can see four of them. They're behind that big storage tank. There's another one angling to get close to the crane."

"Tell me when he's a yard from the crawler tread. I'll take him. You guys take the four you can see. I think a couple more are hanging off the side of the rig holding on to the safety net. I don't know if they've given up or what, so keep an eye out for them."

"Roger that. Your guy's got ten more yards to go."

Juan waited with his back pressed to the warm pipes. Through all the chaos and adrenaline, part of his mind remained focused on the problem of Daniel Singer's timing. No matter how far-fetched the idea, he was convinced that Singer had found a way to make a hurricane do his bidding.

Singer was an engineering genius after all. His invention had made him a millionaire a hundred times over while he was still in his twenties. As Max would say: The man might have a screw loose, but the machine was still humming.

"Five yards," Linda radioed.

Whatever Singer had planned had to be on a large scale, but Juan didn't know what it could be. He knew of nothing that could affect a hurricane's formation, severity, or the path it takes. A new anger hit him. If Singer had developed such a technology, why use it like this? Hurricanes and their Pacific and Indian Ocean cousins, typhoons and tsunamis, caused billions of dollars in damage, killed untold thousands of people every year, and left untold numbers of ruined lives in their wake. If Singer wanted to save the planet, ending such misery would be a fantastic first step, in Juan's opinion. It was the senseless waste that angered him. Like this attack here, like Samuel Makambo's revolution of personal self-aggrandizement, like the corruption that plagued Moses Ndebele's homeland. All of it sickened him.

"Two yards."

God, how he was tired of the fight. When the Berlin Wall came down and the Soviet Union collapsed his superiors at the CIA sat around and patted themselves on the back for a job well done. Juan had known the worst was yet to come as the world splintered on religious and tribal lines and the fighting emerged from the shadows.

He hated being right.

"Take him."

Cabrillo's concentration returned to the fighting without a moment's hesitation. He burst over the top of the drill pipes and loosed a three-round burst that hit the crawling gunman across the side and back. A barrage of fire erupted off to his left as more rebels targeted him. They were cut down by Linda and her team. Juan sprinted from behind the pipes, intentionally drawing fire to get the attackers to show themselves. His remaining people were prepared for this and for the second time since the battle started autofire blazed across the platform as though the gates of hell had opened.

It was the most intense close-quarter combat he had ever experienced. Bullets filled the air, some passing close enough for him to feel their heat. He dove over an oil barrel that had been knocked flat and had it pushed into him by a stuttering burst from at least two AKs stitching its side.

Linda saw one of the men firing at Juan but her snap shot missed as he vanished around a knot of pipes. She ran from her position and chased after him. It was like running into a forest of metal trees. The way the pipes crisscrossed and doubled back on themselves gave the gunman the advantage; no matter where she looked, down low or up high, her view was constantly blocked.

Realizing she could walk into a trap at any second, she started to retreat out of the maze, her eyes never lingering on a single spot for more than a second in case the gunman had outflanked her.

She rounded a vertical pipe as thick as a culvert and a hand reached out and yanked her machine pistol's barrel, sending her sprawling. She wished something profound would pop into her head in the second she had remaining, but her last thought was how she'd gotten herself killed by a rookie mistake.

The gun sounded like a cannon. The rebel who'd been standing over her had his head stretched like a Halloween mask before it simply vanished. She looked up to see Jim Gibson standing a few feet away in his size 13 Tony Lama's holding a huge revolver with its barrel pointing skyward and smoking.

"Strictly speaking, I'm not allowed to have my leg iron on the platform, but I always figured rules are for suckers." He reached down a big hand and hauled Linda to her feet. "You okay, darling?"

"Saved by a real live cowboy. How much better can I be?"

Knowing every rivet, screw, and weld on the rig, Gibson led her unerringly out of the labyrinth. When they got close to where Linda had first entered she realized she could no longer hear any gunfire.

She looked out cautiously. Five of the terrorists were standing up, their arms thrust so high they might have been standing on tiptoe. Two more emerged from where they'd been hiding in the safety net.

"Juan, I think it's over," she said into her throat mike.

Juan slid around the barrel and got to his feet, his aim never wavering from the marauders. He ran to them, shouting, "Down! Get down! Everybody down!"

Linda raced over to help cover them as they dropped flat. The Zimbabweans began to check the injured and dead while Juan cuffed the survivors. When he was finished he called his ship.

"Nomad to *Oregon*, target is secure. Repeat, target is secure."

"Heard you the first time," Max drawled. "I may be older than you but I'm not deaf." Then he added, "Good job. There wasn't a doubt in my mind."

"Thanks. What's the situation?"

"Mike's shut down the power plant. Oil's still flowing from the loading gantries but nowhere near as hard without the pumps. It's just gravity forcing crude through the lines from the tank farm."

"Is Linc ready?"

"Our cue to launch the SEAL boat was five minutes after Mikey took out the generators. He's leaving now."

LIKE a jet fighter being catapulted off an aircraft carrier, an actuator punched the semi-rigid black boat down a Teflon ramp from the boat garage and into the ocean. With a deep V hull for stability and an inflatable curtain for additional payload, the boat had been built by Zodiac's military division in Vancouver, Canada. She could cut across almost any sized wave as nimbly as an otter and hit speeds in excess of forty knots thanks to a pair of 300 hp outboards.

Linc had the wheel while Jerry Pulaski stood at his side. Both men wore two flak jackets over their utility uniforms. Bulletproof shields had been screwed into place so the helm amidships was nearly invulnerable. At their feet sat two long black cases containing Barrett M107 .50-caliber rifles. They had an effective range of a mile, making the thirty-two-pound guns perhaps the finest sniper rifles ever created.

With so much crude contaminating the waters around the loading terminal neither Juan nor Max were willing to risk the *Oregon*'s drive tubes becoming clogged with oil. And neither was willing to risk firing at the sensitive loading gantries if they couldn't guarantee one hundred percent accuracy from her weapons systems. It would be up to Linc and Ski to form the backstop for Mike's charge down the causeway.

They raced across the waves toward the bow of the supertanker lying at anchor and only slowed when the boat started cutting through the slick. The scum of oil was at least six inches thick and clung to the rubber pontoon ringing the hull. Fortunately, the props were below the toxic sludge; otherwise they'd barely make headway.

Behind them the *Oregon* was in motion again, maneuvering to get an oblique firing angle on this critical part of the facility. Though they wouldn't aim directly for the causeway or the acres-sized floating pier, Max had no qualms about tearing up the ocean all around them with the Gatlings.

Peering through a large pair of binoculars, Ski scanned the slab-sided tanker for any signs that the terrorists were using her as an observation platform. She looked clear. Just to be safe they would board her at the bow, more than a thousand feet from the superstructure, the most obvious place for a lookout.

They reached a string of buoys marking the hundred-yard off-limits zone surrounding the massive ship and there was still no fire from above.

"Dumb as we thought," Linc remarked.

From up close the ship's hull under its coat of red antifouling paint looked more like a steel wall rather than something designed to cruise the oceans, and with her tanks nearly empty, the deck rail loomed sixty feet over their heads.

As Linc worked the wheel and throttle to bring them up to the bow, Ski readied a grappling gun with rubber-coated tines. Just before the assault boat slid under the bow's curve he fired the hook skyward, two strands of nanofiber line trailing behind it. It sailed over the rail and when he drew back on the line it caught hard. Linc tossed a painter attached to a powerful magnet against the tanker's hull to secure the assault boat.

Though too thin to climb, the nanofiber was stronger than steel. Ski threaded the line through a winch bolted to the boat's deck and made sure the foot stirrups were secured. When he was ready he saw that Linc had opened the padded cases that held the two sniper rifles. Each already had a ten-round magazine in the receiver and they carried ten more apiece.

"Your chariot awaits," Ski said and stepped into the stirrup.

Linc did likewise and hit the button to start the winch. The nanofiber line started to slide through the pulley on the grappling. Ski's stirrup tightened and he was lifted off the assault boat, holding the rifle in one hand and the line in the other. When he was eight feet off the assault boat, the line took Linc's weight, and both men were lifted up the side of the tanker.

It took just seconds to reach the top. Ski kicked himself out of the stirrup and leapt over the rail. He landed softly and immediately brought the rifle at his shoulder and his eye to the scope, scanning the deck and superstructure for any movement. His stirrup jammed in the small pulley, arresting the nanofiber wire, and leaving Linc to climb the rail in order to reach the deck.

"Clear," Ski said without looking at him.

They started for the stern, each man running fifty feet and finding cover while the other kept the superstructure in his sights. Although there was no sign of activity anywhere on the ship, they maintained the leapfrog technique as a precaution. It took three minutes to reach the wheelhouse and, for the first time, they went to the port side of the tanker to look down at the loading pier. The twin gantries were taller than the ship, but their fat hoses dangled negligently, so the oil spewing from them fell only twenty feet before splashing to the dock and eventually oozing into the sea.

A rough count showed at least a hundred insurgents prepared to defend the dock. They'd had time to build barricades and fortify their position. Trono and his men were in for a tough slog if Linc and Ski couldn't disrupt the defense.

"What do you think?" Ski asked. "Is this good enough or do you want to get higher?"

"The height's good but we're too exposed if there is someone skulking around the ship. Let's get to the roof of the superstructure."

While they made their way into the ship and up a seemingly endless set of scissor stairs, Linc gave Max a situation report and learned that Mike and his men had fought their way across the terminal and were now in position.

A door opened near the top of the stairs. A man wearing a pair of black trousers and a white shirt with epaulettes emerged. Linc had his pistol out and pressed between the officer's eyes before the man had realized he wasn't alone in the staircase.

"No, please," he cried sharply.

"Quiet," Linc said and pulled back his automatic. "We're the good guys."

"You are American?" The officer was English.

"That's right, Captain," Linc said, noting the four gold stripes on his shoulder boards. "We're about to put an end to this situation. We need to get to the roof."

"Of course. Follow me." They started up. "What's going on? All I know is one minute we're taking on our normal load of crude and the next some idiot has yanked the hoses, damaging my ship. I called the marine office but no one picked up. Then my lookouts report armed men on the pier. Now it sounds like my days in the Falklands out there."

"Suffice it to say, your crew is going to be okay. Just don't let any of them near the deck or any open spaces."

"That's been my standing order all morning," the captain assured him. "Here we are."

They'd reached the top of the stairwell. There were no doors but there was a hatch in the ceiling accessible by a ladder. Ski started up without a word.

Linc held out his hand, "Thank you, Captain. We'll take it from here."

"Oh yes, right. Good luck to you," he said and shook Linc's outstretched hand.

Ski got the hatch open, flooding the stairwell with brilliant sunlight. He climbed through, followed by Linc. There was no way to lock the portal from the top, so they would have to keep an eye on it to make sure that no one came up after them.

The roof of the pilothouse was a featureless plane of white-painted steel shadowed by the ship's funnel and an antennae array. When they neared the edge they dropped to their bellies so as not to show themselves and again looked down over the dock. At the end of the causeway they could see Mike's small army awaiting their signal. The UAV buzzed nearby.

"*Oregon*, this is Linc. We are in position. Give us some time to designate targets. Stand by."

After setting up their rifles and placing full magazines along the lip of the roof so they could quickly shift positions, the two men scoped every one of the enemy soldiers, figuring out who the officers and noncoms were so they could decapitate the leadership, as the saying went.

"I'll be damned," Linc muttered.

"What?"

"Eleven o'clock. Guy with the shades chewing out some teenager."

Ski shifted his rifle so he could see who Linc was talking about. "Got him. Yeah? So? Who is he?"

"That, my friend, is Colonel Raif Abala, the sneaky bastard who pulled the double-cross on us when we were selling him the guns. He's General Makambo's right hand."

"Seems to be out of favor if Makambo sent him here," Ski said. "Want to take him first?"

"No, I think I'd rather see his face when he realizes what's what and who's who. You ready?"

"I've got at least four officers on my half of the dock and six more who seem like they know what they're doing. Rest are cannon fodder."

"Okay, then let's rock and roll. *Oregon*, we're ready."

"We're good to go here," he heard Mike Trono say over the tactical net.

Max's reply was letting Mark Murphy unleash a torrent of shells from the Gatling gun. The water and oil soup ten yards off the causeway exploded in a line that extended its entire length. It was as though the ocean had reared up in a continuous wall. The rebels cowered at the sight and sound as they were doused with filthy spray. A soldier stationed on the causeway broke cover to run back to the floating dock.

With the Gatling's scream overriding the sound of their shots, Linc and Ski got to work, firing as fast as they could. One shot equaled one kill. Every time. After firing five rounds they could see confused soldiers start to look around as their leaders dropped. The two snipers backed away from the edge and shifted further aft. When Linc looked through his scope again he could see Abala screaming at his men. By the fear Link could see written in the faces of Abala's troops his rants were having little success. In the distance, Mike and his team were cautiously coming down the causeway.

Again, he and Ski found their targets and again the rebel leadership was decimated. A soldier finally realized the shots were coming from above and behind them and looked up at the tanker. The guerilla was about to shout a warning to his comrades but got no further than opening his mouth before Ski dropped him with one of his Barrett's half-inch slugs.

"Mike, you're about eighty feet from the first ambush," Tiny Gunderson said over the radio.

"What are they doing? My Softscreen's down again."

"If I were a betting man I'd say talking about giving up. No, wait, my mistake. I think one's trying to rally them. No, wait again. He's down. Nice shot, Ski."

"That was me," Linc said.

"And courage has left the building," Tiny crowed. "They've dropped their weapons and are reaching for the sky."

That first sign of capitulation broke the dam for the rest. All along the causeway and on the loading dock men were laying down their arms. Only Abala seemed interested in fighting on. He waved his pistol like a madman. Linc watched him level it at a young guerrilla, screaming at him, presumably, to pick up his AK-47. He shot off half of Abala's foot before the colonel could murder the unarmed man.

Trono's team swept through the defeated rebels, tossing their captured AKs into a pile and patting down each man for additional weapons.

Linc and Ski remained in their sniper nest, making sure there were no holdouts until the entire area had been secured.

"That's the last of them," Mike announced. He was standing over Colonel Abala, who was on the dock writhing in pain. "Who missed on this guy?"

"That was no miss, son," Linc said. "Once he gets out of the hospital that's the cat that's going to lay this whole thing on Makambo and Singer."

It took ten minutes for Linc and Ski to get down to the dock. Linc approached Abala and squatted next to him. The rebel colonel was nearly in shock and didn't acknowledge his presence, so Linc lightly slapped his face until he looked over. Spittle bubbled from Abala's lips and he had a deathly pallor under his dark skin.

"Remember me, numb nuts?" Linc asked. Abala's eyes went wide. "That's right. Congo River, about a week or so ago. You thought you could double-cross us. Well, this is what happens." Linc leaned close. "Never, and I mean never, mess with the Corporation."

* * *

WHEN the Angolan army finally arrived at the Petromax terminal, the *Oregon*—with her equipment, her crew, and all of Moses Ndeble's men, alive or dead—was well over the horizon.

The Angolan forces found that the oil flowing to the loading pier had been shut off and crews had capped the two offshore wells. They also discovered eighty-six corpses laid out next to an administrative building and over four hundred frightened men roped together and locked inside, many of them wounded. One of them, who had a bloody bandage wrapped around his truncated foot, had a sign draped over his neck that read:

MY NAME IS RAIF ABALA. I AM A COLONEL IN SAMUEL MAKAMBO'S CONGOLESE ARMY OF REVOLUTION AND WAS HIRED TO PERPETRATE THIS ACT OF TERRORISM BY DANIEL SINGER, FORMERLY OF MERRICK/SINGER. I UNDERSTAND THAT IF I DO NOT COOPERATE THE PEOPLE WHO STOPPED US TODAY WILL FIND ME.
  HAVE A NICE DAY.

29

THE shabby appearance of the *Oregon* was expertly applied camouflage to make her look neglected, but the dilapidation of the *Gulf of Sidra* was the real thing. For twenty years she'd tracked back and forth across the Mediterranean carrying her loads of oil while her owners eked every penny of profit they could. If something broke it was replaced with a used part, hastily repaired with duct tape and bailing wire, or discarded altogether. When her sewage treatment plant went down it was bypassed and repiped to dump directly into the sea. Her air-conditioning system merely moved hot air around the superstructure rather than cooled it. And with the galley's walk-in cooler not working, the chefs had to balance taking food out of the freezer and letting it thaw but not spoil.

Her black hull was streaked with rust while bare metal showed on her superstructure, and her single funnel was so streaked with exhaust that it was impossible to tell it had once been painted green and yellow. The only modern piece of equipment aboard her was the new escape pod hanging over her stern, put there at the insistence of her captain once he learned where they were sailing.

With a beam of a hundred and twenty feet and the length of three football fields, the *Gulf of Sidra* was a huge ship, though small in comparison to the 350,000-ton tanker that had been berthed at the Petromax terminal. Her outdated design left her seven holds capable of carrying only 104,000 tons of crude.

Though she had become a fixture lying at anchor outside the Mauritanian port of Nouakchott, a hazy silhouette against the western horizon that had been there for weeks, her departure went largely ignored. She'd steamed from the city as soon as Daniel Singer had arrived from Angola and had put more than two hundred miles between herself and the coast.

She was chasing a tropical depression moving across the Atlantic that had the potential to build into a hurricane. It was the storm Singer had been waiting for, the perfect conditions to test what the world's brightest meteorological minds and the most sophisticated computer models said would happen.

With the temperature in his cabin hovering above a hundred degrees, Singer had taken to spending as much time as he could on the wing bridge, where at least the ship's seventeen-knot speed created a breeze.

He'd just gotten word over the BBC wireless service that Samuel Makambo's attack had been foiled by Angolan troops. Nearly a hundred guerillas had been killed in the swift counterattack and four hundred captured. Singer wondered briefly if Colonel Abala, the only rebel who could identify him, was among the living or the dead and decided it didn't matter. If he was linked to the assault the publicity of a court appearance would only spread the word. He'd hire the flashiest lawyers he could find and get his case shifted to the World Court in The Hague. There he would use the opportunity to put humanity's treatment of the earth on trial.

What truly bothered him about the failed attack was that estimates put the amount of oil spilled at about twelve thousand tons. Though an environmental catastrophe, it was far short of the million tons he'd been planning on. There would be no cloud of benzene arsonic acid lacing the storm and spreading its poison across the southeastern United States. It would be a punishing storm, the worst hurricane to hit America in recorded history, but without the noxious contamination he feared it wouldn't touch off the panic he'd expected.

He knew he would have to contact the media and explain once the storm was over—or better yet, when it was about to make landfall—how a chance battle in a remote part of the world had prevented a catastrophe.

It would be one more example of how interconnected the earth was, how we were leaving our future to the vagaries of chance.

Adonis Cassedine, the ship's master, stepped out from the bridge. Unlike his handsome mythological namesake, Cassedine was a sour-looking man with an unshaven face and rodent-sharp eyes. His nose was askew from being poorly set after a break, so the smudged glasses he wore tilted off one of his cauliflower ears.

"I just got a report from a container ship a hundred miles in front of us." Sunset was still hours away and already his breath smelled of the cheap gin he swilled. To his credit, however, he didn't slur his words and his body only swayed a little. "They are encountering Force Four conditions with winds out of the northeast."

"The storm is forming," Singer said. "And just where we need it to be. Not too far out that it has settled on its course, but not too close that it could fail to coalesce."

"I can get you there," Cassedine said, "but I don't like it."

Here we go again. Singer was already angered over Makambo's failure. He didn't want to hear another complaint from this washed-up rummy.

"This ship, she is old. Her hull is rotting and what you have in her holds, it's too hot. It is weakening the metal."

"And I showed you the engineers' reports that say the hull can take the thermal load."

"Bah." Cassedine dismissed the statement with a wave. "Fancy men in suits who know nothing of the sea. You want to take us into a hurricane and I say the ship will break in two when we hit Force Six."

Singer moved closer to the captain, using his superior height to intimidate the Greek. "Listen to me, you damned lush. I am paying you more money than you've seen in your lifetime, enough to keep you in a bottle for decades. For that I expect you to do your job and stop bothering me with your predictions, your concerns, or your opinions. Do I make myself clear?"

"I am just saying—"

"Nothing!" Singer roared. "You are saying nothing. Now get out of my face before your breath makes me sick."

Singer kept glaring at Cassedine until the captain backed off, as he knew he would. Singer believed most alcoholics were weak, and this one was no different. He was so far gone he would do just about anything he was told in order to keep up a constant state of inebriation. He felt no qualms exploiting such weakness, just like he'd felt no qualms exploiting the naïveté of Nina Visser's eco-crusaders or Samuel Makambo's greed. If that was what it took to make people stand up and notice the destruction they were doing to their planet, so be it. Hadn't Geoffrey Merrick exploited Singer's own genius to create their invention? Singer had done the lion's share of the work while Merrick had taken the credit.

All along everyone believed Singer preferred to stay out of the limelight and in the background. What a load of junk. What person wouldn't like to receive the praise of their peers, the accolades, the awards? Singer had wanted all that, too, but it was as if the media only saw one half of Merrick/Singer, the telegenic half, the half with the easy smile and the charming anecdotes. It wasn't Singer's fault that he froze at the lectern and looked like a cadaver on TV or came across as an idiot savant in an interview. He'd been given no choice but a shadow existence—only it was under Merrick's shadow he'd had to live.

Again he cursed that his former partner wasn't here, denying him the opportunity to lord it over him. He wanted to look Merrick in the eye and scream, "It's your fault! You let the polluters keep destroying the environment and now you are going to see the consequences."

He spat over the *Gulf of Sidra*'s side, watching his saliva fall until it became part of the ocean, a drop in the biggest bucket in the world. Singer had been like that once, a small piece of something so much larger than himself it was impossible to believe he could make a difference.

He would be insignificant no longer.

CABRILLO'S first order when he returned to the *Oregon* was to send her charging northward, to where Africa bulged into the Atlantic and where the hot winds blowing off the Sahara eventually evaporated enough water to spawn hurricanes. He didn't return to his cabin until he'd overseen the refitting of his ship. The *Liberty*'s hull was scrubbed and her tanks refueled and she was back on her davit. The two submersibles had had their coating of oil scoured off with solvents and brooms, their batteries recharged, and all the equipment that had been removed put back. The Gatlings, 40 mm, and .30 calibers had all been checked over, their barrels and receivers cleaned and their ammo bins refilled. Armorers were repacking the AK-47s given to Moses' men and tagging the almost five hundred guns they had taken back from Makambo's forces. Juan hadn't forgotten the bounty Lang Overholt had put on those weapons' return.

But as busy as he'd been, he couldn't come close to the work Dr. Julia Huxley and her team were performing in medical. They had twenty-three patients to look after, a total of thirty-one bullets to remove, and enough organs and limbs to put back together it seemed she'd never leave surgery. The instant she stripped off one pair of bloody rubber gloves an orderly snapped on a fresh pair for her to tackle the next injured man. At one point her anesthesiologist quipped he'd passed more gas than a judge at a chili contest.

But after fifteen straight hours of work, she sewed closed a bullet graze on Mike Trono's shoulder, a wound he didn't even remember receiving, and knew there were no more. When Mike had hopped off the table Julia had rolled onto it with a theatrical groan.

"Come on, Hux," Mike teased. "Getting the injuries is a lot tougher than fixing them."

She didn't open her eyes when she replied, "First of all, that little scratch you got doesn't even qualify as an injury. The cat I used to have clawed me worse than that. Second, if you don't appreciate my work I'll be more than happy to pull the stitches and let you bleed a while longer."

"Tsk, tsk, what about your Hippocratic oath?"

"I had my fingers crossed when I took it."

He gave her a kiss on the cheek. "Sweet dreams, Doc. Thanks."

No sooner had Mike left the OR than a shadow blocked the lights hanging over the table. Julia levered open her eyes to see the chairman looming over her. By the grim look on his face she saw he knew.

"I want to see her."

Julia got off the table and led Cabrillo through to another part of the medical bay, a small chilled room with a single table in the center. Four stainless-steel drawers were built into one wall. Without saying anything, she slid open one of them to reveal a nude body enclosed in an opaque plastic bag. Juan tore the plastic covering the head and stepped back to study the pale gray face of Susan Donleavy.

"How'd she do it?"

"It was a nasty way to die," Julia said, ten times more exhausted now than she'd been a moment earlier. "She stuck out her tongue as far as she could and let herself fall forward. Her chin slammed the deck and her teeth severed her tongue. She then rolled over and basically drowned in her own blood. I can't imagine what it takes to fall like that and not try to stop it with your hands."

"She was cuffed."

"She could have turned her head at the last second." Julia looked at the body sadly. "For all we know maybe she did it again and again until she got her courage up for a final attempt."

Cabrillo didn't say anything for a moment. He was remembering the boat chase in Sandwich Bay after he and Sloane had found Papa Heinrick murdered. The driver he'd been following had intentionally crashed his boat into the shore rather than risk capture. He had thought maybe it was out of fear, that he didn't want to face an African prison, but the truth was the guy had sacrificed himself for the cause. Just like Susan Donleavy.

"No," he said with certainty. "She did it right the first time."

"You've reviewed the security tapes from her cell?"

He turned to face her. "Don't need to. I know the type."

"Fanatic."

"Yup. Biting off the tongue was an acceptable alternative to hara-kiri for captured Japanese soldiers during World War Two."

"I'm sorry, Juan. Scuttlebutt around the ship is that she might have known some more useful information."

"She did." He looked at Julia. "And I think Geoff Merrick knows it, too. I need you to wake him."

"Forget it. His blood pressure's still too low. I've barely checked his wound for fragments and am only now getting his infection under control. I admit his coma's much shallower, but his body's refusing to come around."

"Julia, I don't have a choice. Singer ordered the raid this morning at a specific time because he's got something else planned. He kidnapped

Merrick because he wanted him to see what it was. When Linda interviewed Susan she said that Singer spent a few hours at the Devil's Oasis talking with Merrick. I am willing to bet he spilled the whole thing then."

"Are you willing to bet his life?"

"Yes," Juan said without hesitation. "Whatever Singer's up to is likely to involve a hurricane. I think he's devised a way to shape them somehow. Do you need me to lay out what that means? You took leave to volunteer in New Orleans after Katrina."

"I was born there."

"We can stop another city from suffering the same fate. Julia, you have full autonomy over medical decisions on this ship but only because I say you do. If you would prefer me to give you an order, I will."

She hesitated, then said, "I'll do it."

Juan knew he should ask Linda to conduct the interview, it was her area of expertise, but he wasn't extracting information from a reluctant captive, only talking to a half-conscious victim. "Let's go."

Hux grabbed some supplies from the OR and led Cabrillo through to the recovery rooms. Where once Geoffrey Merrick had a room to himself, he now shared the space with three wounded Africans. His sunburned face was covered in gel to help his skin heal, but beneath it Juan could see the scientist remained pale. After checking his vital signs Julia injected a stimulant into his IV drip.

Merrick came around slowly. At first his eyes remained closed and the only sign of movement was his tongue attempting to lick his dry lips. Julia moistened them with a wet cloth. Then his eyes fluttered and opened. His looked from Julia to Juan and back to the doctor again, obviously disorientated.

"Dr. Merrick, my name is Juan Cabrillo. You're safe now. You were rescued from the people who kidnapped you and are now in the sick bay of my ship."

Before Merrick could reply, Julia asked, "How are you feeling?"

"Thirsty," he rasped.

She tipped a glass of water with a straw to his mouth and he took several grateful sips. "How's your chest?"

He thought about his answer for a moment. "Numb."

"You were shot," Juan told him.

"I don't remember."

"Susan Donleavy shot you during the rescue."

"She wasn't beat up," Merrick said as a fragment of the memory came back. "I thought they had tortured her, but it was all faked with makeup."

"Daniel Singer showed up one day when you were being held prisoner. Do you remember that?"

"I think so."

"He did and you two spoke."

"Where's Susan now?" the scientist asked.

"She killed herself, Doctor." Merrick stared at him. "She did that to prevent us from learning what Singer intends to do."

"Oil rigs." Merrick's voice was fading to a whisper as his body fought the drugs in an attempt to return to unconsciousness.

"That's right. He planned on attacking oil rigs off the coast of Angola and causing a huge slick. What else was he planning? Did he tell you?"

"You have to stop him. The oil is especially toxic." His last words were slurred.

"We have," Juan said. "His assault failed. The slick will be contained."

"Ship," he said dreamily.

"There was a ship at the terminal but it wasn't attacked."

"No. Singer has a ship."

"What is he using it for?"

"It was Susan's discovery. She took it to him. I thought it was only a test, but she had already perfected it." His eyes closed.

"Perfected what, Geoff? What did Susan perfect? Dr. Merrick?"

"An organic gel that turns water into pudding."

"Why?" Juan asked desperately, fearing Merrick was slipping away. "What is it used for?"

Merrick said nothing for nearly twenty seconds. "Heat," he finally whispered. "It gives off a lot of heat."

And there was the connection Cabrillo had been looking for. Hurricanes need heat and Singer was going to give one a boost. If he released the contents of a vessel laden with Susan Donleavy's gel into the ocean, probably at the epicenter of a forming storm, the heat would give the weather system a kick start exactly when and where he wanted. That was how he knew when to attack the Petromax terminal. The prevailing winds would carry the oil vapors northward into the hurricane he had helped generate.

Juan knew the seas off Africa's west coast were the logical place Singer would dump the gel, but the area was vast and there wasn't enough time to conduct a search. He had to narrow the parameters. "What kind of ship is Singer using?" A tanker was the most likely candidate, but Juan wouldn't lead the semiconscious man with his suspicions.

Merrick remained mute, his eyes closed and his lips slightly parted. Julia was watching his monitor, and Juan knew the look on her face. She didn't like what she was seeing.

He shook Merrick's shoulder. "Geoff, what kind of ship?"

"Juan," Julia said in a warning tone.

Merrick's head rolled to face him but he couldn't open his eyes. "A tanker. He bought an oil tanker."

The monitor started to wail as his heart rate slowed dangerously. Julia pushed Juan aside, shouting, "He's crashing! Get the cart in here!" She threw aside the sheet covering his chest as one of her staff raced into the room with a portable defibrillator.

Through it all Merrick managed to open his eyes. They were clouded with pain. He reached out to clutch Cabrillo's hand, his mouth forming three words he didn't have the breath to say aloud.

The chirping alarm turned into a continuous tone.

"Clear," Julia said, the paddles poised over Merrick's naked torso. Juan took his hand away so Julia could apply the electrical impulse to restart Merrick's heart. His body convulsed as the charge ran through him and the monitor showed a corresponding spike before returning to flat line.

"Eppy." The orderly handed Julia a syringe full of epinephrine. The needle seemed impossibly long. She speared the area between two of Singer's ribs and loaded the drug directly into his heart. "Up it to two hundred joules."

"Charging, charging, charging," the orderly said watching the machine. "Go."

She applied the paddles again and for a second time Merrick's body jerked partially off the bed. The line on the monitor peaked again.

"Come on. Come on," Julia urged and then the beat was back, widely spaced at first but improving steadily. "Get a ventilator in here." She shot a scathing look at Cabrillo. "Was it worth it?"

He met her gaze. "We'll know when we find a tanker named the *Gulf of Sidra*."

30

THE weather was turning foul as the *Oregon* raced northward, forcing a delicate balance between speed and the need to keep the wounded from being further injured by the ship's motion. Julia had torn a page from the nineteenth century by slinging the worst of the wounded in hammocks so they swayed with the swells and were cushioned when the ship was hit by a particularly tall wave. She hadn't left Merrick's side for more than twenty minutes since getting his heart started again.

After getting the name, it had taken Murph and Eric less than a half hour to discover that a tanker called the *Gulf of Sidra* had been anchored off the coast of Mauritania for nearly a month but had weighed anchor the day before. The ship had been owned by Libya's state oil monopoly until a recent sale transferred her to a newly incorporated Liberian firm called CroonerCo., which Murph recognized as a thinly veiled reference to Singer's last name.

With that information the duo had been able to calculate an ever widening arc where the vessel could be hiding, an area that would soon include a tropical depression swirling six hundred miles off the African coast. They were driving as hard as they dared for that region.

To narrow the odds further, Juan had again called upon Lang Overholt to use the United States' government's halo of spy satellites to search the grid coordinates for the *Gulf of Sidra*. Now that everyone was aware of the stakes, Overholt had taken Cabrillo's findings to the CIA's director. The president was briefed a short while later and orders went out to the Coast Guard and Navy as well as NUMA and the National Weather Service, which was conducting regular patrols of hurricane alley. A guided missile cruiser returning from interdiction patrols in the Red Sea was diverted and a destroyer paying a courtesy call to Algiers cut short her stay and started out of the Mediterranean. There was also a pair of nuclear attack submarines close enough to the area to reach it in twenty hours.

The British government was apprised of the situation and offered to send two vessels from Gibraltar and another from Portsmouth. They would arrive on station days after the Americans, but their help was greatly appreciated.

Juan knew, however, that even with all of these ships streaming in to search for the tanker, the *Oregon*, with her superior speed, would be the first to reach the edge of the storm and it would fall on his shoulders to stop Daniel Singer.

SLOANE Macintyre weaved down the passageway carrying a dinner tray that Maurice had personally prepared. With her arm still in a sling it was awkward, and she found herself leaning a shoulder against the walls to keep herself steady. It was almost eleven and she didn't see another soul as she made her way aft. She came to the door she wanted and had to use her foot to tap on it softly. When there was no reply she hit it a little louder with the same results.

She set the tray on the carpeted deck and cracked open the door. She could see dim lighting from inside.

"Juan," she called softly and retrieved the tray. "You weren't at dinner so I had Maurice fix you a little something."

She stepped over the threshold, not yet feeling that she was intruding. A lamp spilled a pool of light across half of Cabrillo's desk. The other half was blushed with the muted glow of a computer monitor. The chair was pushed back as if Juan had just gotten up from working but he wasn't at the file cabinet or the antique safe. The sofa tucked under a darkened porthole was empty.

She set the tray on the desk and said his name again as she approached his dim bedroom. He lay facedown on the bed and before Sloane took in the whole picture she looked away, thinking he was nude. When she peeked back shyly she saw he wore a pair of boxer shorts nearly the same color as his skin, though a crescent of pale white showed above the boxer's waistband. Then she feared he wasn't breathing until his chest expanded like a bellows.

For the first time she allowed herself to stare at his stump. The skin was red and puckered and looked raw, no doubt from all the fighting he'd been involved in. The muscles of his upper legs were large and even in sleep they didn't seem relaxed. In fact, none of him did. His whole body was tensed. She held her breath to listen carefully and heard his teeth grinding together.

His back was a patchwork of old scars and new bruises. There were six identical marks that looked as though he'd taken a shotgun blast and what she hoped was a healed surgical incision and not a knife wound because it began just over his kidney and disappeared under his shorts.

His clothing had been tossed onto the floor and as she folded it, she wondered what kind of man would pay such a heavy price to do what he did. He gave no outward sign that at night his dreams gave him a case of bruxism that sounded like he was going to pulverize his teeth. And although he was barely in his forties, he had accumulated two lifetime's worth of scars. Some force drove him to put himself in danger despite the cumulative effects it was having on his body.

It wasn't a suicide wish, of that she was sure. She could tell by his easy banter with Max and the others that Juan Cabrillo loved life more than anyone. And maybe that was it. He had put it upon himself to make certain others had the opportunity to enjoy their lives as much as he did. He had made himself a protector even if those he looked after would never know of his efforts. She thought back to their conversation about what he would be if not the captain of the *Oregon*. He'd said a paramedic, an unsung hero if ever there was one.

When she draped his pants over a wooden valet, his wallet fell to the floor.

Sloane looked over at Juan. He hadn't moved a muscle. Feeling a twinge of guilt, but not enough to overcome her curiosity, she opened the wallet.

All it contained was cash in a variety of currencies. No credit cards, no business cards, nothing to identify him in any way. She should have known. He wouldn't carry around anything that could link him back to his ship or give his enemies information about who he really was.

Sloane looked over to the office, where the lighting made his desk seem to dominate the space. She padded silently to it, glancing in his direction again before gently tugging open the middle drawer. This is where Cabrillo kept himself. She found a gold and onyx Dunhill lighter and an ornate cigar cutter. She found his American passport and saw nearly every page had been stamped. She preferred his hair short like he kept it now versus the photo taken six years earlier. There were two more U.S. passports, one with the picture of a great slob of a man named Jeddediah Smith, and it took her a moment to realize it was Juan in disguise. There were others from various countries and under different aliases, as well as matching credit cards for all the personas, and shipmaster's licenses for both Juan and his Smith character. She found a gold pocket watch inscribed to Hector Cabrillo from Rosa and suspected it belonged to his grandfather. Amid the bric-a-brac were a few letters from his parents, his old CIA ID tag, a small four-barreled antique pistol like a riverboat gambler might carry, an ivory-handled magnifying glass, and a rusted Cub Scout pocketknife.

Toward the back of the drawer was an inlaid Turkish box and inside she made a discovery she never expected—a gold wedding band. It was a simple pipe-cut ring, and judging by how little it was scratched, Sloane thought it hadn't been worn much. She wondered what stupid woman had let a man like Juan get away. They were one in a million and if you were lucky enough to find one you did whatever it took to make it work. She looked more carefully into the box and saw a piece of paper folded so it completely covered the bottom.

She was on the cusp between snooping and prying and glanced over her shoulder to where Juan was sleeping before reaching for the slip of paper. It was a police report of a single-car accident in Falls Church, Virginia, that had claimed the life of Amy Cabrillo. Tears pricked Sloane's eyes. As she read through the dry report she learned that Juan's wife's blood alcohol level was nearly three times the legal limit.

A man like Juan would marry once in his life, to the woman he felt certain he could grow old with. The fact that this woman had taken that from him made Sloane hate her all the more. She wiped at her cheek and care-fully refolded the report and set everything back into the drawer the way she'd found it. She picked up the tray of food and retreated from the cabin.

Linda Ross rounded a corner just as Sloane got the door closed.

"Hi, roomie," Sloane said quickly to cover her embarrassment. "I didn't see Juan at dinner so I brought him some food. He's asleep."

"Is that why you're crying?"

"I . . ." Sloane could say nothing more.

Linda smiled warmly. "Don't worry about it. It'll be our secret. For what it's worth he's probably the best man I've ever met."

"Have you and he?"

"I'll admit he's as handsome as the devil and the thought crossed my mind when I first came aboard; but no we haven't and never will. He's my commander and my friend and both are too important to screw up with an affair."

"But that's all it'll ever be, isn't it? I sense he's a one-woman man and any opportunity has passed."

"You know about Amy?"

"I was snooping and saw the police report."

"Don't tell Juan you saw that. He doesn't think any of the crew knows he's a widower. Max made the mistake of telling Maurice once and, well, Maurice gossips like an old woman. And yeah, it would probably only be a short-term thing but not because he's in mourning over Amy. He's got another love, one no woman can compete with."

"The *Oregon*."

Linda nodded. "So think through what you want to do before you do anything."

"Thanks."

As they walked away Juan's cabin door opened slowly and he peered down the corridor. The sound of his desk drawer opening had wakened him but he'd feigned sleep so as not to embarrass Sloane. He would have to talk to Max about his inability to keep a secret and Maurice, too, for that matter. He closed the door again, thinking that what he overheard made a decision he'd been contemplating a bit more difficult.

* * *

JUAN was in the living room of the guest cabin talking with Moses Ndebele. His men were resigned to their beds, nearly incapacitated by seasickness. He enjoyed Ndebele's intellect and his ability to forgive considering how harshly he'd been treated by his government. Unlike some men, who when they gain power trample freedoms and impoverish their people in a quest for wealth and personal glory, Ndebele really did want what was best for Zimbabwe. He spoke of economic reforms, of getting the country's once thriving agriculture sector back to its former capacity. He talked about power sharing among the tribes and an end to the nepotism that ruined many African nations.

More than anything else he wanted his people to no longer fear their own government.

Cabrillo was more convinced than ever that making his bargain with Moses had been the right call. They had the chance to restore what had once been a shining beacon in sub-Saharan Africa and make it again the envy of the continent. Of course, all it would take was to find a boat lost for a century that had sunk somewhere in about a thousand square miles of ocean.

He felt the ship suddenly veer. He judged the turn to be at least fifteen degrees and was getting to his feet when his phone chimed.

"Someone found her," he said, knowing it was Max with the news they'd been waiting thirty hours to hear. He mouthed an apology to Moses as he strode from the room.

"She was detected by something called Mag-Star," Hanley said. "Apparently it's a new military satellite that can detect the distortion a large steel-hulled ship has on the earth's magnetic field."

Juan was familiar with the technology. "How far are we from her?"

"Another hundred and fifty miles and, to answer your next question, we're still the closest of all the vessels vectoring in."

Calculating speed and distances Juan said, "That'll put us on her about sunset, not that we've seen the sun in a while."

The *Oregon* had been steaming under a roiling veil of cloud cover since before dawn, while the seas had built to fifteen-foot waves that pounded her hull. The ship had no problem shouldering aside the swells; she was designed to absorb much worse and at speeds greater than she was making, but the wounded were taking a beating despite Hux's best efforts. The wind hovered around thirty knots with gusts edging Force Eight on the Beaufort Scale. Although the rain hadn't started yet, the forecasts predicted it would hit within a couple of hours.

"Taking down the *Gulf of Sidra* in this storm's going to be tough enough," Max remarked. "Darkness is only going to make it worse."

"Tell me about it," Juan said. "I'll be there in a second."

Moments later he strode into the operations center. The regular watch standers were being replaced by the Corporation's best team. It was difficult because the ship was pitching violently and the crew had to keep one hand continuously braced against a counter or bulkhead. Eric Stone was already at the helm; Mark Murphy, sporting a shirt that advocated nuking the whales, was sliding into the weapons station while Hali was jacking into the communications systems. Linda Ross arrived while Eddie and Linc stood against the back wall, as different as Mutt and Jeff in every aspect but competence.

Max came over from where he was monitoring his beloved engines as soon as Juan got into the center chair. On the main monitor was a satellite picture of the Atlantic. The clouds were beginning to curl into the familiar pattern of a burgeoning hurricane. The image shifted every few seconds to show the past several hours of the growing storm. The eye was just beginning to form.

"Okay, where are we and where's the *Sidra*?" Juan asked.

Stone tapped at his computer and two flashing icons appeared on the monitor. The *Gulf of Sidra* was positioned right at the edge of where the eye was growing, with the *Oregon* driving in hard from the southeast.

They watched the screen for more than an hour as it was updated by the National Reconnaissance Office, the secretive government agency that oversaw nearly all U.S. spy satellites. The more the storm took on a hurricane's distinctive shape, the tighter Singer's tanker turned, keeping just inside the strengthening eye wall.

"I'm getting some more information from Overholt," Hali said, staring at his computer. "Says here the NRO has some additional data on the target. Checking back through their logs they've been able to re-create her course for the two hours before they ID'd her. Eric, I'm sending this over to you."

When he received the e-mail from across the room Eric typed in the coordinates. "Coming up now," he said and hit Enter.

The icon for the *Sidra* bounced back a couple of inches on the screen then tracked forward. It looked as if the eye was forming along her course rather than her running along its edge.

"What the hell?" Juan muttered.

"I was right!" Eric cried.

"Yeah, yeah, you're a genius," Mark said, then turned to face Cabrillo. "He and I were back in my cabin brainstorming. Well, we also did a little hacking into Merrick/Singer's mainframe. Susan Donleavy didn't keep notes on the computer. She either had a stand alone or just wrote stuff out longhand. Anyway, all we found about her project was her original proposal and even that was pretty thin. Her idea was to create an organic flocculent."

"A what?"

"It's a compound that causes soils and other solids suspended in water to form into clumps," Eric answered. "It's used in sewage treatment plants, for example, to settle out the waste."

"She wanted to find a way to bind the organic material found in seawater in order to turn water into a gel."

"What for?" Max asked bluntly.

"Didn't say," Mark replied, "and apparently no one on the peer review committee cared because she got the go-ahead without explaining the need for something like this."

Stone continued, "We know from your talk with Merrick that the reaction is exothermic and, from what I can guess, it probably isn't sustainable. The heat will eventually kill off the organics and the gel will dissolve back into ordinary seawater."

"I'm following you," Juan said, "but I don't see a point to all this."

"If Singer lays down a line of flocculent it will spread for a while and then just fizzle out." Mark blew a raspberry to emphasize his point. "The hurricane would absorb some of its heat as it passes over it but not really enough to make any major changes to its severity or direction."

Eric butted in, "My idea is that if he spreads it in a circle just as the hurricane begins to revolve he will be able to dictate where and when the eye will form—and most important, how big it will be."

"And the tighter the eye, the faster the wind can whip around it," Max added.

"Andrew's was eleven miles across when he came ashore in Miami," Murph said. "Natural processes limit how small it can be, but Singer can push that so the hurricane goes above five on the Saffir-Simpson Scale. He might also be able to control where the storm tracks as it heads across the Atlantic, in essence pointing it like a gun at whatever coastal region he chooses."

Cabrillo studied at the monitor again. It looked as though the *Gulf of Sidra* was doing exactly what Eric and Murph predicted. She was in the beginning of a spiraling turn, using the heat generated by Susan Donleavy's gel, which she was doubtlessly discharging as fast as her pumps could go, to tease the storm tighter and tighter. Singer would make the eye smaller and thus the hurricane more powerful than anything nature was able to create.

"If he finishes that turn there won't be a damned thing we can do," Eric concluded. "The eye will be formed and no force on earth will be able to stop it."

"Any idea where he's sending it?"

"If it were me I'd take out New Orleans again," Murph said, "but I don't know if he'll have that level of control. Safest bet would be to slam it into Florida where the warm coastal waters won't weaken it. Miami or Jacksonville are the highest profile cities. Andrew caused something like nine billion in damages and that was Category Four. Hit either city with a Category Six and it'll topple skyscrapers."

"Max," Juan said without looking at him, "what's our speed?"

"Just a tick under thirty-five knots."

"Helm, take us to forty."

"The doc ain't gonna like that," Max chided.

"I'm already in Dutch for making her wake Merrick," Juan said humorlessly.

Eric followed the order, ramping up the magnetohydrodynamics to eke more electricity from the sea to feed into the pump jets. The *Oregon* began to ride even rougher as she cut across the waves. An external camera showed her bow almost being swamped as she slammed into the swells. Water sheeted across the deck in a three-foot-deep surge when she lifted free.

Cabrillo tapped at his communications console to dial up the hangar.

A technician answered and went to get George Adams per Juan's request. "I don't like that you're calling me," Adams said by way of greeting.

"Can you do it, George?"

"It'll be a nightmare," the pilot replied, "but yeah I think I can as long as the rains don't hit. And I don't want to hear any grief if I damage the Robinson's landing struts."

"I won't say a word. Place yourself on ten-minute standby and wait to hear from me."

"You got it."

Juan killed the connection. "Wepps, what's the status on our fish?"

On each side of the *Oregon*'s prow below her waterline was a tube capable of launching a Russian Test-71 torpedo. Each of the two-ton weapons were wire guided, with a range of nearly ten miles, a maximum speed of forty knots, and four hundred and fifty pounds of high explosives loaded into its nose. When he'd designed the *Oregon* Cabrillo had wanted American-made MK-48 ADCAP torpedoes, but no amount of sweet-talking would budge Langston's refusal. As it was, the surplus Soviet torpedoes were powerful enough to sink any but the most heavily armored ships.

"You're not considering torpedoing the *Sidra*, are you?" Mark asked. "That'll dump her entire load of gel in one concentrated spot. At this stage that much heat could have nearly the same effect as if the ship had completed her circle."

"I'm just covering all my options," Juan reassured him.

"Okay, good." Mark called up a diagnostic on the torpedoes. "They were pulled from the tubes three days ago for routine inspection. A battery on the fish in Tube One was replaced. Both are showing full charge now."

"So what's your play?" Max asked Juan.

"Simplest solution is to chopper a team over there, take control of the tanker, and shut off her discharge pumps."

"You know, Chairman," Eric said, "if we sail her far enough away from the eye and start dumping the gel again, the heat should generate excess evaporation and create another powerful low pressure zone. It would disrupt the storm and literally tear it apart."

"Oh, God!" Hali exclaimed suddenly. He hit a switch on his panel and a strident voice filled the control room.

"I repeat, this is Adonis Cassedine, master of the VLCC *Gulf of Sidra*. A storm has cracked our hull. We are under ballast so there is no oil spill but we must abandon ship if she breaks up any more." He gave his coordinates. "I am declaring an emergency. Please, can anyone hear my signal? Mayday, mayday, mayday."

"Under ballast, my eye," Max grumbled. "What do you want to do?"

Cabrillo sat motionless, his hand cupped around his chin. "Let 'em sweat. He'll keep making reports even if nobody answers him. Eric, what's our ETA now?"

"Still looking at about three hours."

"The *Sidra* won't last that long in these seas with a cracked hull," Max said. "Especially if her keel's affected. Hell, she could break apart in three minutes."

Juan couldn't argue the point. They had to do something but his options were limited. Letting the tanker break up on her own was the worst of them and it seemed Eric's idea of using her to defuse the storm was out. The best he could hope for was to put the ship on the bottom with the least amount of spilled gel. The Test-71 torpedoes could do the job, but it might take hours for the hull to finally disappear under the waves, which meant hours of her continuing to disgorge her cargo.

Inspiration came from his experience on the *Or Death* with Sloane, when the boat was hit by a missile fired from the yacht guarding the wave-powered generators. She'd sunk in an instant because her bow had been ripped off while she was at speed. Cabrillo didn't consider the countless pitfalls in his crazy idea, he just set about getting it organized.

"Linc, Eddie, go down to the stores and get me two hundred feet of Hypertherm, the stuff with the electromagnets on the casings." The plastic explosive–like material was a magnesium-based compound capable of burning at nearly two thousand degrees Celsius and was used in salvage operations to cut steel underwater. "Meet me in the hangar. Eddie, kit up on your way. I can't guarantee what kind of reception we're going to get on the *Sidra*."

"What about me?" Linc asked.

"Sorry, but we've got weight limitations."

Max touched Juan's shoulder. "Obviously you've come up with something devious and underhanded. Care to enlighten us?" After Cabrillo explained his plan, Hanley nodded. "Like I said, devious and underhanded."

"Is there any other way?"

31

GEORGE Adams's face was a mask of concentration, his fingers curled tightly around the Robinson's controls. Wind and the furiously spinning main rotor blades made the small chopper jittery on the raised helipad, but he wouldn't take off until the timing was just right.

The *Oregon* dropped down the back of a large swell and a wall of water suddenly loomed up over the deck, its crest curled and threatened to swamp the helicopter and its three occupants.

"Talk to me, Eric," he said as the ship started to climb the next wave.

"Hold on, the camera's almost reached the top. Okay, yeah, there's a large trough on the other side. You've got plenty of time."

The instant the ship reached the apogee of its ascent Adams gave the Robinson a bit more power, knowing that when they took off the *Oregon* would drop from under them rather than rise up on a hidden wave and crash into the chopper. As they took to the air the tramp freighter plummeted. George dipped the nose to gain airspeed and then lifted out of the reach of the surging sea and into a maelstrom of wind. He had to turn with the wind to gain more speed and altitude before swinging back into the gale. Hammered by a fifty-knot headwind, the Robinson was making only sixty knots over the ocean, not much faster than the

Oregon herself, but Juan had wanted to get to the *Gulf of Sidra* as quickly as possible.

If the plan held, his ship would be in torpedo range by the time he and Eddie had finished laying the Hypertherm charges.

"I calculate our flight time to be an hour and twenty minutes," George said after settling in for the difficult flight.

"Juan?" It was Max over the radio.

"Go ahead."

"Cassedine's sending another SOS."

"Okay, go ahead and answer it just like we talked about."

"You got it." Max left the channel open so Cabrillo could hear the conversation. "*Gulf of Sidra*, this is the MV *Oregon*, Captain Max Hanley. I have heard your distress call and am making all possible speed to your location but we're still two hours away."

"*Oregon*, thank God!"

"Captain Cassedine, please advise on your situation."

"There's a split in the hull amidships port side and we're taking on water. My pumps are going at full capacity and we don't appear to be sinking, but if the tear gets any worse we will have to abandon ship."

"Has the hole gotten any bigger since it first occurred?"

"Negative. A rogue wave running across the wind hit us and tore the plating. It has been stable since."

"If you turn due east we can reach you quicker." This wasn't true but if the *Gulf of Sidra* turned as she spewed her poison it would distort the hurricane's eye somewhat. Basically it was a test to see who had control on the ship, its master or Daniel Singer.

Static filled the airwaves for almost a minute. When Cassedine came back there was a new current of fear in his voice. "Ah, that isn't possible, *Oregon*. My engineer reports damage to our steering gear."

"Most likely a gun to his head," Juan said to Max.

They had considered this scenario, so Max went on as if it wasn't a big deal. "Understood damage to your steering. In that case, Captain, we can't risk a collision in these conditions. When we are ten miles from you I will request that you man your lifeboats."

"What, so you can put a line on my ship afterward and claim her for salvage?"

Juan chuckled. "This guy's facing death and he's worried we'll steal his vessel."

"Captain, the *Oregon* is a thousand-ton commercial fishing boat," Max lied smoothly. "We couldn't tow a tanker on a millpond let alone in the teeth of a hurricane. I am just unwilling to risk a runaway derelict ramming us in the middle of this storm."

"I, ah, I understand," Cassedine finally said.

"How many souls aboard?"

"Three officers, twelve crew, and one supernumerary. A total of sixteen."

The extra man would be Singer, Juan thought, realizing that was a small number even by tanker standards, which were so automated nowadays that they typically carried just a skeleton crew, but he supposed it was enough for what Singer intended.

"Roger that," Max replied. "Sixteen people. I will call you when we are in range. *Oregon* out."

"Affirmative, Captain Hanley. I will radio immediately if our situation changes. *Gulf of Sidra* out."

"Don't get too used to that Captain Hanley stuff," Juan said when the tanker was off the air.

"I don't know," Max said airily. "Has a nice ring to it. So do you think Singer will abandon with them?"

"Tough to say. Though he's hit a setback he might try to complete his mission without the crew aboard. They will need to slow in order to launch the lifeboat, but if Cassedine shows him how to get her back to speed then he could finish tightening the storm into an eye less than six miles across."

"Would you?"

"If I were him and I'd come this far, yeah, I think I would see it through to the end."

"Which means two things. One is that Singer's crazier than an outhouse rat and two, you and Eddie better keep an eye out for him when you're laying the cutting charges."

"We'll be careful."

An hour later George radioed back to the *Oregon* that they had reached their first waypoint on the flight. It was time to clear the *Gulf of Sidra* of her crew.

"This is the *Oregon* calling Captain Cassedine." Max said over the radio.

"This is Cassedine, go ahead *Oregon*."

"We are ten miles from your position. Are you prepared to abandon ship?" Max asked.

"I do not want to argue, Captain," Cassedine replied, "but my radar shows you are nearly thirty miles from us."

"You're trusting radar in twenty-foot seas?" Max scoffed. "My radar doesn't even show you. I'm relying on my GPS and by our estimates you're ten miles from us." Hanley rattled off the longitude and latitude numbers of a spot ten miles due east of the *Gulf of Sidra*. "That is our current location."

"Ah, yes. I see that you are correct and are within the ten miles."

"We can come in closer if you've made repairs to your rudder."

"No, we have not, but the supernumerary has volunteered to stay aboard to keep working on it."

"The rest of you are abandoning him?" Max asked, playing the part of a concerned mariner.

"He is the vessel's owner and understands the risk," Cassedine told him.

"Understood," Max said with mock unease. "After you launch the boat and get clear of the tanker steer a heading of two seventy degrees and transmit a tone on the EPIRB emergency frequency so we can home in on you."

"A heading of two seventy degrees and a tone on 121.5 megahertz. We will launch in a couple of minutes."

"Good luck, Captain. May God go with you," Max said seriously. Even if Cassedine and his crew were knowingly helping Singer, the sailor in him understood the dangers of getting into a lifeboat in this sea state.

A quarter hour later, Hali Kasim put the 121.5 MHz marine distress band on the op center speakers so everyone could hear the high-pitched directional tone.

"Got that, Juan?"

"I hear it. We're heading in."

Even flying at five hundred feet they only broke through the clouds when they were less than a mile from the supertanker. At ninety thousand tons heavier than the *Oregon* she rode the waves much more smoothly with only occasional spray breaking over her blunt bows. They could just make out a tiny yellow speck motoring away from the red-decked behemoth. It was her lifeboat and, like he'd been ordered, Cassedine was heading due west, well away from the *Oregon* so there would be no chance he could interfere. They could also tell that the tanker was picking up steam again after slowing to send the lifeboat down its rails.

"Check that out," George said and pointed.

Near the *Gulf of Sidra*'s stern a jet of fluid arced from her side about eight feet below her rail. It was discharge from her sea-suction intake, a system of pipes and pumps that allowed her to take on or expel ballast water.

Only she wasn't pumping water. The fluid gushing from the three-foot-diameter hole was thick and viscous, like the oil that had contaminated the bay around the Petromax terminal in Angola. Only this was clear and seemed to spread across the ocean faster than the pump was ejecting it from the ship.

"It's growing on its own," Eddie said from the backseat. Next to him were the thick ropes of Hypertherm. "The organics within the gel are contaminating the surrounding water and turning it into goo."

They circled the supertanker to take a look at that damage on her port side. There was a gash in the hull rising up from her waterline and extending to her railing. As the hull flexed with the waves the rend opened and closed like a vertical mouth. The sea around the tear was coated with a growing skin of gelatin-thick flocculent.

"Where do you want me to drop you?" George asked.

"As close as you can to the bow," Juan said.

"I don't want to risk getting doused by spray so it'll have to be at least a hundred feet back."

"We won't have the time to hunt for Singer, so make sure when you come back to grab us you can do it quickly."

"Trust me, Chairman, I don't want to hover over anything in this wind one microsecond longer than necessary."

Adams looped them around and into the wind, coming at the tanker from an altitude of a hundred feet, the restless sea seeming to pulse just below the landing skids. They crossed over the ship's rail and George reined in the little chopper, holding her steady against the gusts in an expert flying demonstration as he dumped altitude. He maintained a hover twenty feet higher than the deck rose on even the biggest waves.

"Eddie, go."

Eddie Seng pushed open the door opposite him, fighting to keep it open with one foot while he used the other to kick the coils of Hypertherm out of the helicopter. The explosives fell to the deck below like an entangled nest of snakes. When the last of it disappeared over the sill he straightened and the wind slammed the door closed.

"Now for the hard part," George muttered, keeping an eye on the horizon, gauging the swells and the frequency of the gusts. A few drops of rain pattered against the windscreen. He didn't let this ominous development crack his concentration.

Juan and Eddie both waited with their hands poised on their door handles, their machine pistols slung across their backs.

An explosion of spume erupted across the width of the tanker's bow as she plowed into another monster wave; as she started riding up it, George started to lower the Robinson. He'd judged it perfectly. The deck was no more than five feet from the chopper's skids when the ship started to settle again.

"See ya, boys."

Cabrillo and Seng opened their doors and jumped without a moment's hesitation, freeing Adams to lift away from the ship before she slammed another wave in the unrelenting cycle.

Juan hit the deck and rolled, immediately surprised at how hot the metal was. He could barely stand the temperature through the thick weave of his fatigues and he got to his feet as fast as he could. He knew the heat would seep through the rubber soles of his boots in minutes. He didn't care about his prosthesis, he'd never feel it, but his other foot and Eddie's were in for first- or second-degree burns if this took too long.

"This is going to suck," Eddie said as if reading Juan's mind.

"The spray hitting the bow should make it a little cooler there," Juan said as they reached the pile of Hypertherm. He waved up at George in the Robinson hovering five hundred feet above them. Adams was their lookout in case Singer appeared.

Because of the *Gulf of Sidra*'s inertia, Juan had decided changing the ship's course or ramming her engine into full reverse would have little effect. The best chance of stopping Singer was laying the Hypertherm as quickly as possible.

The metal-cutting explosives were configured in twenty-foot lengths with electricity-conducting clips on their ends so sections could be joined into a single charge. The detonator and battery pack could be set between any two segments, but in order to produce the desired results they would need to set it as close to the middle as possible.

Juan lifted ropes of the Hypertherm over his shoulders until he felt his knees about to buckle. By the time he was finished his left sock was soaked with perspiration.

"Ready?" he grunted.

"Let's go."

Staggering under their hundred-and-fifty-pound loads, the two men marched toward the bow, both trailing dreadlocks of gray explosives. The wind and the ship's motion made them lurch drunkenly but they fought on. When they finally reached an area soaked by spray they saw tendrils of steam spiraling up from the deck. It reminded Juan of a visit to the hot springs at Yellowstone when he was a kid. He dumped his burden thirty feet from the prow. It was as close as they could get without risking being swept overboard by the eruptions of spray.

"How are we looking, George?" Juan panted.

"I did a flyby of the bridge but didn't see anyone. The decks are a mess of pipes and manifolds. I don't see Singer anywhere."

"How about you, Max?"

"We're within the torpedoes' range and waiting for your signal."

"Okay."

What Juan thought was an eruption of spray blasting over the front of the ship turned out to be a microburst of heavy rain. It slackened after a few seconds but didn't entirely abate. They had been running under two unforgiving deadlines. One was to prevent the tanker from completing its turn, and the other was to lay the explosives and be back aboard the *Oregon* before the rain made flying impossible. He could only hope they had better luck with the former.

Eddie started laying the explosives across the width of the ship along one of the seams where two hull sections had been welded together. Juan was busy with the detonator, testing it a couple of times with the remote control he carried in his pocket before jacking it in to the first length of Hypertherm. It took six twenty-foot segments to span the tanker's beam. Each one contained a battery that when activated generated a magnetic field that anchored the explosives to the steel deck and prevented it from rolling with the ship.

Eddie and Juan had to work together to lower a length over each of the tanker's sides so that some of the Hypertherm dangled in the water. Again the electromagnets clamped it to the hull along one of its welded seams. When they were finished they had a line of explosives that covered every inch of the ship above the waterline. The extra lengths they left piled on the deck.

Juan radioed George for extraction as soon as Eddie made the final connection. The rain was growing heavier, near horizontal sheets that cut visibility so the distant superstructure was as nebulous as a ghost. As Adams prepared to make the trickiest pickup of his distinguished career Cabrillo called Hanley.

"Max, the charges are laid. Go ahead and fire the torpedoes. We should be out of here by the time they arrive."

"Roger that." Max replied.

Back in the op center Mark Murphy opened both outer tube doors and brought up the torpedo control program on his computer. Linked through the ship's radar and sonar systems, a three-dimensional wire frame representation of the tactical picture came up on his screen. He could clearly see the *Gulf of Sidra* steaming seven thousand yards from the *Oregon*. In the parlance of World War Two submariners, this was going to be a turkey shoot.

"Wepps, on my mark fire Tube One," Max ordered. "Mark."

Cocooned in a bubble of high-pressure compressed air, the twenty-one-foot torpedo shot from the tube and put nearly twenty yards between itself and its mother ship before the silver-zinc batteries engaged its electric motor. It took just a few seconds for the Test-71 to ramp up to its operational speed of forty knots.

On Mark's screen he could see the torpedo streaking toward the tanker, tiny filaments representing her wire guidance cables trailing in its wake. For now he let the fish run free, but he had a joystick control for when he needed to steer the weapon.

"Fire two."

Murph launched the second torpedo, the sound of its discharge ringing through the ship like a hollow cough. After moment he said, "Both torpedoes away and running true."

"Juan," Max called, "you've got a pair of fish on the way so now's the time to get out of Dodge."

"Working on it," Cabrillo replied.

He was looking up into the storm as George brought the Robinson lower and lower. It was his third attempt to put the chopper on the deck. The shrieking winds had aborted the first two when the helo was still fifty feet above the ship. A gust hit the helicopter and George compensated instantly, crabbing the aircraft to keep pace with the *Sidra*'s seventeen-knot forward speed.

"Come on, Georgie boy," Eddie said, lifting his feet to keep the soles from searing. "You can do it."

The Robinson came lower still, its rotor wash whipping the rain off the deck in a circular pattern. They could see Adams behind the Plexiglas windscreen. His movie star–handsome face was taut with concentration, his eyes unblinking. The skids hovered a tantalizing ten feet above the deck and as the *Sidra* rose on another swell the gap shrank. Eddie and Juan got into position so they could open the chopper's rear doors and dive in as quickly as possible.

Adams managed to keep the helicopter exactly on station for nearly fifteen seconds waiting for the tanker to reach the top of the wave. When it started to drop again, he let the Robinson fall the last couple of feet. Cabrillo and Seng whipped open their doors and dove inside headfirst even as the helo bounced back into the sky. Adams twisted the throttle sharply and they lifted away from the supertanker.

"That was one fancy piece of flying," Juan said, getting himself settled and his safety belt fastened.

"Don't congratulate me yet. I still have to land on the *Oregon*," Adams replied. Then he grinned. "But that was damned smooth if I do say so myself. Oh, just so you know, that crack amidships has gotten bigger. The deck's starting to split, too."

"Won't make much of a difference now," Juan said and keyed his radio. "Max, we're away. Where are the torpedoes?"

"Two thousand yards and closing. Call it four minutes to impact."

The Atlantic was too rough to see the weapons' tracks as they moved through the water, though the three men in the chopper hovering at eight hundred feet were going to have a spectacular view of their detonation.

"I'll trigger the Hypertherm ten seconds before impact," Juan said. "Hitting her on both port and starboard will shear everything below her waterline and the explosives will burn through everything above. The bow will come off like a piece of sliced bread."

Murph came on the tactical net. "I'll call out the ranges. At fifty yards go ahead and blow it."

A tense three minutes passed as Mark guided the torpedoes so they would slam into both sides of the *Gulf of Sidra* in the exact spots below where Juan and Eddie had laid the Hypertherm. Juan had the remote detonator in his hand, his thumb poised.

"One hundred yards," Mark reported.

As the torpedoes converged on the tanker they drew closer to the surface, so it was possible to see the faint line of their wakes. Murph was vectoring them in perfectly.

"Seventy-five."

With his keener vision Adams was the first to spot it. "What the hell is that?" he suddenly shouted.

"What? Where?"

"Movement on the deck."

Cabrillo saw it then, a tiny figure running from the *Gulf of Sidra*'s bows. He was wearing a rain suit that was nearly the same shade of red as the tanker's deck, the perfect camouflage to stalk the maze of pipes in order to reach the bow unseen. "It's Singer! Look away!"

He mashed the detonator button and turned his head to shield his eyes from the intensity of the burning Hypertherm. When he didn't see the sun-bright luminescence in his peripheral vision he stared at the ship. The Hypertherm was still in place but hadn't cooked off.

"Wepps, abort! Abort! Abort!"

Mark Murphy could have triggered the torpedoes to self-destruct but instead he sent a signal to slow the hurtling weapons and used both joysticks to send them diving. On his screen he watched their descent. The angle looked all wrong for them to pass below the tanker's tremendous draft but there was nothing more he could do. They were close enough now that an autodestruct order would stave in the *Sidra*'s hull and consign her to a lingering death that would allow her entire load of gel to escape.

"Dive, baby, dive," Eric Stone said from his station next to Murph's.

Max was holding his breath watching the main monitor where it displayed the torpedoes' paths. They passed within six feet of the tanker's flat bottom and within eleven feet of each other. Everyone in the op center let out a collective breath.

"GET me down there," Juan shouted, pointing at the tanker.

Adams threw the chopper in a steep dive before saying, "I can't guarantee I can pick you up again. We're low on fuel."

"Doesn't matter." There was fury in Cabrillo's voice.

The Robinson rushed over the tanker's bow like a hawk coming out of a stoop, its skids no more than ten feet off the deck as Adams chased Singer down the length of the ship. Juan already had his safety belt off and was ready with his shoulder braced against his door. He unslung his MP-5 and dumped it on the seat. When he'd jumped the first time the machine pistol had gouged painfully into his back. This leap was going to be even tougher.

Singer must have heard the chopper because he looked up over his shoulder. His eyes went wide and he started running even harder. There was a dark object in his hand that Juan recognized as the detonator battery. Singer cut to his right, trying to get his pursuers to fly into a manifold tower rising forty feet from the deck and also to reach the rail so he could hurl the battery into the sea.

Juan forced open his door. The drop was ten feet and the chopper was moving at least ten miles per hour, but he leapt anyway.

He hit hard, tumbling across the hot steel plates until he crashed into a pipe support. He hauled himself to his feet, his body feeling the collective result of so much punishment. He took off at a dead sprint, his pistol out of its holster and clutched tightly in his fist.

Singer had seen him jump from the chopper and redoubled his pace, his long strides eating distance like a gazelle. But no matter how badly he wanted to toss the battery overboard and complete his mission the man behind him was driven even harder. He glanced over his shoulder again to see Cabrillo gaining ground, his face a mask of rage.

A fresh waved surged under the tanker, making her hull moan with the stress. The tear along her port side slammed closed as the swell buckled the keel. Then, as it passed by, the split opened again, tearing wider than before. Singer had seen the gap and was far enough from the rail to avoid it when it closed but when it yawned opened he never thought it would rip the deck so easily.

Singer tried to avoid it, and was awkwardly shifting his weight when his foot fell through, shredding his rain pants and the flesh of his leg against the jagged edge. The paperback-sized battery pack went skittering. He screamed at the pain and his other leg fell into the hole, dangling above the slick surface of the flocculent still sloshing in the tank. The searing metal blistered his hands as he struggled to pull himself free before the gap slammed shut.

Cabrillo dove into him at full speed just as the tanker shifted again and the two sides of the tear scissored closed. He tumbled with Singer amid a spray of warm liquid and a keening cry that pierced his brain. When he recovered from the fall he looked at Singer. Everything below the top of his thighs had been cut off and had dropped into the tank. Blood spilled from the clean slices in torrents that turned pink in the rain.

He crawled to Singer and turned him faceup. He was ghostly pale and his lips had already turned blue. His scream suddenly ended as his brain refused to feel anymore pain. He was slipping into shock.

"Why?" Juan demanded before the man succumbed to the trauma.

"I had to," Singer whispered. "People have to act before it's too late."

"Haven't you figured out that the future takes care of itself? A hundred years ago you never saw the sun in London because of the industrial pollution. Technology evolved and the pall went away. Today you say the problem is cars causing global warming. In ten or twenty years something will come along that makes the internal combustion engine obsolete."

"We can't wait that long."

"Then you should have spent your millions on inventing it sooner rather than squandering it on a demonstration that can't possibly change anything. That's the problem with your movement, Singer. You're all about propaganda and press releases, not concrete solutions."

"The people would have demanded action," he said weakly.

"For a day or a week. To effect change you need alternatives, not ultimatums."

Singer said nothing, but as he died it was his defiance that was the last thing to fade from his eyes.

Fanatics like him would never understand the nature of compromise and Juan knew he shouldn't have bothered. He lurched to his feet to recover the battery pack and started running for the bow.

"Talk to me, Max."

"You've got three minutes before the torpedoes run out their charges."

Because of the guide wires spooling out from the *Oregon*, the outer tube doors couldn't be closed to load any more torpedoes from the ship's store. If Juan didn't set off the Hypertherm now it would take thirty minutes to get two fresh torpedoes into the water and he knew the *Gulf of Sidra* would break up before then.

"Don't wait for me no matter what. If I can't detonate the Hypertherm, hit the ship with the torpedoes anyway. Maybe we'll get lucky and the blast will ignite the cutting charges."

"I hear you, but I don't like it."

"How the hell do you think I feel?" Juan said as he ran.

The tanker seemed impossibly long, her bows like a horizon that never grew closer. The heat radiating from the deck made his pores run with sweat and each time his left foot slapped the ground he could feel the blisters popping. He ignored it all and sprinted on.

"Two minutes," Max said over the radio when Cabrillo finally reached the string of Hypertherm bisecting the ship.

When Singer had yanked the battery from the detonator, he had torn the wires that carried the electricity to set off the charge. Juan had to first disconnect the detonator from between two lengths of the explosives so he didn't accidentally complete the circuit. Using the pocketknife Eddie had recovered at the Devil's Oasis, he had to peel back the plastic insulation to expose the copper before he could twist the wires back together. There were three of them and it took twenty seconds each.

A status light embedded in the detonator turned green. He had a complete circuit.

"One minute, Juan."

He clipped a length of Hypertherm to one side of the detonator and was moving to the second when he heard over the radio. "Chairman, it's Murph. Torpedoes are a hundred and fifty yards out."

"Keep them coming. I've almost got it. There!"

The string was complete. He turned and started running aft, hampered by the stinging pain radiating from his charred foot. He was now in a race against two torpedoes homing in on the ship at forty knots. He'd covered a hundred feet when Murph reported the torpedoes were a hundred yards away. He accelerated through the agony, not caring that he was crying out with every step.

"Fifty yards, Chairman," Mark said as if it were his fault.

Juan let it go for another few seconds, gaining a couple more feet before pressing the remote.

In a blazing arc that rivaled the sun, the Hypertherm ignited, its magnesium core spiking to two thousand degrees. The burn raced from the center of the ship like lightning, making the steel deck as soft as wax and then heating it further so it dripped into the hold like water. The bow was wreathed in a noxious cloud of smoke and scorched metal. The light it gave off filled the sky, turning the cheerless gray into brilliant white. The explosive cut completely across the deck and then continued on, slicing open the hull down to the waterline in a blink of an eye.

Juan could feel the intense thermal shock on his back from three hundred feet away and had it not been for the rain he probably would have lost the hair on his head.

As quickly as it had ignited and burned through the ship, the Hypertherm exhausted itself, leaving in its passing a long narrow gash with edges that glowed with residual heat.

He managed to cover another twenty yards before the Test-71s hurtled into the ship directly below where the charge had cut the hull. The concussion from the twin explosions lifted him off his feet and threw him down the deck as water and torn metal geysered up from the blasts. The bow was torn free of the rest of the tanker and sank in an instant. The force of her passage through the ocean caused water to surge into her holds, forcing the nearly three quarter load of flocculent to squeeze toward the stern through the pipes that connected the tanks. A gout erupted from the tear in her side, sending gel squirting more than a hundred feet. They had known this would happen, but accepted it as a small price to pay as the remainder of the organic flocculent remained trapped within the ship.

Juan staggered to his feet, his head pounding with an unholy ring. Looking forward he could see the ocean climbing up over where the bow had been in a wall of water that seemed to grow in height as the ship settled into the sea's embrace. The *Gulf of Sidra* was sealing her own fate as her massive diesel engine continued to turn the propeller, ramming her under the waves at seventeen knots.

"Juan, it's George." He looked up to see the chopper hovering above him. "I think I have enough fuel to make one attempt."

"You won't have time," Juan said as he ran aft again. "This pig's sinking faster than I thought she would. She'll be gone in less than a minute."

"I'm going to try anyway. I'll meet you at the stern rail."

Cabrillo just kept running.

"And we're coming in," Max Hanley called from the *Oregon*. "Rescue crews are gearing up now if you go into the drink."

Juan ran on, coming down the starboard side of the ship so he could avoid where the hull had been breached. Behind him the sea climbed higher. Already a third of the tanker was awash and every second saw more of her go under.

He reached the superstructure and raced down the narrow space between it and the rail, his legs pumping up the ever steepening deck. He reached the *Sidra*'s jack post with its soaked Liberian flag just as water reached the leading edge of the accommodation block. There was no sign of George Adams in the Robinson. Cabrillo would just have to hold on and pray he didn't get sucked too deep when the ship plummeted out from under him.

He had just started climbing over the rail when the chopper careened from around the crazily tilted superstructure. From its back door dangled a patchwork rope made of assault rifle slings, a fatigue jacket, some lengths of wire pilfered from somewhere in the cockpit, and Eddie Seng's pants looped at the bottom.

A line of portholes one story above Cabrillo exploded, blown outward by the buildup of air pressure as water filled the superstructure. He turned away from the shower of glass that rained downward and looked up again in time to see Eddie's pants swinging at him.

He leapt as they arced just above his head, slipping an arm through the pant legs, and was jerked into the air, spinning and twisting like a coin on the end of a string. Below him the *Gulf of Sidra* vanished under the waves, her grave marked by a pool of gel many thousands of times smaller than what Daniel Singer had intended.

The first person to greet them in the *Oregon*'s hangar after George's unbelievable landing was Maurice. He was dressed impeccably in his trademark black suit with a crisp white towel over one arm. In the other he held aloft a serving dish with a silver cover. As Juan staggered from the Robinson, and Max, Linda, and Sloane arrived in a jubilant rush, Maurice approached and whipped off the cover with a flourish.

"As per your earlier request, Captain."

"My earlier request?" Dulled by fatigue, Juan had no idea what the steward was talking about.

Maurice was too dour to ever smile, but his eyes glinted with merriment. "I know this isn't technically a hurricane but I believe you would enjoy your Gruyère cheese and lobster soufflé with a baked Alaska for dessert."

His timing had been so perfect that the delicate soufflé hadn't settled and steam curled from its top. Laughter echoed throughout the hangar.

IT would be the tenth squall of the year to form in the Atlantic powerful enough to become a tropical storm and thus deserve a name. Though it had started to evolve into a hurricane with a massive potential for destruction, the eye never seemed to fully form. Meteorologists had no explanation why. They'd never seen a phenomenon like it.

It was just as well. It was early in the season to have this many storms and a weary public wasn't really concerned with a hurricane that never was. In keeping with tradition, each storm was named after the corresponding letter in the alphabet so that the first storm always has a name starting with the letter A, the second with the letter B, and so on. So when it came to the tenth storm, a storm that never made landfall, few would recall that it had been given the moniker of Tropical Storm Juan.

32

THE dune buggy carrying Cabrillo, Max, Sloane, and Mafana flew across the desert on its fat tires, the souped-up engine roaring as Juan drove it at breakneck speed. Moses Ndebele had wanted to make the trip, but his doctors at a private South African hospital refused to let him leave so soon after the surgery to repair his shattered foot. He'd sent his old sergeant in his place, although he trusted Cabrillo implicitly.

They were running late for their appointment. The man at the company who rented them the vehicle was also a volunteer with the Swakopmund police. He had been delayed because he'd been out arresting a group of Europeans stranded in the desert who were responsible for a kidnapping that took place in Switzerland.

The open-topped buggy crested a hill and Juan whipped them into a slide that dug furrows into the ground. The vehicle rocked on its suspension as the four passengers gaped at the valley below.

The *Rove* looked as though she was under way on an ocean of sand. Small dunes lapped at her hull like gently rolling swells. If not for her missing funnel and her broken cargo derricks and the fact that every fleck of paint had been scoured from her, she would have looked like she had before being buried for a hundred years by the worst sandstorm in a century.

A short distance from her was a huge cargo chopper painted a bright turquoise with the name NUMA emblazoned on its rotor boom. Near it were two small excavators that had been used to remove the thirty feet of sand that had entombed the ship and a cluster of workers lounging in the shade under a white tent canopy.

Juan leaned over to kiss Sloane's cheek. "You were right. Congratulations."

She beamed at the compliment. "Was there ever any doubt?"

"Tons of it," Max said from the backseat. Sloane reached back and slapped his leg playfully.

Juan put the buggy in gear and raced down the side of the dune. Their appearance made the workers get to their feet. Two of them detached themselves from the others and started across the desert floor to where a ramp had been rigged to give access to the *Rove*'s main deck. One carried a box under his arm.

Cabrillo braked just shy of the ramp and killed the engine. The only sound was a gentle breeze that stirred the air. He unstrapped his belts and climbed from the bucket seat as the two men approached. Both were solidly built and were maybe a year or two younger than him, though one had pure white hair and eyes that were as blue as his own. The other was darker, a Latino with a perpetually amused look on his face.

"I don't know a whole lot of people in the world who truly impress Dirk Pitt," the white-haired man from NUMA said. "So when I had the chance to meet one of them I took it. Chairman Cabrillo, I presume?"

"*Juan* Cabrillo." They shook hands.

"I'm Kurt Austin and this rogue here is Joe Zavala. By the way, thanks for getting us away from cleanup duty in Angola where NUMA's leading a hand."

"Pleasure to meet you. How's it coming?"

"Better than expected. Our ship happened to be nearby on a survey mission. Joe was able to modify a suction dredge used to take samples into an effective oil vacuum. We can pump the crude directly to storage tanks onshore. With Petromax deploying everything they have from other facilities in Nigeria, the spill should be totally cleared up in less than two weeks."

"That's great to hear," Juan said, then added with a touch of self-recrimination. "Had we been a couple hours earlier there wouldn't have been a need for such a cleanup effort."

"And a couple hours later would have doubled it."

"True." Cabrillo turned to his companions. "This is the president of the Corporation, Max Hanley. Mafana here represents Moses Ndebele, and this is Sloane Macintyre, the reason we're all standing eight miles from the ocean but looking at a steamship."

"Quite a sight, huh?"

"Not that I'm complaining, but how did you find it so fast?"

Before answering, Joe Zavala produced bottles of Tusker lager from the box. The glass was icy cold and blistered with condensation. He popped the tops and handed them around. "It's about the best way I've discovered to beat back the dust."

They saluted each other and took long gulps.

"Ah!" Zavala breathed. "That's the stuff."

"To answer your question," Austin said, wiping his mouth, "we turned the problem over to our resident computer genius, Hiram Yeager. He pulled together every scrap of information about the storm that hit the night the *Rove* disappeared, gleaning it from old ships' logs, memoirs of people living in Swakopmund, missionaries' journals, and a report filed with the British Admiralty concerning navigational changes to the coast of South West Africa after it was over.

"He fed everything he could into his computer and then added meteorological data about this area for the century since the storm. About a day later Max spit out the answer."

"Max?" Hanley asked.

"It's what he calls his computer. It created a map of the coastline as it is today with a line running parallel to it, ranging from a mile to more than ten miles inland. Had the *Rove* been close to shore, like to pick up passengers who'd made off with a fortune in diamonds, she would be buried somewhere along that line."

"The distance variances are caused by different geological conditions and wind patterns," Zavala added.

"Once we had our map we flew along the line in a chopper trailing a magnetometer."

"I did the same thing for days," Sloane told them, "but I was searching out at sea. Guess I should have done more research."

"It took us two days to get a hit that could be the *Rove*, and it was less than thirty feet from where Max said she'd be."

"That's amazing."

"I've been trying to convince Hiram to make his computer predict lottery numbers for me," Zavala quipped. "He says it can do it, but he won't let me ask."

"We used ground-penetrating radar to confirm it was a ship and not a mass of iron, like a meteorite," Austin went on. "The rest was just a matter of moving sand."

Zavala opened a second round of beers. "Moving *a lot* of sand."

"Have you been inside her yet?" Sloane asked.

"We were saving that honor for your arrival. Come on aboard."

He led them up the gangplank and onto the *Rove*'s teak deck. They had done a masterful job removing the overburden, going so far as to sweep out the corners so the only sand on her was what blew with the wind.

"The bridge windows were smashed in, either by the storm or later when she was buried, so it was filled with sand. However . . ." He left the word hanging in the air and slapped a hatch. The metal echoed. "The desert never entered her crew's quarters."

"I've already loosened the dogging wheel," Zavala said. "So Miss Macintyre, if you'd please."

Sloane stepped forward and spun the locking wheel another half turn to disengage the latches. She pulled it open and a trickle of sand spilled over the coaming. The wardroom beyond was lit only by a couple shafts of light from small portholes along two walls. Other than the drifts of sand covering the floor, it looked as though a hundred years had never passed. The furniture was all in its place. A stove sat ready to warm the teakettle sitting on its top and a lantern hanging from the ceiling appeared to need just the touch of a match to glow.

But as their eyes adjusted they all saw that what at first looked like sacks of cloth draped over the table were actually the mummified remains of two men who'd died facing opposite each other. Their skin had turned gray as their bodies dried out and seemed as brittle as paper. One wore nothing but a loincloth around his waist and the stalks of feathers that had lost their fletching in a band around his skull. The other wore rough bush clothes and next to where he lay his head sat an enormous slouch hat that had been white eleven decades earlier.

"H. A. Ryder," Sloane breathed. "The other must have been one of the Herero warriors their king sent to retrieve the stones."

"They had to have attacked just as the storm hit," Austin said, returning from down a short corridor. "There are a dozen or more bodies lying in the cabins. Most looked like they died in a fight. Lots of stab wounds. The bodies of the Hereros don't have a mark on them, so they probably died of starvation when the *Rove* was buried."

"But they didn't kill him." Juan pointed at Ryder's corpse. "I wonder why?"

"From the looks of it, these two were the last of them, Zavala remarked. "Probably died of dehydration when the ship's water supply ran dry."

"Ryder was well known in his day," Sloane said. "It's possible they knew each other. They could have been friends from before the heist."

"That's one mystery we'll never be able to solve," Max said, stepping forward to reach for one of the bags placed under the table. "As to another one."

When he lifted the saddlebag the dried-out leather split and a cascade of diamonds tumbled into the sand. Unpolished and in poor light, they still dazzled like bits of captured sunshine. Everyone began cheering at once. Sloane picked up a twenty-carat stone and held it to the porthole to plumb its depths. Mafana scooped up handfuls of diamonds and let them sift through his fingers. His expression told Juan he was thinking not of himself but of what wealth these stones meant for his people.

The old sergeant broke open the other bags and began sorting through the stones, plucking out the largest and clearest. There were many to choose from because the original miners who'd brought the diamonds to their king had taken only the finest they had wrested from the earth. When his hands were brimming he turned to Cabrillo.

"Moses said that you gave him one handful of stones as a down payment," Mafana said solemnly. "He ordered me to give you back two as our people's way of saying thank you."

Juan was overwhelmed by the gesture. "Mafana, this isn't necessary.

You and your men fought and died for these stones. That was our deal."

"Moses said you would reply that way so I was then supposed to give them to Mr. Hanley. Moses says he is less sentimental than you and would accept them on behalf of your crew."

"He's got a point there," Max said and held out his hands. Mafana gave him the stones. "Having played a master jeweler not too long ago I'd say there's about a million bucks here."

"You couldn't have done a very good job of playing at it." Sloane took the largest stone from the pile and showed it to him. "This one alone will fetch about a million when it's cut and polished."

Max just stared at it goggle-eyed, bringing a fresh round of laughter.

AN hour later, after everyone had explored the ship, Sloane found Juan standing at the *Rove*'s prow, his hands clasped behind his back.

"What's that line?" she asked as she approached him. "Give me a tall ship and a star to sail her by."

He turned and smiled. "Only look out for the sand dunes."

"I've been reading the ship's log. H. A. Ryder continued to write in it after they were buried. Kurt was correct about the Herero attacking at the height of the storm. They slaughtered the crew to a man, all except Ryder. The Herero leader had once worked for him as a guide and owed him his life following a lion attack. Not that it mattered. The reprieve was temporary."

"What happened?"

"The storm raged for a solid week. When it was finally over they couldn't push open any doors, including the one leading to the bridge, and the portholes were too small to fit through. They were trapped. There was enough food and water to last them nearly a month, but the end was inevitable. One by one they died off until only Ryder and the Herero chief remained. I have to assume that Ryder went next because there was nothing in the log about his companion succumbing."

"That is definitely on my top ten list of ways not to die," Juan said with a shudder.

"There was something else in the log that Ryder mentioned, something pretty interesting. He wrote that when he and his companions plundered the Herero's diamonds they left behind four beer pots brimming with stones. I know from history that their king never used them to buy protection from the British against the Germans occupying his lands so the stones are still out there."

"Forget it," Juan said, grinning. "Last time I helped you I ended up stranded on a giant metal snake in the middle of the ocean and had a supertanker sink from underneath me. If you want to go looking for more diamonds, be my guest. I'm going to stick to something safe, like hunting terrorists."

"It's just a thought," she said, teasing.

Cabrillo shook his head. "While we're on the subject of diamonds there's a couple of things I'd like to ask you."

"Fire away."

"Are you sure you'll be able to get a good price for these stones?"

"My company will pay close to full market value for them just so they can maintain their monopoly. They won't like it much that I didn't bring them back myself, but in the long run they'll have no choice. Don't worry. Moses will get more than enough money to see the leaders of his country get sent packing."

"That brings me to my second question. I assume that once the deal is done you aren't going to win employee of the month any time soon. I was wondering if you'd consider changing careers."

"Are you offering me a job, Chairman Cabrillo?" Her smile was brighter than any one of the diamonds they'd found could ever be.

"The hours are long, the work's dangerous but, as you just saw, the pay can be pretty good."

She stepped closer to him so that their chests were almost touching. "I had a chat with Linda not too long ago and I got a sense that there isn't a whole lot of fraternization among the crew."

"Office romances are tough enough. It's even worse when you all live together."

She ran a fingertip along his bare arm and looked into his eyes. "In that case there's something I need to get out of my system first before I'd even consider going off and playing pirate."

"What's that?" he asked, his voice husky.

"This," she said as their lips met.

COMING SOON IN HARDCOVER